THE GLASS ROOM

DI Vera Stanhope is not one to make friends easily, but when one of her neighbours goes missing, she feels duty-bound to find out what happened. It's an easy job to track the young woman down to the Writers' House, a country retreat where aspiring authors gather to work on their novels. But things get complicated when a body is discovered and Vera's neighbour is found with a knife in her hand. Calling in the team, Vera knows that she should hand the case over to someone else. But the investigation is too tempting, and she's never been one to follow the rules. Working with Sergeant Joe Ashworth, she starts the hunt for a murderer who has turned killing into an art form.

Books by Ann Cleeves
Published by Ulverscroft:

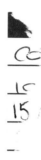

Ann Cleeves is the author behind ITV's *Vera* and BBC One's *Shetland*. She has written over 30 novels, and is the creator of detectives Vera Stanhope and Jimmy Perez — characters loved both on screen and in print. She is a multimillion-copy bestselling author, and her books are sold worldwide. Ann worked as a probation officer, bird observatory cook and auxiliary coastguard before she started writing. She is a member of 'Murder Squad', working with other British northern writers to promote crime fiction. In 2006 Ann was awarded the Duncan Lawrie Dagger (CWA Gold Dagger) for Best Crime Novel, for *Raven Black*, the first book in her Shetland series. In 2012 she was inducted into the CWA Crime Thriller Awards Hall of Fame, and in 2017 awarded the CWA Diamond Dagger. She lives in North Tyneside.

You can visit the author's website at www.anncleeves.com

ANN CLEEVES

◆

THE GLASS ROOM

Complete and Unabridged

CHARNWOOD
Leicester

First published in Great Britain in 2012 by
Macmillan
London

First Charnwood Edition
published 2018
by arrangement with
Pan Macmillan
London

The moral right of the author has been asserted

A catalogue record for this book is available
from the British Library.

ISBN 978–1–4448–3800–8

Published by
F. A. Thorpe (Publishing)
Anstey, Leicestershire

Set by Words & Graphics Ltd.
Anstey, Leicestershire
Printed and bound in Great Britain by
T. J. International Ltd., Padstow, Cornwall

This book is printed on acid-free paper

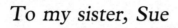

To my sister, Sue

Acknowledgements

Thanks to everyone who helped in the writing of this book, especially Julie, Helen, Naomi and Catherine at Macmillan and Sara Menguc and her team worldwide.

I'm grateful to Paul Rutman who sparked the idea, and to Brenda, David, Wunmi and Elaine who have helped bring Vera to a wider readership.

1

Vera Stanhope climbed out of Hector's ancient Land Rover and felt the inevitable strain on her knees. Hector's Land Rover. Her father had been dead for years, but still she thought of the vehicle as his. She stopped for a moment to look down the valley at the view. Another thing her father had gifted her: this house. Sod all else, she thought, maybe she should forgive him because of this. It was October and the light was going. A smell of wood-smoke and ice. Most of the trees were already bare and the whooper swans had come back to the lough.

She'd stopped at the supermarket outside Kimmerston on her way home from work and there were carrier bags piled on the passenger seat. She took a guilty look round to make sure the coast was clear. Her eco-warrior neighbours despised the use of plastic bags, and after a day in the office she couldn't face a right-on lecture about saving the planet. But there was no one in the yard next door. A couple of hens poked around a weed patch. No sound, and if Jack was working in the barn there'd be loud rock music. Or howling blues. She lifted the bags out of the Land Rover, then set them down on her doorstep to search for her keys.

But the door was already open. She felt a shiver of tension, but also of excitement. No way would she have gone to work without locking it.

1

She'd never believed all the romantic crap about it being safe for country folk to leave their doors open. The rural communities experienced crime too. She'd read the reports and knew there was as much drug use in the pleasant middle-class high schools in Northumberland as in the ones in town. It was just that teachers were better at keeping it quiet. She pushed the door open, using her elbow, thinking that really the last thing she needed was a burglary. She didn't have much to steal. Any self-respecting robber would turn up his nose at her Oxfam clothes and her pitiful PC, her ten-year-old telly. But she hated the thought of anyone being in the house. And she'd have to call in the CSIs, and they'd leave the place in chaos, fingerprint powder over every surface. Then they'd go back to the office with tales of the squalor in which she lived.

Despite her considerable weight she moved quietly. A skill she'd learned in childhood. She stopped in the hall and listened. Nobody was moving in the house. Unless they were as quiet as she was. But there was sound, a cracking of twigs, of sparks. A fire had been lit. The smell of wood-smoke was coming from her home, not from the cottages in the valley as she'd first thought. But it surely wasn't a fire out of control. There were no fumes seeping into the rest of the house. No roaring flames. No heat where she was standing.

She opened the door into the small living room and saw Jack, her neighbour, sitting in the most comfortable chair. The chair where Hector had always sat. He'd put a match to the fire she'd already laid in the grate and was staring at the flames. Shock, and relief of the tension she'd felt on coming into the house, made Vera angry. Bloody hippies! She'd given them a key for emergencies, not so that they could wander into her house whenever they felt like it. They had no respect for personal boundaries.

'What the shit do you think you're doing?'

Jack looked up at her and she saw there were tears running down his cheeks. She swore under her breath. What was it? Some domestic crisis? A family bereavement? It had been a mistake to get to know these people. Let folk into your life and they started making demands. She hated people making demands.

Then she remembered the times Jack and Joanna had dug the snow from the track so that she could get down the hill to work. The nights she'd gone uninvited into their house to steal bottles of homebrew when she was desperate for a drink. Evenings of good food at their kitchen table and the three of them laughing at some daft joke.

He nodded towards the fire. 'I'm sorry,' he said. 'It was bloody cold. And I hated waiting at home, once I'd made up my mind to speak to you.'

'What is it, Jack? What's happened?'

He shook his head. 'It's Joanna. I don't know where she is.'

Jack was a Scouser, soft and sentimental. He'd been in the merchant navy once, travelled the world, had stories enough to keep you entertained from teatime until a drunken early morning. Later he'd got hooked by the dream of the good life and, reaching the age of forty, he'd bought the smallholding next to Vera's house. A city boy, his only experience of rural living had been his annual pilgrimage to the Glastonbury Festival, yet somehow he'd made a go of it. Worked from dawn to dusk and even longer. Often, coming home close to midnight after a difficult case, Vera would hear him in the barn, would tip her head round the door to say goodnight. And that brief contact allowed her to believe that her colleagues were wrong. She did have friends. She did have a life away from the job.

'What do you mean?' Vera tried to keep her voice patient, although something about a weeping man made her feel like slapping him.

'She's been away for two days. No word. I think she's ill. She won't talk about it.'

'What sort of ill?' A pause. 'Cancer?' Vera's mother had died of cancer when she was a child. She still had a kind of superstition about speaking the word.

He shook his head. His greying hair was pulled back into a ponytail. 'I think it's her nerves. Depression. She went on Monday while I was at Morpeth farmers' market. Must have got a taxi. She said she needed some space.'

'She warned you she was leaving?'

He shook his head again. 'Nah, she left a note.' He pulled a scrap of paper from his jeans pocket, set it on the small table next to him, moving a mug with five-day-old coffee dregs so that Vera could see it.

4

Vera recognized the writing. Joanna often communicated by notes. Purple ink and immaculate italic, spiky and beautifully formed. *'Septic tank emptied.'* *'Parcel in barn.'* *'Fancy coming in for supper tonight?'* This one read: *'Gone away for a few days. Need some space. Soup in pan. Don't worry.'* No signature, not even J. No x.

'A few days,' Vera said. 'She'll be back. Or she'll phone.'

He looked up at her bleakly. 'She hasn't been taking her drugs.'

'What drugs?' Vera knew Jack smoked dope. Their house smelled of it. Sometimes, after a few beers too many, he rolled a giant spliff when he was in her place, not thinking that she might be compromised. Once he'd even offered it to her. She'd been tempted, but had turned him down. She knew she had an addictive personality; best to keep her vices legal. She'd presumed Joanna smoked too, but couldn't remember having seen it. Red wine was Joanna's poison, drunk from a large Bristol Blue glass. 'My only inheritance,' she'd said once, holding the glass to the light. 'All that I have left from home.'

'Pills,' Jack said. 'Lithium. To keep her on an even keel, like.'

'And that's why you're so worried?'

'I've been worried for weeks. She's been acting weird. Not talking. And now she's disappeared.'

It had been clear to Vera from the moment she'd seen the couple that Jack adored Joanna. He stole looks at her, basked in her presence. She was big-boned with long, corn-coloured hair

5

worn in a plait down her back. Dramatically dark eyebrows. A wide mouth and large brown eyes. All her features big and generous — hands and feet to match. She wore red, boat-shaped leather shoes and patchwork dungarees, hand-knitted sweaters in bright colours. If Vera had been asked to describe her in one word, it would have been 'jolly'. She'd never thought of Joanna as being depressed. Maybe a bit the other way, laughing too loudly sometimes and always the last one to leave a party, hugs and kisses all round. Not really in a sexy way, but flamboyant. Vera thought in an earlier life Joanna could have been in the theatre, or an artist. Or a lady. She spoke like an aristocrat, the sort of voice you'd have heard on the BBC in the Sixties. But life before Jack was never mentioned.

Vera went back to the bags still standing on the doorstep and pulled out a couple of bottles of beer. There was a bottle opener on the coffee table next to the mug. So much for her planned evening of domesticity: changing the sheets on her bed, sticking a few towels in the washing machine.

'Go on,' she said. 'Tell me all about it.'

'I never knew what she saw in me.' His voice was weedy, the Liverpool accent even more pronounced.

'Stop fishing for compliments!' Vera barked. 'I've no time for games.'

He looked up at her, shocked. He'd expected sympathy and an easy ride.

'Where did you meet her?' Vera wasn't sure how relevant this was, but she was curious

6

anyway and thought it would get him talking.

'Marseilles,' he said. 'A cafe by the harbour. I'd been working out of there, just finished the contract with the shipping company, money in my pocket. She was sitting alone, halfway through a bottle of wine. Drinking to get drunk, not because she was enjoying a glass with her fish supper. She heard me talk to the waiter, realized I'd never get myself understood and translated for me. She's always been a bit of a show-off. We got talking. You know.'

'What was she doing in Marseilles?'

'She'd run away from her husband,' Jack said. 'Some rich bastard.' He changed his voice, made it music-hall posh: '*He was heading up the office in Paris.* Some businessman. Or banker. Or wanker. Marseilles was about as far away from him as she could get.'

'Why didn't she go back to the UK?' Vera thought if you left your man, you'd want friends about you. Family even.

'Nothing for her there. She's like the black sheep in her family. They threatened to have her sectioned if she left her husband. You know, like locked up in a loony bin.' He paused. 'She tried to kill herself. There's a scar on her wrist. I saw it that first time, sitting in the sun outside the cafe in Marseilles. It's still there. She calls it her war wound.'

'I've never noticed.'

'That's why she always wears all those bangles. Anyway, that was a long time ago. I got her sorted out. Took her to the GP. She's fine if she takes her pills. They said she had bipolar

7

disorder. I dunno, *I'd* have gone crazy if I'd lived what she'd been through.'

'But she's stopped taking the pills?'

'Aye. Says she's okay now and doesn't need them.' He paused again and looked up, straight at Vera. 'I think there's another man.' Then: 'I think she wants the high of being in love. That's why she stopped taking the lithium.'

'Where would she meet another man?' Vera thought he was letting his imagination run wild. 'Besides Chris in the pub and Arthur the vet, who does she ever meet?'

'She has her own friends,' Jack said. 'Her own interests. That was the deal from the start. I wasn't going to run her life for her.' He hesitated. 'Last week she was on the phone and hung up when I came into the room. She wouldn't say who it was.'

'So where do you think she's gone?' Vera realized she'd finished the beer. She thought she'd like to get rid of Jack before she opened another. Then she'd be able to enjoy it in peace.

'I don't know,' he said. 'If I knew, I'd go and find her.'

'Even though you don't want to run her life for her?' Vera looked at him, challenging him to come up with a rational answer. 'Maybe it's just as she says in the note, and she needs a few days away.' She was thinking it would be easy enough for her to find out where Joanna had run away to. There was only one taxi firm within ten miles of the farm and everyone used it. If she had a word with Tommy Wooler, she'd soon know where Jo was hiding out. If Jack hadn't been so

8

anxious, he'd have thought of that too.

'She's stopped taking her pills,' he said again, bending forward to make sure Vera understood the gravity of his words. 'She's been up and down for days: one minute high as a kite, singing and laughing, the next all angry and shouting the odds. She's not herself. I'm not going to drag her back against her will. Do you think I'd live with her if she didn't want to be with me? Do you think I'd force her to be unhappy? Look, I know you think I'm a soft git, but I'd die for Joanna Tobin.' He paused for breath. 'I'm worried about her, about what she might do to herself.'

'You think she might attempt suicide again?'

'Yeah,' he said. 'That's what I think. If it doesn't work out for her. If whatever she's dreaming about doesn't happen.'

Vera pushed herself to her feet. There was frozen stuff in her bags that would soon be melting. 'So what do you want me to do?'

He looked at her as if she was mad. 'Find her, of course. Make sure she's safe.'

'And then?'

'That's all.' He'd stood too and they'd moved to the front door. Outside it was freezing and the sky was spattered with stars. 'Just make sure she's safe.'

2

God, Vera thought, *if any of the others considered doing this — going freelance, playing the private eye — I'd give them such a bollocking.* She stood in the lean-to putting the contents of her shopping bags into the freezer. It was a chest freezer, too big for her, living on her own. Exactly the same size, she realized for the first time, as the one in which Hector had kept all his dead animals and birds, the core of his illegal taxidermy business. She'd got rid of that when he died. It had been stinking. So why had she bought another, exactly the same? Some shrink could make a big deal out of that. Or decide that she was an idle bugger with no imagination.

And why had she agreed to do as Jack asked and chase around the county looking for Joanna? *Because I'm soft as clarts. Because I enjoy happy endings and want to bring the couple together again, like I'm some great fat Cupid in wellies. Because it would be bloody inconvenient living here without them next door.*

In the kitchen she opened another beer, put a pork pie and a tomato on a plate, with a quarter of a crusty loaf and butter still in the packet, then carried the lot into the living room on a tray. The fire was low and she threw on another couple of logs. The round 1930s clock that stood on the mantelpiece said it was nine o'clock.

10

She'd better try Tommy Wooler now. He usually caught the last couple of hours before closing in the Percy Arms in Sallyford.

He recognized her mobile number. 'Where are you then? Pissed and incapable and needing a lift home?'

'Not a drop has touched my lips, Tommy. Well, not so you'd notice, and I'm home safe and well. I'm after some information.'

'What sort of information?' Defensive now. In his younger days he'd been a bit of a tearaway. Not malicious, just a tad wild and daft. He kept up with a couple of the bad lads he'd met in the Young Offenders Institution at Castington. Vera had never asked him about them, but that was the way his mind was working.

'You picked up Joanna Tobin two days ago.' A statement not a question.

'Aye, that's right.' There was no suspicion in his voice. He was just relieved she wasn't asking him about his old unsavoury acquaintances. Vera wondered what they were up to and why he was so jumpy, made a mental note to check on them. Or get Holly to do it.

'Where was it you took her?' As if she knew really, but it had just slipped her mind.

Tommy didn't care any more. He just wanted to get out to the pub.

'Out to the coast. Howick way.'

'Where exactly, Tommy?' She could feel her stomach rumbling, felt somehow that the pie was taunting her.

'I don't know exactly. She had to direct me. In the middle of nowhere. She didn't have the

11

postcode, so I couldn't get it on the satnav. Nightmare!' He paused. 'She called it the Writers' House. Strange name.' He paused. 'What do you want her for anyway?'

But Vera didn't answer. She'd replaced the phone and her mouth was full of pie.

★　★　★

The next morning Jack was lurking in the yard waiting to catch her on her way to Kimmerston. She was earlier than usual and she'd thought she might miss him. How long had he been out there? He was pretending to work on his old tractor, but Vera knew fine well he was waiting to check up on her. She went up to him and stood, legs apart, hands on hips, and put on the fierce voice she used occasionally to show her team she meant business.

'I've promised I'll look for her. But I'll do it in my way and in my time. I'll tell you as soon as there's any news.'

He nodded, but said nothing, and Jack — who was all words, flowery and flowing, whose life was a series of stories — made this silence speak volumes. She got into the Land Rover and drove away, aware of him watching her all the way down the lane.

In the office she googled the Writers' House and found it at once. It seemed there was nothing sinister about the place. Unless you found poets and novelists sinister. This was a retreat for writers of all sorts, and throughout the year it hosted a number of residential courses for writers with different levels of experience. What had she been expecting? A Gothic tower, where Joanna had been trapped by a madman who'd persuaded her to fall in love with him? The pictures on the website showed a large whitewashed farmhouse. Part of it was very old, according to the advertising pitch, and fortified against the Scots who had raided across the border. One view *did* show a bare-stone outside wall with crenellations. And there was a small, dark chapel. But inside it was all very tasteful and not Gothic at all. Flagstones on the kitchen floor, bare beams, stripped wooden doors. Low sofas and easy chairs, with only the occasional flipchart to indicate it wasn't a private home. The place was run, apparently, by a company of the same name, headed by someone called Miranda Barton.

There were pictures of the tutors, and even Vera recognized a couple of names: a poet who appeared on television occasionally, talking about the decline of British culture; a playwright. The fees seemed to her to be exorbitant, and certainly well beyond Joanna's pocket. Unless Joanna had a secret fund left over from her marriage. In large red letters it said that bursaries were available to writers who showed talent, and it occurred to Vera that Joanna's disappearance was no more disturbing than that: she fancied herself as a writer. Perhaps she'd been awarded one of the bursaries, but had been embarrassed to tell Jack what she was up to. Perhaps she wanted to wait until she'd finished a piece of work before telling him.

A course had started the day Joanna took herself off from Myers Farm: 'Short Cuts. The art of the contemporary crime short story.' *Cuts*, Vera thought. *Very witty. You could tell they'd be good with words.* She had just clicked onto the link when she heard footsteps outside her office: her sergeant, Joe Ashworth, dead on time for their daily morning meeting. She turned off the PC, feeling faintly guilty without really understanding why.

* * *

Mid-afternoon, she wandered through to the open-plan office where Joe was filling in his overtime form.

'I'm off,' she said. 'Taking back some of the time I'm owed from the Lister case.'

'Going to the gym?' A sly little grin. He knew she'd been told to lose weight.

'Piss off!' But there was no animosity in it. After a week of strategy meetings and appraisals she was looking forward to being away from the office. It was still clear and bright and, driving east past the newly ploughed fields, where the low sun threw long shadows from the trees lining the road ahead of her, she felt more optimistic than she had for ages. Since the last major inquiry.

She'd printed out a map from the Writers' House website and had to stop every now and then to check directions. This wasn't work, not really, so she was back in Hector's Land Rover. No satnav. She felt the wonderful liberation of the truant. Rounding the brow of a hill, she had a view of Alnmouth, with its pretty painted houses, and the bay, and turned north past the masts and domes of RAF Boulmer. Then after a series of missed turns and narrow lanes, she could see the house. It was in a steep valley that led to the coast, sheltered on the landward side by trees. The old fortified farmstead with a newer extension leading away from the sea. The chapel forming one side of a courtyard. She pulled into a farm gate to get her bearings and decide what tack to take with Joanna. Now she was here, she wasn't sure how she should play the situation. What if the group was in the middle of some intense discussion on the meaning of literature and life? Vera pictured them seated round the room she'd seen on the Internet, writing pads on their knees, brows furrowed in concentration. She was sure everyone would enjoy the drama of the interruption: Vera walking in demanding to talk to Joanna. Everyone except Joanna, who'd be mortified. *Time for a bit of tact, girl.*

There must be, Vera thought, staff. An office manager, a cook, someone to make the beds and clean the toilets. People she could talk to and get a feel for the place. If the punters paid that much for a week in the wilds, they would expect to be looked after. She decided she'd leave the vehicle where it was and go in on foot, get the lie of the land, wait until any group activity or workshop was over and she could get Joanna on her own.

The light was fading quickly now and the temperature had dropped. Walking east down the lane into the valley, she was entirely in shadow. In the morning the house would be filled with light, but now the place had a gloomy air. The trees in the copse had dropped their leaves and the lane was covered with them. Once she almost slipped. She arrived at the gate to the Writers' House. There was a professionally painted sign and the logo of a quill pen that she recognized from the website, and beyond, a large garden. After the house the lane petered into a track that was no more than a footpath. It led steeply down to the small shingle beach that she'd seen from the car. There were no other buildings within sight. If you wanted a place to write without distraction, this would suit the bill. But it occurred to Vera that it would be a long trek to the pub.

Approaching the house, she felt nervous. Here she was well out of her comfort zone. She couldn't flash her warrant card and demand respect and attention. No crime had been committed. And she'd never really got on with arty types: people who used words with ideas behind them, but had nothing real to say. She was more comfortable with the villains she brought to court.

Now she could see the place in more detail: a big house and then some old outbuildings, stables perhaps, that had been turned into a cottage. Both faced into a paved area that must once have been a farmyard. To her right the tiny chapel that must once have served the extended family that had lived here. In the house they'd switched the lights on, but they hadn't drawn the curtains. This was Vera's favourite time of day. She'd always been curious, loved the glimpses of other folks' domestic existence as she walked down the street. And what was it to be a detective, after all, but to pry into other people's lives? There was a big front door, but she avoided that. It looked as if it locked automatically from inside, and she didn't want to ring the brass bell that hung outside. Not until she knew Joanna was still there and she had some idea of what was going on.

She walked round the side of the big house, avoiding the shingle path, keeping to the grass border that ran right up to the wall. She made no sound. Arriving at the first window, she stopped with her back to the house. It came to her suddenly that she must look completely ridiculous. If there were someone further up the bank looking down — a couple of birdwatchers, for example, with binoculars — they'd take her for a madwoman, or an inept burglar. Still standing close to the wall of the house, so that she couldn't be seen from inside, she looked in. The kitchen. A young man in chef's whites stood with his back to her, stirring a pan. There was a teapot on the table and two blue mugs. An older woman sat at the table, reading a typed manuscript. She was rather glamorous, with dyed blonde hair. The finger that turned the page had red nails. Was that Miranda Barton? At any rate, there was no sign of Joanna and, crouching so that she was lower than the windowsill, Vera moved on.

The next room was empty. It looked like a

library, the walls lined with bookshelves. There were a couple of small tables and leather-seated, upright chairs. Now Vera had turned another corner and was on a paved veranda that looked out over the sea. On the grass below was a bird table and a set of elaborate feeders filled with nuts and seed. She could see the lighthouse at the Farne Islands to the north and Coquet Island to the south. In the summer this would be a magnificent place to sit. Vera pictured them here after a day's writing, drinking fancy wine and sharing their ideas. Posing. Why did she feel the need to sneer? Because people who talked about books or pictures or films made her feel ignorant and out of her depth.

She'd stopped right on the corner, because most of the wall facing out to sea was made of glass. There were two long windows, almost floor-to-ceiling, and between them double glass doors. A long, light room. The place featured on the website, with the sofas and the easy chairs. And there were people inside. It seemed to Vera that the group had just broken up. They were standing and chatting. Tea must have been served, because they were holding cups and saucers, balancing scones on paper napkins. Now it was almost dark outside, and Vera thought there was little danger of her being seen. The people in the room were pre-occupied with their own concerns. Their faces were animated. There were six of them, but the door leading further into the house was open, so it was possible that some people had already left. Certainly there was no sign of Joanna.

Vera stood for a moment and wondered how Joanna might fit into this group. Joanna, with her big hands and feet, her loud laugh and her dirty fingernails. Her brightly coloured home-made clothes. If she was here, had she escaped already to the privacy of her own room, daunted by the confidence of her companions?

Vera had decided that it was time to go back to the front door, ring the bell and ask to speak to Joanna. She had a cover story prepared. There would be a domestic crisis: a relative's illness, which Joanna should know about. That was when Vera heard a sound that shocked the people on the other side of the glass from their self-indulgent conversation. A scream. It seemed hardly human and was without age or gender: loud and piercing and terrifying.

3

Vera couldn't tell where the noise was coming from. Inside the house? If so, why did it seem so loud, even out here? The sound seemed to surround her, almost to swallow her up. Perhaps it was the pitch, but it was as if she was feeling it through her bones, rather than hearing it with her ears. There was no escape from it. She took a few steps back and looked up. At the top of the house, double glass doors, mirroring the ones here out onto the terrace, led onto a stone balcony. The woman from the kitchen was there, lit from behind, leaning over, emptying the noise from her lungs into the cold air. Vera was reminded of a drunk spewing. Suddenly the noise stopped.

It seemed to take Vera hours to get into the house. The struggle to be heard, to get inside, reminded her of one of her recurring nightmares: she was a child, locked out of a house where her mother was dying, and she could never find a way in to save her. Now the adult Vera banged on the patio doors, where moments before the guests had been drinking tea. Nobody responded. They must all have rushed away to find the source of the screaming. She retraced her path round the house to the front door. Now the light had gone and she stumbled from the path, losing her way in the thick vegetation of the shrubbery. She pushed through the bushes, struggling to fight off the panic, and decided she must be walking in the wrong direction because there was still no path. The branches scratched her face and pulled at her clothes. She forced herself to stand still. She was no longer a child and she wasn't lost.

In the distance she heard the faint sound of waves on shingle. As she turned away from the sound, the solid shape of the building became clear against the sky above the shrubs. Vera climbed back to the path and walked round the house to the front door. There was no sound from inside. Checking her watch, she saw that she'd been wandering round in the garden for nearly twenty minutes. She ran her fingers through her hair and pulled a dead leaf from her jacket, then rang the brass bell by swinging the rope, which was attached to a heavy clapper. There was no response. There was a light in the cottage on the other side of the yard and she considered going over. Then the door of the main house opened and she saw the young chef, who had been working in the kitchen. He was still wearing his whites.

'This way,' he said. Then he added distractedly, 'How did you get here so quickly?'

Vera thought for a moment that she felt like a very fat Alice in a strange Wonderland. The chef darted away from her down a narrow corridor, leaving her to follow. He was thin and very dark. As he'd opened the door she'd seen black hairs on the backs of his hands and his lower arms. *A wolf in chef's clothing.* She glimpsed the guests through a half-open door, but he was walking so

21

quickly that she couldn't make out individuals as she hurried to keep up. If Joanna was in there, Vera didn't see her. The house was much bigger inside than she'd have guessed, a warren of passages and small rooms. He led her up a short flight of stairs. By now Vera was completely disorientated; she must have seen just the outside of the newer extension, and now there were no windows to help her make out which way they were going.

'I was in the area anyway.' Finally she got close enough to him to answer the question. The speed of their progress had left her a little breathless.

'I phoned for an ambulance too. I don't know where that is.'

'Ah,' she said. 'They might take a while to get here. They'll be coming from Alnwick, most likely.'

'Actually . . . ' The young man paused. 'I don't think there's much rush. They won't be able to do anything, after all.' He stopped at the end of a corridor and opened the door.

It was not at all what she had been expecting. She'd thought she'd be stepping into a bedroom, a grand bedroom because of the balcony. But this was another Alice moment. Another contradiction. It was as if an outside space had been brought indoors. Everything was green and alive. She stood at the threshold and looked in.

The room was a first-floor conservatory. It was tall and narrow and glass doors led onto the balcony, but there was glass too in the sloping ceiling. From the terrace below she hadn't seen that. And glass walls on each side. There was a tiled floor and painted wicker chairs. Pots of enormous plants with shiny dark leaves formed a mini tropical jungle. All the plants were fat and fleshy and one had a tall spike of pink flowers. The smell was of compost and damp vegetation. In the daylight there would be a magnificent view over the sea. A large mirror in a green frame hung on the one solid wall. The glass must be old with flaws in it, because the reflection was slightly distorted and, glancing into it, Vera felt the queasiness of seasickness. The room was very warm.

'So what am I here to look at?' She shook her head in an attempt to clear her mind.

'Didn't they tell you? They made me repeat the details.' The young man walked past the plants and the garden furniture and opened the glass door to the balcony. There was a rush of cold air, and in the distance the sound of the tide sucking on shingle. The balcony was wider than the glass doors and each end was in semi-darkness. He turned to Vera impatiently. 'Out here!'

She followed him outside and in the faint light from the room saw a man crouched in the corner of the stone parapet, his knees almost up to his chin. The pose seemed strange because his cropped hair was grey; he was in late middle age. Older men didn't sit on floors because they found it hard to get up again. Their joints creaked. And nobody would sit on a stone floor in late October. The angle of the lights from inside the room threw odd shadows onto his face. He looked angry. Outraged.

He was wearing a pale-coloured shirt under a

23

black jacket. In this light it was hard to make out the exact colour of the shirt. Most of it was covered in blood. And there was blood on the stone floor and on the wall. Looking closer, Vera saw that there was spatter on the glass door. It seemed that he'd been stabbed, but there was no immediate sign of the knife.

'Who is he?'

'I told them when I phoned 999.' The young man was beginning to get suspicious. 'Who are you anyway?'

'Aye, well, not everything gets through.' Vera showed him her warrant card, pleased that she could find it on the first trawl of her bag; tilted it so that the light caught the photo. 'I'm Detective Inspector Stanhope. What's your name?'

'Alex Barton.'

'Your mother runs this place?' She'd had him down as the hired help and couldn't keep the surprise from her voice.

'We run it together. I'm a partner. Though sometimes you wouldn't think so.' The tone was resentful and it was obvious that Alex regretted the comment as soon as it was made. He realized this wasn't the right time to air family grievances. 'Don't you want to know what's happened here? Shouldn't you be speaking to– '

'Of course, pet. First of all, tell me about the victim.' Vera had never liked being told how to do her job. She took his arm and led him back through the strangely shaped glass room and into the corridor. 'But out here, eh? We don't want to muck up the crime scene more than we already have.'

On her way to the room she'd noticed a small sitting area where two corridors formed a crossroads. There was a chaise longue and a low coffee table, covered with upmarket newspapers and literary magazines. There was still no window and the only light came from a dim wall lamp covered by a red shade. Vera thought you'd struggle to read anything much here, and that the whole house was more like a stage-set than a place for practical activity. She lowered herself carefully onto the seat and Alex followed.

'Where's everyone else?' she asked. An event like this, there were always spectators.

'I told them to wait in the drawing room.'

'And they always do what you say, do they, pet?' He didn't answer and she continued. 'What do you know about the chap on the balcony?'

'Didn't you recognize him?' There was something supercilious about the question. Vera had got the same reaction when she asked for chips in a posh restaurant.

'Famous, is he?'

'He's called Tony Ferdinand. Professor Tony Ferdinand. Academic, reviewer and arts guru. You must have seen him on *The Culture Show*. And he did that series on BBC4 about the contemporary novel.' The man didn't wait for a response. Perhaps he'd already worked out that Vera wasn't a natural BBC4 viewer. 'Oh, God, this'll be a nightmare. We'll never get any of the professionals from London up after this. Imagine the publicity! Lunatic students cutting the lecturers' throats! It's hard enough to prise the sods away from London as it is.'

'So he was working for you?' But not much liked, Vera thought, if Alex's first thought was for the business rather than the man.

'He deigned to grace us with his presence.' He must have seen that Vera still needed an explanation. 'He came to the Writers' House once every couple of years to act as tutor. Making it clear that he was doing my mother an enormous favour. They go back a long way. But his support made a big difference when we set up the writing courses.' He paused, seeming to realize that he sounded callous. 'I'm sorry. It's hard to believe that he's dead.'

'How long have you known him?' Vera found herself amused. This young man was hardly more than a child to her and surely couldn't have been involved in this business for more than a few years.

'Pretty well as long as I can remember. Since I was a child. Tony worked with my mother at St Ursula's, and when she was first published his positive reviews made a big difference to her career.'

Vera wasn't sure how any of this worked. St Ursula's? This was a world about which she knew nothing.

'She's a writer too, is she?'

'Of course. Miranda Barton!' He paused. 'I suppose she's not that well known now. But don't let on you've never heard of her. She'd be mortified.'

'Sorry, pet. I don't get much time for reading in my line of business. Not stories, at any rate.' Through the thick walls she heard the muffled sound of a police siren in the distance. The local cavalry arriving, showing off for all they were worth. What did they need a siren for? To scare one tractor and a bunch of sheep from the lane?

'What was Mr Ferdinand doing here?' Vera went on. 'Was he lecturing on this course, 'Short Cuts'?'

'In theory.' Again she thought she sensed bitterness in the young man's voice. It seemed there were lots of complications in this case. At least she hoped there were. She liked something she could get her teeth into, something to prove what a brilliant detective she was.

'And in practice?'

'He was here to massage his ego, to convince himself that he was still as influential as he'd always been. In 1990 *The Observer* called him a star-maker. I think he's always on the lookout for more stars, to prove his importance in the literary firmament.'

Again Vera wasn't sure what this meant, and now wasn't the time for another show of her ignorance.

'Who found the body?' she asked.

Alex leaned back against the end of the chaise longue as if he was suddenly exhausted. 'My mother. Tony was scheduled to run an informal session before supper. Questions and answers. All about how to find an agent or a publisher, how to submit work. It was often the most popular workshop of the week, the practical side of getting work into print. It was what a lot of the students came for. Of course they all hoped

27

Tony would recognize their genius and recommend them to an agent or publisher. He was charismatic, you know. One word of praise from him and they'd believe in themselves as writers. Tony hadn't appeared for tea, so Mother went to find him. The glass room was one of his favourite places.'

'That's what you call it? The glass room?'

'Yes.' Again he regarded Vera with suspicion.

'Was that unusual? Mr Ferdinand not arriving to work on time?'

'It was, rather. Tony wasn't the easiest person to work with, but he was professional.'

'Your mother came up here and saw him on the balcony?' Vera wasn't sure that made sense. If you were looking for someone, wouldn't you just poke your head round the door to see if they were inside? How could she know that Ferdinand would be crouched in a heap in the corner?

'Yes,' Alex said. 'Then all hell broke loose.' Despite his expression of shock at the professor's murder, it seemed to Vera that the young man was devoid of emotion. He was going through the motions. Which couldn't be said of his mother. Vera could still hear the sound of Miranda Barton's screaming in her ears, feel it reverberating through her body. The sight of the man on the balcony — the fixed and angry glare on his face, the blood — would be shocking of course. But she thought that there had been more than shock in that noise. It was more personal. Like a mother keening for a child. Or a woman grieving for her lover.

'This room is just above the drawing room,' Alex went on, 'so everyone who was having tea could hear her. They all ran out to see what was going on. The last thing I wanted was some sort of circus, so I told them to wait downstairs. It didn't take much to wind my mother up. If anything, I was embarrassed. I thought she was just causing a scene. When I saw Tony, I brought Mother downstairs and asked another tutor, Giles Rickard, to take her into our cottage. I went back to the office to phone the police.'

'And the ambulance,' Vera said.

For the first time he gave a wry little smile. 'I know, that was ridiculous. But I'd never seen anybody dead before. I suppose I needed confirmation, someone medical to tell me I wasn't making it all up. I wasn't sure what I was supposed to do.'

The front doorbell started to ring. 'That'll be the local police,' Vera said. 'You'd best go and let them in. Tell them I'm here and bring them up. They can secure the scene for us, and I can start my investigation.'

Alex stood up and gave her a strange look. 'What investigation?'

'Why, that's what I do for a living. I catch criminals.' Again, trapped in this small space, with the low red light throwing odd shadows on the white walls, she felt as if she'd wandered into someone's weird dream. She needed her sergeant, Joe Ashworth, to turn up full of youthful energy and common sense.

'But I told them on the phone!' Now the man seemed to be losing patience with her altogether.

'We know who killed Tony Ferdinand.'

'Your mother saw the murderer?'

'No! I did. As I've just said. And as I told your colleagues. On my way to the glass room, while Mother was still screaming, I bumped into the woman here in the corridor. She had a knife in her hand.'

'Very convenient.' *Bugger*, Vera thought. So it was back to working the boring stuff, the pathetic druggies and the pub brawls, just when she'd thought there might be something more exciting to sustain her interest. Then she had another thought, which was even more disturbing. 'I suppose your murderer has a name?'

'It's one of the students. We've shut her in her bedroom. She's called Joanna Tobin.'

4

Joanna's room was small. A single bed set against one wall, and against another a desk, with an anglepoise lamp and a chair. A narrow wardrobe. There was a red carpet on the floor and the duvet cover and the curtains were a deeper red. A door led to a tiny shower room. This was slightly more comfortable than the cell in Low Newton prison where she'd more than likely end up, but not much bigger. Of course, Vera thought, the court might decide Joanna was mad, and then she'd go to a secure psychiatric hospital instead. Vera wasn't sure which would be worse. If she had a choice in a similar situation, she would probably opt for the prison. It would still be full of psychos, but at least you'd have a date for getting out. Places like Broadmoor, you were dependent for a release date on the whim of a team of psychiatrists and politicians.

There'd been a man standing outside the closed door of the room. He was tall and heavily built. She thought he'd been fit once, but had slightly run to flab. Dressed in cheap jeans and sweatshirt, he stood with his legs apart and his hands on his hips. Classic bouncer posture. You couldn't tell from his face, but Vera thought he was probably enjoying himself. Deep down, everyone loved a murder almost as much as she did. They loved the drama of it, the frisson of

31

fear, the exhilaration of still being alive. People had been putting together stories of death and the motives for killing since the beginning of time, to thrill and to entertain. It was different of course if you were close to the victim. Or to the killer. Vera hadn't begun to think yet how she would tell Jack what had gone on here.

'Who are you?' Vera had demanded of Joanna's warder before he opened the door.

'Lenny Thomas.' In those four syllables she could tell this was a voice that came from Ashington or one of the other ex-pit villages in the south-east of the county, not from rural Northumberland.

'Work here, do you? Or are you one of the writers?' Vera saw him as a handyman or gardener, but she'd met more scruffy academics.

'I'm a writer.' He looked suddenly astonished, as if he'd never said the words before.

'Student or tutor?'

'Student, but that Professor Ferdinand had said I had the potential to be published. He said he might take me on as one of his postgraduate students. Imagine that! Me doing an MA in creative writing, and I only scraped five GCSEs. He said that wouldn't matter. He was going to put in a word. And a word from him would make a difference. Everyone knew that.' Lenny gave a little laugh that had no resentment in it. 'But that'll never work out now, eh? I knew deep down it was too good to be true. People like me never get that sort of luck. But it was nice to believe it, like, while it was happening.'

'If he thought you were good enough, other

people will too,' Vera said.

'Aye, maybe.' And Vera saw that Lenny probably didn't want success enough, or wasn't confident enough to push his work. She nodded to the door. 'How is she?'

'No bother,' Lenny said. 'Calm as owt.' And he moved away to let Vera in. 'Do you want me there with you, like?'

'Nah,' Vera said. 'We'll be fine. Go off and get yourself a cup of tea.'

She could tell the man was disappointed, but he wandered off without comment.

Joanna was sitting on a window seat, looking out into the garden. It was quite dark by now, so there was nothing for her to see. She must have heard the door opening, but she didn't turn her head and seemed lost in a world of her own.

'Why, lass, you've got yourself into a bit of a pickle.'

Vera sat on the edge of the bed. She could have chosen the chair by the desk, but the bed was more comfortable and closer to Joanna. If Joanna shifted her head just a bit, Vera would be within her line of vision.

'One question,' Vera went on. 'Did you make him sit out on the balcony before you stabbed him, or did you do it in the room, then stick him outside? It doesn't quite make sense. We'll know, of course, once the pathologist gets here, but it'd save us a bit of time if you explain how he ended up there. I couldn't see any blood in the room itself, so I guess you got him outside.'

Now Joanna did twist her body so that she was looking into the room. It was as if she noticed

33

Vera for the first time. Her posture, sitting on the window seat, her back to the glass, was almost regal.

'I didn't kill him at all.' She was, as Lenny had said, quite calm.

'Come on, pet. You were wandering around the corridor outside the glass room with a knife in your hand!'

'So I was,' Joanna agreed, in the posh southern accent that made Vera think of a lady of the manor opening a village fete. Or the wife of a colonial governor. 'How very Lady Macbeth!'

'I'll need to take your clothes for forensic examination.' Vera decided the woman must be quite insane, and that it was best to get the clothes away from her while she was being cooperative.

'I was there in the room,' Joanna said. 'But I didn't kill him. I didn't even see him. I suppose he must have been dead already.' Despite the denial, she slid off the window seat and began to strip. She'd never been embarrassed by nudity. One very hot July day, Vera had caught her swimming naked in the tarn close to the farm. She'd laughed out loud at Vera's surprise: *Why don't you come in. It's lovely!*

Her body was still brown from working in the fields all summer. She was soft and supple. Vera saw a dressing gown on a hook on the door and threw it to her. She thought it might be better to start this story from the beginning. 'What are you doing in this place, anyway?'

Joanna pulled the dressing gown around her and tied the cord. It was made of silk and looked like a kimono. She'd have picked it up for a few

34

pence at a charity shop and brought it home in triumph to show off to Jack.

'Should you be talking to me, without a lawyer?' This was Joanna at her most imperious, and Vera was surprised.

'Probably not,' Vera said. 'If you like, we can wait until we're in the station and I can talk to you there. Lawyers, tape recordings. The works. Probably for the best. I haven't cautioned you yet, and I'll only get into bother when we get to court.'

A shadow seemed to pass over Joanna's face. 'I'm sorry,' she said. 'I always get arsey when I'm scared.'

'Jack said you'd stopped taking your pills.'

The mention of Jack threw her and, for a moment, Vera thought she might cry. 'I did for a couple of weeks, but I'm back on them now. I saw it wasn't the right time to stop. Maybe it never will be.' She looked into Vera's face and gave a wide smile. 'You don't need to worry. I'm not mad.'

And Vera thought now that was probably true. This was the Joanna she knew: loud and quirky, but rational enough. In which case, why had the woman stabbed a professor of English literature to death?

'Tell me,' she said again. 'Why are you here?'

'I thought I could write.' Joanna seemed to be struggling to choose the right words. 'At least, I thought I had something to say. I read an article about the Writers' House in the *Newcastle Journal*. They were running a sort of competition. I sent in a piece. It was about France, about my life there. Bits of details that had stuck in my head. Anyway, I won and they awarded me a bursary. A week's tuition. All free.'

'Why didn't you tell Jack you were coming to stay here? He wouldn't have minded. He'd have been proud of you!'

'He thinks it's wrong to rake over the old days.' Joanna turned briefly again to look out into the dark. All she would have seen was her own reflection in the glass. 'He takes it personally. He thinks he should be enough for me.'

'Because you're enough for him?' Vera said.

'He adores me,' Joanna said. 'I should be grateful. I *am* grateful.'

Vera thought this was an odd sort of conversation to be having with a woman who'd been accused of sticking a knife into a man's heart, but at least Joanna was now talking freely to her.

'It's a tricky sort of emotion, gratitude,' Vera said. 'It's never come easily to me. I'd rather have people owing *me* a favour than the other way round.'

'Yes,' Joanna smiled again. 'I've always felt that too.'

'So winning this competition was a way for you to take off for a few days? Have a bit of time to yourself? Get away from Jack and the farm?'

Joanna leaned forward so that the long plait fell over her shoulder. 'It wasn't just that. It was a way of exploring my past, making sense of it. Of taking the time to go back and look at the events of my first marriage with fresh eyes.'

'Eh, pet, that sounds more like therapy than stories to me!'

Joanna threw back her head and gave the rich, deep laugh that Vera remembered from parties and dinners at the farm, which took her away from this strange house with its piles of books and paper, back to a real world of lambing and freshly turned soil and rain. 'You should have been here,' Joanna said. 'They should employ you to sit in on the workshops to stop students writing pretentious crap.'

'I'm here,' Vera said, serious again, 'because a man's dead.'

They sat for a moment, looking at each other in silence.

'I didn't kill him,' Joanna said. 'I didn't like him very much, but I didn't kill him.'

Vera was aware that if she continued to question Joanna she'd be crossing a line. In fact the line had already been crossed when she'd decided to come into this room on her own. The prime suspect in the case was Vera's neighbour, could even be considered a friend, so there was a conflict of interest. She was on her own with the woman. No witness and no tape recorder, as she'd said before. She should call immediately for one of the local bobbies to escort Joanna to a waiting police car and drive her back to the station. They'd find her a duty solicitor and another member of the team should interview her. But Vera stayed where she was and said nothing. She was a detective, and listening was what she did best.

'Tony wanted sex with me,' Joanna went on.

37

'In a way, it was quite flattering and for a moment I was tempted. He was good-looking in a smooth, boring kind of way, and it's a long time since I've been propositioned. Completely out of the question of course.'

'Why out of the question?' Vera asked. She had imagined that the hippies went in for free sex. They seemed so relaxed with their bodies, and wasn't that what hippies were famous for?

Joanna looked up sharply. 'I didn't fancy him,' she said, as if the answer was obvious. 'He wasn't my type. And he was rather a horrid man.'

'In what way horrid?' Again Vera had intended not to ask any further questions. Soon Joe Ashworth would be here. She'd phoned him before coming to talk to Joanna. Then they could progress the interview in a more orthodox way. He could take the lead. But Vera wanted to know what had happened to provoke such grotesque violence, and at the moment Joanna was her best source of information, whether she was a suspect or witness.

'He was greedy,' Joanna said after a moment's consideration. 'I hate greed, don't you? It's such a mean, small-minded vice. As if money matters at all!'

'It matters to lots of people,' Vera said.

'Only to people who have nothing of real value in their lives!' There was the imperious tone again. 'But I shouldn't be rude about him, should I? He didn't deserve to die. Nobody deserves to die before their time.'

'Why did you go into the glass room?' Vera asked. 'Everyone knew it was his favourite place,

38

apparently. If you disliked him so much, what were you doing there?'

'I went because he asked me to. Obviously it was a foolish thing to do. But wisdom has never really been my bag.'

'Perhaps you should explain.' Again Vera felt that the conversation was spinning away from her. She needed facts. Time of death. Cause of death. A list of the people in the house. Something to anchor her to reality. She looked at her watch. Joe Ashworth could drive like a cautious sixty-year-old without Vera to urge him on. And she wouldn't have put it past him to call in on his wife and bairns on the way through from Kimmerston. But even allowing for all that, he should be here soon. Joe had as much imagination as a louse and, when he arrived, she'd let him look after Joanna. The woman would be safe with him, mad or not, and he wouldn't let himself be distracted by her ramblings on morality.

'I knew he wanted to get inside my knickers,' Joanna said. 'So it would have been more sensible to stay away. But this was so exciting. I had to go, didn't I? When I got the note, no way was I going to stay away.'

'What note?' Vera leaned forward. The bed was soft enough, but she could have done with something to lean against and there was a crick in her neck. She wanted to stretch, but that might have given Joanna the impression that she was bored.

'We each have a pigeonhole near reception. If there are outside phone messages or the tutors want to leave work for us, they leave them there. I had this note from Tony. *Come to the glass room after lunch. A major publisher has expressed interest in your work.*'

'How did you know it was from Tony?' Vera asked. 'It could have been from any of the tutors. And he was a university lecturer, wasn't he? Not a publisher.'

'It was signed,' Joanna said. Vera could tell the woman was making an effort to be patient. 'Not a proper signature, but initials. And I knew Tony liked to sit in the glass room. He'd escape there most days after lunch with coffee and a brandy. I think he liked looking down on us. Literally, I mean. From the balcony he could see onto the terrace and that was where the smokers all gathered and chatted. I caught him once, listening in.' She paused. 'And he was much more than a university professor. He had influence, contacts in the industry.'

'What did he get out of it?' Vera asked. 'I mean if he'd found you a publisher, would he get a cut?'

'No!' Joanna was losing patience now and struggled to make Vera understand. 'It wasn't about the money. It was about power. If he'd helped me become a best-selling author, I'd always have to be grateful to him, wouldn't I? It would be like he'd created me. That was what turned him on.' She considered her earlier assessment of Ferdinand. 'It was power he was greedy for, not money.'

Vera still wasn't sure she got it, and decided to stick to the facts. 'What happened next?'

40

'I knocked at the glass-room door. It's a public room, but Tony tended to treat the place like his own. There was no answer, so I went in. There was nobody there. I thought Tony had been there. There were two coffee cups and a glass on the table. The chairs were arranged differently from usual, and I wondered if he'd been chatting to one of the other students, if someone else had received a similar offer. That was when I saw the knife.'

'Where was it?'

'On the floor. Next to that big plant pot. I picked it up to take back to the kitchen. I mean, in my experience that's what knives are for. Chopping meat and peeling vegetables. Not killing people.'

'You didn't go onto the balcony?'

'Obviously not.'

It was possible, Vera thought. The body wouldn't have been visible. Not from the table.

'Didn't you hear the screaming?' She would have liked to believe Joanna, but none of this made sense.

'What screaming?'

'Miranda Barton yelling fit to bust! I could hear her from outside. You'd surely have passed her in the corridor.'

'I didn't pass anyone,' Joanna said. 'Until I met Alex in the corridor. And I didn't hear anyone screaming. The walls here are very thick. I wouldn't, unless I was in the drawing room or standing outside.' She stood up and suddenly towered over Vera, seeming very tall and strong. Had she towered over Ferdinand with a knife in

41

her hand? 'All I heard was music. Someone with a CD player in his room, I suppose. The Beatles.' She looked down at the detective. 'That was what happened. You can believe me or not, as you like.'

5

Joe Ashworth got the call from Vera just as he was on his way home. He'd left work a bit early because it was his birthday and his wife Sarah, known in the family as Sal, had planned a family tea party. It was supposed to be a surprise — the kids adored surprises — but he knew how it would be. A home-made banner on the wall, balloons and a cake covered in candles and chocolate buttons. The bairns wild with excitement, topped up with a sugar-high after licking out the cake bowl and dipping their fingers in the icing. He loved these family events, of course, but it'd be a bugger putting them to bed afterwards, and he had his own ideas about what constituted a birthday treat. The last thing he needed was Sal fraught and knackered.

So Vera's call, taken on the hands-free, provoked a mixed response.

'You slipped out of the office smartish tonight.' Her voice was amused rather than disapproving, just wanting to let him know that she was aware of what was going on, even in her absence. She'd phoned the station and they'd told her he'd already left.

'Aye, well, it's my birthday.' He slowed down to pass a cyclist in helmet and lime-green Lycra.

'I've got a birthday treat for you, lad.' And he listened as she talked about the murder, recognizing her excitement. Hearing too his wife's voice in his head: *That woman's a ghoul — the delight she takes in other people's misery.* He pulled over to the side of the road so that he could write down the details, the post-code and the OS coordinates.

'I'm on my own at the moment,' she said, 'apart from a couple of plods. So quick as you can, Joe, eh?'

He sat where he was for the moment, deliberating. Should he call in quickly to the house, so that the family could do the hiding behind the sofa, jump out and wish Daddy happy birthday? It was only a couple of miles out of his way, and Vera would never know the difference. Or should he send Sal a text, explaining? But a text was the coward's way out, and if he did that, Sal would be seething when he finally got home, even if it was at some unearthly hour of the morning. He couldn't imagine life without Sal, thought she was the best wife in the universe, but she knew how to hold a grudge. Better face her now. He started the engine and drove off, thinking that at least he wouldn't have the nightmare bathtime and bedtime hour to deal with.

Half an hour later he was on the road again, two slices of chocolate cake wrapped in foil on the passenger seat beside him. For some reason the kids had taken to Vera and always remembered her. They sent her gifts and paintings, which he seldom passed on. He thought she'd sneer and chuck them in the bin. She wouldn't turn up her nose at cake, though.

He drove slowly down a narrow lane, worried

44

that he might miss the turn to the house. There was woodland on either side of him, the bare trees caught in his headlight beams as he turned a corner. No moon. He leaned forward, his hands tense on the wheel. A shadow crossed the road ahead of him, caught just on the edge of his line of vision, and made him brake sharply, skid on the frozen fallen leaves towards the verge. He regained control of the car in time, but found he was shaking. He told himself it was nothing. A deer perhaps. Too big for a fox. Just as well he was on his own. Vera would have ridiculed his panic. *What's wrong with you, Joey-boy? Scared of your own shadow now?*

He crossed the brow of the hill and suddenly the valley below him seemed full of light. He passed Vera's Land Rover parked in a farm gateway on his left. There was no possibility after all that he would miss the place; it was the only house for miles. The entrance to the drive was marked by a lamp. To one side of the house there was a car park. As he walked towards the front door he saw a minibus with *The Writers' House* painted on one side.

A uniformed female officer stood at the door. She must have recognized him because she let him in with a smile. 'DI Stanhope said to send you straight upstairs. She's expecting you.'

'Where am I going?'

'I'll take you.' He was a large man, the size and shape of a bear. 'Lenny Thomas, one of the students.' He held out a hand. 'Is that big woman your boss, then?'

Pots and kettles, Joe thought. 'That's right.'

45

'I've written a crime novel,' Lenny said. He ambled away and Joe followed. 'But from the perspective of the villains rather than the cops.' He stopped suddenly. 'I don't suppose she'd let me in to look at the crime scene. For research, like.'

'Not a chance.'

'Aye, well.' Lenny sounded unbothered by the rejection. It seemed to Joe Ashworth that he was probably used to it. 'No harm in asking. You know what they say: *shy bairns get no cake.*' He stopped at a door. 'They're in there.' Lenny added hopefully, 'Do you need me for anything else?'

Joe thought he was like one of those big soft dogs that follow you round, desperate to be taken for a walk. 'No thanks, mate.' He waited for Lenny to disappear back down the hall before knocking and going inside.

He recognized Joanna Tobin at once. He'd taken a dislike to Vera's neighbours when he first met them, thought them feckless and irresponsible, though over the years he'd recognized the work they put in on the small hill farm and had developed a grudging respect. By keeping an eye out for Vera, they took some of the pressure off him. But this was probably the first time he'd looked at Joanna properly, and now he stared at her as if she were an artist's model and he was about to paint her. She sat against the uncurtained window in a dressing gown of blue and green silk. Her clothes were in a transparent scene bag on the floor, and a blue jersey inside matched the blue of the silk. Her legs and feet

46

were bare and brown. There were a few remnants of polish on her toenails: vivid pink. Her hair had been tied into a loose plait, but strands had become loose and fell across her face. She was frowning and it seemed that she'd hardly noticed him come in.

'You know Joanna Tobin,' Vera said. 'It seems she's mixed up in this, one way or another.'

He nodded. Joanna looked at him and smiled.

'We need to get Joanna back to the station to take a proper statement,' Vera went on. 'She admits to picking up the murder weapon, but not to killing the man.'

Joe found himself with nothing to say.

'Organize it, will you, Joe? Don't just stand there.' Vera was losing her patience. 'Get a couple of the uniforms downstairs to take her in, and ask Holly to do the interview. Drag Charlie in too. I'll stay here while Joanna makes herself decent. You'll have other clothes you can put on, won't you, pet? Tell Holly to drop her home afterwards.'

'You're not arresting me?' Joanna turned her gaze slowly towards Vera. Joe thought she was almost disappointed. Was she a drama junkie then? One of the weirdos that turned up at the station on occasions, admitting to crimes they'd seen on the television news.

'Not if you didn't kill the man,' Vera snapped back. 'What's the problem? Don't you want to go home? Scared of facing Jack, are you?'

'I don't know what to say to him.'

'Whatever you like, as long as it doesn't hurt him,' Vera said. 'I don't want him turning up in

47

my house again, like some sort of whipped mongrel.' Then she turned to Joe and let her anger loose on him too. 'Are you still there? Sort out transport for Joanna to the station, then tell all the other guests and staff that I want to talk to them. Herd them into one place and start putting together a list of names and contact addresses. And find out where Tony Ferdinand's bedroom is. Tape it, and get an officer on the door. I'll be down as soon as I can.'

Joe nodded and left the room. He was used to Vera yelling at him. It was like him shouting at the kids when he'd had a bad day — just a way of letting off steam. The time to worry was when she was being pleasant.

He wandered along the corridor and must have taken a wrong turn, because instead of coming down the narrow stone steps that Lenny had taken him up, he found himself at the top of rather a grand staircase, all curves and polished wooden balustrades.

Joe looked down into an entrance hall and beyond to a double door, which must once have been the main way into the house. Another uniformed officer stood just inside the door. The sound of a gong reverberated through the space, startling him for a moment. The noise was loud and must have been made just outside his line of vision. It seemed that murder wouldn't stop the residents eating dinner, and a line of people crossed the hall at the foot of the stairs into what was obviously a dining room. Most carried drinks in their hands. Somewhere there must be a bar. Walking further down the stairs, he could see them inside a panelled room with an arched ceiling. A long table had been laid with silver and a white cloth, and glasses reflected the candlelight. Joe thought some of the diners had dressed especially for the meal — there were long skirts, and a couple of the men wore suits. It seemed there was no dress code, though. Lenny was still in his jeans and sweatshirt. They all took their places at the table and sat with a hushed reverence. They could have been waiting for someone to say grace. Usually, Joe supposed, they'd be talking over the matters of the day. Today there was an air of anticipation, as if nobody knew quite what to expect.

A large middle-aged woman walked to the head of the table. She was dressed in wide black trousers and a raspberry-coloured velvet jacket that was so long it reached her knees. Her unnaturally blonde hair was pinned to the top of her head with a tortoiseshell comb. She wore a string of large, diamond-shaped black beads around her neck. She seemed to Joe to be terribly pale. Was this the woman Vera had described shouting to alert the company to the tragedy? If so, there was no sign of hysteria now, and only the pallor of her skin indicated her distress.

'You'll all have heard of Tony's death,' she said. 'A terrible tragedy. A loss to the literary life of the country. And a sadness for poor, unbalanced Joanna and her family too. The police are in the house and have promised to cause as little disruption to our lives as possible. There is, after all, no mystery about what happened here this afternoon. I'm sure Tony would want us to continue with our programme, and we'll do that, and although it'll be impossible for some of his old friends to concentrate on fiction at this terrible time, we owe it to him to try.' She poured red wine from a bottle on the table into a glass. 'Let's drink,' she said, 'to the memory of Professor Tony Ferdinand.'

The group stood up and raised their glasses. The scene had, Joe thought, a strangely theatrical air. It was as if they knew they had an audience watching them from halfway up the sweeping staircase.

He wondered what Vera would make of it, and of the general assumption that Joanna Tobin was a murderer.

6

It seemed to Joe that Vera's bad-tempered
instructions, issued from Joanna's room, had
already been carried out. He'd found Ferdinand's room. It had the same layout as Joanna's,
but was bigger and rather more grand. He'd
stood at the door and looked in, tempted to look
in drawers and pockets, but knowing the CSIs
would want to be there first. The residents of the
Writers' House were all in one place. He'd give
them time to eat, then he could start taking their
contact details. Or perhaps Vera would be free by
then. She loved being the centre of attention,
and it would be like all her Christmases had
come at once, to walk into that fancy dining
room and lay down the law. He didn't really do
public speaking and still got nervous at the team
briefings, if someone from outside was there.

He continued down the stairs. The dining-
room door had been shut. He called over to the
officer standing by the main entrance, 'Keep an
eye on things in there and give me a shout if it
looks as if they're coming to a close. I should be
back in plenty of time, but just in case.' He
passed over a card so that the man had his
mobile-phone number.

While it was quiet he wanted to get a feel for
the space. Especially in the dark, with no views
from the windows, he'd lost all sense of
direction, of the way the house was laid out. He

51

presumed the big double doors faced east towards the sea. He wandered around the ground floor, peering into empty rooms. It was a large house with the feel of a country hotel, and too plush for a college. There were dark wooden floors and the furniture was large and looked comfortable. The smell of flowers and furniture polish. In one room the chairs had been pulled into a semicircle facing a whiteboard, which still contained a list of underlined headings: *Crime scene? Weapon? Suspects?* A strange parody of the board they'd soon be looking at in the incident room back at the station. On the lecturer's table there was a pile of handouts. He glanced down briefly. They seemed to contain a book list. The sheet was headed *North Farm Press*.

He realized that there were books everywhere. They were piled on coffee tables and on the arms of chairs in the room with the whiteboard. One large room looked just like the public library in his village. There were even books in the small bar and the public lavatories. Joe wondered what his wife would make of it. She'd recently joined a book group, but he thought the attraction was more about a night out with her mates, giggling over the Pinot Grigio and nosing into someone else's home, than a serious study of literature.

He opened the door into a large and well-equipped kitchen. A mix of industrial catering and farmhouse traditional. An Aga and a stainless-steel range cooker. A big scrubbed pine table and gleaming worktops. On one of the benches desserts had already been placed in fancy glass bowls on two big trays and covered with tea towels. Some sort of mousse, he thought, lifting the corner of the cloth. Lemon or orange with a raspberry sauce. He felt hungry and wished he'd stopped to eat his birthday cake. A big pan was still bubbling on the slow plate of the Aga. It smelled of beef and wine, herbs and garlic.

A swing door on the opposite wall opened, letting in the murmur of voices from the dining room beyond and a skinny dark man.

'Who are you?' The man stopped in his tracks — startled, it seemed, by the intruder into his territory.

'DS Ashworth. And you?'

'Alex Barton. Director, cook and bottle-washer. Murder doesn't seem to have dulled their appetites. They want more casserole.' He took a set of oven gloves and lifted the pan onto the table, before shutting the lid of the Aga. His face was flushed and Ashworth thought he'd been drinking. 'Can I help you?'

Make sure there's some of that stew left by the end of the evening. 'Not at the moment. Just getting a feel for the lie of the land. That okay with you?'

Alex shrugged. 'Sure. Make yourself at home.'

'We'll need to talk to your guests when they've finished dinner. And to you, of course. Can you make sure nobody leaves?'

'Of course. Why don't you join us for coffee? In about half an hour.'

He gave a sardonic little wave, before picking

53

up the pan and disappearing again through the swing door. Ashworth was left with a tantalizing glimpse of the room beyond, candlelight throwing shadows on the faces of the diners.

He left the kitchen and found himself back at the place where he'd first come into the house, the back door that led into the car park. Vera was there with Joanna. They were waiting for one of the local cops to bring a police car to the door. Joanna was now dressed in clothes that Vera had retrieved from her room — jeans and hand-knitted sweater — and seemed unusually quiet and passive. Vera helped her carefully into the vehicle and gave her shoulder a little pat. They watched the lights disappear up the lane.

'What do you think?' Joe said. 'Did she do it?'

'I don't see that she had any motive. She claims Ferdinand was a lechy old goat. But she'll have dealt with a few of those in her time, without resorting to stabbing them in the belly.' *But really,* Vera thought, *how well do I know her?*

Joe nodded in the direction of the dining room. 'They say Joanna was unbalanced.'

'Eh, pet, *they* all seem like a bunch of loonies to me, but I'm not accusing them of murder.' She paused. 'Billy Wainwright's taking a look at the scene now. Let's see what he comes up with before we come to a decision, eh? As it stands, I don't see we have enough to charge her with anyway. The CPS would laugh at us.'

'Billy will place her at the scene. She's admitted to that. And her fingerprints will be all over the knife.' Joe was wondering how he could

54

tactfully tell Vera that she'd have to step back from this one. 'Most cases, that would be enough.'

She stopped in her tracks and threw him a vicious look. 'Are you telling me how to do my job, Sergeant Ashworth? Think you could do it better, do you? Looking to move a couple of rungs up the ladder, at my expense?'

'I think you should just be aware that you're taking this personally. Your judgement could be clouded.'

Then he found Vera's face right in his. So close he could only see her eyes, bloodshot and furious. 'I take every killing on my patch *personally*, Sergeant Ashworth. If I didn't care, I wouldn't be doing my job right.'

Joe took a pace backwards and said nothing. He wasn't paid enough to stand up to Vera Stanhope when she was in one of her strops. Let one of the suits in HQ sort her out.

Instead, he nodded again towards the dining room. 'They haven't started the pudding yet. We've got time to check with Billy before we talk to them. We've been invited to have coffee with them there when they've finished eating.'

'Have we now! How civilized.'

When they arrived at the glass room, the crime-scene manager Billy Wainwright was on the balcony with Keating, the pathologist. They'd rigged up powerful lights, so that Ferdinand was floodlit. His skin looked white and the blood looked black. It was hard to see the good-looking charmer Joanna had described. Vera called Billy out into the corridor.

55

'How's the wife, Billy?' A standing joke. Well, more a routine greeting now, and perhaps not so much of a joke. Billy was a serial adulterer and seemed proud of the reputation. He ignored her. 'What happened here, Billy?' Vera went on. 'Did he sit on the balcony and wait to be stabbed to death? Or was he moved afterwards? I mean, this all seems madness to me.'

'Could he have been hiding out there?' Billy asked. 'You wouldn't see him from just inside the door, despite all the glass.'

'Who'd he be hiding from?' It was Vera at her most sceptical. 'He asked Joanna to meet him. He wasn't a bairn playing hide-and-seek.'

'Mr Keating thinks Ferdinand was killed where he was found,' Billy said. 'But he won't commit himself until the post-mortem.'

'Is there anything either of you *will* commit yourselves to?'

'Aye. That knife they retrieved from the woman you've sent off to Kimmerston for questioning . . . '

'What about it? Don't stand there grinning and playing games with me, Billy Wainwright. Just spit it out.'

'It wasn't the murder weapon. Nothing like. We're looking for something about the same length and width, but the murder weapon had a serrated blade.'

7

Vera threw a triumphant grin to Joe and turned on her heels. As he hurried after the shadow thrown by the red light, she turned and called back to him, 'You'd best organize a search of the residents' rooms. God knows where we're going to get the manpower for that this evening. Our mistake. We shouldn't have taken it for granted that Joanna Tobin was the murderer.'

She spoke about *our* mistake, but it seemed to Joe that she was blaming him for the assumption that Joanna had been Tony Ferdinand's killer. She swept on and down the grand staircase so quickly that Joe almost had to run to catch up with her. Vera could move very quickly when she wanted to, even though she was so unfit.

'Where are we going?' he asked. 'There's no rush. They won't have started coffee yet.'

'We're looking for knives, Joey-boy. Or rather we're looking for a place where knives might once have been. The absence of knives. Both the one that Joanna Tobin was wandering around the corridor with, and that's now safely on its way to the lab. And the other one, that killed Tony Ferdinand. Where do you think we're going?' She arrived at the kitchen before he had the chance to answer.

The room was much as it had been when Joe had looked in earlier, though the trays of desserts had disappeared. Alex Barton was pouring coffee

57

from a filter machine into pots.

I should have checked about the knife when I was here before. Joe was feeling foolish, knew this was a mistake Vera would never have made. *But I thought Joanna was the killer. I thought there was no urgency.*

'If you want to go into the dining room,' Barton said, 'I'll bring the coffee through in a minute.'

'It smells fabulous, pet,' Vera said. 'But I'm not here for the coffee. Show me where you keep your knives.'

Alex set the jug back on the filter machine and stood for a moment looking at her. Joe couldn't make out what the man was thinking, or even if he recognized the implications of the request. Alex pointed to a chef's block on the bench. 'My mother gave it to me when I graduated from college. They're the best you can get.' Again the voice was flat, and Ashworth found it impossible to tell whether he was proud of the gift or resented it.

Vera walked over to the bench. 'There seem to be a few missing.'

'Of course some are missing.' Now Barton did sound impatient. 'I've been cooking with them.' He nodded towards the draining board, to a pile of dirty pots and cutlery.

'I know you're busy,' Vera said. 'But can you check that they're all there. It shouldn't take more than a moment.'

'You think Joanna stole a knife from here to kill Tony?'

'I don't think anything at the moment, Mr

58

Barton. Not until I understand the facts.' Vera gave a thin little smile. 'Are guests allowed into the kitchen?'

'We don't encourage it,' Alex said. 'Hygiene regulations. But the room's never locked.' He seemed about to ask another question of his own, but thought better of it and nodded. 'Just let me take this coffee through before it gets cold, then I'll check for you.'

When he returned he pulled three knives from the draining board, wiped each with a white cloth and slotted it into a hole in the wooden block. 'There's one missing,' he said.

Vera had stood, watching. 'You're sure?'

'Of course I'm sure. They're the tools of my trade. I work with them every day.' He paused, frowning. 'I hope I'll get it back. It'd cost a lot to replace.'

It seemed to Joe that Alex wasn't troubled so much about the cost of the knife as about the fact that one of the set was missing. 'Can you describe it?' Joe leaned forward.

'Like this, only with a finer blade.' Barton took out a wedge-shaped knife.

'Not serrated?'

'No! Not serrated. The only serrated knife here is the bread knife, and that's over there.' Barton nodded towards a breadboard in the corner. A black-handled knife lay across it, taunting them.

'Has it been here all afternoon?' Vera asked.

'Yes! I used it at lunchtime and made myself a sandwich this afternoon.'

'You and your mother were here, drinking tea,'

Vera said. 'Just before she found Professor Ferdinand's body.'

'How did you know that?' Barton looked at her as if she were a witch.

Vera smiled at him mysteriously. 'I'm a great believer in traditional detective work,' she said. 'It always pays dividends. Isn't that right, Sergeant?'

But Joe wasn't listening. He was thinking that the knife with which Joanna had been found had most likely come from the Writers' House kitchen. Not the murder weapon, though. That was still missing.

'Thank you for your help, Mr Barton,' Vera said. 'Perhaps now we could talk to your guests.'

★ ★ ★

She stood for a moment outside the door of the dining room and composed herself. Watching her, Joe thought she was like an actress preparing to play a major role. She shut her eyes briefly, then walked inside. He followed. *Always in her shadow*, he thought. *But maybe that's the way I like it.*

Vera walked the length of the table, just as Miranda Barton had done earlier. Joe closed the door and stood with his back to it. On these occasions Vera preferred him to be unobtrusive. *You're my eyes and my ears, Joe. I'm a simple soul; I can't talk and observe at the same time.* So he watched the reaction of the people sitting at the table. There were twelve of them plus Miranda Barton, fewer than he'd thought when

60

he'd seen them parade into the room after the dinner gong had been struck. Did people with big personalities and big egos take up more space? Because there was nobody here who was ordinary. The voices were louder than Joe would have expected and the gestures slightly more dramatic. Even Lenny, the working-class guy from Ashington, seemed to be playing a caricature of himself.

The desserts had been eaten, the glass bowls pushed to one side and napkins rolled into balls on the table. Alex had returned from the kitchen with a second pot of coffee. He set it down for the diners to help themselves. Vera waited at the head of the table until everyone was served. Biding her time. Eventually the conversation faded and she had their full attention.

'Ladies and gentlemen, I'm sorry to have disturbed your dinner like this.'

No reaction. The audience didn't notice the sarcasm. Perhaps dinner was as important to them as the fact that there was a man upstairs with his throat cut. Even Miranda Barton, who had created the disturbance when she saw the body, had managed to eat all her pudding and now reached out to take a chocolate from the plate that was circulating with the coffee.

Vera continued, 'I'm sure you appreciate that our investigation will cause some disruption to your programme. Obviously we'll need to take statements from you all, and we'd like to begin that this evening, while your memories are fresh.' She looked around her and gave the fixed, icy smile that terrified her team more than her

61

anger. 'Are there any questions at this point?'

Ashworth saw that the assembled writers had underestimated Vera. They despised her for her ill-fitting clothes and badly cut hair. It showed in their posture as they slumped over the table or back in their chairs. They saw no danger in her, certainly not in the smile.

'What's happened to Joanna?' It was a woman, with very short black hair and striking red lipstick. Joe found it hard to tell her age. Her face was angular and ageless. Mid-thirties, perhaps?

'And who are you?' Vera's smile flickered for a moment, then returned. Ashworth almost expected her to add *dear* to the question. That was one of her tactics, to play the maiden aunt. Concerned, but a little simple. A tad patronizing.

'Nina Backworth. I'm one of the tutors on the course. I'm an academic specializing in women's writing and short fiction.'

'A colleague of Professor Ferdinand's then?'

'No!' The woman sounded horrified at the idea. 'He supervised my work briefly when I was a post-graduate student, but now I'm based in Newcastle. I'm sure you know that Tony set up the creative-writing MA in St Ursula's College, London. The course has achieved international fame. Any student accepted there has a head-start in finding a publisher.'

And what about you? Did you find a publisher after being taught by him? But Vera kept that question to herself. 'Any good, was she? Joanna Tobin? As a writer, I mean?'

'I thought she showed great potential.' Nina

paused. 'I don't believe she would have attacked Tony Ferdinand without good cause. I hope you'll treat her with some sensitivity.'

'Are you saying Professor Ferdinand deserved to die, Ms Backworth?'

There was a sudden tension in the room, a spark of excitement or energy. The audience was more attentive. The woman regarded Vera warily. 'Of course not. Nobody deserves to be killed like that. I want to alert you to the fact that there could have been an element of self-defence in what happened here today.'

Vera looked at her. 'But you believe that Joanna Tobin killed the professor?'

'Of course!' Then, when there was no response from Vera, her voice became uncertain. 'That's what we were told. That's what I assumed.'

Joe watched and found he was holding his breath. Sometimes, when she was angry, Vera let her mouth run ahead of her brain. And Joe knew that the assumption that Joanna was a murderer would make her very angry. *Don't let her mention the knives*, he thought. *Don't let her give away more than she needs.*

Vera looked across at him and her face twitched into what might have been a wink. It was as if she'd known what he was thinking and was saying: *Give me credit for a bit of sense, lad!*

'Joanna Tobin is helping the police with our enquiries,' she said blandly, challenging them to ask more questions. 'She hasn't been formally charged, and our investigation continues.' She took a sip from the coffee cup in front of her, though by now, Joe thought, the drink would be cold. Vera had better timing than a stand-up comedian and knew the importance of a pause. 'I understand that the writing course is planned to run for two more days. I see no reason why this arrangement should be changed. My colleagues and I will need to talk to you individually, and we'll begin that process this evening. Our officers will remain here overnight to provide protection and to prevent any intrusion from the press.' She paused again and swept her eyes around the room. 'And to stop anyone from running away.' She looked around the room once more. 'I assume all the course members are still here.'

'We had a visiting tutor this morning,' Miranda Barton said. 'Chrissie Kerr, who owns and runs North Farm, a small literary press based in the county.'

'When did she leave?'

The question was directed to the whole room, but again Miranda answered. 'After lunch. I saw her drive away. And Tony was still very much alive at that point, so I don't think she'll be much of a witness for you.'

'Excuse me!' This was Nina Backworth again, on her feet, scarcely able to contain herself. Joe thought she'd make a decent defence lawyer. 'Are you saying that you intend to keep us as prisoners in this house while you carry out your investigation?'

'Of course not, Ms Backworth.' Vera gave a chuckle. 'The comment just now was one of my little jokes. Certainly you're free to leave, but please tell my officers if that's your intention. You're witnesses to a murder, after all.'

8

The drawing room had a huge inglenook fireplace and an ornate wrought-iron basket where logs burned. It seemed to Vera that all the heat went up the chimney and the fire was just for show. Typical of this place. All show and no substance. And just like these people, who were acting their hearts out in an attempt to persuade her that they were sophisticated, intelligent and entirely blameless in the matter of Tony Ferdinand's death.

She and Joe moved around them, taking contact details and plotting a timeline for their activities, from the coffee served after lunch to the time when Ferdinand had last been seen alive. She doubted Keating would give her a more accurate time of death than the victim's leaving the meal and the discovery of his body. Some of the Writers' House residents could be ruled out of the murder immediately. They were in the company of others for all but a few minutes during that period. She wondered what Joe made of these loud, showy people, who reminded her of exotic birds, all brightly coloured plumage and irritating squawk, caged in a luxurious aviary. When he'd first started working for her he'd been anxious in the presence of the articulate middle classes. He was more confident now. She'd given that to him, at least.

Upstairs, a team was searching bedrooms. Not Ferdinand's. She'd do that herself, once the CSIs had been in. God knows how Joe had pulled in the officers so quickly. With the promise of overtime, which she'd have to pay for from her budget? None of the residents had objected to the search, but then Vera didn't expect the knife or any bloody clothing to be found. Hours had been wasted, while they'd assumed Joanna to be the murderer. Anything incriminating would surely have been disposed of. There was an acre of garden, thick undergrowth, dense shrubs. But now it was dark and the search there would have to wait for the morning.

When the timeline was complete she looked at the clock. Gone eleven. Not the time to begin individual interviews; Nina Backworth would be on her feet again, talking about police harassment. Vera needed to get in touch with Holly and Charlie and she supposed she should get some sleep herself. She stood up and stretched and caught Joe's eye.

'Thanks for your cooperation, ladies and gentlemen. That's all we need for tonight. No doubt I'll see you at some point tomorrow.'

Outside, the hearse had arrived to take Ferdinand to the mortuary. The cold air hit her and made her feel suddenly awake and alive. At this point she felt she could go on all night, and for most of the next day.

'Do we know when Keating plans to do the post-mortem?'

'Not until the morning. Around ten.' Joe

66

Ashworth *did* look tired. Nearly half her age, but he couldn't match her for energy. *Don't be smug, Vera pet. That's all down to genetics. Hector was still climbing trees at seventy, stealing birds' eggs.*

'Team briefing at eight-thirty then,' she said. 'We'll come back here after the post-mortem. Lull the bastards into a sense of security by giving them the morning off.' She grinned at him. 'Get yourself home, man. It's your birthday. Your lass will be waiting for you, all frilly knickers and fishnet stockings. I'll see you in the morning.'

Back inside, the house seemed quiet. In Ferdinand's room she found Billy Wainwright; she pulled on the paper suit and boots that he threw to her, and joined him.

'No signs of violence or disturbance in here,' he said. 'I was just off home.'

'Hang on for a few minutes, will you, Billy, while I just have a quick look at the man's things.'

He shrugged to show that he wasn't happy, but he wasn't about to make a fuss. The place smelled of cigarette smoke, despite the sign on the door saying smoking wasn't allowed. That, and some sort of fancy aftershave. The clothes in the wardrobe felt expensive to her — the shirts were heavy cotton and the jerseys cashmere. She looked at the labels and recognized some of the designer names. She hadn't thought university lecturers were so well paid.

On the desk under the window there was a black ring binder and a diary. Again she turned to Wainwright. 'Have you finished with these? Can I take them with me?'

He nodded, and it seemed to Vera suddenly that the man was exhausted, too tired even to speak. Perhaps the effort of lying to his wife, of keeping up with his bonny young lovers, was finally catching up with him.

★ ★ ★

She got Wainwright to drive her up the lane to her Land Rover. The internal light had never worked, but there was a torch in the glove compartment for emergencies, and she punched numbers into her phone. There was no reply from Charlie, which was only to be expected. He could be an idle bastard, Charlie, though for some jobs — the meticulous searching through a suspect's background, for example — there was nobody to match him. Most likely now he'd be in his bed. Or a lock-in at his local pub, his phone switched off.

Holly did answer, and Vera could have predicted that too. Holly was young and fiercely ambitious. A good detective, but not as good as she thought she was. Sometimes Vera took it upon herself to remind her DC of that fact.

'How did the chat with Joanna go?' No need to introduce herself. Holly would know who it was at this time of night.

'Okay. Joanna Tobin stuck to the story she gave you. All very calm and collected. You'd have thought she'd been through a police interview a dozen times. She'd had a message from Tony

68

Ferdinand asking to meet her, and she went to the glass room at the top of the house. She didn't go out onto the balcony, and just assumed that he'd changed his mind about the meeting. She saw the knife on the floor and decided to take it back to the kitchen.'

'If she's the killer,' Vera said, 'what did she do with the murder weapon?'

'Could she have chucked it over the balcony?'

'She could have done.' Vera allowed herself to sound a bit impressed. 'But Billy Wainwright has already been down with his torch to check. Nothing. Anything else from the interview?'

'Not much. Joanna says she didn't like Ferdinand, but she had no reason to kill him.'

'Nobody liked him much,' Vera said slowly. 'At least, that's the impression they give.' She paused. 'Do you think Joanna was set up?'

'You mean the murderer sent the message, not Ferdinand?' Holly was openly sceptical. Vera thought she hadn't yet learned the importance of suitable manners when she spoke to her superiors. The lass could do with a bit more respect. 'In that case, why leave a knife that wasn't the murder weapon lying around? He must have realized we wouldn't be misled for long into thinking Joanna was the killer.'

'Unless he's an ignorant bugger.' Vera was playing devil's advocate. Really, she didn't know what she thought about all this. Except that someone was playing games.

'Come off it!' Holly said. Only adding 'Ma'am' at the last minute. That lack of respect again. 'They were all on a crime-writing workshop. They'd understand the basics of forensics, if they write that sort of stuff.'

This time Vera had to concede defeat. 'Aye. Maybe.' In the house in the valley below it seemed that the writers were going to bed. The lights on the ground floor were being switched off. 'Did you get Joanna home all right?'

'Yes, I dropped her off myself. It wasn't too far out of my way.'

'Was Jack at home?' Vera imagined his relief as he opened the door and saw Joanna standing there. She hoped he'd contained himself and not made too much fuss. Joanna wouldn't like tears and hugs.

'Someone opened the door. I assumed it was him. I didn't hang around.'

'I'll see you in the morning then. Eight-thirty for a briefing. I've left a message on Charlie's phone.'

Vera clicked off her phone and sat for a moment in silence. She opened the window to clear her head and thought she could hear the waves on the rocks at the end of the valley. She started the engine, drove down to the house to turn round, then headed home. She felt an unexpected surge of relief when she'd negotiated the lanes and reached the road that would take her inland. It was as if she'd escaped from a prison.

At home the farm was in darkness. She got out of the Land Rover in the yard, almost expecting to find Jack lurking in the barn with his questions or his gratitude, but she unlocked her house without interruption. On her kitchen table were three big bottles of their home-brew and half a dozen mucky eggs in a bowl. A card in Joanna's writing. *Thanks.* Vera wondered if Joe Ashworth would consider that bribery and corruption. Then she thought she'd better get back her bloody key. The last thing she wanted was the hippies wandering in and out of her house whenever they felt like it.

★   ★   ★

In bed she looked at Ferdinand's diary. It had been fingerprinted and tested, but the only contact traces came from the dead man. It contained no insights into his mind, just a list of appointments. In the week before his journey to Northumberland he'd recorded an episode of *The Culture Show* for television and appeared live on *Front Row* on Radio 4. Vera occasionally listened to that when she was having her supper and wondered if she'd heard him — he'd be one of those self-satisfied prats who criticized any poor bugger who had the nerve to put his thoughts on paper. As far as she knew, Ferdinand had never been published himself. Since arriving at the Writers' House he'd marked in the schedule of his responsibilities: *tutorial 1, tutorial 2.* No names. And for today: *5 p.m. lecture. Nuts and bolts of the business.* Also a single initial and a question mark: *J?* So he had expected to meet up with Joanna. The extra scraps of information were merely tantalizing.

Vera left home early the next morning and still there was no sign of Jack or Joanna. Holly was in the incident room before her, printing off the information she'd found on the Writers' House on the Internet. The equivalent, Vera thought, of an over-eager pupil sharpening the teacher's pencil. Then: *My God, that shows my age. When did they last have pencils in classrooms?* The others wandered in afterwards, Charlie last as usual. Holly handed out the notes.

Vera stood at the front and talked them through it. 'Our victim is Tony Ferdinand, professor, reviewer and all-round media star. So there'll be lots of press interest. He was in Northumberland to act as visiting tutor at the Writers' House, the place up the coast where wannabe writers go to get inspiration. They run residential courses in all forms of literature, but this week they're doing crime fiction. Is that significant? It seems a bit of a coincidence that they've spent three days planning a perfect murder, and then one of the lecturers dies in a very theatrical way. Is one of them playing games with us? I've had a quick look in Ferdinand's diary. He made a note of the appointments he'd set up with other students, but no names are mentioned. He might have had a meeting with someone he calls J yesterday, but it all seems very vague. We need to be aware that Joanna Tobin could be lying or could have been set up.'

She paused and checked that they were all with her. 'Then there's this business with the knife. Another game? Or does the killer not know enough about forensics to realize we'd tell the difference between blades? Did he think getting Joanna to the scene would be enough to convict her? Again, the whole business seems very theatrical to me. In any event, the murder weapon is still out there somewhere. I've organized a search of the grounds and that should start this morning.

'Holly, will you get on the phone and check out Ferdinand? Talk to his university, St Ursula's College, London, to broadcasters, publishers, anyone else he might have worked with. Usual stuff. Any enemies? Any recent scandals or problems? You'll have the guest list of the Writers' House, so see if one of those names crops up.' Vera thought that Holly, with her clipped southern voice, would go down well with the London intelligentsia. You could almost see her as a pushy publicist, with her long legs and sharp suits. 'And have a word with a woman called Chrissie Kerr. She runs a small publishing company based not very far from here. According to the woman in charge, she left the Writers' House before Ferdinand was killed, but she might have picked up on tensions or problems, and she'll have background on the whole organization.

'Charlie, I want you digging around into the background of Joanna Tobin. She's my neighbour, and I need to keep a bit of a distance, so this is your responsibility and, anything you find, you let Joe know as well as me. Seems as if she might have been set up. Or is she the one who's playing games? We know she has a history of psychiatric illness and, according to her partner, there was at least one serious suicide attempt. Her family comes from Bristol or somewhere in the West Country, and I think she lived for a while in France. Check for any overseas convictions.' Vera stopped for breath and looked across the room towards her sergeant. 'Joe, you were there last night. Anything I've missed?'

He'd been sitting at the back, a biro in his hand, and she hadn't even been sure he'd been listening. Maybe the squiggles on his notepad were doodles. From this distance it was hard to tell. Maybe he was remembering the delights of the night before, his very special birthday treat. But he answered immediately.

'The people who run the place. Mother and son. The mother's a professional writer and apparently she was a friend of the deceased.' He glanced up at Vera to check that the information was accurate. She nodded. 'Something about her response to the murder seems odd. She found the body and apparently screamed the place down, yet later over dinner she appeared completely composed. Certainly she ate everything on her plate.'

'Nothing wrong with a middle-aged woman having a healthy appetite, even in a crisis,' Vera put in and was rewarded with a laugh from her audience.

'It says from Holly's notes that the place gets some Arts Council funding,' Joe said. 'It might be worth checking how the finances of the place work. If there were some sort of scam and Ferdinand found out, that would be a motive. I don't know how these things work, but he *could* have suspected that something dodgy was going on. And Ferdinand was a tall man. He wasn't

74

going to just stand there and allow himself to be stabbed. Maybe the mother and son worked together to kill him. Or one of them kept watch.'

'Good thinking.' There were times, Vera thought, when Joe Ashworth was a credit to her. Maybe occasionally she should tell him so.

★ ★ ★

Paul Keating, the pathologist, was an Ulsterman. Straightforward and a little dour, he had a rugby player's nose and a grown-up family. He conducted his post-mortems with respect and little fuss. Vera knew colleagues, even experienced colleagues, who hated being present at the post-mortem, but she'd never seen the logic in that. She was scared of people when they were alive and dangerous. At least the dead could do you no harm.

'Why was there so much blood?'

'The heart continued to pump and there was a gaping wound for it to escape from.'

'Was he killed out on the balcony?' This had troubled Vera from the beginning. There had been no sign of a struggle in the glass room. The place was like a rainforest, thick with tall plants, and none of the pots had been knocked over. Although Joanna had said the furniture had been arranged differently, it hadn't been tipped up. Everything was orderly. But it had been a cold October afternoon, not the weather for sitting outside. Vera remembered Joanna's description of Ferdinand's habit of eavesdropping. Had the killer caught him on the balcony, listening in on the discussion below? Or had Ferdinand heard a previous conversation, something that might ultimately have led to his death?

'I think he must have been. There's no blood spatter in the room, but plenty outside.'

'Ferdinand was a big man,' Vera said. 'Tall at least. You'd have thought he'd have put up a fight, but none of our witnesses have scratches or abrasions.'

'That struck me too.' Keating looked up from his work. 'I looked for skin under the fingernails, but there was nothing.'

'So why did he stand there and let someone take a knife to him, without a struggle?'

'He'd have been sitting,' Keating said. 'As you said, he was a tall man. And the angle of the wounds show that he was stabbed from above.'

'Why would he sit on a stone floor? There were chairs in the room and he could have taken one out, if he wanted to look at the view.' Again Vera had the image of a child playing hide-and-seek. 'Or did the killer block the door to the house and Ferdinand went onto the balcony to escape? Perhaps he hoped to attract attention from there. He was stabbed when he was cowering in the corner.'

'It's a possibility, I suppose.' But Keating was always cautious and ruled little out as impossible. 'My thoughts were running another way. I'm waiting for tox reports.'

'You think he might have been drugged?'

Keating shrugged. 'An unconscious man isn't going to fight back. You could put him where you wanted and kill him there.'

In the hospital car park Vera breathed deeply to get rid of the smell of chemicals and dead body. Joe stood beside her. They'd come in his car. 'You were very quiet in there,' she said.

'I had nothing to contribute.'

'What is it, Joe? You sound like a sulky teenage girl. I can't stand moods.'

'I don't think you should be working on this case. You were at the house when the body was found, and you know one of the suspects. You can't keep your distance.' He stood with his legs apart and his hands on the car roof, almost like a suspect told to stand in the brace position for searching, in American cop shows.

'You're questioning my integrity?' She wondered why she was so angry. She'd told Joe often enough that he should stick to his guns, have the courage of his convictions. She just hadn't expected him to take a stand against *her*.

'No!' It came out almost as a howl. 'No! I'm just worried about how it looks.'

'Eh, pet, I've never been one to worry much about appearances.'

He relaxed briefly and gave a little grin.

'Would it make you feel better to know I've got an appointment with the Super this afternoon? I might have to leave you in charge of taking witness statements.'

He turned round so that he was facing her. 'You've already talked to him about your involvement in the case?'

'Do you really think I'd jeopardize a

conviction in a murder inquiry? That's why I've got Charlie digging around in Joanna's past, and why you'll be copied in on anything he finds.' Vera saw that she was starting to win him round. She climbed into the passenger seat and waited for him to join her in the car — thinking that she'd better find a quiet moment as soon as they arrived at the Writers' House to phone the Super and set up that appointment.

9

Nina Backworth slept badly. Even at the best of times she seldom slept through for a whole night and usually managed only four or five hours. It had come to haunt her, this need for sleep, and she searched almost obsessively for a remedy. She kept off any form of caffeine, took note of her diet. Did a particular food have an adverse effect? Or a positive one? She drank little alcohol, because that seemed to make the problem worse. She hated the idea of taking drugs, but away from home — especially when she had to work the following day — she took sleeping pills prescribed by a sympathetic GP. She'd taken a tablet the night before and had fallen asleep almost immediately, but she'd woken again in the early hours, her mind fizzing with ideas and anxieties. Now, dressing for breakfast, she felt sluggish and tense.

How had she been persuaded to take part in this venture? She was employed by the Department of English at Newcastle University, and lectured on the undergraduate course, with women writers her speciality. She didn't do popular fiction. Not professionally. She read detective stories when she wanted to escape, when she had flu or when she needed to forget some man or other. Though these days there wasn't often a man she needed to forget. The elderly Penguins in their green jackets, stolen from her grandparents' house, or the Collins Crime Club hardbacks borrowed from the library had been her best weapon against insomnia when she was an undergraduate. But this wasn't literature to be taken seriously or to be taught on a residential course. Her editor, Chrissie Kerr, had persuaded her: *You're published by a small press with a tiny marketing budget. Even if everyone on the course buys one of your books, that'll be a help. And the brochure goes everywhere. Miranda Barton has promised a big article in* The Journal.

So Nina had gone along with the idea. She'd been seduced by the idea of a week in the country. And by the fee. She had to admit even now that the fee would be very useful.

And then there'd been a murder. It seemed trite, almost ridiculous. If someone had come up with such a scenario in a story presented to her for appraisal, she'd have mocked the idea. *Too Christie for words.* That Tony Ferdinand had been the victim was a complication she had yet to explore properly. She was too tired to think. Perhaps there would be time for a walk on the beach before her first workshop, and that would clear her head.

In the dining room breakfast was served from a sideboard from heated dishes. Miranda liked to preserve the atmosphere of an Edwardian country-house party, though here there were no housemaids in frilly aprons, only Miranda herself and her son. Nina saw that she was almost the last person to arrive for the meal. Again they sat round one large table, but dinner was the only formal meal. At breakfast, guests helped themselves. She gathered, as she spooned fresh fruit salad into a bowl and dipped the bag of herbal tea into a mug of hot water, that people were acting as if the murder had never taken place. Across the table from her, novelist Giles Rickard had his nose in the *Telegraph*. Among the students, the conversation was about writing and the fruitless search for agent or publisher. Was that a sign of the self-obsession of the aspiring writer? Perhaps it had more to do with the fact that the two police officers who had been posted there overnight were in the room too, tucking into a pile of bacon and egg.

Nina had expected the appearance of the fat female detective of the evening before, but there was no sign of anyone in plain clothes. The officers changed shift and two more arrived, but they just stood awkwardly, one at each of the external doors, as if they were unsure what they were doing there. She fetched her jacket from her room.

'I'm just going for a walk on the beach,' she said. 'That is all right?'

The man was very young, fresh-faced and eager. She presumed it was his first murder and he was excited to be there. Had he woken up this morning thinking that life was good, and that he had chosen the best job in the world? 'You'll not be long?'

She promised that she would not be long. She was teaching in an hour. But she needed fresh air and exercise. She gave a little smile. 'I'll go mad if I'm stuck in there all day.'

He stood aside and let her out, shouting after her, 'Have a nice stroll!'

Alex Barton was filling the bird feeders below the terrace, but was so concentrated on the task that he didn't notice her. She watched for a moment and saw how tame the small birds had become. They sat on the table within inches of him, apparently unconcerned by his presence, and a robin perched on the wooden strut that held the narrow cage of feed. The path led straight from the garden to the beach. It was low tide, so there was sand; at high water only rock and shingle were visible. They'd woken to mist, but the sun was already burning through it and shone straight into her eyes. There was that familiar smell of salt and rotting seaweed that reminded her of childhood holidays. Gulls calling. At one point she looked back at the house. From there she could see the glass room, the windows reflecting the sunlight. A screen hid any activity that might be taking place on the balcony. After the oppressive claustrophobia of the Writers' House, it was a pleasure to be outside. The water was calm and oily and she searched for flat pebbles to skim across it, and felt a rush of jubilation when she managed five skips. Again she thought of being young, on holiday in her grandparents' home — Enid Blyton summers of exploration and picnics.

As she returned to the house she was amused to see the relief in the young policeman's eyes when he glimpsed her approaching through the garden. Perhaps he'd been reprimanded for letting her out, warned he'd be in big trouble if she escaped. There was still no sign of Vera Stanhope or her colleague. *Perhaps it's all over,* she thought. *Perhaps they've arrested Joanna Tobin and need nothing more from us.* That made her think of the short story Joanna had submitted the day before, and how she'd have been proud to have written it. But just as she was turning into the door, a minibus arrived and a group of uniformed men and women spilled out, chatting and laughing. She hesitated long enough to discover that they were there to search the gardens. All day she would catch glimpses of them, walking in lines across the lawns and through the trees.

Alex had moved inside and was clearing the grate in the drawing room. He was bending over the fireplace sweeping the last of the ash into a big, flat rusty dustpan. He was wearing jeans and a tight black T-shirt. Nina had noticed before that he never seemed to be affected by the cold.

He heard her come in and turned round. 'Sorry. I should have done this last night. But after all that happened . . . '

'How's Miranda this morning?' Really, Nina didn't care how Miranda was feeling. She'd taken a dislike to the woman from the minute she'd arrived here. From before that, even. But it seemed the right thing to say.

He straightened. He'd tipped the ash into a metal bucket. 'She's okay. It's not as if she was particularly close to Tony. Not recently. I don't think they'd had much to do with each other professionally for years. It was the shock, I suppose, that made her so hysterical.'

'Oh, I thought they were great friends.' *That, certainly, was the impression Ferdinand had given all those years ago.*

Alex looked up sharply. 'Once perhaps. Not now.'

Nina brought out her notes. This was her standard lecture on the structure of the short story. She'd given it so many times that she could deliver it standing on her head. She looked at her watch. Ten minutes to go. Soon the keen ones would be dribbling in.

An hour later they stopped for coffee. The lecture had gone well enough. The students had laughed in the right places, had seemed focused, had taken notes. Nina enjoyed teaching mature students more than she did lecturing to undergraduates, who were usually super-cool and unengaged. And yet this morning she had the sense that they were all just going through the motions. Wasn't everyone actually thinking about a real crime while she'd been speaking of fiction?

'Storytelling is all about *what if?*' she'd said. '*What if* this character acts in this particular way? *What if* things aren't quite what they seem?'

Now, drinking her black decaff coffee, listening to the murmured conversation all around her, she thought she had her own questions, which could affect the narrative of these particular events: *What if Joanna Tobin didn't kill Tony after all? What if I tell the detective everything I know about Tony Ferdinand?*

84

After the break she set the group an exercise. The room was quiet and warm, from the background heat of the radiators, but also from the sun that flooded in through the big windows. Nina found that she was drifting into a daydream, part memory and part fantasy. This is what writers do, she thought. We create fictions even from our own experience. None of our recollections are entirely reliable. For she considered herself a writer, even though her work was only published by a small independent press based in the wilds of Northumberland.

In her story (or her memory) she was twenty-one, a bright young woman, newly graduated with a First in English Literature from Bristol University. She spent the summer in her grandparents' home in Northumberland, working in the local pub every evening and writing during the day. A novel, of course. A great young woman's novel about growing up and love. It had been a joyous book, Nina thought now — the writing as glittering as the water had been that wonderful summer, when she sat in the garden of her grandparents' house, with her laptop on the rickety wooden table, tapping out her 2,000 words a day. She would be far too cynical to write a novel like that now. And her grandparents had watched admiringly, interrupting only to bring her cold drinks, bowls of raspberries from the garden, slices of home-made cake.

Nina stirred in her chair and glanced at the clock. The time she'd allowed her students for the exercise was over. Now they would read their work aloud and she would find something intelligent, helpful and kind to say about it. Her own story would have to wait for another occasion.

★ ★ ★

The fat detective appeared suddenly at lunchtime. She was there with the good-looking sidekick, ladling soup into her bowl, as if she hadn't eaten in weeks, chopping off thick slices of newly baked bread and spreading it with butter.

Nina watched her from the other side of the table. She tried to listen in to the conversation between the detectives, but beside her Lenny Thomas was demanding her attention, needing her reassurance.

'So you think, like, that I have a chance of getting onto the course at St Ursula's? Even now Tony Ferdinand's dead?'

'I think you could find a publisher now, Lenny. I'm not sure the St Ursula's course is what you need at this point in your writing career. You have a fresh and original voice. A publisher will see that. He wouldn't need Tony Ferdinand to point it out to him.' *And you'd be any publicist's dream. Ex-offender from a former pit village. Much easier to promote you than a middle-class female academic in a provincial university, already approaching middle age. In fact everything mid, everything mediocre.*

She realized how bitter she had become. And how jealous she was of this enthusiastic man with his newly found passion for writing, his ability to hook the reader in with the simplicity of his prose and the authenticity of his characterization. She turned to the neighbour on her left. Mark Winterton might be boring, but at least he wouldn't make her feel inadequate. His writing was well crafted, but pedestrian, lacking any spark or humour, and his value to this particular class was that he was a retired police inspector. He was tall, grey-haired and polite and answered the group's questions about procedure, forensics and the judicial system with consistent good humour.

'This must seem very strange to you, Mark,' Nina said. 'To be at the receiving end of an investigation, I mean.'

'It is rather.' He wasn't local and had a northern accent that she didn't quite recognize.

'Does it make you regret leaving the job?' She was genuinely interested. After having such responsible and demanding work, wouldn't life seem a little tame afterwards? 'Is that why you decided to start writing about it instead, so you can recapture some of the excitement?'

He shook his head gently. 'You can't know,' he said, 'how glad I was to leave the stress behind. I'm more than happy to be an observer on this one.'

'Why choose crime then, when you decided to write?'

'I read all the text books,' he said, as if the explanation was obvious. 'The ones on how to be an author. They all tell you to write about what you know. I joined the force when I was sixteen.

I don't know about anything else.'

'There's more to life than work!' Nina wondered in her own case if that was true. She used her work as an escape, an excuse to avoid relationships. 'Are you married?'

He smiled. 'Divorced,' he said. 'The stress of the job took its toll early on. Two sons and five grandkids.' He paused. 'There was a daughter too, but she died when she was young.'

'Then you could write children's fiction. Or about what it is to lose a child. You know about those things.'

'Is it possible to make a story out of something so personal?'

'It's not always easy,' Nina said. 'But it's certainly possible. If you want to try, I'd be happy to look at it.'

'Thank you. I might take you up on that!' And his face suddenly lit up, so Nina thought she had probably earned her fee, just in that conversation.

On the other side of the room Inspector Stanhope had already finished eating. She hoisted herself to her feet. Nina noticed that there was a splash of soup on her jersey and felt the urge to pick up her napkin and wipe it off.

'Ladies and gentlemen, I'm sorry that we're obliged to disturb you again.'

No you're not, Nina thought. *You love all this. You're not like Mark Winterton. You thrive on the stress. You probably think that we're a load of pretentious morons anyway, and that we deserve to be inconvenienced.*

The inspector was continuing: 'This afternoon

we'll take individual witness statements. Sergeant Ashworth and I will set up in the chapel and call you in when we're ready for you. We'd be grateful if you don't leave the Writers' House while the process is under way.' Nina wondered if that was a dig at her, for her comment about being imprisoned yesterday and for daring to go for a walk this morning.

That impression intensified when the inspector paused for a moment and looked around her.

'We'll start, shall we, with Ms Backworth?'

10

Vera took over the chapel as her interview room. She wanted a base where she wouldn't be interrupted or overheard, and it had come to her that this would work well. There were no fixed pews inside and she arranged the chairs around the table that stood where once an altar had been. She'd asked Alex to show the chapel to her. She found him easier to deal with than Miranda, and she'd always had a soft spot for a man who could cook.

'We keep it heated to stop the damp,' he'd said. 'The students use it as a quiet room, a place where they can write in peace.'

It was a bare and simple space. No stained glass in the windows. No ornate carving. Hardly bigger than Vera's living room, it had unplastered walls and a wooden ceiling like an upturned boat.

Vera thought there was no harm in asking Nina Backworth to wait while she prepared the room. In theory Vera liked strong women; in practice they often irritated her. Nina, with her strident voice and her emphasis on rights, the challenge to Vera's authority, had certainly irritated. And Vera had to admit there was something intimidating about the woman that coloured her response. It was the expensive haircut, the red lipstick, the fitted linen jacket and wide trousers, all in black. The black boots with the heels and the pointed toes. According to the lad on door duty, Nina had gone for a walk on the beach before taking her lecture this morning. Had she gone out in those clothes? It was hard to imagine her scrambling over rocks and shingle. If Nina Backworth had been ugly and poorly dressed, Vera would have considered her much more kindly. Now the inspector thought it would be good for the woman to wait to be interviewed, as if *she* were the student and Vera were her tutor.

'Bring her in, pet.' Vera had arranged the table so that she was facing the door. There was a chair for the witness in front of her. Joe Ashworth would take a place to one side, out of the eye-line. He'd make notes.

Joe returned followed by Nina. She took the seat offered and looked, to Vera, pale and uncertain. Vera felt a twinge of sympathy. Perhaps the make-up and the sophisticated clothes were protection. Everyone had their own way of facing a hostile world.

'Would you like anything?' Vera asked. 'Coffee? Water?' She could tell it was the last thing Nina had expected. Kindness could be a great weapon.

Nina shook her head. 'No. Thank you.'

'This is an informal chat,' Vera said. 'Nothing official. Not yet. Later we'll take a formal witness statement that could be used in court. But I need to get a feel for what happened here, the people involved.' She looked up sharply. 'Seems to me writers must be nosy buggers. A bit like cops. You collect characters and places, don't you, for your books? You'll be interested in everything and everybody, because you never know when the detail will come in handy for a story.'

'Yes,' Nina said. 'Yes, it is exactly like that.' It seemed to Vera that the woman looked at her with a new respect.

'I'm the same myself,' Vera went on. 'Other people call it gossip; I say it's research.'

Nina relaxed and gave a little grin.

'So tell me about Professor Tony Ferdinand. What sort of character was he? Did you know him before you met here at the Writers' House?'

It was an undemanding question and Nina must have realized it was one she'd be asked, but she hesitated. Vera thought she was debating how much she should say. She leaned back in her chair as if she had all the time in the world, as if the woman's silence was entirely natural.

'As I explained, he supervised me for a while at St Ursula's.'

Vera put her elbows on the table. 'Tell me how that works,' she said. 'I never went to college myself. This is a new world to me.'

'I'm not quite sure how it works generally,' Nina said. 'I think perhaps I had an unfortunate experience.'

'Then tell me how it worked for you.'

Nina looked out of the long window, and spoke without looking at Vera at all. 'I was very young when I wrote my first book. I'd just left university and I spent the summer not very far from here. My grandparents lived on the Northumberland coast and I felt more at home

92

with them than I did with my parents.' She shrugged apologetically. 'Sorry, none of this is relevant.'

'But it *is* gossip,' Vera said. 'Nothing I like better than gossip.'

'It was the sort of book you write once in a lifetime. I didn't understand the rules of storytelling — all this information we're passing on during this course would have meant nothing to me — but the story and the characters came together like a sort of magic. I have never been so happy as I was that summer.'

Vera thought sometimes a case worked out that way. Everything falling into place. Instinct and solid policing coming together. Then there was nothing more exhilarating. Nina seemed lost in her memories and Vera prompted her. 'So how did Tony Ferdinand come into your life?'

'I'd heard him on the radio, read his reviews and I admired him. He seemed passionate about literature and about championing new, young writers. He'd just set up the new creative-writing MA at St Ursula's. I suppose he was some sort of hero. Then I met him, quite by chance, at a party. Friends of my grandparents, not very far from here, were celebrating a wedding anniversary. I'm not sure how he came to be there. I think he happened to be in the area. On holiday perhaps. Later I found he was very good at getting himself invited to parties, fancy restaurants.' Nina stopped speaking for a moment. 'He'd been a freelance journalist. I don't suppose he was paid much. And he had very expensive tastes.'

Vera nodded, remembering the clothes in his wardrobe. 'Must have seemed like a stroke of luck,' she said. 'Just bumping into him like that.'

'I could hardly believe it. I'd only gone to the party to keep my grandparents happy and as soon as I walked into the room I heard his voice. I'd have known it anywhere.' Nina paused again. 'You must understand that I was very young, very naive. Easily flattered. Tony encouraged me to talk about my novel. Later I realized I was the only female under fifty there and that *he* was flattered by my admiration. I entertained him for an hour or so while he drank a bottle of our hosts' champagne. 'Why don't you apply to St Ursula's?' he said when we left. 'And let me see a copy of your novel.' And he gave me his card.'

'That must have been exciting,' Vera said. 'To have someone that famous asking to look at your work.'

'Unbelievably exciting!' Nina faced Vera to make sure she understood the importance of what she was saying. 'Like being six and waking up on Christmas morning and getting just the present you'd been dreaming about secretly all year.'

'So you sent the book to him?' Vera didn't want to give Nina the impression she was rushing her, but neither did she want to be here for hours. She had that appointment with the superintendent, and if she was going to be grovelling, she'd better not be late.

'I phoned him as soon as I got back to my parents' house in London, and went to see him. His office in St Ursula's was so full of books there was hardly room for a desk. I thought anyone who owned that many books must be honest and true. How could you read so widely and not be a good person? And he said he loved my novel, that I should join his course.' She paused. 'After that interview I was happier than I've ever been in my life. It was as if I was flying home.'

'But it didn't work out?'

'No,' Nina said. 'It didn't work out.'

'Tell me.' Still Vera was aware of time passing, but this was the first time she had a sense of Tony Ferdinand as a real person. He'd been a con man, she thought. A bit of a chancer. But bright enough to make people think he had influence. And in the end so many folk believed he could pull strings, and make things happen, that the perception became truth. 'Tried it on, did he?' Nina had been a bonny young woman after all. And it seemed he'd tried it on with Joanna.

'No not that. He was unpleasant in an old-fashioned sexist way. Touching as if by chance. The occasional invitation that could have been taken as a proposition. But I could have coped with that.'

'So what did he do?' Vera asked. 'What did he do that was so terrible?'

'He ruined my novel. Him and the rest of the group.'

'How did they do that?'

Nina struggled to find the words to explain. 'The teaching sessions were brutal. I'd had to take criticism as an undergraduate, but this was

95

horrible. A form of intellectual combat. We'd sit in a circle, discussing an individual's work, but there was nothing constructive in the comments. It was more like a competition to see how hard and unpleasant each student could be. Tony told us things were like that in the publishing world: tough, uncompromising. We should get used to it. But it wasn't done for our benefit. He enjoyed moderating all that bile and aggression. He was entertained, and it made him feel powerful. It wasn't just me he had a go at. He picked on anyone vulnerable. I remember him and a visiting tutor tearing apart one student, who fell to pieces in front of us. I found myself joining in. It was horrible.' Nina looked up at Vera. 'I tried to edit the text to meet the group's comments. Most of the other students seemed so much more confidant and articulate than I was. And Tony seemed to agree with them. But of course that was a mistake. In the end my original vision was quite lost.'

'So you left?' Vera still couldn't quite make sense of this. Usually she enjoyed dipping into worlds that were quite different from her own, but this seemed so far from her own experience that it was unfathomable. She'd never understood before that words could be a profession, a matter of pride, an income.

'Eventually. It felt like a failure, but I was making myself ill. I found a more conventional postgraduate course and became an academic. I dumped the first novel. There was no way I could recapture the excitement. Recently I've started writing again.'

'Published, are you?'

'Not by anyone you'd have heard of.' Nina managed a grin. 'I'm with a small press, North Farm, based in rural Northumberland. I've got a passionate and intelligent young editor. It's almost impossible to get my novels into mainstream bookshops, but Chrissie has a number of imaginative marketing strategies, and at least I don't feel that I've sold my soul.'

'What I don't understand . . . ' Vera leaned forward across the table ' . . . is why you agreed to run this workshop. You must have known in advance that Professor Ferdinand would be one of the tutors.'

For a moment the woman sat in silence. Nina Backworth, usually so good at words that she made a living from them, said nothing. Her attention seemed held by the dust floating in the shaft of light that came through the narrow window above her head.

'At first I didn't know Tony would be here,' Nina said at last. 'The Writers' House has an international reputation and it's considered an honour to be invited to lecture here. I was interested to see how it works. A number of my friends have attended workshops and came back raving about the place. My managers at the university thought it would be a good thing to do — my being chosen as tutor reflects well on our courses — and so did my editor. The fee is generous, and that always helps.'

She paused for breath and Vera thought there were already too many explanations. She wasn't sure she believed any of them. She said nothing

97

and allowed Nina to continue.

'When Miranda sent me the list of tutors, it was too late to back out. Besides . . . ' The woman gave the same strained smile. 'Sometimes it's important to face one's demons, don't you think? I hoped I'd give my students here a more positive experience than Tony had given me. And I decided it would be good for me to meet the man again.'

'And was it?' Vera knew all about demons. She was living in the house where her dead father had kept bird skulls and skins in the basement. He regularly came to haunt her. She heard him muttering in her head late at night.

'It was quite scary the first time we sat down to dinner together. I felt like an anxious young woman all over again. Then he started to patronize me and, instead of being frightened, I found myself hating him.'

Vera paused for a second. 'Hate's a very strong word.'

The answer came back immediately. 'I'm a writer, Inspector. I choose my words carefully.'

'What was going on between him and Joanna Tobin?' Vera was remembering Nina's intervention the night before. The other guests had assumed that Joanna was the killer, but Nina had stood up to defend her.

'Joanna was a talented writer, Inspector, with an interesting story to tell. It doesn't always work when real experiences are turned into fiction, but she managed a witty and sardonic voice, combined with real menace, that I found very fresh.'

'And Ferdinand was grooming Joanna for stardom, was he? Offering to put a word in for her with his publisher mates?' Vera wondered if Joanna's writing had been good enough to turn her into a star. What would Jack make of that?

'He was trying,' Nina said. 'Joanna wasn't as naive as some of the other students. She wasn't taken in by the flattery.'

'So how were things between them?' Vera kept her voice casual.

'Tense. Tony could be unpleasant here if he didn't get his way, given to snide and sarcastic remarks. Not quite as brutal as his St Ursula seminars, but getting that way.' Nina hesitated.

'You might as well tell me the whole story, pet,' Vera said. 'If you don't, some other bugger will.'

'Once she fought back. With words, I mean, not literally. *Get off my fucking back, Tony. This is my story and I'll tell it in my own way. Sometimes you remind me of my ex-husband.* It was in front of the whole group. The animosity seemed almost personal. I even wondered . . . '

'Spit it out!'

Nina looked up sharply, shocked by the barked order. 'I wondered if they'd met before. If there was a history between them, as there was between Ferdinand and me. But that was ridiculous. How would a small farmer from Northumberland meet an academic from London?'

But Joanna hadn't always been a farmer, Vera thought. She caught Joe's eye to check that he'd understood the significance of the remark and watched him write a note in his book.

'When did you last see the professor?' Vera sneaked a look at her watch. Soon she'd have to leave for Kimmerston and her meeting with the boss.

'At lunch yesterday.'

'How did he seem?'

Nina hesitated. 'Really much as usual. In fact he was rather mellow. He'd had several glasses of wine. He started to reminisce — the highlights of his intellectual career. His favourite topic of conversation.'

'Do you remember who was sitting next to him?' Vera felt that she was pushing the conversation on too quickly. If she were allowed time, Nina might provide answers to questions Vera hadn't yet thought to ask. The woman was an observer, with an insight as sharp as Vera's own.

'Lenny Thomas was on one side and Miranda Barton on the other.'

'Tell me about the relationship between Miranda and Tony Ferdinand.' Sod the superintendent, Vera thought. If she were late for their meeting he'd have to understand that she was in the middle of a murder investigation. This was more important.

'They worked together for a while at St Ursula's. Miranda was assistant librarian in the college's library. And of course Tony discovered her. She'd been published, but to very little notice. Then Tony wrote a glowing review in one of the broadsheets. Called her one of the best writers of her generation. It made a huge difference to her. For a couple of years she was in the best-seller lists here and in the US.' Nina's tone was measured and Vera could only guess what she'd made of Miranda's success. She'd be jealous, wouldn't she? Only a saint could watch a rival outperform and not feel bitter. And Miranda must have been a rival, mustn't she?

'Was that at the same time as you were at St Ursula's?'

'She topped the best-seller lists the year I was there,' Nina said. 'Tony held Miranda up as a role model. *This is what you might achieve if you play things my way.* There was a television adaptation of one of her novels. It was called *Cruel Women.* I suppose the money she made then helped to pay for this place. She was never so successful again.'

Vera saw Ashworth pointing at his watch and saw she really would have to go now. All the same, she couldn't help asking, 'What was Miranda's book about?'

Nina blinked as if startled by the question, then gave another of her rare smiles. 'I really don't know. I didn't get beyond the second page. In my opinion the writing was pretentious crap.'

11

Later that afternoon Nina felt a compulsion to write. The hours before tea had been marked as free for students to concentrate on their own work: on the exercises set by tutors or on suggested edits to submitted manuscripts. Downstairs the house was empty and quiet. The residents must be writing in their rooms or searching for inspiration outside. The police had taken up residence in the chapel, so that was now out of bounds.

At the introductory meeting on their arrival at the Writers' House, Nina had said, only partly joking, that she was there under false pretences. Certainly she could talk about short fiction — the form had been her area of study since she was an undergraduate — but she'd never written crime. Now, with the tension and drama of a real murder investigation in the background, she began to understand the attraction of the genre. Nothing was more shocking than murder, yet the traditional structure of crime fiction provided a way of examining the subject with distance and grace. The idea that she might create her own detective story had grown slowly and insidiously all day, but by mid-afternoon she could think of nothing else. She felt as excited as she had as a new graduate, the ideas buzzing in her head, the fingers twitching to hold a pen. The exercise she'd set for the students was that they should choose a place in the house or garden as a setting for a crime scene. They should describe it, and use the description as a jumping-off point for their story. A good discipline: to make the scene real for the author and for the reader. Nina thought now that it would be a sensible way for her to get started too.

She prowled through the house looking for a setting for her piece. Nothing indoors sparked her imagination. The house was quiet. From the kitchen she heard the sound of cooking and the door banged as Mark Winterton returned from his interview with the good-looking sergeant in the chapel, but nobody else was about.

She fetched her coat from upstairs and went outside. The police officers on the doors had gone and she slipped through the back door and into the car park. The light had almost disappeared and the mist had returned like a fine drizzle on her skin. On the terrace the wrought-iron furniture appeared ghostly and insubstantial, a distorted memory of warm summer days. Water dripped through the ornate holes cut into the tables, and the chairs were tipped forward to allow rain to drain away. A lamp had been switched on in the drawing room beyond the glass, but nobody was inside. A fire had been lit in the big grate.

Nina imagined this as her crime scene. The terrace designed for use in sunshine, now gloomy on a grey October afternoon. One of the white chairs set upright and occupied by her victim, the moisture like pearls on her hair and skin. Nina dried a chair with a tissue and sat down, taking the place of the victim. Who would it be? Important, surely, to get inside the head of the person who'd been murdered, even if he or she were already dead when the story started. *She,* Nina decided. Her victim would be a woman, but someone quite different from herself.

Her concentration was broken by a sound from inside the drawing room. Raised voices. She turned to look, but from where she was sitting she couldn't see them. Nor could they see her.

'Really, Mother, you have to be careful.' That was Alex Barton. Alex the son, who must have left the dinner preparations for a while. Nina supposed she should make herself known. There was something shabby about sitting here in the fading light eavesdropping on the conversation inside. But she didn't move. Writers were like parasites, preying on other people's stress and misery. Objective observers like spies or detectives.

Except I'm not objective, Nina thought. I don't like Miranda. I don't know about her son. He seems harmless enough, but I certainly don't like her.

The boy continued to speak, sounding concerned and exasperated at the same time. 'Why don't we just cancel the rest of the course?'

'We can't do that!' His mother's voice was sharp. 'We'd have to give them a refund, and we can't afford to throw money away. You know how tough things are at the moment. Besides . . . '

'Besides, what?'

'I'd rather have the investigation taking place

104

here, where we can keep an eye on what's going on. If we send everyone home we won't know what's happening.'

'I don't want to know!' Alex said. 'I want to forget all about Tony Ferdinand. You don't know how pleased I am that he won't be part of our lives from now on.'

'You should be careful.' The mother repeated her son's words, so that it sounded like a mantra. 'You don't want people to think you're pleased he's dead.'

'Of course I'm pleased!' The words were high-pitched and childish. 'Given the chance, I'd dance on his grave.'

The spite in his voice took Nina back to St Ursula's, to one of the dreaded seminars. She'd heard the same note in her own voice that afternoon in London. The afternoon she'd described to Inspector Stanhope, when for once she hadn't been the object of the group's criticism. When the relief of someone else bearing the brunt of the bullying had caused Nina to join in, to be almost as cruel as the rest of them. Throwing insults as if they were rocks.

A sudden noise brought her back to the present: wood splitting in the fire, sounding loud as a gunshot in the silence.

'Ssh,' Miranda said. 'You don't know who might be listening.'

I'm listening, Nina thought, relishing her role as observer. Oh yes, I'm certainly listening. It occurred to her that Vera Stanhope would be proud of her. Then she heard the door shutting and assumed that both people had left the room.

She got up quietly and looked inside. The space was lit by a single standard lamp and Miranda was sitting in a chair by the fire. Her eyes were closed and tears ran down her cheeks.

★ ★ ★

By the time Nina had replaced her coat, scribbled some ideas for her story in a notebook and returned to the drawing room, it was filled with people. Miranda was talking to Giles Rickard, one of the tutors. He was an elderly novelist with a red nose, a large shambling body and arthritis. His crime fiction was superficially gentle and rather old-fashioned, though it contained moments of malicious wit. His detective was a Cambridge don, a mathematician. Rickard had had a late burst of success when a television readers' group had picked one of his books for discussion, and now he regularly appeared in the best-seller lists. Nina thought it was rather a coup for Miranda to have attracted him to teach on the course. He wore a perpetual air of surprise as if he couldn't quite believe that fame had come to him at last. With the students he could be occasionally waspish and demanding, but he'd taken to Nina.

'You write well,' he'd said when they'd first met in the house, so she'd assumed that he must have got hold of one of her recent books, and that in itself had endeared him to her. And perhaps Chrissie would persuade him to give a blurb for the next title. 'You'll see, my dear, it could happen for you too. But success isn't all

106

it's cracked up to be, you know. You give up a good deal.' She'd wondered what a man like him could have to give up. He'd never married, had no family. Privacy perhaps. Or leisure. But surely he could turn down the speaking engagements and the book tours. Why, for instance, had he agreed to spend this week at the Writers' House? It couldn't be that he needed the money.

Now he waved at her across the room. Miranda, still speaking to him, seemed not to notice. Nina made herself camomile tea and went to join them.

'What are your plans for the rest of the evening?' Nina's question was directed at Miranda. In her room she'd looked at the programme. Ferdinand had been scheduled to lecture on the editorial process in the time before dinner.

Miranda showed no sign of her earlier distress. The tears had been wiped away and fresh make-up applied. 'We had a good idea about that. I've asked Mark if he'd give us a talk on the crime scene and the role of the CSIs. It would fit in nicely with the writing exercise you set today. What do you think?'

Nina paused. 'I do wonder if a lecture on true crime might be a bit close to home. Rather lacking in taste?'

'We're all *thinking* about poor Tony's murder,' Miranda said, 'even if we're too tactful to discuss it. I don't suppose a lecture on the subject will upset anyone, especially as poor Joanna was something of a stranger in our midst. We seem to have very thick skins here.'

Nina saw that was true. The only person who'd shown genuine emotion at Ferdinand's death had been Miranda herself, and it seemed she could switch that on and off at will. She was astonished that Mark Winterton had agreed to speak to them. Perhaps Miranda had bullied him into it, because he'd always seemed a shy and retiring man.

His lecture, however, was surprisingly entertaining, and he seemed to come to life talking about his work. He began by explaining the process of securing a crime scene. The students were more attentive than Nina had seen them — certainly more focused than when she'd been speaking on literary matters — and she found herself fascinated too. What was it about the ex-policeman's talk that intrigued and even titillated? Why this bizarre interest in the process of managing the crime scene? Because, like crime fiction, it gave violent death a shape and a narrative? It turned an inexplicable horror into a process, into people's work.

Winterton's voice was pleasant and light. 'The first officer called to a crime is responsible for securing the scene,' he said. 'Even if he's a new constable and a senior officer turns up, his duty is to restrict access until the CSIs give permission. It wasn't always like that! One of the first murders I investigated, the chief constable turned up with half a dozen friends — all in evening jackets and dicky-bow ties. They'd been at some smart do, and gawping at a poor woman who'd been battered to death by her husband provided the after-dinner entertainment.' He paused. 'And some officers call those the good old days.'

Lenny Thomas stuck up his hand. 'What do you think of the way the police are handling Tony Ferdinand's murder?'

Winterton gave a little laugh. 'Oh, I'm not prepared to comment on a colleague's work. If you're personally involved, even as a witness, you have a very different perspective on an investigation.' He glanced to the back of the room.

Turning, Nina saw that Vera Stanhope had returned and was standing there next to her good-looking young sergeant. Ashworth gave the inspector a wry grin and she flapped her hand at him, a gesture that said: *Don't you have a go at me too.* So perhaps Inspector Stanhope had a tendency to become personally involved in her cases. Perhaps her perspective on the investigation was flawed. The rest of the audience realized the detectives were there and fell silent as if they were expecting an announcement from Vera — news perhaps that Joanna had been charged and that the investigation was officially over. But Vera only said, 'Don't mind us, folks! We're just here to pick up a few tips.'

The interruption and the arrival of Vera Stanhope and Joe Ashworth seemed to put Winterton off his stride. He continued to lecture, but in a dry and formal way as if he were talking to a group of young trainees, emphasizing the need to follow procedure. It was about bagging evidence and taking photographs. All interesting enough, but without the human element that had captured their interest previously. It seemed to Nina that the appearance of the detectives had reminded him of a real death — the death of someone they'd all known — and, even if the victim hadn't been particularly well liked, he no longer considered murder a fit subject for entertainment.

Yet it was fictional murder that had captured her imagination. She now had her central character and the germ of an idea, which was both simple and audacious. *What fun if I can pull this off!*

While all around her the residents were asking Mark Winterton questions about fingerprints and DNA, in her mind Nina was out on the terrace in an October dusk, watching a murderer kill a woman who was sitting on a white wrought-iron chair.

12

Vera's meeting with Ron Mason, the superintendent, had gone surprisingly well. She thought she couldn't have handled it better. Her boss was a small man, given to fits of irritability, but she'd caught him on a good day. Perhaps he was so unused to Vera consulting him about anything that she'd flattered him by appearing to ask for his advice. Certainly he had no idea that he was being manipulated.

'So the prime suspect is a neighbour of yours?' He leaned forward across the table. He'd once had red hair and, although it was grey now, his eyebrows were still the colour of powdered cinnamon and there were freckles the same colour all over his forehead. Vera had never noticed that before. She thought that spending time with all these writers was turning her brain, making her look at things in a different way.

'It certainly seemed like that at first, though we don't have enough to charge her.' Vera explained about the knife Joanna had been carrying not matching the wounds on Ferdinand's body.

'Complicated then.'

'I wondered if you'd like to take over as senior officer in charge of the inquiry,' Vera said. 'In view of what might be considered a conflict of interest.' Mason was a competent administrator, but hadn't taken a personal interest in a major crime investigation for years. Word in the canteen had it that he'd lost his nerve.

'No need for that,' Mason said quickly. 'A rural police area like this, we're always going to bump up against the odd acquaintance.' He paused. 'I take it that's all you are, acquaintances?'

'I don't really move in arty circles,' Vera said, encouraging him to smile at the thought. 'Like I said, Joanna Tobin and Jack Devanney are just neighbours.'

And that was all it had taken for Mason to confirm her place in the investigation. At the end of the interview he stood up and shook her hand. 'Thanks for keeping me informed,' he said. 'Good luck.'

★ ★ ★

Back in the Writers' House, Vera thought they'd need it. It seemed that many of the people there with the opportunity to commit the murder had disliked Tony Ferdinand, but she had no sense yet of why anyone should choose this particular time and place to do it. She arrived just as Winterton's lecture had started. She could have told them her own stories about balls-ups at crime scenes, and had been tempted to put in her two penn'orth, but had seen that would hardly be professional. When the talk was over and the residents were preparing for dinner she took Ashworth across the yard and into the chapel.

'What did you make of Winterton, then?'

'He had opportunity,' Joe said. 'I don't see how he could have motive. He's never moved in literary circles. He only retired from the job twelve months ago.'

'What's he doing here then? Police pension is better than it was, but you'd not think he'd have the spare cash for this sort of jaunt. Have you seen the fees? Or did he get one of those bursaries?' Vera wondered briefly what she'd do when she retired. She saw herself in Hector's house, too fat and unfit to get out, watching daytime telly and drinking beer for breakfast. Then the hippy-dippy neighbours would be her only link to the outside world. Maybe after all she had more of a vested interest in Joanna's innocence than anyone realized.

'No, he applied for a bursary, but he didn't get one. I get the impression his writing's not up to much.'

'So maybe he had a reason for killing Tony Ferdinand and he came here specially to do it. He used the course as a cover.'

'Yeah,' Joe said. 'And that's a piggy I can see floating past the window.'

Vera smiled. She liked it when Joe stood up to her, as long as he didn't do it too often. 'He'd have the knowledge about how an investigation works. He'd understand enough to pull the stunt with the knives.'

'But he wouldn't have got it wrong, would he?' Joe said. 'He'd have made sure the right knife was in Joanna's possession.'

'So he would.' Vera was feeling hungry now, but she didn't want to eat her dinner in front of

113

a party of suspects. Let Mark Winterton play the performing cop for them.

'I was thinking Winterton might be useful,' Joe said. 'An insider. They'll say things to him that they wouldn't say to us.'

'He's a suspect,' Vera said sharply. 'A witness, at the very least. Sometimes you have to keep your distance.' She saw it was on the tip of Joe's tongue to make some comment about her own lack of objectivity. Instead he looked at his watch.

'I should get home. If I don't see the kids before they go to bed tonight, they'll forget what I look like.'

'I was going to talk to Joanna Tobin,' she said. 'Now that she's had a while to think about things and we know what questions we want to ask. I can't do that on my own. But no problem, of course. Your family has to come first, Joe, I understand that. I'll ask Holly if she can come along. She could do with the practice. I might get her to take the lead. What do you think?' Vera smiled sweetly. Joe Ashworth would know exactly what she was playing at. There was no love lost between Holly and Joe, and he wouldn't want the bright young lass to take credit for any information gained in the interview. Vera lifted up the canvas shopping bag that did as a briefcase, a sign that she needed a decision.

'The wife'll kill me.'

'Like I said, pet, no pressure. Holly could use the experience. You get an early night.' But she knew now that she had him hooked.

'I'll do it.'

114

Vera beamed. 'Champion,' she said. 'There's a casserole I made a couple of days ago when I was feeling domestic. I get the urge sometimes, but it soon passes. We'll have a bite to eat before we talk to the dippy hippies, shall we? I can't concentrate when I've got an empty stomach.'

'And you'll let me lead the interview?'

'Of course, bonny lad. It's only right. We can't compromise the inquiry.'

★　★　★

The house was cold and Vera put a match to the fire. From the kitchen, heating up the chicken casserole and sticking a couple of jacket potatoes in the microwave, she heard Ashworth grovelling to his wife.

'Yeah, I know I promised, but this is something I can't get out of.'

They ate sitting by the fire with plates on their knees.

'Is there anything I should know,' Ashworth said. 'Before we go in there?'

'I wouldn't want to influence you.' And that was true enough, Vera thought. She'd be glad of Joe's take on the pair. He disapproved of them instinctively, just because of their clothes and the way they looked, the fact that they didn't have a real job or the whole 2.4 kids thing. Vera wasn't sure of the way her sergeant voted, but she knew that by temperament he was conservative. He'd be sceptical about the pair and wouldn't be taken in by the romance of their relationship. That was just what Vera needed.

115

They saw the couple before they realized Vera and Joe were there. Again the lights had been switched on, but the curtains — if there were any at the Myers Farm kitchen window — hadn't been drawn. Jack and Joanna were sitting at the table. Supper plates were piled on the draining board. Jack was wearing thick woollen socks. His feet were stretched towards the ancient Rayburn and he drank beer from a bottle. The pose suggested complete exhaustion, and Vera thought he couldn't have slept much even after Joanna's release from custody. Joanna was sitting at an old-fashioned sewing machine, turning the handle with her right hand and guiding the fabric under the dipping needle with the other.

'My nana used to have one of those Singers,' Joe Ashworth said. He sounded wistful. Perhaps he thought his wife should spend her time sewing clothes for the kids instead of making a life of her own.

'No time for nostalgia, lad.' Vera knocked sharply at the door and marched in without waiting for a reply. Jack jumped to his feet. It was almost as if they'd woken him from a deep sleep. Joanna just looked up from the sewing.

'What is it, Vera? Have you come to arrest me?' The question was amused and impassive, as if the answer would have been of purely academic interest.

'Nothing to make a joke about.' Vera took a seat at the end of the table, leaving the one opposite the woman free for Joe. 'We've just got a few questions.'

'What will you have?' Jack said. 'Beer? Coffee?'

116

Now he was on his feet, it seemed he couldn't keep still. He bounced towards the dresser on the balls of his feet, shook the stiffness out of his arms and shoulders.

'This isn't a social call.' Vera looked at him. 'Maybe there's something you could be getting on with. We could do with some privacy.'

'I'm not sure.' He glared at them. 'I think I should stay. You hear all sorts of things about the police. You might need a witness.'

'This is Vera, Jack!' Joanna threw back her head and laughed. 'She's not going to fit me up.'

He seemed about to respond, but glowered at the detectives and walked out without a word. They all watched him leave the room. After Jack's bluster, the place seemed very quiet and calm, like a house after all the kids have been put to bed. Eventually they heard his boots cross the yard as he made his way to the barn.

'Someone's trying to fit you up,' Joe Ashworth said. 'That's how it seems at least.'

Oh yes! Vera said to herself. *Good opening, Joey-boy. Nice way in!*

'What do you mean?' Joanna was sitting very upright in her chair.

'The note, apparently from Ferdinand. If it wasn't from him, perhaps the killer wanted you at the murder scene. What did you do with it, by the way? The note, I mean.' The question was thrown in as an afterthought, although it was what he'd wanted to know from the start.

'I'm not sure. I have looked for it. I thought perhaps you'd be able to test the handwriting, though only the initials were written. The rest was done on the computer and printed out.'

'Didn't that strike you as odd?' Joe said. 'A note as short as that, why not just scribble it on a bit of paper? Why not speak to you, if it comes to that? Ferdinand must have seen you at lunch. He could have told you whatever he wanted then.'

'Everything about that place was weird,' Joanna said. 'And I did wonder if the note was a ruse and Ferdinand just wanted to get me into his room on our own. But while there was a chance he had information about a publisher I decided to play along with it.' She paused and returned to Joe's initial question. 'I rather think I must have chucked the thing into the basket by the fire in the drawing room as soon as I got it. I put all my waste paper in there. They use it to lay the grate every evening.'

'So it's probably burned?'

'Yes,' she said. 'It probably is. And if that's the case, there's no proof I received it at all.' The last words were thrown towards Ashworth like a challenge: *I dare you to call me a liar!*

Ashworth looked at her for a moment and then changed the subject. 'Had you met anyone at the Writers' House before?'

Sitting at the end of the table, Vera thought this was another good question.

This time Joanna paused before answering. 'It's possible.'

'You don't seem very sure,' Ashworth said.

'That's because I'm not.' Joanna frowned. 'Look, it's probably not relevant to Ferdinand's death. I don't see how it can be.'

'But . . .'

118

'But I thought I recognized one of the tutors. An old guy. Giles Rickard. The name was familiar when I got the list of participants.'

'He's a writer,' Ashworth said. 'They tell me he's famous. Maybe you've read one of his books.' The tone was sceptical: *Don't play games with me, lady.*

'I'm trying to be honest here, Sergeant.' Joanna was holding her temper, but only just. 'I'm telling you how it is. Maybe I only recognized the name because I'd seen it on a bookshelf somewhere, but I don't think so. And then when I saw him on the first night of the course, I was convinced I'd met him before. Even before I was told who he was. It was a long time ago and he'd changed, got bigger, softer. Old. But the features were the same. I've got a good visual memory.'

'Where do you know him from?' Vera asked the question. Ashworth frowned at the interruption, but she hadn't been able to help herself. She'd become involved in the conversation. She looked at Joe, a sort of apology, before turning back to Joanna to wait for the answer.

'He was a friend of my ex-husband's,' Joanna said. 'If it's the man I believe him to be, that's how I know him.'

'Didn't you ask him?' Ashworth demanded. 'I mean, he's a famous writer and you're trying to get published, so surely you'd use any contact you had in that world.'

Again Joanna took time before replying. 'It wasn't a happy time for me,' she said at last. 'The marriage was a disaster almost from the beginning. I was young. The separation was brutal. My husband was so convinced of his brilliance that he believed I must be mad to want to leave him. Literally mad. And by the end of the experience I probably was. Giles knew me from that time.'

'So it would have been embarrassing to introduce yourself to him?' Ashworth said. 'Because the last time you met, you were . . . ' he paused to find an acceptable term. Vera saw that *mad* would be too stark for him. Too unkind. ' . . . mentally ill.'

'No!' This time Joanna's response was immediate. 'I've never been embarrassed in my life. People can take me or leave me.'

'Then I don't understand.' And Vera saw that Ashworth really didn't understand. His experience of domestic life was limited and suburban. People married. If they separated, usually it was because one party had an affair. And Joe disapproved of affairs.

'Paul, my husband, was an unpleasant man. Controlling and violent. Also rich, which was a complicating factor. Giles was his closest friend, despite the difference in their ages. Like a surrogate father. I thought that if Giles recognized me, he might tell Paul where I was.' She looked up and stared first at Ashworth and then at Vera. 'I was scared,' she said. 'It all happened nearly twenty years ago, but still I was scared.'

13

Vera watched Joe drive down the lane. She waited until his lights had disappeared and then she went back to Myers Farm. Through the kitchen window she saw Jack standing behind Joanna, his arms around her shoulders. Was Joanna telling him about Rickard? Sharing her anxiety. This time when Vera knocked she waited for them to call her in.

'What is it now?' Jack was reproachful. 'Don't you think Joanna needs to be left alone? It's late. We were thinking of going to bed.'

'I'm here as a friend,' Vera said. 'Not as a cop. I should have nothing to do with this investigation. Conflict of interests. When we come to courts the defence could use that. You do see?'

'So you'll have a beer then?' Jack stood away from Joanna. 'If you're here as a friend. If it's not a professional visit.'

'Aye, why not?' Vera leaned across the table towards Joanna. For the first time she saw how tense and strained the woman was. The performance for Joe had been a brilliant effort. 'You submitted a piece of writing to get the bursary for the writing course.' Her voice was low, and Jack, in the pantry, wouldn't have been able to hear.

'Yes.'

'It was about your marriage,' Vera said. 'Your

121

marriage turned into fiction. You told me that and so did Nina Backworth. Very personal, she said. It must have been hard to write.'

'No.' Joanna was drinking wine from the Bristol Blue glass. Jack had obviously poured it for her as soon as Ashworth and Vera had left. 'It wasn't hard at all. I'd been bottling up the hatred for years and when I saw the advertisement for the Writers' House, I sat here one afternoon and spewed it all out. Then I sent the story off, before I had a chance to change my mind.'

'Did the writing come easily because you'd stopped taking the medication?' Vera asked. 'Is that why you came off it?'

'To make me more creative, you mean?' Joanna was self-mocking. 'No, it wasn't that. Not in that sense, at least.'

'In what sense then?' Vera thought of Jack's words before all this had started, his fear that Joanna had found a new lover.

But he came back into the room then and Joanna just shook her head and refused to answer.

'Can I read the story?' Vera was leaning back in her chair, the bottle raised towards her mouth. She could tell the question came as a surprise. 'Ashworth should have asked to see it, but I didn't want to make a deal of it while he was here.'

'I can't see what that could have to do with Tony Ferdinand's death.'

'Ferdinand had read it, hadn't he? And he was known as something of a sexual predator.'

'You think it might have turned him on?'

Joanna threw back her head and laughed. 'Nah, he was just an ordinary perv.'

'Rickard had seen it too?' Vera was trying to grope her way through the complexities of the' situation. She didn't care if her ideas seemed ridiculous.

'A copy of all submitted work was shown to every tutor,' Joanna said.

'Did Rickard recognize you?'

'If he did,' Joanna said, 'he didn't say anything.'

'What did he make of your story?'

'I don't know. I was due to have a tutorial with him the afternoon Tony Ferdinand died.'

There was a silence while they considered the implication of that fact. 'So it might be important,' Vera said. 'Probably not, but you see how it could be?'

When Joanna didn't answer, Vera went on:

'I could get a copy from Miranda Barton, you know. But I wanted to ask you first.'

Joanna nodded. She went to a drawer in the dresser and took out an A4 envelope. 'This is all I have left,' she said. 'I deleted it from the computer.'

'Because you didn't want Jack to read it?' Vera kept her voice light. On the other side of the table Jack seemed about to speak, but said nothing. Not like him to keep quiet, Vera thought. Maybe he's growing up at last.

'Not because there's anything secret,' Joanna said. 'And nothing really I'm ashamed of. Except being taken in by a bastard. But you know what Jack's like.' She turned towards her partner and

123

gave him a smile that was almost maternal. 'I thought it would make him angry. I thought he'd decide to go off and play the hero.'

'Eh,' Jack said, trying to keep it light. 'Stop talking about me as if I'm not here.'

Vera ignored the interruption. 'You thought he'd confront your ex, you mean?'

'Something like that. He'd have had a go at Paul, if he'd been able to find him.'

'And would you have done that?' Now Vera did look at Jack. The knuckles were white on the hand that clasped the bottle. If he squeezed it much harder it'd smash into pieces.

'Yeah I would,' Jack said. 'If I'd found him I'd have killed him.'

'And I wouldn't have wanted that,' Joanna said, suddenly serious. 'I don't blame Paul Rutherford or Giles Rickard any more. They didn't turn me into a victim, Vera. I did that all by myself. Sometimes you just have to take responsibility.'

★ ★ ★

Vera sat up in bed and read the manuscript Joanna had given to her. The bedroom was cold. The fire she'd lit for Joe had long gone out and she hadn't bothered switching on the central heating. She had two pillows at her back and a spare duvet wrapped around her shoulders. On the bedside table some hot milk with a good splash of whisky in it. Outside it was still; there was no sound at all. In her head she heard the voices of the people in the story.

This was fiction, but the central character, Maggie, was a barely disguised version of Joanna, and when Vera read the piece, she found Joanna there, speaking in her aristocratic tone, confused and angry.

Maggie grew up in a house in Somerset governed by unspoken and unwritten rules. Everything from the correct folding of napkins to her inadequate schooling was prescribed in advance. Then she met Paul and every rule was broken or irrelevant. He was her saviour and her devil. He walked into her life one evening, rangy and spare, a hungry lion looking for food. For a woman and admiration. For money and a woman to worship him. In his life there were no rules, except one: take what you want. And she was seduced by his wickedness, by the absence of rules. It liberated her from the tedious life of duty. That evening, a guest in her father's house, he made love to her while the other guests were at dinner. The next morning she ran away with him.

That was the start. Very melodramatic, Vera thought. She remembered snatches of a book programme on Radio 4 and came up with a different word. Very gothic. She wondered if it had really happened that way, or if Joanna had re-created a story to suit her heightened mood. Perhaps her relationship with Paul had been more mundane, almost sleazy. She was a schoolgirl who wanted to escape from strict parents and a boring home life. And he was an older man who wasn't going to turn away a bonny lass when she'd thrown herself at him. Was the overblown language of the story the result of Joanna's lack of medication at the time of writing? Or had she first seen her husband as the romantic figure described in the story? And as the theatrical villain he later became in the work?

As she read on, the lack of factual detail in the piece irritated Vera. She'd hoped there would be something here to help her in the investigation. But while the scenes of the couple's life in Paris, especially those describing Maggie's unravelling into depression, were vivid, little was specific. Paul left the apartment every day to go to work, but there was no mention of the address of their home or of exactly what he did to earn a living. Of course Vera could ask Joanna about her life in France, but Joanna was still a major suspect.

Besides, how could this be relevant to the murder? Did Vera really think Joanna's ex-husband had manipulated events at the Writers' House? The notion that a stranger had been murdered just to implicate Joanna, to torment her further, seemed fanciful even at this time of night. Why bother now after all these years? Perhaps Joe Ashworth had been right not to pursue the idea. After reading the pages through for a second time, Vera put them on the floor beside the bed. After all, she could hardly justify spending more time and energy on this line of enquiry. She fancied another whisky as a nightcap — she deserved it after reading all that stuff — but by now the room was freezing and she couldn't face her cold feet on the bare kitchen floor. Her last thought was that she should have brought the bottle to bed with her.

★ ★ ★

At the team briefing the next morning the question of Joanna's past came up. Joe Ashworth was leading the session. Vera sat at the back, determined to keep her mouth shut and let him get on with it. She didn't want to compromise the investigation by taking a leading role. Nor was she keen to let slip that she'd been back to visit Joanna the night before. He began with a recap.

'Of all the folk staying at the Writers' House, only seven had the opportunity to kill Tony Ferdinand. The rest were together between lunch and the discovery of the body. There's no news yet from the search team on the murder weapon.'

Holly stuck up her hand. Vera thought she would have been the sort of child to sit in the front row of the classroom and tell the teacher if he'd got something wrong.

'Yeah?' Joe reacted just as the teacher would have done.

'There's Chrissie Kerr, the publisher, too. She was at the Writers' House in the morning to give a guest lecture. She stayed for lunch.'

'And drove away before Ferdinand died.' Joe glared at her.

'Nothing to stop her pulling in at the top of

the bank and coming back on foot.'

Vera thought they were like squabbling kids and decided it was time to step in or they'd be there all day. 'Any connection between Kerr and Ferdinand?' she asked. 'Any possible motive?'

'Not that I can find,' Holly said.

'Let's put her down as an outsider and carry on, then.' Vera sat back in her chair and waited for Joe to continue.

He pointed to the photos of the Bartons, stuck on the whiteboard. 'So we have mother and son, Miranda Barton and her son Alex. They run the place.' He turned to Holly, icily polite: 'You were going to dig around into the business's finances. What have you come up with?'

'Well, it's hardly making them a fortune,' Holly said. 'But they're not on the verge of bankruptcy, either. Miranda bought the house years ago when she was making a decent living out of her writing. There's hardly any mortgage. She must have got the idea of setting it up as a writers' retreat when her books stopped selling. It makes sense really. A sort of value-added B&B. And New Writing North covers the cost of the bursaries, so it's all profit.'

She looked at Ashworth over her specs. 'I don't see any motive for either of them. If anything, they have something to lose if the murder has an impact on bookings.'

Vera thought there was an edge of competition in every conversation between these two. Holly was waiting for Joe to contradict her and was looking forward to another argument, but he didn't give her the satisfaction.

128

Vera raised a finger. 'They seem an odd pair to me,' she said. 'The woman's all showy emotion, and you'd think the lad was made of ice. Chalk and cheese.'

Joe looked at her expecting more, but she shook her head. 'Just making the point.'

He turned back to the whiteboard and pointed to another photo. 'Next, Lenny Thomas. Worked for Banks Open-cast until he developed back problems two years ago. Since then he's lived off invalidity benefit. He's got a council house in Red Row. Divorced with one kid. A bit of a history when he was a kid — car theft, burglary. One period of probation and six months' imprisonment. Nothing recent. Not since he started with Banks.'

'How does he fit in with the arty set?' This from Charlie, bags under his eyes you could carry golf clubs in, last night's takeaway curry on his jersey.

Vera was tempted to jump in again at this point, but she allowed Ashworth to speak first. 'They've adopted him as their own working-class pet,' Ashworth said. 'They're kind, but patronizing. They wouldn't want to be thought snobby.'

Well done, lad!

'Motive?' Holly asked. She was still sulking because Joe was getting all the attention.

'According to Lenny Thomas, Tony Ferdinand had said he could find him a publisher and turn him into a star. Maybe it was all talk, and Lenny got resentful and lost it.'

'The trick with the knife, and the forged note to Joanna, would hardly be his style, would it?'

129

This was Holly betraying her own prejudices.

'You mean he's not bright enough to think of it, because he once drove a truck on an open-cast for a living?'

Don't let her bug you, Joey-boy, Vera thought.

'Besides,' Joe went on, 'we don't know the note to Joanna was forged. And we're not going to find out. She claims it was burned. She's still got to be our prime suspect.' He pointed to the photo of Joanna. It had been taken recently, and Vera wondered where they'd got hold of it. She was wearing a red sweater and her hair was blowing away from her face. 'Joanna Tobin. Living the good life with her partner, Jack Devanney, in the hills above Clachan Lough. Like Thomas, she was one of the students who'd been awarded a free place on the writers' course. She was found close to the body with a knife in her hand. Problem is, the knife doesn't fit the wound. So was she set up? Or was she playing some sort of elaborate game with us? A sort of double bluff.'

He paused and turned towards Vera. 'She spent ten years of her married life in France, and records of that time only came through this morning. She assaulted her husband, attacked him with a knife, then attempted suicide. The doctors diagnosed some sort of psychotic episode and she was never charged. She escaped from a French psychiatric hospital and made her way back here, with the help of Devanney. It seems she's been on medication ever since.'

Except she stopped taking it for a few weeks before going to the Writers' House. Because she fancied herself in love, as Jack had feared?

'Case over, then!' Charlie looked up from the paper cup he'd been staring into since he'd sat down.

'That's dangerous talk, Charlie, and you know it.' Joe's voice was sharp. Vera wasn't sure if he was really angry or if this was a show for her benefit. 'There's no evidence to connect her to the victim. If you start looking for proof to nail an individual, you'll likely try too hard and find it. Doesn't mean it's real. Now's the time to keep an open mind. So let's move on.'

Joe pointed to the next photo on the board. The photo was old and looked as if it had been dug out of an old HR file. 'Mark Winterton. Former inspector with Cumbria Police. Not much use as a writer, according to the staff at the place. So what was he doing there? It would be good to establish some link between him and the victim. Or with Joanna Tobin. Charlie, can you do that? There's an address near Carlisle for him. Not so far from where Tobin lives, as the crow flies.' Charlie nodded. He was used to being shouted at and didn't bear resentment for long.

'The last two are tutors. Nina Backworth, academic and writer. She admits to hating Ferdinand and blames him for screwing up her writing career. So she has the most plausible motive, but again there's no forensic evidence to link her to the victim.' Ashworth paused and looked round the room to check he had their full attention. 'Then there's Giles Rickard. He's done very nicely from his writing recently. A

131

house in Normandy and a flat in Highgate.' He looked at Charlie 'That's a flash part of London. And he's got a holiday cottage up the coast in Northumberland. Which is how he came to be invited as a tutor on the course. He claims that he had no professional contact with Ferdinand, and they seem only to have met at the occasional publishers' party. According to Rickard, who seems a nice old chap. But maybe we can't entirely trust him. Because he forgot to tell us that he was best mates with Joanna Tobin's ex-husband, Paul. And when I googled him I found a scathing review of one of his books in the *Times Literary Supplement*. Written by our victim.'

14

Nina Backworth woke with a start and she didn't know where she was. It was still dark. At home, in her flat in Newcastle, there would be enough light from the street lamps for her to make out the shadow of the wardrobe, and she'd hear the background buzz of distant traffic. Here, briefly everything was strange. She heard footsteps in the corridor outside her door and there was a moment of panic. Her body was rigid with fear and her pulse raced. Someone had broken into her flat. The image of a bloody body crouching in a dark corner flashed into her mind, half-nightmare, half-daydream. Her body? Her flat? A premonition of her own death? Then a beat later she remembered where she was and began to breathe again. Tony Ferdinand was dead, but she was still alive. She turned on her bedside light and saw that it was six-thirty. After all she hadn't slept badly. The footsteps outside her door would be one of the other residents.

She tried to settle back under the sheets, but could tell immediately it would be impossible to rest. The shock of waking suddenly had made her muscles tense and she'd never been any good at relaxing. She got out of bed and opened the curtains. Her room looked over the sea and in the distance a light-buoy flashed. There was no wind; it would be another quiet day. She pulled a jersey over her pyjamas and made tea. Then, sitting in the easy chair by the window, her notepad on her knee, she continued to work on her short story. The words came easily and she thought that this was what she was made for.

* * *

At breakfast she found herself sitting next to Giles Rickard. Still exhilarated by the hour's writing, she was tempted by the smell of coffee. Usually she never drank caffeine, and now, sipping from the mug, enjoying the smell and the taste, she found her body responding immediately to it. She felt alert, more awake than she had for months. She saw the arthritic hands of her companion and wondered how she would describe them if she were writing about them. It occurred to her that hands like that could never hold a knife with the firmness needed to push the blade through skin and muscle. This man at least could be no suspect. She said as much to Rickard.

'You'll have to tell the inspector that, my dear. I've already had a message from her asking if I could make myself available for a chat in the chapel this morning. That was her word. *Chat.* Of course she hopes that we'll underestimate her — we'll see her size and her clothes, and discount her obvious intellect.'

'What are you working on at the moment?' Nina didn't want to discuss Ferdinand's murder or Vera Stanhope's investigation. She had noticed in the few days that she'd known him that

134

Rickard enjoyed gossip. He revelled in it like a lonely old woman, could be spiteful and bitchy, though he was always charming to one's face. She suspected that she might have been the object of his venom herself on occasions and didn't want to give him further ammunition.

Besides, this was an opportunity to pick the brains of one of the most successful crime writers of his generation. Did he plan his work in detail in advance? And what were the commercial pressures? Did he feel the need to turn out the same kind of book each time?

'I've more or less given up writing altogether,' Rickard said. 'It became rather a chore, you know. A means to an end. I considered the last six books as my retirement fund.'

'Then why did you agree to come here?' Recklessly Nina reached out to pour more coffee. She saw that her hands were trembling very slightly, the effect already of the caffeine. 'If you don't even enjoy writing, it must be tedious for you, discussing your work with the students.'

For a moment there was no answer, and Nina wondered if the old man had considered her question impertinent.

'It was a matter of unfinished business,' Rickard said at last. 'Yes, I think that's how you might describe it.'

She was going to follow up with another question when she heard a loud voice in the reception hall outside the dining room. Around her the other residents fell silent and Joanna Tobin walked through the door. She stood just inside the room, making an entrance.

'I hope you've all saved some bacon for me,' Joanna said. 'I'm starving.'

She was dressed even more flamboyantly than she had been at the beginning of the writers' course, in black canvas trousers and a silk top of clashing oranges and pinks. The equivalent of war paint. But Nina thought she looked white and strained.

There was a moment of awkward silence while the other residents stared at the newcomer. 'Come and sit next to me,' Nina said. Her voice sounded forced, overly jolly. 'I'll get you something.' She found the hostility embarrassing, and was glad to turn her back on the group to fetch Joanna's breakfast.

Walking back from the serving table, Nina saw that Joanna and Rickard sat without speaking, the space where she'd been sitting an invisible wall between them. She was disappointed; she'd hoped the old man might make some gesture of welcome, even if only to irritate the rest of the house. She set a plate of food in front of Joanna, but the woman hardly seemed to notice.

'Why did you come back?'

Joanna looked up at her, and her voice was loud enough for the whole room to hear her answer. 'The bursary was for the whole course. Why wouldn't I?'

'What did Vera Stanhope make of your decision to stay on the course?'

'The police haven't charged me,' Joanna said. 'I'm a free woman. It doesn't have anything to do with bossy Vera.'

As if on cue, Vera Stanhope appeared at the

136

dining-room door. Nina thought the whole meal had the air of a tense Whitehall farce. Everyone was overacting like mad and making dramatic entrances. Soon people would be diving out of windows and taking their clothes off.

Vera walked towards the table and nodded to Joanna. The room was still quiet, so they could all hear. But if they were expecting an angry confrontation, and to see Joanna being led away again, they were disappointed. 'I thought I saw your Jack's van driving away up the lane,' the inspector said easily. 'I hope he's sorted out his MOT. We wouldn't want him picked up by the plods on the A1.'

Joanna grinned, but didn't answer. Giles Rickard was struggling to get to his feet. Vera moved towards him, and Nina assumed she was there to help him out of his seat, to take him into the chapel for their *chat*.

'You stay where you are, Mr Rickard,' Vera said. 'I'm afraid I'll have to postpone our little meeting. I need a few words with another of the guests first, and it's a bit more urgent.' She turned to Nina. 'If you wouldn't mind coming with us, Ms Backworth. We've just got a few more questions.'

It was the last thing Nina had been expecting. She began to blush. She followed Vera out of the dining room, aware that everyone was staring at her. She felt like a girl pulled out in front of a school assembly for a misdemeanour she hadn't realized she'd committed.

★ ★ ★

In the chapel the lamps were lit because the narrow windows let in so little daylight. The table and chairs were as they'd previously been, at the head of the nave, like a stageset in a theatre. The inspector lowered herself into one of the seats and gestured Nina to take another. Nina was aware of Joe Ashworth leaning against the bare wall as she walked in, but from where she sat he was outside her line of view.

'Can I help you, Inspector?' Nina knew she could come across as haughty. She thought that she and Joanna had a similar defence against the world: they became hard and brittle. Confrontational. 'I've already given you a very full statement.'

'So you did.' Vera shut her eyes for a moment. It was as if she was rerunning the previous interview in her head. She opened them suddenly. 'But other facts have since come to light.'

'I don't understand.'

'Mr Ferdinand died from knife wounds. He was stabbed repeatedly. It seemed odd to us from the start that he put up so little resistance. He was a tall man. Middle-aged, perhaps, but physically fit and, if someone came at him with a knife, you'd have thought he'd put up a bit of a fight.' Vera paused. Nina saw that she was expected to comment, but what could she say? She pictured an intruder in the glass room, the damp heat and the plants, the knife and the blood, but still she could feel little sympathy for Ferdinand. So she remained silent.

'Ferdinand didn't fight back because he was

drugged,' Vera went on. 'He'd hardly have been aware of what was happening. Maybe he was killed on the balcony because that was where he lost consciousness. He'd have been given the pills earlier in the day. During lunch perhaps. Or maybe Ferdinand fell asleep in one of the chairs in the glass room and the killer yanked him out and half-carried him outside. Thoughtful enough not to make a mess on the smart tiled floor. We probably won't know, unless the murderer tells us.'

'This is very interesting, Inspector,' Nina said, 'but I don't understand what it has to do with me.' And the first part of the statement at least was true. She did find the means of Tony Ferdinand's death interesting. Could she work something similar into her story? All writers are parasites, she thought again.

'It has everything to do with you, Ms Back-worth.' The detective's voice seemed unnaturally clear, jerking Nina away from her fiction. 'You take sleeping pills.'

'Yes, I suffer from insomnia. My GP prescribes them.'

'And your pills have the same chemical composition as the drug found in Ferdinand's body, according to the toxicology report that we received from the pathologist this morning. He'd have taken them earlier in the day. As I say, they could have been added to his lunch or his coffee. You'll know yourself that they don't work immediately. You told me that you were sitting close to Professor Ferdinand that lunchtime.'

There was a silence. Nina felt the mindless

panic that had struck her when she'd woken that morning, the sense that her world had been invaded and that there was nothing she could do to control it. Then things started to come to life again. Her brain slipped back into gear.

Her first impulse was to fight back, to protest about her personal belongings being searched, invoke her human rights, threaten an action for breach of privacy. She realized in time that such a response would be counter-productive. She had to present herself as a reasonable, intelligent woman. 'I didn't kill Tony Ferdinand,' she said calmly. 'I didn't poison him and I didn't stab him.'

Vera flashed her a smile. 'Aye, well, pet, no doubt you would say that. Even if you were the killer. Have you noticed if any of your pills have gone missing?'

Nina pictured the brown plastic bottle, kept in her washbag. She hadn't taken any tablets the night before. Her doctor had told her they'd be ineffective if she used them too often.

'I don't know,' she said. 'I mean, no, I haven't noticed.'

'Had you told anyone here that you had them in your possession?'

Nina thought back. Had she mentioned her insomnia on the first evening of the course? Everyone had seemed so tense and ill at ease, talking too much as they clasped their glasses of wine, trying to make an impression, and she'd admitted that she too felt anxious in this new place and in this gathering of strangers. 'Most people knew I had problems sleeping,' she said.

'I didn't talk about taking stuff for it.'

'But someone might have put two and two together?'

'I suppose so.' But Nina was sceptical. This all sounded too elaborate to her. Murder wasn't a parlour game, the moves planned out in advance. Surely it was usually a brutal outburst of anger, sudden and unforeseen? Not in her story, of course. The action there was as elegant as a Regency dance. But in real life.

'I'm trying to help you out here!' Vera said. 'If your pills weren't stolen, you become the murderer. You do see that?'

Nina didn't answer.

Vera suddenly seemed to lose patience. 'Take Sergeant Ashworth to your room and show him your tablets,' she said. 'We'll have to take them away, of course. Do you keep your room locked?'

'Only from the inside at night,' Nina said. 'Not during the day.'

'Ever had the feeling that someone's been in there, rifling through your things?'

'No,' Nina said. 'Never.'

It seemed to be the answer Vera was expecting. 'Get along!' she said. 'I have other people to see.'

15

Ashworth didn't know what to make of Nina Backworth. She was the sort of woman who would usually terrify him. But following her up the main stairs away from the lobby he found himself aware of her body, a sudden and powerful attraction that left him breathless. At her bedroom door she turned and gave an unexpected grin:

'I thought police officers were supposed to be fit.'

He felt confused, unsure what to make of the observation — had she noticed the effect she was having on him? His words came out as brusque, almost rude.

'The pills, Ms Backworth, if you don't mind.'

Her room was on the same floor as those of all the other tutors. While she went into the bathroom, he stood by the window and looked out at the sea, trying to regain his composure. At an angle below him was the terrace, with its wrought-iron furniture. The garden, rather overgrown and unkempt, sloped steeply to a path that led down to the beach.

He looked back into the room. It had a faint smell of citrus. Her perfume. He'd noticed it as he'd come up the stairs. Everything was ordered. She'd made her own bed, and her pyjamas — white silk — were folded on the pillow. On the desk were a notebook and a fountain pen, neatly aligned. He hadn't realized that anyone wrote with a real pen and ink any more. He was thinking how classy she was, well outside his sphere, when she returned from the bathroom carrying a red toilet bag.

'The pills are inside,' she said. 'I didn't touch the bottle. I thought I might smudge finger-prints. Something like that.'

Her prints would already be on the bottle, of course, but he should have thought of that, should focus now entirely on the task in hand. This was ridiculous. He was behaving like a teenager. Though when he'd been a teenager he'd already had his future mapped out. He'd met his wife when he was still at school. *Sixteen years old and I was already middle-aged.*

He took a clear plastic evidence bag from his pocket and, using it as a glove, he slipped the bottle inside. Then he held it to the light and tilted it so that he could count the tablets.

'There are four left,' he said. 'Is that what you would have expected?'

'No.' He couldn't tell what she was thinking. Her face was white and set. The red lipstick like a splash of fresh blood on her face. 'My GP gave me a prescription for a month's supply. I'd used about ten.'

He did the arithmetic in his head and checked it before he spoke. He didn't want to make a fool of himself in front of this woman. 'So there are sixteen missing?'

'I can't be precise, but certainly about that. At least a dozen.' She slumped, so that she was sitting on the bed, leaning forward. The straight spine and upright posture were so characteristic of Nina Backworth that it seemed another, more vulnerable woman was there. A stranger. 'Someone came into my room,' she said. 'They went through my things.'

He wanted to sit on the bed beside her and put his arm around her shoulders. 'It's a horrible feeling.' The words seemed inadequate to him.

'So you believe me? You know I didn't poison Tony Ferdinand?' Something of the old spark returned. 'You know I wouldn't be so foolish as to use my own sleeping pills!'

Ashworth took a moment to answer. 'My job's not about belief,' he said. 'It's about fact. Evidence.'

She looked up at him. 'Then do your job,' she said. 'Find your evidence. Prove that I didn't kill Ferdinand.'

⋆ ⋆ ⋆

Downstairs Vera was waiting for him. 'Charlie's coming over to pick up the pills,' she said. 'He's bringing some stuff he's dug up about Ferdinand and Lenny Thomas.'

Ashworth nodded. He knew it was ridiculous, but Nina's words had given him a new energy, a new determination. 'We've got time to fit in an interview with Rickard, then. And Charlie won't mind waiting if he can get his hands on coffee and a home-made biscuit.'

Vera looked at him. 'Did your lass put something in your tea this morning?'

'What do you mean?'

144

'You seem like a new man.' She paused. 'Do you want to lead on the interview with Rickard? I mean, I know there might be some history with Joanna, so maybe you're better doing it.'

But Ashworth shook his head. Rickard was a writer, intimidating, and anyway at the moment he wasn't sure he'd be able to concentrate. 'Nah, you do it. I'll sit in.' And from the beginning of the interview he could tell he'd made a wise decision. Vera was at her sharpest, her most outrageous and clever.

From the moment Rickard came into the chapel, leaning on a stick and struggling to push open the heavy door, Ashworth couldn't get past the fact that this was an old man. Old men weren't murderers. It wasn't just that it seemed physically impossible: Rickard couldn't have stabbed Ferdinand, and certainly couldn't have lifted him from the wicker chair in the glass room and out onto the balcony. It was more than that. In Ashworth's mind, old people weren't wicked. Vera seemed not to share this inhibition, and Ashworth wondered if that had something to do with her relationship with her father. *Horrible Hector*, she called him, or *my beastly father*, though she'd spent most of her life looking after him.

Now Vera was leaning forward across the desk towards Rickard.

'What I don't understand,' she said, 'is why you're here at all. You're a famous writer. Even I've heard of you. Seen your books in WH Smith at Central Station in town. So why give up your precious time to spend a week on the Northumberland coast?' She smiled and stretched back in

145

her chair, waiting for the old man to speak.

Rickard hadn't expected the question. Ashworth thought he'd anticipated a gentle and routine interview, that he'd be treated with deference because of his age and his celebrity.

'Perhaps, Inspector, I feel the need to give something back to the writing community. Success is such a matter of luck, and mine certainly has little to do with the quality of my work.' He gave a little smile, apparently pleased with his answer.

'Don't give me that crap.' Her voice was icy. 'Did you know Joanna Tobin would be here, before you agreed to be a tutor?'

There was another silence. Through the window Ashworth saw that the sun had come out. From here, the blue sky gave the initial appearance of a summer's day, but even with this restricted view he saw that the light was different. Colder. And the shadows would be longer. There must be a coffee break; students had spilled out into the courtyard. He couldn't see them from where he was sitting, but Rickard had left the chapel door open and he could hear the voices outside and smell the cigarette smoke.

'Miranda showed me the work of the students who had received bursaries,' Rickard said. 'An attempt to persuade me to sign up. She should have realized that authors hate seeing good writing by newcomers. It only proves to them how pitiful their own attempts are.'

'You recognized Joanna's name?' Vera had narrowed her eyes.

'Not immediately. She's using her maiden

name again. I only knew her when she was married.' He paused. 'I recognized some of the details of her story.'

'Rather gothic, I thought,' Vera said. Ashworth was astounded. You'd have believed she dealt with books for a living. And how could she talk with such authority about a story she'd never read?

'You've read it?' Rickard too seemed astonished.

'Don't you think police officers can read, Mr Rickard? Just because I don't go much for your kind of fiction, it doesn't mean I don't like a good story, especially when it has some basis in truth.'

They stared at each other across the table.

Vera spoke first. 'I take it Joanna's story *did* contain some element of truth? You'd know. After all, you were close to the parties concerned.'

'I'm a friend of her ex-husband's,' Rickard admitted at last. 'At least I was close to his family.'

'I've heard Joanna's version of events,' Vera said. She seemed suddenly more cheerful. 'Why don't you give me yours?'

'I knew Paul's father very well,' Rickard said. 'We met at university. Oxford. Both reading English. We came from different backgrounds. Roy was a grammar-school boy and he had an eye for business even then. He spent the summer vacation working in his father's print company. My family were landowners. Very little ready cash, but a big pile in the country. You know.'

147

Ashworth didn't know at all, but Vera nodded as if she understood exactly.

Rickard continued, 'What we had in common was a love of the English language. Roy's passion was Dickens. I focused on the dramatists of the sixteenth and seventeenth centuries. Shakespeare and his successors. Though, in personal reading, my taste was less grand.' He smiled at Vera. 'I always took pleasure in the gothic, and in detective fiction too. Sherlock Holmes, of course, then I moved on to the Golden Age stories of the Thirties.'

Ashworth was wondering what all this had to do with a murder investigation in Northumberland in the present, but Vera just nodded again as if she had all the time in the world.

'When we graduated,' Rickard said, 'I retreated to the family home to write. There was just enough money that I never had to work for a living. Roy set up a publishing house. Rutherford Press. You might have heard of it. He became one of the most-established independent publishers in the country. In time Paul, his son, joined him. Paul was an ambitious man. He understood business, but he never understood books.' Rickard paused and rubbed his left shoulder as if it was giving him pain. 'One of the big multinationals put in a bid for Rutherford. Roy was against it, but Paul persuaded him. I found out later that Paul had been promised a lucrative post with the company, if the deal went ahead.'

'So that was how he went to Paris,' Vera said. 'Taking his young bride with him.'

'Yes, he was to head up the European operation. A poisoned chalice. I think they wanted him to fail. They'd fulfilled their commitment by giving him a leading role in the company, but they didn't really want him.' Rickard took a sip of water from the glass that had been put for him on the table. 'I was living in Paris too then. I had the idea that I might write the great contemporary gothic novel, and really I couldn't continue living in the country with my mother and her incontinent dogs. My income just about stretched to a flat in a not-very-fashionable district.' He paused again. 'Roy, Paul's father, died. A heart attack. Or a broken heart.'

'He felt that his son had betrayed him?' Vera asked. Her voice was gentle now.

Rickard seemed surprised. 'No, nothing like that. He was proud that Paul was so driven. But he missed the business, the meetings with authors and the excitement of new scripts arriving every day. I suggested that he should set up on his own again, but he said he didn't have the energy. Perhaps he was already ill.' He stared through the window, lost in thoughts of his own.

'So you're in Paris,' Vera said briskly. 'You and Paul and Joanna. Did you see a lot of them?'

'Yes, we met up at least once a week. Paul's idea, not mine. I'd go to their grand apartment for dinner. A way to get the quality of wine I couldn't afford on my meagre income. And I suppose I felt a responsibility for Paul after his father died. I never married, never had children. Roy had made me Paul's godfather. From the

149

beginning it was clear Paul's position in Paris was untenable. His French was appalling, and he had no knowledge of how things worked in Europe. The attitude to books and writers is still very different there. He was under considerable stress.'

'Did you know he was beating up his wife?' Vera's tone was conversational.

Watching the old man's face, Ashworth saw that his first impulse was to lie. Then Rickard thought better of it.

'I guessed,' he said.

'That he kept her virtually a prisoner?'

'If that was the case, it was a very comfortable prison. The height of luxury.' Then Rickard saw that the flippancy wouldn't do. 'Paul was ill,' he said. 'Completely irrational. He had a sort of breakdown.'

'And Joanna was so depressed that she attacked her husband with a knife and then attempted suicide! And, thanks to Paul's family and friends, she was locked up in a French psychiatric hospital. If I'm not mistaken, you were one of those friends.'

'If it wasn't for me, she'd have found herself in a French jail!' The retort was sharp, and Ashworth saw that Rickard regretted the outburst as soon as it was made.

'And you expect Joanna to be grateful to you, do you?'

'Of course not,' Rickard said. 'But that was a long time ago and she seems to have rebuilt her life.'

They looked at each other.

'What about Paul?' Vera asked, in a way that made Ashworth see that she already knew the answer. 'Mr Paul Rutherford. What's he up to now?'

'He moved on from publishing,' Rickard said. 'Remarried, had a family.'

'And what line of business is he in today?'

Rickard looked her straight in the face. 'He's an MEP.'

'So he is.' Vera gave a little smile. 'And doing very well, I understand. It seems he developed an understanding of Europe after all. He's still ambitious, though. Intending to stand for Westminster next time, so the rumours have it.' She leaned over the desk towards Rickard. 'I looked him up, you see, when I knew we'd be having this conversation. Now, you shouldn't trust the Internet, but I'd say the articles I saw were right about Mr Rutherford.' She straightened up and her voice hardened. 'So that's what you're doing here, is it, Mr Rickard? Still protecting your godson's interests? The last thing a prospective MP needs is a charge of domestic violence against him.'

'No!' Rickard attempted to stand up to make his point. 'Since we spent that time together in Paris I've felt guilty about Joanna. I wanted to meet her, to check that things were going well for her. It was an impulse when I saw her name on the list of bursary students. An old man's folly.'

Vera looked at him and said nothing. The silence stretched. The students had gone back to work and there was no sound from the garden. At last she spoke.

'Things *were* going very well for Joanna. She'd met a man who adored her and they'd set up home in the most beautiful place in England. She'd found a way to make sense of the nightmare of her younger days, and there was a chance that the story of the abuse she'd suffered might be published. Then she was implicated in a murder. Some might consider that could be a way of getting your pal Paul off the hook. Who's going to believe a murder suspect when she accuses a respectable MP of domestic violence? And of course she wouldn't dare, would she? Not in her position now. Last thing she'd want would be to attract the attention of the press.'

'That's ridiculous,' Rickard said.

'Aye, isn't it? Just like something out of those gothic novels you were so fond of in your youth. All madness, conspiracy and drama.'

Rickard struggled to his feet. He was on his way to the door when Vera called him back. 'How well did you know Tony Ferdinand?'

He turned slowly to face her. 'I didn't. I met him a couple of times. Nothing more.'

'But he reviewed you, I understand.'

Rickard gave a little laugh. 'The piece in the *TLS*? Unkind, perhaps but very amusing. It did me no harm.'

'I read it,' Vera said. 'Rather personal, I thought. And it's hard to believe that you were no more than acquaintances. Publishing seems a very small world.'

'A world, Inspector, of which I wanted no part. Literary success came late to me and I never believed I deserved it.'

152

16

When they'd finished with Giles Rickard, Charlie was waiting for them in the main house. As Ashworth had predicted, he'd blagged coffee and a slice of home-made cake from Alex Barton and was sitting in the lobby, the front of his jacket covered in crumbs, reading a copy of the *Sun*.

'That Alex seems a nice enough lad,' Charlie said, nodding in the direction of the kitchen.

'Eh, Charlie, man, you'd like anyone who fed you.' Sometimes Vera despaired of Charlie. It wasn't that he was stupid. Not really. Just unobservant, with the judgement of a gnat.

* * *

Now they were back in the chapel. They'd shut the door against the cold and Vera thought if she didn't get some fresh air soon, she'd throw a fit. In the house there had been cooking smells coming from the kitchen and she tried to remember if there was a decent pub along this part of the coast, somewhere they could get a bar meal for lunch and maybe a pint. Though perhaps it would be simpler just to stay here. Alex Barton was a skilful chef. Her mind began to wander. She thought it was an odd existence for a young man like Barton: to be locked up in this house with a load of middle-aged arty types,

153

the only real company a mother who seemed to pine for a more glamorous past.

She thought suddenly that Alex was a bit like Giles Rickard, who had also spent much of his adult life with his mother. Until he came to his senses: *Really I couldn't continue living in the country with my mother and her incontinent dogs.*

And like me. I spent my whole life in my parent's shadow. Hector would have liked a son to create in his own image. Someone with a passion for guns and birds of prey and breaking the law. Instead, he got a daughter with a mind of her own.

Then she realized that Charlie and Joe were staring at her and she snapped her attention back to the present.

'So what have you got for us then, Charlie? What have you and the lovely Holly conjured up between you?'

'I don't know what Holly's been up to,' Charlie said. 'I think she was hoping to track down Lenny Thomas's ex, see if there was any history of domestic violence. I've been on the phone to an old mate of mine who's a DS in the service in Cumbria. He remembered Mark Winterton.'

'Did he now? And what did he come up with?'

'Not a lot,' Charlie said. 'My mate described him as one of the quiet ones. Regular church-goer. You know the sort. A good enough boss and a stickler for procedure. Management loved him. He was a bit tight with his money apparently. Never first in the queue when it came to getting in a round. And you had to get him in a corner and rattle him, to get him to shell out for the tea fund.'

'So respected, but not popular.' Vera thought it wasn't a bad thing to have an officer like that in the team. Someone who wasn't going to play to the gallery.

'Aye, though there was a lot of sympathy when his daughter died.'

'What happened?' Vera looked up sharply.

'She got mixed up with the wrong crowd at uni apparently, ended up taking a heroin overdose. The coroner couldn't decide if it was suicide or an accident.'

'But what was the word on the street?'

'Uh?'

'What did your DS think had happened? Winterton's colleagues must have had an opinion.' She thought it would have been the talk of the station for weeks. There'd be sympathy, of course, but also malicious gossip maybe. A secret satisfaction that a God-botherer who'd given them stick over their expenses had a daughter who'd gone off the rails.

'I don't know,' Charlie seemed confused. 'My mate didn't say.'

'Well, ask him! If he's based in Carlisle, it's not that far away. An hour down the A69. Go and see him and buy him a pint.'

'Aye, okay.' Charlie brightened.

'Where was the lass at university?' Vera asked suddenly.

'I don't know!' Now he was feeling got at. 'Does it matter?'

'It might explain what Winterton's doing here,' she said. 'I mean if she was at Newcastle or Northumbria when she died. The place might provide an emotional pull for him.' *Or she might have been at St Ursula's. That would make an interesting connection between the victim and the retired cop.* She looked up at two sceptical faces. 'Otherwise, what the hell is he doing in this place? He's not much of a writer, so he didn't get a bursary. But Charlie said he's tight with his money. It doesn't hang together.'

'Perhaps he thought writing about his daughter's death — putting it into a story — might help.' Ashworth spoke for the first time. He'd had a vacant look all morning and Vera hadn't even been sure he'd been listening. She wondered if his wife had been giving him grief again. 'I don't know, a way of coming to terms with the loss.'

'Do we know what he wrote about?' Vera was remembering Joanna's work. *All these words,* she thought. *All I seem to be doing on this case is sit around talking. About words written by the suspects.* Again she felt the need for fresh air and a longing to escape this house. She envied Charlie his excuse for a drive to Cumbria. But she was the boss after all. She could create her own excuse.

Ashworth shook his head and Charlie looked blank.

'What now then?' Ashworth asked.

'Charlie's going to take Nina Backworth's pills back to HQ and get them off to the lab. You and me are going out for lunch. Then if Holly has

156

found out where Lenny Thomas's ex-wife's living, we'll pay her a visit.'

'What about this place?' Ashworth asked.

Vera thought this place could be left to its own devices for a few hours, and really she didn't care as long as she had a break from it. Then she had an idea. 'Let's get Holly over and ask her to have a chat with Mark Winterton. Two cops in the same mould, I'd say. She might get more out of him than I could. And we've kept her in the office for too long.'

'What about going to Carlisle to chat to my mate?' She could tell Charlie was pissed off because he hadn't been invited to lunch.

'That, Charlie, you do in your own time.'

★ ★ ★

They had lunch in the pub in Craster, sitting upstairs so there was a view over a quiet sea. Crab sandwiches and smoked salmon from the smokery over the road. The day was still cold and clear and Vera felt like a truant. She'd got Joe Ashworth to drive and had spoken to Holly on the way. Lenny's ex-wife worked in a nursery in Cramlington and she'd be expecting them at three.

'I felt I couldn't breathe in the Writers' House,' she said. She'd gone for a glass of dry white with the sandwiches. Beer at lunchtime sometimes made her sleepy. 'And I couldn't think straight. This is more like it.'

'So you've cracked it then, have you?' There were times when Joe could be facetious. 'You know who killed the letchy old goat, and why?'

'Eh, pet, I haven't got a clue. But at least now I feel I've got a *chance* of working it all out.'

★ ★ ★

The nursery was part of a Sure Start centre, and at first they went the wrong way and ended up with a group of pregnant women who were lying on the floor, doing breathing exercises. They reminded Vera of seals, hauled onto a beach, all round and sleek, gleaming in the sunshine. Vera had had a broody phase in her late thirties. There'd been a man then — the only man she could have contemplated living with — but he hadn't thought the same way about her and nothing had come of it. Now she wasn't sure she'd ever have felt the need to go through all this palaver.

Helen Thomas was in the baby room. A couple of the children were so tiny that they were lying in cots, the rest were sitting with the carers on a brightly coloured rug, surrounded by plastic toys. Ashworth, always a sucker for bairns, squatted down to make silly noises at them.

'Don't get any ideas, Joe,' Vera said, only partly joking. 'Three is enough for anyone, and they get in the way of your work.'

Lenny's ex-wife called over to a colleague, 'Take over here, will you, Gill. I'll be in my office if you need me.' Vera had been expecting their interviewee would be a nursery assistant, someone who changed nappies and wiped up sick, not this confident woman who seemed to be in charge.

The office was small, but impressively tidy. Helen Thomas nodded for them to take the two chairs and perched on the edge of the desk. On the walls there were charts and rotas, and posters about healthy eating and the importance of play.

'How can I help you? The officer who phoned didn't say.'

'It's about Lenny Thomas. You were married to him?' Vera found it hard to imagine this neat little woman in the same bed as the man she'd met at the Writers' House.

'Yes.' There was a pause. 'Is he in some sort of trouble?'

'Probably not. You must have seen in the press that there was a murder at the Writers' House up the coast. Lenny was one of the witnesses.'

'Not a suspect then?'

'Only in the same way as all the other residents are.'

'Oh, come off it, Inspector! How many of the other residents have a criminal record and speak like Lenny does? I bet you're not speaking to everyone else's partner.'

Vera was about to snap back, but then she thought of the summary she'd heard of Lenny's background at the morning briefings. 'Sometimes the police make assumptions,' she said. 'It doesn't always mean that they're right. So why don't you put us straight?'

Helen didn't reply immediately. It seemed she needed time to think about her answer. 'Would you like tea? Coffee?'

They shook their heads.

'Lenny is a good man,' Helen said. 'A

159

romantic and a dreamer, but basically a good man.'

'Is that why you divorced? Because you couldn't live with his dreams?'

'That was why I had an affair, Inspector.' The retort was immediate. 'I needed a man who lived in the present and not in the future. When he was made redundant from Banks, Lenny was full of wild plans and I was just concerned about paying the mortgage. My lover was stable, reliable, but very boring, and I soon got rid of him. The divorce was Lenny's idea. He'd thought I was perfect, and he couldn't forgive me for spoiling the image.' She paused. 'We're still good friends. We have a son, Daniel, and we see each other often. Sometimes I wonder . . .'

' . . . if you'll get back together?' Vera completed the sentence.

'Yeah!' She smiled. 'Daft, isn't it?'

'How long were you married?' Joe asked. Vera thought he was genuinely interested and wondered if he'd been having dreams of his own.

'More than fifteen years. I'd known Lenny when we were still at school, though. He was the class clown, desperate to please. I went away to college and he got into trouble. Nothing serious. One of the Blyth hard men was pulling his strings, made him believe he could make easy money. More daft dreams. I met Lenny again when he'd just come out of prison, at a wedding of an old school friend. He made me laugh.'

'And he adored you,' Vera said. She thought of Jack, who adored Joanna, and wondered again if somewhere there was a lover in the background in that relationship too. Someone secret and unlikely.

'Aye, maybe he did.' Helen gave a little laugh.

'It's hard to live up to, that sort of adoration.'

'It was very good for me.' Helen became serious. Somewhere down the corridor a baby was crying. She listened for a moment and seemed to decide that there was nothing wrong. 'I'd been a terribly shy child. Bright enough, but not willing to stand out or give an opinion. Lenny gave me the confidence to take more exams and try for promotion. He always believed in me, but somehow I could never quite believe in him.'

'In his dreams?' Vera prompted.

'Aye, in the dreams.'

'How long had he wanted to be a writer?' The baby had stopped crying. Just outside the office there was a conversation between two mothers.

'Since we got together,' Helen said. 'He'd got some education in prison and the teacher had encouraged him. Sometimes he'd read out his stuff and I thought it was good too, but what would I know? I did know that we had a child, and I wanted more for Daniel than Lenny or I had had growing up, and Lenny didn't seem to mind working on the open-cast. He made friends there and the money was more than he'd ever had before. He seemed happy enough.'

'Then he got the back trouble?'

'Aye, folk make fun of back pain, as if it's something you make up to fool the doctors, but Lenny was in agony.' Again Helen was distracted for a moment by a noise outside. This time it

161

came from a group of older children singing nursery rhymes. 'At first I encouraged his writing. I thought it would take his mind off the pain. Then his back got better, and I thought he was ready to find another real job. It wasn't so much the money. By then I was earning enough to keep us. I didn't want Daniel seeing a dad who sat around the house doing nothing all day. But all Lenny could talk about were the stories, how he was going to get a publisher and what he'd buy for us when he was rich and famous.'

'The man who died at the Writers' House,' Vera said. 'He was a bit of a celebrity. On the telly all the time talking about books. Apparently he'd told Lenny that his work was good enough to get published. He'd offered to put him in touch with a publisher. Told him he had a good chance of seeing his books on the shelves.'

Helen looked up, horrified. 'And then he died, and all that hope was all taken away. Oh, poor Len.'

'The man, Tony Ferdinand, has rather a reputation.' Vera chose her words carefully. 'It seems he could be ruthless in his dealings with his students. Is it possible that Lenny might lose his temper with the man, if he felt he was being criticized or mocked?'

'No,' Helen said. 'Lenny's never lost his temper all the time I've known him. Even when I told him about the affair he was sad, not angry. He's just a big softie.'

They sat for a moment in silence. Vera hoped Helen might continue, but she sat on the desk, her feet swinging like a child's, challenging them not to believe her.

'Did Lenny phone you from the Writers' House,' Vera asked at last, 'to tell you about the murder? If you're still close . . . '

'Yes, he phoned,' Helen said. 'He thought we might hear about the death and he wanted to let me know he was okay.'

'So it's not unexpected, us turning up like this. You'd have had time to prepare your story.'

'I didn't need to prepare a story, Inspector.' The original hostility had returned. 'I'm telling you the truth.'

Vera saw they'd get nothing more out of the woman and she got to her feet. Ashworth followed her lead. At the door Vera paused and turned back.

'How did Lenny find out you were having an affair?'

'He didn't find out. Once it was over, I told him. I hated having a secret from him.'

'I hope that made you feel better.' Vera spoke so softly that the woman probably couldn't even hear her. Joe had heard, however, and she saw that she'd shocked him again. Still she continued, 'It certainly wouldn't have done a lot for Lenny.'

17

At lunch Nina found herself sitting next to Lenny Thomas. She'd almost decided to stay away, to hide in her room while the meal was taking place. After the interview with Vera Stanhope, since Joe Ashworth had come into her room and stood, stony and pale, looking out of her window, she'd had the terrible thought that everyone in the Writers' House would think she was a murderer. Certainly it had seemed to her that the young detective thought of her in that way. They'd know about her pills, the drugged victim. They'd string those facts together to make a convincing narrative. And who could blame them? She'd reach the same conclusion, presented with the same facts.

But it seemed that the police had been discreet, as of course she should have realized they would be. The residents had forgotten that she'd been summoned away from breakfast to talk to Vera Stanhope. This would be the last full day of the course. Tonight there would be a special dinner and everyone would read a short piece of work. A celebration of their time in the house. And that was the main topic of conversation over lunch. Nobody considered that this feast might be inappropriate. If Tony Ferdinand had been well liked, the consensus might have been different. He'd been a major literary figure with the potential for changing

164

careers, and would certainly be missed on those grounds, but the students had seen through his arrogance and his superficial charm. The other tutors had considerable influence too, and the students were reluctant to lose the opportunity of bringing their work to these people's notice. Now the conversation around the table was cheerful, almost excited. It seemed that even Joanna had been accepted back into the fold. She was chatting to Mark Winterton. Nina heard her laugh, musical and infectious, across the table.

'I can't believe that tomorrow everything goes back to normal,' Lenny said.

'What do you mean?' It seemed to Nina that nothing would ever be normal again.

'Well, this has been fantastic for me. Like, suddenly, for the first time in my life, I'm with people who think the same way I do. I mean, Helen, my wife, she was great when we were living together, but she didn't really get the writing thing. She's more practical.'

Nina saw that Lenny had loved every minute here. The whole deal: the fancy rooms, and being cooked for, and being taken seriously as a writer. She could see that it would be hard for him to go back to the flat in the ex-pit village. He'd feel like Alice emerging from the magic of Wonderland and having to go back to a boring schoolroom. 'But you'll carry on writing,' she said.

'Yeah,' he said. 'I can't imagine ever stopping that. But the being published thing. That was never going to happen, was it? Tony Ferdinand was a bullshitter. Even if he hadn't died, men

165

like me don't get their names on books.'

'That's not true, you know.' But Nina could tell that her words were unconvincing. 'What will you read at the party tonight?'

'I thought the first page of the novel. I'm pleased with that. It's part of what I put in to get the grant. What about you?'

'Oh!' She was surprised. 'I don't know. I hadn't thought that I would.'

'This isn't just a student gig, you know,' he said. 'I asked Miranda. Tonight everyone reads a bit. Even her. You'll have to give us something.'

'I've been working on a short story,' Nina said. 'I'll read a piece from that, perhaps.'

★ ★ ★

Later Nina went onto the beach. Rickard was giving a masterclass and, though she'd considered going in and sitting at the back, in the end she thought she needed exercise and a break from the house. If everyone was planning to read at the farewell party, it would be a long night. She walked round the side of the house to get to the terrace and the path to the coast. Passing the drawing room where Rickard had already begun to talk, she saw Joanna sitting right at the front of the room, her face rapt, giving her full attention.

The sun was low and it was cold. Tonight there would be a frost; the sky was still clear. Nina walked along the tide line, stooping occasionally to pick up a piece of sculpted driftwood or a pretty shell. There was no wind, and the water slid onto the shingle beach, the waves hardly breaking. A small party of gulls floated just out to sea. Tomorrow she'd be back in her flat in Newcastle. She thought she'd invite friends to dinner later in the week. Usually she despised university politics, but she thought she needed to hear gossip, to drink a little too much. She'd tell them about the murder. They'd have read about it. She'd have fun describing Vera Stanhope to them. The fact that her sleeping pills had been used to drug the famous victim would just make a better story.

She looked at her watch. Rickard's session would last for another half-hour, but she was starting to feel chilled and she decided to go to her room and choose which piece of her work she'd read. She began to climb the path into the garden and was shocked by a figure blocking her way. The garden was in shadow and at first all she could see was a silhouette, squat and bulky, partly hidden by overgrown shrubs.

'Ah, Nina, I've been waiting for you. I saw you on the beach from my room in the cottage. I wanted your advice.' It was Miranda. At the same time as Nina recognized the voice, the figure became clearer. Miranda was wearing a cord skirt that reached almost to her ankles, a thick jacket and a scarf. Boots.

'How can I help you?' Nina assumed this would be something about course content, about how to attract more students. She was a professional after all, with useful contacts in the university. She found her dislike of the woman was almost like a taste or a smell, so unpleasant

167

that she felt compelled to keep her distance. She stood on the sandy path a couple of yards away from Miranda and tried to analyse the antipathy.

'It's about the murder,' Miranda said. Then she broke off. 'Why don't you come into the cottage? I'll make us tea. We can talk there, where it'll be warm.' Miranda lived with her son in a cottage in what must once have been part of the farm's outbuildings. Students and tutors were never invited inside. Miranda made a big issue of her privacy: *Living on the job, I can only survive if I have my own space.* Nina supposed she should feel honoured to be asked in, but still something about the woman made her reluctant to agree.

'I was hoping to do some work on my story before supper.'

'Please come.' Miranda was almost pleading, and Nina remembered her howling when Ferdinand's body was found. She shouldn't be so hard on the woman; her dislike was irrational and unkind.

'All right,' Nina said. 'Why not?'

The door from the old farmyard led straight into the kitchen and the heat seemed suffocating after the late-afternoon chill. There was a cream Aga, with a pile of underclothes airing on the covered plate. Nina found the sight of Alex's pants and his mother's bras faintly embarrassing and turned away, but Miranda just lifted the clothes onto the wide windowsill, raised the cover and put the kettle on the hotplate. The edge of the beach closest to the water was visible from the window. The thin white strip of shingle showed as a shallow crescent in the last of the light. From upstairs the view would be clearer. The idea that she'd been watched from Miranda's lair made Nina uncomfortable and she hoped the conversation would soon be over. But now that she'd secured Nina's presence, Miranda seemed in no hurry to explain why she'd asked to speak to her.

'Ordinary tea or herbal?'

'Neither thanks, I really do want to look at my story before this evening.' Nina felt trapped. Why didn't the woman just come out with what she wanted? Had she heard that Ferdinand had been drugged? Was it just a prurient curiosity that had got her outside on a cold October afternoon?

'What's the significance of Joanna's reappearance?' Miranda had turned from the Aga to ask the question. The cold had made her eyes water and her mascara had smudged. Or perhaps, Nina thought, she'd been crying again. Still, she found it hard to feel sympathy for the woman. Miranda was frowning. It seemed that Joanna's return to the house had bothered her.

'I'm not sure I understand what you mean.'

'Well, the fact that's she's free to come and go at will, does that mean the police don't believe she killed Ferdinand after all?'

'I have no idea!' Nina tried to give a little laugh. 'Inspector Stanhope doesn't confide in me any more than she does in you.'

'She's a strange woman, Vera Stanhope. Don't you think so?' Again the question was asked with an odd intensity. The kettle whistled and

Miranda moved it off the plate, but didn't bother to make herself tea.

'I think she's more intelligent than she'd like us to think,' Nina said carefully. 'If she believes Joanna's innocent, then she's probably right.'

There was a moment of silence. A large tabby cat appeared through an open door at the far side of the kitchen and wound itself round Miranda's legs. 'This is Ophelia,' the woman said. 'With my name, I have an affection for Shakespearean heroines.' She looked at Nina as if expecting a response, but Nina didn't know what to say. Miranda scooped up the animal and held it under one arm. With the other she opened the fridge door, took out an already-open can of cat food and spooned it into a bowl on the floor. The smell made Nina feel like retching.

Miranda set down the cat and straightened up. 'So the killer might still be here!' she said. 'Do you see?'

So this, Nina thought, was what had unsettled Miranda. This was why she had lurked in the garden waiting for Nina to approach. Had it really just occurred to her? Had she been so certain Joanna had committed the murder? *But we were all certain.*

'I suppose that was always a possibility,' Nina said. She was sitting in a rocking chair, which had been covered in a patchwork shawl. The cushions were soft and she felt overcome now by lethargy. She'd lost her initial impetus to get out of the cottage as soon as possible. She looked up and saw that Miranda seemed lost in thought.

'Do you think you know who the killer might be?'

'I *thought* it was Joanna.' The woman's voice was almost petulant. It was as if Joanna had let her down.

'But if it's not?' This time Nina's words were sharper. She still felt tired and thought if she were to go to her room now, there was a chance that she might sleep for an hour before dinner.

'I'm not sure.' Miranda was leaning with her back to the Aga. The cat had stopped eating. It had climbed onto the windowsill, settled on the pile of clothes, and was snoring. She looked sharply at Nina. 'You have no idea? I wondered if it might relate back to his old St Ursula days.'

'How could it?'

Miranda shrugged. 'I thought the police might have told you something. I've noticed the way that young sergeant looks at you. He's obviously smitten.'

'Nonsense!'

'I had to walk round the house this morning and I saw the three of you in the chapel. Believe me, he couldn't take his eyes off you.'

Nina again had the feeling that Miranda had been spying on them all. She knew the building so well that she could move around it almost unnoticed. If the group at the Writers' House had the atmosphere of a country-house party, the director's social status was ambiguous. She might be a partner in the company, but on these occasions she was not quite gentry and not quite below-stairs staff. Like a Victorian lady's companion, Nina thought. Or a governess. And that made her strangely invisible.

'That's ridiculous,' Nina said. 'Sergeant Ashworth is a professional and I'm a suspect. As I suppose we all are.' She summoned the energy to lift herself out of her chair. 'And in any event the police have given me no more information about the identity of the killer than they've given the rest of you.'

The women stood for a moment, looking at each other. 'This is a difficult time,' Miranda said. 'It's the police's role to pry, and we all have secrets. We've all done things of which we're ashamed.'

It was such an odd thing to say that for a moment Nina couldn't move. Then without a word she opened the door and went out into the cold. Crossing the yard, she wondered what Miranda could have meant. Were her words a confession? Had she hoped Nina would make a sympathetic response, so that she could unburden herself further? Or were they a threat?

18

Walking into the house from the yard, Nina almost bumped into a strange woman. She recognized her at once as a possible ally in the Writers' House, at least as different from Miranda as it was possible to be. The newcomer could have belonged to Nina's gym; she was smart, confident, and gave the impression that she'd be at home in the city. The woman looked at Nina, took in the style of the clothes and the quality of the haircut, and seemed to have the same response. The same recognition of a kindred spirit. She smiled.

'I'm sorry,' Nina said. 'It's freezing outside and I just wanted to get indoors. I should have looked where I was going.'

'No problem.' The woman held out her hand. 'DC Holly Clarke.'

'Ah,' Nina said. 'Part of Inspector Stanhope's team.'

'And you must be Nina Backworth.'

'Oh dear.' Nina pulled a face. 'It's a bit worrying that you recognized me so easily. How did they describe me? Uppity academic. Wears black. Red lipstick.'

'I'm not sure,' Holly said, 'that the inspector notices lipstick.'

They both grinned.

'Can I help you?' Nina was suddenly anxious. Had they sent this pleasant young woman to arrest her? Had the results from the lab on her sleeping pills come back already?

Holly shook her head. 'I've been taking more witness statements. Routine. You know how it is. The youngest member of the team . . . '

' . . . and a woman! I know, it's just the same in the university. Everyone thinks things have changed, but sexism lives on.' Here, Nina was on safe and familiar territory. 'You've got a female boss, though. I'd have hoped that might make things a bit different.'

'It doesn't always work like that, does it?' Holly said. 'A woman climbs to the top, then hauls the ladder up behind her. She doesn't want the competition.' She paused and gave a sly, conspiratorial smile. 'Not that I'm saying Inspector Stanhope would operate in that way.'

'Of course not!' Nina said in mock horror. They stood for a moment in comfortable silence, then she added, 'Are you finished for the day? On your way home?'

'I'm not sure. I've done all the interviews, but I wondered if I might stay here for a while. Stanhope's a great one for picking up the atmosphere. She says that listening is the best skill a detective can have.'

'So you hope to earn a few brownie points?'

'Yes,' Holly said. 'Something like that.'

'Why don't you stop for dinner?' Nina thought the evening ahead would be less daunting with a sympathetic companion. She imagined the amusing whispered comments they might pass between them after the less-inspired readings. And it would be reassuring to have a friend on

174

the inquiry team. Someone who might put Nina's case to Inspector Stanhope. 'There's probably even a spare room here, if you can't face a long drive at the end of it. We can ask Alex. He'll be in the kitchen preparing the meal. He's in charge of most of the domestic arrangements.' Nina didn't want to go back to the cottage to ask Miranda. 'Unless there's something you need to get back for?'

'Nothing and nobody.' Holly grinned. 'And that way, at least I'll be able to have a couple of glasses of wine!'

The last comment made Nina even more relaxed. Police officers didn't drink on duty, did they? This would be just as Holly had said: unofficial overtime to allow her to understand the place and the residents better. Nina could have nothing to fear from her. She knocked on the kitchen door and spoke to Alex about Holly spending the night. He nodded as if there was no problem, even giving the impression that the whole thing had already been arranged as he handed over a key to an empty room. Nina could see that he was preoccupied with his cooking and that he wasn't really listening.

'Sorry about that,' Nina said. 'He's a perfectionist. But the food here is *very* good.' It was as if she were recommending a fancy new restaurant in Jesmond.

★   ★   ★

They all gathered in the lounge for pre-dinner drinks. Even Lenny had made an effort and was dressed in a dark suit. Nina thought it had probably last been worn at a funeral. The trousers were painfully tight at the waist and his belly hung over his belt. The room too was dressed for the occasion. There were flowers, huge dahlias and chrysanthemums — the colours, Nina thought, of fire. Candles on the window ledges and the mantelpiece. Nobody mentioned Tony Ferdinand at all. It was as if he'd never been here, never given his ego-laden lectures, never sat in one-to-one tutorials making promises he was unlikely to keep, or assessing the possibility that he might persuade a student into his bed. Tonight the residents pretended that they were at a fashionable book launch; for most, after all, this was the nearest they'd get to the real thing. Nina, who had attended a couple in her time — her own and her friends' — thought they'd be disappointed by the reality. Here, the wine was a great deal better.

She'd prepared carefully for the evening. There'd been a bath, her favourite oil, a cup of camomile tea within easy reach. Then make-up. Perfume. Long silver earrings. A red dress. Her students would be shocked to see her in colour. She was known for wearing black. A moment to read through the paragraphs she'd chosen for the presentation. Then shoes and a small evening bag. Halfway down the stairs she'd gone back to check that her room was locked. She was still troubled by the recurring image of an intruder. When she'd arrived in the drawing room most of the students had been there already, though she'd been the first of the tutors. She'd walked

176

into the room to a little round of applause.

Holly was there, still in the clothes she'd been wearing in the afternoon of course, but they were smart enough for her not to look out of place. She'd added more make-up and was holding a glass of wine. She was talking to Joanna, who tonight *was* wearing black. Another statement perhaps. Soon after, Giles Rickard came in. He sported a little bow tie, this time in blue velvet. His movement seemed a bit easier than it had; perhaps he too was relieved at the prospect of leaving the place, of returning to the real world.

But I'm not sure that I am pleased to be leaving, Nina thought. And though she'd considered the place as a prison all week, now she had a moment's anxiety about going. In some circumstances prison might be comforting. A place of safety.

Miranda was handing out drinks and canapés. She had on a long black skirt and white silk blouse — clothes that, Nina thought, reflected her ambiguous position in the house. The colours of a waitress's uniform, but in a rather grander style. As Nina took a glass of white wine, Miranda gave a tight smile. 'I'm so glad we had that little talk this afternoon.'

She moved on before Nina could answer, and the academic was pleased not to be expected to make a reply. What would she have said? In her memory the exchange had been acrimonious and disturbing.

★ ★ ★

177

Dinner was more elaborate than on the previous evenings. There were bottles of wine on the table. Alex had changed from his chef's whites into a shirt and jacket, and after helping Miranda to serve the meal he sat beside her. Usually he ate alone in the kitchen. Again there were flowers and more candles, thick and cream, the sort you might see in a church. Nina sat next to Holly, but during dinner they spoke very little. The young detective's attention seemed to be on the conversation going on all around her. It seemed she'd taken to heart Vera Stanhope's advice about listening. But when the dishes were being cleared, Holly turned to Nina.

'Go on then! Give me the gossip. Who's sleeping with whom.'

Nina was shocked. 'Oh, I don't think anything of that sort is going on.'

'It's different from any residential course I've ever been on then,' Holly said easily. 'A hothouse atmosphere like this and away from the office, a couple too many glasses of Chardonnay and you can believe that you fancy almost anyone. The problem is sitting next to them at work the following week, and realizing what a prat you've made of yourself.' She nodded across towards Alex. 'He's fit enough. If I weren't a police officer, I could be tempted!'

Nina gave a little laugh, but found that she was shocked.

The main business of the evening started during coffee. It was clear that Miranda considered herself the star and the mistress of ceremonies. Any notion that she was there

178

simply to serve them was quickly dispelled. They were still in the dining room, and she took her natural place once again at the head of the table.

'This has been a disturbing and unusual week,' she said. 'And I'd like to thank the tutors and students for their concentration and their focus at such a difficult time. The quality of work produced has been outstanding and, instead of dwelling on the tragedy that occurred here, I think it right to celebrate this evening the fine writing that has been achieved.'

There was no further reference to Tony Ferdinand. Again Nina remembered the pain the woman had expressed when she learned of his death, and she wondered at Miranda's poise.

'Tonight we each have the opportunity to share a short piece from work created this week.' Miranda looked around the table. 'Do we have a volunteer to begin?'

A number of hands shot into the air. Diffidence, it seemed, was not a problem within the group. The students probably thought interest would wane as the evening progressed and more wine was drunk.

'Lenny,' Miranda said, 'would you like to start us off?'

Lenny got to his feet. He'd shaved since the afternoon and Nina had noticed that throughout the meal he'd only been drinking water. Despite sounding so defeatist at lunchtime, it seemed that he now intended to give this his best shot. As he picked up the sheet of paper from the table, Miranda saw that his hands were shaking.

'Before I do my reading,' he said, his accent so

179

broad that Nina wondered if the southerners in the audience would understand him, 'I'd just like to thank all the people who made this possible for me. The Bartons and the tutors, and the rest of the folk here who've given me so much support. It's been like a dream come true.'

Then he launched into his reading. Nina had expected a piece from the beginning of his novel, an action scene, following two teenage lads racing a stolen car round Blyth housing estate. That was what he'd told her he'd read, when they were discussing it at lunchtime. It was well written, fast, and developed the characters immediately. Instead, he'd chosen something else, something he'd written at her insistence after their first tutorial.

'This is great writing, Lenny,' she'd said. 'But the story's all told at the same pace. It's fast and furious from beginning to end. Occasionally the reader needs time to catch her breath and it's good to change the mood a bit too. Try to write something tender for me. A love scene or a conversation between a parent and child.'

Now he stood, the paper shaking in his hand, like a sail hauled in too close to the wind, and started speaking. His voice was slow and almost without expression, but the tone of the piece was so unexpected, so sad, that he had them hooked from the first words. *She stood at the window watching her man walk out of her life.*

He read for only a couple of minutes, then he stopped abruptly. Nina wasn't sure if he'd intended to end the piece there or if he'd become so moved, by his own writing and by the

180

occasion, that he was unable to continue. He sat down to applause and looked around him, confused, as if he'd just woken up.

'Wow!' Miranda got to her feet. 'Well done, Lenny. I don't envy the person who has to follow that.' She looked around the table and Nina thought she would ask for another volunteer. She was deciding she might raise her hand herself and get the ordeal over with, when Miranda focused her attention on the ex-policeman, Mark Winterton. 'Mark, would you like to try?'

He stood up. He seemed unflustered. Nina supposed he'd be used to giving evidence in court.

'I'm not going to read,' he said. His face was thin and the small, square spectacles he wore gave him the appearance of a rather pedantic teacher. His words too were clipped and precise. 'One of the great benefits of the course has been the development of an ability to assess one's own work. And I've realized that my work really isn't very good at all!' There was a sympathetic murmur from the other end of the table. 'I'm not going to put you lot through any of my stuff. But, like Lenny, I want to thank all the staff and students for their support. This was something I had to try. I gave it a go, and it didn't work out. Maybe I'll have to find another outlet for my creativity. But in the meantime I look forward to seeing some of your books on the shelves and to telling my friends: *I knew them before they were famous.*'

He smiled at them all and took his seat. Nina thought this was all going much better than

181

she'd expected. It might not end up as the turgid, smug event that she'd dreaded. She turned to watch Miranda take centre stage once more. *She wears too much make-up: all that powder is very ageing. I wonder who she'll pick on next.* Miranda's gaze moved around the table. *Really, the woman's like a stage medium, looking for an easy target.*

'Joanna,' Miranda said. 'I know you've not had an easy week, but would you feel up to reading, dear?'

At once the patronizing tone made Nina want to jump to her feet and come to Joanna's defence. It occurred to her that Miranda disliked the woman more, now that it seemed she was innocent of Ferdinand's murder, than when it was assumed she was the killer. Joanna, though, seemed capable of looking after herself. She stood slowly, reached out to fill her glass with red wine and took a sip. Then she surveyed her audience.

She looked striking in the candlelight. The long corn-coloured hair was pulled back from her face and the simple black dress made Nina think of a young widow, a woman certainly in mourning.

'I came to the group with a story,' Joanna said. 'Something very personal. But I was too close to it and the language was all wrong. Too elaborate. It took the help of the tutors, especially Nina, for me to realize that I needed to keep it simple. To keep it real.' She started reading without further introduction. It was the description of a young woman being beaten up by a man. The words

182

were carefully chosen, clear and without emotion. The piece was written from the woman's point of view, but there was no self-pity. She described finding herself on the floor, feeling the cold tile against her cheek, seeing a piece of bread dropped from the morning's breakfast.

Joanna paused to catch her breath, and in the distance they heard the sound of a door banging. Nina sensed Holly tense beside her. Everyone in the house was present in the room. Perhaps a window had been left open and the wind had blown the door to. But that night there was no wind. Joanna continued to read. Then the dining-room door was thrown open, so hard that the handle knocked against the wall.

Joanna stopped in the middle of a sentence and turned to look at the man who stood just inside the room. He was wiry and middle-aged, his greying hair tied back in a ponytail. When Joanna spoke, it was in the weary tone of a mother who's had a tiresome day with a fractious child, at once affectionate and irritated.

'Jack, man. What the fuck do you think you're doing here?'

That was when the man lost his temper and started shouting.

19

Vera sat in her house in the hills waiting to hear from Holly. There was still some light outside — it hadn't been worth going back to the station after the interview with Helen Thomas and she'd come straight home. She'd let Joe get off early too, expecting gratitude, because he always claimed that he liked to spend time with his bairns before bedtime, but he'd been in an odd mood all day and he'd slunk away without a word. It was freezing — this year, it seemed, winter had come early — and she'd got a good fire going. She was warming her feet in front of it, drinking a mug of tea when her phone rang.

'Holly. How did it go with Winterton?'

When Vera had suggested that the younger officer should spend the afternoon at the Writers' House, talking to the ex-detective, Holly had looked like a greyhound let off the leash. Almost quivering with enthusiasm.

'Okay.' Reception wasn't brilliant in the house, and Holly sounded as if she were at the end of a long tunnel.

'So why do you think he decided to do the writers' course? Anything to do with the daughter's death, do you think?'

'Not directly. I had the impression that he just wanted some time away from home. Retirement didn't suit him as much as he'd expected. He

184

misses the routine of the job. And feeling useful. He did an English-literature evening class and that gave him the writing bug.'

'Aye, well, I can see it might take some folk that way.' Vera hated thinking about retirement. She dreaded it more than she feared illness or sudden death. 'But why the writing thing?'

'Everyone told him he wrote a good report,' Holly said. 'And he was reading thrillers where they got all the police procedures wrong, and he thought he could do better. I don't think there's any more to it than that. His daughter was at university in Manchester, so there was no contact with Ferdinand or the North-East.'

Vera found that her tea was almost cold. She'd have to make some more. 'Did Winterton have anything useful to say about the other residents? Anything we might have missed?'

There was a pause at the other end of the phone.

'Come on, Holly, you did ask, didn't you? You did stroke his ego, like, and let him think we needed his help and experience?'

'I did my best!'

'But it didn't work?' Vera tried to be reasonable. Maybe it was *her* fault. She should have taken on Winterton herself.

'He said he'd left that life behind him. It was tempting to meddle, but he knew how he'd feel if he was working an investigation and some retired officer tried to tell him how to run a case.'

There was a moment of silence. Vera thought she heard the sound of an engine outside. It was

185

probably Jack working in the barn, though it'd be bloody cold in there now that the light was starting to go.

'Nothing more you could have done then,' Vera said. No point blaming Holly this time. She didn't want to knock the spirit out of her so early in the evening. Vera wanted her on top of her game for the rest of the night. 'At least you gave it a go.' She paused again, couldn't help giving it one last try. 'What was your feeling when you were talking to Winterton? Did he have his suspicions, do you think? That old detective's instinct? He's been living with them all for nearly a week. You'd think he'd have a notion which of them could be a killer.'

'If he likes one of them for the murder, he's not letting on.'

There was a moment's silence. Vera was just about to speak when Holly went on.

'I've arranged to stay on here, just as we agreed.' Her voice was suddenly clear and bright as if she were in the same room. 'I'll go to the dinner when they all read out their work, and I'll stay the night. There's a spare room. This is the last chance we've got to see them all together. They're on their way home tomorrow.'

'Lock your door when you go to bed.' Vera kept her tone light and amused. 'I don't want to lose a promising young officer.' She switched off her phone before Holly could answer. She'd only be fishing for more compliments.

★　★　★

186

Vera put on the kettle again. No alcohol tonight. She wanted to keep her brain sharp. As Holly had said, tomorrow all her suspects and witnesses would be on their way home. Out of her patch, many of them. Beyond her control. This was a time for reflection. She wished she had Joe Ashworth here. He wasn't much one for original thinking, but he let her know if her ideas were daft. For a wild moment she was tempted to give him a ring, to demand that he come over. Then she saw how unreasonable that would be. Let him have one night with his family. She didn't know when he'd get the next one. She reached out and switched on the television.

On the screen her victim had come back to life. An arts programme was running an obituary for Tony Ferdinand and showing clips of his broadcasts. He was sitting, relaxed, in a chair, talking about a writer of whom Vera had never heard. It must have been summer because sunlight was streaming in through a window. He was wearing a white collarless shirt and loose linen trousers, and his face was brown. It was impossible not to look at him. Vera found she wasn't taking in the words, but her attention was fixed on his body, tight and fit for his age, and on his grey eyes. Someone in the investigation had described Ferdinand as charismatic and for the first time she understood what they'd meant. Then suddenly the piece was over. She switched the television off.

She wished she'd met Tony Ferdinand. She found it hard relying on the descriptions of the other witnesses. Most of them had disliked him, and that was unusual after a murder. Usually there were contradictions. This almost unanimous hostility made her suspicious. Had the suspects discussed their attitude to the man before giving their statements? It seemed unlikely. She'd been on the scene almost as soon as the body had been found. Unless there'd been some sort of collaboration surrounding his death, an agreement about alibis and timing. That would be a nightmare. It would widen the circle of possible suspects. But even among a covey of writers, people who created impossible situations for a living, this seemed fanciful.

So what had the man been like? A predator, it seemed, sexually and in his academic life. At least according to Nina and Joanna. What had made him that way?

She pulled a file from her bag: notes Holly had made following her phone calls to Ferdinand's staff. The notes contained the home phone number of one of them who'd worked with him on the creative-writing MA. *Sally Wheldon*, Holly had written. Then: *Poet*. It was seven o'clock. Was this a good time to catch a poet at home? Vera had never met one before. She fetched the phone and returned to her chair by the fire. Hector's chair. Looking out, she saw that there was already frost on the windscreen of the Land Rover, a hazy moon.

The voice that answered the phone was older than Vera had expected. A London voice. Motherly and without pretension.

'Yes? Sally Wheldon.'

Vera explained who she was. 'I think you've

188

already spoken to one of my colleagues, but I wonder if you've got time to talk to me. Informally. Younger officers don't always take the time. They get the facts, but they're not so good at listening.'

'If you think it would help.' The woman sounded pleased to be asked. It seemed time wasn't a problem for her. Perhaps she wasn't a mother after all, but middle-aged and lonely. There were no young kids at home this evening, certainly. You'd hear them, wouldn't you, this time of night? Or a television in the background. Those computer games that made noises. Or were the children of poets not allowed television and computers? Vera realized the woman was waiting for her to continue the conversation.

'I'm just interested in the sort of man Professor Ferdinand was,' Vera said. 'I never met him, so it's hard to tell.'

There was a pause on the other end of the line. Ms Wheldon was choosing her words carefully. A good sign. But then a poet *would* be careful with words. 'He was one of those people who need an audience,' she said at last. 'None of his relationships lasted very long and he lived by himself, but he never seemed comfortable with his own company. He'd walk into a room and look for someone to perform to. That made him rather a selfish teacher. He wasn't really interested in the students' work, only in his own reaction to it.'

'Is that why people didn't like him?' Vera wished she were in the same room as Tony Ferdinand's colleague. She imagined them chatting over tea and biscuits, then she could pick up the gestures and small smiles that would reveal more than words.

'He never really fitted into academia,' the woman said. 'Not into St Ursula's at least, which always considered itself a cut above the other London colleges. He was too brash and too full of himself. He'd been a freelance journalist, of course, before he started here. He'd never published any fiction or poetry and there was a lot of resentment when he was invited to set up the course. There were people in college who thought they'd be better suited. People who'd been to university together, who spoke in the same way. Tony wasn't prepared to play their games. He didn't have to. He was a celebrity and he could pull in quality students, the kids of playwrights and film-makers. Of politicians. He made the course and the college famous.' Sally paused. 'He gave the rich kids a hard time sometimes. We argued about it. Just because they came from affluent families, it didn't mean they had the confidence to take his stick. But he didn't listen. He had a chip on his shoulder about anybody with a posh voice and a fancy degree. I didn't have either of those things, though. I was a working-class girl from Essex, so he treated me okay.'

And perhaps that was why he was so encouraging to Lenny Thomas, and felt it was okay to ridicule Nina Backworth, a well-brought-up graduate with supportive parents.

'He was quite a sad man,' Sally went on. 'A lonely man, despite his need to be the centre of

190

attention. Six months ago he was mugged in the street outside college and he ended up in hospital for a couple of days. Nobody visited him except me.'

Vera replaced the receiver and felt almost cheerful. If she were in hospital, *she'd* have visitors: Joanna and Jack, Joe and Holly and Charlie. They'd bring her grapes and make her laugh.

She'd listened to ten minutes of the radio news when her phone rang again. Holly. 'Are you okay to drive?'

'Aye, of course.' Implying that she was sober as a judge every evening.

'I think you'd better get over here. Your mate Jack's turned up and is shooting his mouth off. Throwing his weight about. If you don't sort it out, someone will phone 999 and he'll end up in the cells overnight.'

'Tell them that I'm on my way.'

★ ★ ★

She scraped enough ice off the windscreen to give her a hole to peer through, and then switched the heater up full, to blast away the rest. By the time she hit the road to the coast she could see where she was going. Approaching the Writers' House she could make out the reflection of the moon on the sea. There was no sign of Jack's van in the car park, but maybe he'd hidden it in the lane somewhere and come down on foot. He'd go in for that sort of drama.

Holly was waiting for her in the lobby. The rest

of the house was quiet.

'I'm really sorry to have called you out.' She seemed mortified because she hadn't managed the situation herself. 'I probably overreacted. It's sorted now, I think. But your neighbour was furious, and I couldn't get him to listen to reason.' With the last sentence she seemed to shift the blame, to imply somehow that it was Vera's fault.

'Aye, well, it was never one of Jack's skills, seeing reason. Has he gone home then?' Vera wondered if she'd passed him, but she could remember seeing no other cars driving up the lane.

'No, he's on the terrace with Joanna and Giles Rickard.'

'Is that a good idea?' Though Vera couldn't see Jack having a go at Rickard. Not physically. The man was too old and frail, and Jack was too sentimental to take on a lesser opponent. Tilting at windmills was his thing.

'Joanna took them both out there. She seemed to know what she was doing.'

Vera saw that Holly had been shaken by the episode, by Jack bursting into the dinner and letting rip. She hadn't felt able to summon the authority to control the situation. Certainly she wouldn't have the strength of personality to stop Joanna doing just what she wanted.

'Where are the rest of the crowd?'

'In the lounge,' Holly said. 'They were reading out their work after dinner. Some of them felt a bit cheated, I think, that they hadn't had the chance to do that, so they've taken their coffee

192

and drinks in there to carry on.' She paused and added in a desperate attempt for approval, 'I was getting on very well with Nina Backworth.'

'I'm sure you were, pet. Kindred spirits.' Vera turned away and went outside. She walked round the house, as she had on her first visit, until she reached the terrace. The curtains in the drawing room had been closed and the only light to the terrace came from a candle on the wrought-iron table where the three people were sitting. There was not a trace of breeze and the flame didn't move. Joanna, Jack and Rickard sat staring at each other. Rickard was wearing a big, black overcoat and a scarf. Joanna had wrapped a shawl around her shoulders, but still, Vera thought, she must have been freezing.

'What's going on here, then?' As soon as the words were out, Vera realized she sounded like a cartoon constable in a kids' TV show, and she added, 'Trying to raise the dead? Looks like some kind of seance.'

She pulled up a chair and joined them. In the house there was the sound of muted laughter, but outside there was silence.

'What were you playing at, Jack man?'

There was no response. It was as if they were all frozen. In the end it was Joanna who answered.

'He got this daft idea into his head that I was in touch with Paul again.'

'Your husband, Paul?'

'My ex-husband. The politician, who spends his time floating between Brussels and Strasbourg. Who has never, as far as I'm aware, come further north than Birmingham — and that was well outside his comfort zone.'

'I didn't think the man was actually here.' Jack made a feeble effort to fight back. 'I thought Rickard was here on his behalf.'

'And I'm supposed to be the mad one!' Joanna rolled her eyes, so that the candlelight caught her chin and threw strange shadows over her face. But she was softening, Vera thought. Perhaps she liked Jack's dramatic gestures. It must be exhilarating to be at the centre of her man's world, to drive him crazy.

'I knew something was wrong,' Jack said. 'I lay there night after night and stories would come into my head. Scenarios, like. Possibilities. *What if?* Then I started to believe some of them. I couldn't just sit at the farm waiting for you to come home. Or not come home.'

Throughout the exchange, Rickard hadn't moved. Now he got slowly to his feet. 'This was a mistake,' he said. 'I should never have accepted Miranda's invitation to the Writers' House. I thought I might make things better, but I've only made them worse. I'm sorry.' He walked away and was lost in the dark.

20

Nina woke when it was still dark. No panic this time. Instead the tired, grainy eyes and taut limbs that came from too little sleep. She had no sleeping pills now to help her. It had been late by the time she'd got to bed and she'd lain there, tense, reliving the shock of the stranger's appearance in the dining room. She wondered now why the arrival of Joanna's partner had so disturbed them? He'd posed no real threat. He'd stood there, yelling at the group, inarticulate with anger, but it had all been words. He hadn't carried a weapon or indicated that he might become violent.

Was it that, in that moment, they saw themselves as Jack saw them? As pathetic wasters. He'd ranted at them all, turning his head from one end of the table to the other. *You're a bunch of self-indulgent posers. Why don't you get off your backsides and do a proper job?* The magic of the evening was lost as soon the door had swung back and he'd opened his mouth. The reality of the outside world had intruded into their ridiculous fantasy of a civilized writers' salon.

Holly, the young police officer, had tried to calm him. She'd left her place and scuttled round the table until she was facing him. *There's no need for this. Let's go into another room and chill out a bit.* Her voice shrill, part panic and part excitement.

But she'd only antagonized him and increased his fury: *Don't talk to me, you stupid little girl. What do you know about anything?*

It had been Joanna who'd gone up to him and put her arms around him as if he were her son, not her lover. At first he'd pushed her away, still yelling, still demanding some explanation. Then he'd broken down and begun to cry.

It occurred to Nina now that Jack hadn't sworn at them. There hadn't even been the casual bad language she used herself to show that she was tired or cross. But still he'd shocked them because his anger was deep and real. They'd spent a week carefully putting words together, but his rage had a greater effect than any of their stories.

She got out of bed and drew the curtains. The room was warm, but through the glass she felt the chill from outside. There was a faint light from the east over the sea. On impulse she pulled on jeans and a sweater, took her jacket from the cupboard. Her last morning at the Writers' House and she'd make the most of it. This afternoon she'd be back in the city.

Downstairs there was still evidence of the evening before. The dining room had been cleared of plates, but in the drawing room there were empty coffee cups and wine glasses. They'd sat here, the memory of Jack's words still in their heads, and pretended that their work was of value. They'd read and listened and clapped politely. Not Nina, though. She hadn't been able to face reading her story. She'd sat in a corner, half-listening to her students' work, applauding

196

only when she saw it was expected of her. Until Miranda had read. Nina's response to her work had been real.

The kitchen door was open and she saw the room was empty. Usually at this time Alex was there, preparing for breakfast. Last night at dinner she'd been sitting across the table from him. He'd been in her line of vision when Joanna's partner had arrived, and she'd seen his face as the accusations had spewed from Jack's mouth. Alex had been shocked by the interruption, as they'd all been, but there had been something else too. Amusement? Perhaps even a touch of admiration? When they'd moved on to the drawing room to continue the readings, Alex hadn't gone with them. He'd claimed to be tired and said he wanted an early night.

Looking across the yard, she saw that there was a light in the cottage. She didn't want to face him or Miranda, and soon surely they'd come to the house to start cooking breakfast and clearing up. She put on her boots and went outside. The cold took her breath away. There was enough light now to see that every blade of grass was covered in frost. She was tempted to walk away from the house, up the track to the lane. But that would have meant walking past the cottage, and she thought again that any moment one of them would come out and she couldn't bear discussing the events of the previous evening with them. Instead she moved quickly down the shingle path to the seaward side of the house.

Still, it was only just dawn. Everything was grey and insubstantial. The trees surrounding the house were blocks of black and for a moment, in their shadow, walking between them and the house, she lost all visibility. Then she came out onto the terrace and into the open and the sea was ahead of her, and suddenly everything seemed very light and clear.

She was back at the place where she'd set her story. Now she was pleased that she hadn't read it out the evening before. Jack's interruption had saved her from that. It wasn't finished, she thought now. Not fit to be read. This scene hadn't been properly described. She came closer, though her attention was fixed more on the horizon, where soon the sun would rise over the line of the sea, than on the group of garden furniture. What words would she use to make the scene — this dawn — real for the reader?

Suddenly she was aware that she wasn't alone. Someone was sitting on the wrought-iron chair closest to her, facing away. On the table were signs that people had been here the night before: a candle, burnt very low, the wax spread over the blue ceramic holder and through the lacy holes in the table, making strange stalactite shapes where it had dripped. Two wine glasses. A coffee cup. An ashtray. The scene was oddly familiar and for the first time Nina felt a tingle of fright. Part superstition and part disbelief. On the floor under the table she saw a piece of white cloth and she had a jarring sense that this was out of place. It shouldn't be there.

Her companion was Miranda. Nina recognized the thick jacket the woman had been wearing the afternoon before, the gleam of the dyed blonde hair piled high on her head. It seemed she hadn't heard Nina's approach; she was too preoccupied perhaps with her own thoughts. Nina almost crept away — after all, the last thing she'd wanted this morning was to speak to this woman — but the dressing of the scene, the candle, the glasses, the ashtray, kept her there.

'Miranda.'

There was no answer, and really by now she hadn't expected that there would be.

She walked round the table so that for the first time she could see the woman's face. Her throat had been cut and was gaping and bloody. It looked almost like a large and smiling second mouth. The idea was immediate and shocking. Not just because of the horror of the image, grotesque and macabre, but because Nina had used the simile before. She'd described this scene. This was her story brought to life.

★　★　★

Later, over strong coffee — she couldn't imagine ever sleeping again, so caffeine was the least of her worries — she tried to explain to Vera Stanhope. They were back in the chapel. Outside, professionals in blue paper suits, looking oddly androgynous, had covered the whole terrace in a white tent. The other participants of the course had been taken away in taxis to a nearby hotel. Statements would be taken, Vera said. Their belongings would be returned to them once they'd been searched.

199

Then they'd probably be allowed to go home. Holly was in the room too, taking notes. There was no sign of the young male detective. Nina would have preferred him there. He was less intrusive than Holly. Throughout the interview she was aware of the young woman's presence. Even when taking notes she demanded attention.

'So how many people would have read your story?' Vera asked.

'Nobody. I was going to read part last night. That scene. The body on the terrace. Then Joanna's Jack arrived and interrupted.'

'Coincidence then.'

Nina set her notebook on the table. 'Read it,' she said.

Vera bent down and took a pair of latex gloves from her bag, then pulled the book towards her and began to read. Once she had problems deciphering the handwriting and asked Nina to give her the word. When she'd finished, she closed it carefully.

'The way the furniture is arranged is exactly as I described it in the story,' Nina said. 'The candle, the colour of the holder, the position of the glasses, the cup and the ashtray. Surely more than a coincidence.'

'No mention of a handkerchief. We found a handkerchief under the table.'

Nina didn't know what to say to that.

'Maybe it had been dropped there during the day.' Vera seemed lost in thought. 'Or maybe not.'

'You think the killer could have left it?'

'That'd be good, wouldn't it? Check for DNA and case closed.'

Vera gave a little laugh, and Nina saw she didn't think it would be that simple.

'The candle was there last night,' Vera said. 'Joanna and her bloke were sitting there, having a meaningful discussion with Giles Rickard.' She paused.

Nina thought at least the detective was taking her seriously. Otherwise she might think she was going mad.

'But it was a different-coloured holder. And no ashtray,' Vera went on. 'And there were only wine glasses. No coffee cup. And the chairs were in different places. So it was deliberately set up later to resemble your writing. Some bugger's playing games.'

She leaned forward so that her face was only inches from Nina's. 'You do see how it looks? Your sleeping pills used to drug Professor Ferdinand. Now you've described in detail the manner of Miranda's death, days before it happened. As if you're some kind of fortune-teller. You're implicated, whether you like it or not.'

'Why would I kill Miranda? I didn't know her.' Nina heard the hysteria in her voice and tried to breathe through it. 'If someone went into my room to take the pills, they could have gone in to read my story too.'

'You haven't started locking your door?' Vera said. 'After the pills were taken?'

'Yes.' Nina tried to work out the timescale. 'I'd started writing the story before you told me Tony

Ferdinand had been drugged. Besides, I've been carrying the notebook around with me all week. Anyone could have picked it up and read it.'

'Of course they could.' Vera lay back in her chair. 'I *had* already thought of that. I might be old, but I'm not daft.'

Nina found herself smiling in agreement. Whatever she was, Vera Stanhope wasn't daft. 'I had a strange conversation with Miranda yesterday afternoon.'

'Aye. You were seen going into her cottage.'

Nina shot a look at Vera. 'So that makes me even more of a suspect?' She wondered who'd seen her with Miranda, again had the feeling that everyone here was being watched.

'Might have done, if you hadn't told me about it,' Vera said. 'What was going on there then? I didn't have you down as best mates.'

'I don't know,' Nina said. Now she thought about it, the encounter with Miranda in the late afternoon seemed surreal. It was hard to believe that the woman on the garden terrace had offered her tea, fed the fat tabby cat. All the small domestic interactions that would never happen again. She looked up suddenly at Vera. 'How's Alex?'

Vera shrugged. 'Hard to tell. I don't think it's sunk in yet. But tell me about your chat with Miranda Barton.'

'I was walking on the beach and she was waiting for me. In the garden, where the path flattens out between the shrubs. She startled me. It seemed very out of character. Thinking about it, you hardly ever saw Miranda outside. I wonder why she bought a place right out in the wilds. She seemed more of a city person.' Nina realized she was rambling, and paused.

'What did she want from you?' Vera seemed not to mind the diversion, but prompted Nina back on course.

'To talk about the murder. And about Joanna. Did I believe Joanna was innocent? I think it had only just struck her that the murderer might still be free. It was almost as if she hoped Joanna had killed Tony.' Nina closed her eyes for a moment and remembered the warm kitchen, her lethargy. Perhaps that wasn't quite accurate. Had the possibility of Joanna's innocence sparked some emotion in Miranda? Had she seemed almost excited?

'There were lots of people here who hoped that,' Vera said briskly. 'How did Miranda seem? Scared?'

Nina struggled to come to an answer. 'I'm sorry. I just couldn't work out why she wanted me there. Was she scared? Maybe. But also wired up. Prepared to put up a fight, I'd say.'

'What sort of fight?'

Nina shook her head helplessly. 'Nothing was spoken of clearly. It was as if she expected me to know what she was talking about. But in the end I was just confused.'

'Do you think she knew who the killer was?' Vera leaned forward again, waiting for the response, and Nina could see how important this was to her.

'Not for certain,' Nina said. 'But I think she might have guessed.'

21

Joe Ashworth arrived just as Vera finished talking to Nina Backworth. He pushed open the heavy door and peered inside.

'Come in!' Vera said. It disturbed her how glad she was to see her sergeant; she realized that she'd come to depend on his presence at these interviews. It wasn't the same with Holly. Vera couldn't relax with her to the same extent. Not the girl's fault, and probably not fair. 'Holly, take Ms Backworth up to her room and help her to pack.'

'I can manage on my own.' Nina's hands were fiddling with a tissue. She looked at the moving fingers as if they didn't belong to her.

'I know you can, pet. But the murderer would have scattered lots of blood around when they made that wound. Spatter, we call it. You can see it on the terrace floor. We'll need to look at your clothes and take some of them away. It's not personal: it's not just you that we've helped to pack.' Vera stood up and gave her a little pat on the shoulder.

They waited until both women had left the room. 'I came as quickly as I could,' Joe said.

'I know.' Vera saw he was expecting a bollocking for arriving late, but she was thinking about Miranda Barton. If the novelist had had suspicions about the murderer's identity, why hadn't she shared them with the police? Because her thoughts were still too vague? Or because she'd seen the opportunity for making money? Vera wouldn't have put it past Miranda to try a spot of blackmail. This was a big place to keep up and maybe, with money tighter all round, folk weren't willing to pay a fortune to sit round talking about books. Maybe it had occurred to prospective visitors that they could stay at home and write and it would cost them nothing. 'Come and look at the scene,' she said. 'Then I want to show you something.'

The sun was up now and the garden flooded with cold light. It was still slippery underfoot and their breath came in clouds. 'My bloody car wouldn't start,' Joe said. 'And then there was an accident on the A1 caused by the ice.'

'Nightmare!' Vera said automatically, but she wasn't really listening.

They put on scene suits and stood just outside the tent. Vera pulled open the flap door so that they could see inside. At the same moment one of the CSIs took a photo of Miranda's body. It came to Vera that, in life, the woman would have loved this attention — the photographs, the audience. Perhaps that was why she had established the Writers' House. Not for the money, but because she needed the admiration and envy of the young writers who had yet to be published. She needed to feel that she was still part of the publishing world, in the same way as ageing television actresses made guest appearances to open supermarkets or award prizes to schoolchildren.

'What do you think?' Vera stood aside so that

Ashworth had a clear view.

'Multiple knife wounds,' Ashworth said. 'The same cause of death as Tony Ferdinand. Same style too. Unnecessary violence.'

'But not quite the same,' Vera said. 'That gash across the throat. It's post-mortem, according to Paul Keating. Ferdinand was stabbed repeatedly, but there was nothing as showy as that here.'

'Is that relevant?'

'It certainly is. Come back inside and I'll read you a story.'

She was about to leave, then stopped and called to one of the CSIs, 'What have you done with the hankie that was on the floor?'

'Already bagged ready for testing. I thought you'd want it fast-tracked for DNA.'

'Let's have a look before it goes off.'

The young CSI held it out for them. 'Distinctive,' he said. 'Plain white, but it's got some embroidery in the corner. Looks home-made. Something a child might have done for a Mother's Day present? Or Valentine's? It looks like a little red heart.'

★　★　★

Back in the chapel, Vera showed Joe Nina's notebook. 'She's written that since she was here. Look at the detail. Everything's the same in the description of the scene: the candle, the number of glasses, the way they're arranged on the table. Nothing about the handkerchief, though, which could suggest it was dropped by accident.'

'If the killer used the story as a model, this

murder wasn't planned that far in advance,' Joe said.

'Well, Miranda Barton might have been chosen as the intended victim, but the execution of the plan couldn't have been decided until the killer had seen the story.'

Vera thought execution was a good word. That was how this seemed to her. There was a ritual to the killings. But then these people were experts in crime fiction. Perhaps that was the intention: to provide layers of meaning that were only for distraction. In Vera's experience, the motive for most murders was simple. It came down in the end to money or sex.

'Keating thinks the same knife was used as to kill Ferdinand,' she said. It was time to get real, to concentrate on concrete facts. 'Where the hell had it been hidden? The search team did a pretty thorough job of the house and garden. And where is it now? Barton must have been killed sometime after I saw Joanna, Rickard and Jack out here on the terrace last night. We might get something a little more precise from Paul Keating on time of death, but I won't hold my breath. So the killer could have had all night to get rid of the weapon.'

'Would the son be able to help with time of death?' Joe had been listening intently. She loved that about him. The way he hung on her every word.

Vera shook her head. 'I had a quick chat with him earlier. He says he took himself off to bed after that ruckus kicked off with Jack. 'The whole thing was just embarrassing,' he said. 'I knew what it would be like. The whole lot of them, slagging off the chap for daring to interrupt the stupid dinner. Actually, I thought Joanna's partner spoke a lot of sense.''

'That's a strange attitude to take when he makes a living from the writers.' Joe paused. 'And when his mam's just been killed.'

'Aye, well, I have the impression he's a strange sort of chap.' Vera still had a picture of the young man, as he'd been when she'd first arrived that morning. She'd found him in the kitchen, still in his whites, lifting a tray of croissants from the oven. It was as if he couldn't take in the fact that his mother had died. Or as if he didn't care. He still felt the need to feed his visitors.

'He didn't hear his mother come in last night?' Joe interrupted her daydream.

'He says not.'

'You'd think,' Joe said, and she thought he could be a persistent bugger, 'after all the fuss, he'd want to talk to her about it. Jack's scene in the dining room, I mean. He'd want to know how it all ended.'

'Well, I'm not the person to ask about that, am I? We need to chat to the boy.'

'Where did Jack stay last night? Did he go back to the farm?'

'No.' Vera spoke slowly. 'Joanna didn't want him driving back, the state he was in. They bunked up together in Joanna's room. This morning I shipped them both off to the hotel with the other residents. Why? What are you thinking? That Jack was the murderer? Unlikely surely. He wasn't in the place when Ferdinand was killed.'

'We don't know that, do we?' Joe looked up at her and Vera saw he had some sort of theory. And that he thought it'd take a hard sell to convince her. 'When I was driving on the afternoon Ferdinand was murdered, something — or someone — ran across the track in front of my car.'

'You think it could have been Jack?'

He looked at her. He hadn't expected her to take him seriously. 'I don't know, but we've always assumed the killer was someone staying in the house. No reason that has to be the case.'

'You're right,' she said. 'We'll check any CCTV between here and the farm for Jack's van. Though I don't know what his motive might have been.'

'Probably a stupid idea,' Joe said. Now she'd agreed to look into it, he was happy to let the notion go. 'Why don't we go and have a chat with Alex Barton? Where is he?'

Vera gave a little smile. In the end she always did get her own way. 'I didn't send him off to the hotel with all the others. It seemed a tad heartless. Besides, I thought we might get more out of him on home territory. He's in the cottage with a minder.'

They walked into the yard, and into sunshine so bright that it made Vera's eyes water.

'You always call him a boy,' Joe said suddenly. 'How old is he?'

'Twenty-three.' Vera fished into her jacket pocket for a tissue and found half a roll of toilet paper. She tore off a handful and wiped her eyes. 'Still a boy to me.'

Alex Barton was sitting in the kitchen of the cottage, with an overfed cat on his lap. Vera had knocked at the door, then walked straight in without waiting for an answer, but he didn't seem surprised or startled to see them. A uniformed constable sat at the table and looked relieved when Vera waved for him to go.

'I always hated this cat,' Alex said. 'It stinks. And when it was more active, it killed birds.'

'I could never see the point of pets myself.' Vera leaned against the Aga and felt the heat penetrate her jacket and warm her spine and her buttocks. 'Your mother liked it, though?'

'Spoilt it rotten,' Alex said. 'It's ancient. When I was growing up I thought she loved it more than me.'

'It's a tricky relationship: single parent and only child. Too much guilt and duty swimming around.' Vera knew Ashworth would think she was speaking from personal experience. So she was.

'I should have got away,' Alex said. 'But I couldn't see how she'd make a go of this place on her own. Not any longer. She needed me.'

Vera realized that he hadn't yet referred to his mother other than by *her* or *she*. 'You'll have a chance now,' Vera said. 'To get away, I mean. This place must be worth a few bob, even if it's got a mortgage. Sell it and you're free to go wherever you like.'

He pushed the cat off his lap and looked at her with big, sad eyes. He was a pretty boy, she saw. There was something feminine about him, despite the dark hair on his arms. When she'd

210

first seen him she'd described him to herself as a wolf. Now she wasn't so sure. He didn't seem sufficiently cruel. She'd expected a response to her words. Anger. A denial that he would choose to benefit from his mother's death, an outburst that such an idea was the last thing on his mind. But he said nothing.

'Have you got a girlfriend?' Again she was deliberately trying to provoke him to speech.

Alex shook his head.

'Of course, why would you? A young lad like you wouldn't want to be tied down. And plenty of chance for sex without commitment here. I'd guess most of the women would be here on their own. Away from home. From their husbands and kids. And it must be intense. Older than you, but there's nothing wrong with experience. All this talk of emotions. They'd be looking for a fling.'

He looked at her as if she was mad and she saw she'd have to try a different way in. Simple questions, she thought. Facts. Maybe that would work.

'How long have you lived here?'

Now he did answer. 'Nearly fifteen years.'

'So you arrived when you were a small boy?'

He nodded. 'I went to the village school up the lane, then to the high school in Alnwick.'

'What brought your mam to this place then?'

There was a pause and Vera thought again there would be no answer. It required judgement, opinion, and it seemed Alex still wasn't ready for that. But in the end he spoke.

'She grew up in Newcastle and always dreamed of living on the coast. One of her books was adapted for television that year. Tony had written an article the Christmas before and described her as one of the best writers of her generation. It made a huge difference to her career. Until then she'd still been working in London, in the university library. Suddenly we had money to spend. She saw the house as an investment for our future. And a pleasant place to bring up a child.'

It was, Vera thought, almost as if he were reciting a story he'd learned by heart. The words were Miranda's, not his own.

'So at first you just lived here?' Vera said. 'She hadn't set up the Writers' Centre.'

'No.' Alex sounded dreamy now, half-asleep. 'Then it was our home. A proper home. I loved it. We'd been living in London, a tiny flat because my mother was just assistant librarian at St Ursula's — and even when her first book was published, it made peanuts — and suddenly I had the garden to play in and the beach. All that freedom.'

'When did your mother start the business?' Vera wondered what it must have been like to have the place overrun with strangers. Surely Miranda must have felt as if her home had been invaded. Or had she relished it? The talk about writing and the gossip, the like-minded people sitting round the table for dinner. It must have been lonely for her here, with only her son for company.

'I was twelve,' Alex said. It was clear that he, at least, hadn't relished the intrusion. 'Mum's books weren't doing so well. She'd thought that the TV adaptation of *Cruel Women* would be the start of a great flowering of her career. It turned out to be the high point. We needed the money. Mum had always enjoyed mentoring younger writers, so she had the idea of running the residential courses.'

'How did that work?' Vera asked. She was genuinely interested. Hector had claimed lack of money as the reason for his night-time adventures, had made Vera feel guilty — *How can I get a proper job when I have you to look after?* He'd drawn her in that way. 'You can't have done the cooking then?' she said. 'You'd still be at school.'

'I helped. But the students cooked for themselves then. There was a sort of rota. That was when I first got interested in food. I loved it: an activity that's practical and satisfying at the same time.'

'What happened to your dad?' She hadn't meant to be so abrupt, but the question had come to her suddenly.

He shook his head. 'I never knew him.'

'Dead? Divorced?'

'Neither,' Alex said. 'My mother never married him. I never met him.'

'But you knew who he was?'

'She *told* me who he was.' Alex bent down to stroke the cat that was rubbing against his legs. 'I'm not sure I believed her.'

'What did she tell you?' Vera demanded. This was like wading through treacle. 'Let's hear the fiction — if that's what it was.'

'My father was an older man. A publisher.

She'd met him at a book launch and fell for his intelligence and his wit. They had an affair. It was the most exciting and wonderful time of her life. He introduced her to theatre and opera, took her away for romantic weekends — Barcelona, Rome, Paris. He was charming and attentive, and she'd never known anyone like him.'

'But he was married,' Vera put in.

Alex nodded. 'With a child whom he adored. When she discovered she was pregnant she finished the affair. She didn't want my father to be forced to choose between the families.'

'Did the man have a name?' Vera failed to keep the scepticism from her voice.

'I'm sure he did, Inspector.' For the first time Alex showed a flash of humour. 'If he existed at all. But my mother never told me.'

'You didn't try to find him?'

Alex shrugged. 'I was worried what I might discover. Like my mother, I preferred the fantasy.'

'I did wonder if Tony Ferdinand might be your dad,' Vera said. She looked at Alex, hunched in the rocking chair. *He's still just a child himself*, she thought. *A bright, screwed-up child.*

'So did I,' Alex said bitterly. 'Like I said, I preferred the fantasy.'

'Did you ask your mother about him?'

'No. I was scared she might tell me the truth. Tony was a manipulative man and I wanted nothing to do with him.' He looked up at Vera. 'He never liked me, you know. I wasn't bright enough to catch his interest.'

214

They sat in silence. Joe Ashworth seemed to be looking out of the window. He managed to make himself still — almost invisible — during interviews, but Vera knew he was completely engaged with the conversation.

'Are you sure you didn't hear your mother come in last night?' he said now, turning back to the room. Vera took the interruption as a sort of rebuke: Joe thought she should focus on the time of death. Important information that might move the investigation on. There would be time enough for all the relationship crap later. When Alex didn't answer immediately, Ashworth continued, 'You do see how it might be important? If your mother came in yesterday evening after the readings had finished and then went out again, or if she went to bed and went out early this morning, that would make us look differently at her death.'

But Vera knew Miranda hadn't gone to bed. She was still wearing the garments she'd been in the night before. White silk shirt and long black skirt. Not the clothes for an early walk on a freezing October morning.

'I didn't hear her,' Alex said. He looked up at Joe. 'I didn't want to hear her. I listened to music until I fell asleep.'

There was another moment of silence. Then outside a shout, so loud that it penetrated the thick walls of the cottage. 'Has anyone seen the boss? They've found something!'

Joe slipped out of the door, but Vera stayed where she was. She pulled herself slowly to her feet. 'Where did your mother keep her books then?' she asked. 'I'd have thought they'd be in pride of place in the main house, but I couldn't find any in the library.'

'She didn't want the students noticing that it's years since she's been published,' Alex said. 'They're upstairs in her bedroom.'

'I'll see myself up there, shall I?' Vera said.

He seemed not to hear her and sat where he was.

22

Joe Ashworth stood outside the cottage door and took a deep breath. Inside the house there'd been a sweet and unpleasant smell. Chemical. Air freshener or some kind of cleaner? Maybe trying to hide the smell of incontinent cat, maybe something more sinister. The CSIs would move on to the cottage when they'd finished on the terrace.

The yard was busy. A couple of men in overalls and navy uniform jackets were deep in conversation, and a CSI, peeling off her crime-scene suit close to the van, hopping as she pulled it over her foot, shouted to a colleague, 'Where are the toilets? I am *so* desperate for a piss.' Beyond the end of the track Joe saw the aerial of a radio van. So the press were there already. The journos, who'd been camping out there since Ferdinand's death, had dwindled away the day before, and now they were back. He was glad someone had had the sense to keep them well away from the house. And Charlie was there, leaning against the bonnet of his car, drinking tea from a mug with the Writers' House logo on it. The whole place was still lit with the sunshine that bounced off the car windscreens and the frozen puddles and turned faces the colour of butter.

Joe called over to Charlie, 'Someone was

shouting for the boss. She's busy. What have they got?'

Charlie pushed himself upright. 'The murder weapon,' he said. 'They think.'

'Where?'

'Down on the beach. I'll show you. Apparently they were lucky to find it.'

Charlie bent to put his mug on the doorstep and walked round the house until they were looking out to the sea. On the terrace, work continued in the white tent. The nylon fabric, with the sun behind it, displayed the figures inside as slowly moving shadows.

Walking through the garden, Joe remembered what Alex Barton had said about moving here from London, about how much he'd loved the place when it was still just a family home. This would be a paradise for a child. Trees to climb and dens to build, rock-pools to poke around in, and on the odd good day when it was warm enough there'd be the sea for swimming. And a child would know every inch of it. If anyone could find a hiding place close to the house, it would be Alex Barton.

Charlie had started on the steep path down to the beach. He slipped once, ripping a tear in the leg of the crime suit, and swore, and by the time they'd reached the shingle he was breathing heavily and sweating despite the cold. He leaned forward, rubbing the stitch in his side.

'You're out of condition, man.' But Joe was feeling the effort too. Too many greasy breakfasts and not enough exercise. There were times, kicking a ball round with the kids, when he felt age creeping up on him.

Three figures stood at the base of the cliff. From this distance and in this light it was impossible to tell if they were men or women. A small flock of wading birds ran along the tide line and took off, calling, as Joe and Charlie approached, black commas against the white sky. The figures near the cliff became clearer, more than silhouettes. Two men and one woman. One was the crime-scene manager Billy Wainwright, who would have been at the house already, working on the terrace. Two others Joe didn't recognize. Members of the search team.

They'd heard Joe and Charlie approach over the shingle, and Billy waved at them. Closer still and they saw he was grinning.

'What have you got?' Joe asked the question. Charlie was wheezing.

Billy moved to one side. Still Joe saw nothing unusual. There'd been a small rock-slide, a pile of boulders at the foot of the cliff. Water leached from the ground, a spring or a hidden stream, and ran across the sand to the sea. Joe imagined his bairns playing here, building dams, castles and moats.

'The rock-fall's not recent, is it?' He was starting to lose patience. Billy was a great one for playing games. Practical jokes. 'What am I looking for?'

'Here!' And in the shadow of the rock-slide there was a rusting outflow pipe, more than half a yard in diameter. 'Once it would have carried the waste water from the house. They use mains drainage now, I guess.' He shone a torch into the pipe, at an angle so that Ashworth could see inside. In the distance, an arm's length from the cliff face, there was a glint of metal and something soft and dark.'

'What is it? The knife?'

'Definitely the knife. But something else. Clothing? I've done all I could *in situ*. I was just going to pull it out.'

He spread a plastic sheet over the shingle beneath the outflow pipe and reached inside. First out was the knife. A black handle with a serrated blade.

'Similar to the one in the kitchen up there,' Joe Ashworth said. 'The bread knife.'

'Similar to knives you'd find in every kitchen in the county.' Billy dropped it onto the plastic sheet.

'The murder weapon?'

'Not for me to say.' Billy straightened for a moment. 'You'd need to ask Mr Keating. But I'd bet my pension on it.'

He lay on his stomach and reached in once again. This time it was harder to retrieve what was inside. It was a snugger fit and caught on the jagged edge of the pipe.

'This might help you, though.' He pulled the bundle free and allowed it to fall onto the sheet. 'A waterproof jacket. Gore-Tex. Large. And I'd guess that those stains aren't just salt water and rust.'

'Blood.' Ashworth squatted to get a closer look. He felt relief, the comfort of tangible evidence. Let Vera Stanhope get deep and meaningful with her witnesses. He preferred forensics. Fingerprints and DNA. 'I don't suppose there's anything on the jacket to identify the owner. Anything in the pocket?'

Billy Wainwright turned the jacket over and felt with his gloved hands into the outside pockets: a tissue, a biro and thirty pence in change. 'You should get DNA from the tissue. Though surely someone will recognize the coat anyway.' He slipped his hand into the inside pocket and pulled out a piece of paper. A newspaper cutting. Or rather, Ashworth decided, a cutting from a colour magazine. Billy laid it carefully on the plastic and smoothed it out so they could read it. A picture of a younger Miranda Barton. The blonde hair shorter and more flattering, the body slimmer. The caption read: *One Cruel Woman*.

'What is it?'

'Looks like something from a women's magazine,' Billy said. 'I don't think it's a Sunday supplement from a paper. An interview with the victim. I didn't realize she was famous.'

'She's not.' Ashworth stood up. 'Not any more.' It occurred to him that this was no coincidence. The piece had been put in the jacket pocket specially. The killer had expected it to be found. They'd thought they'd been clever finding the evidence, but all the time the murderer had been playing with them.

'Look at this.' Billy had moved his fingers to the neck of the jacket. A white label had been sewn inside. On it in permanent marker the words: *For use by Writers' House residents. Feel free to borrow in bad weather, but please return*

221

to cloakroom after use. 'It belonged to the house,' he said. 'Not to any individual. I guess any of your suspects could have worn it. Let's hope we can get DNA on the tissue.' He sounded almost cheerful. Ashworth couldn't bear the flippant tone and turned his back on the group and looked out towards the sea. He knew they'd get nothing useful from the contents of the pockets. This was a set-up, a piece of theatre. The coat and the knife were props, just there to distract them. He resented being made to look a fool.

Someone was making their way down the path from the house to the shore. The figure was tall, wearing a full-length black coat. It took a while for Joe to realize it was Nina Backworth.

'What the shit's she doing here? Who let her onto the beach?' He was glad to have an outlet for his frustration. Nobody answered, and he took off suddenly and strode towards the woman, allowing the salt water and the wet sand to splash his trousers.

'You shouldn't be here, you know,' he said, while she was still at some distance away from him. His voice was raised.

'Why?'

She was very pale. He knew she'd found the body. Her story had predicted the murder. Her sleeping pills had knocked out Tony Ferdinand. And now she was here. Checking they'd found the coat and the knife? But still he couldn't imagine her as a killer.

'Because the area's forensically sensitive,' he said.

'Don't be ridiculous!' She spoke to him as if he were a particularly stupid student. 'The tide's been over here this morning. Any evidence will be halfway to Norway.'

They stared at each other. He didn't know what to say to her.

'I've been sitting in the library all bloody morning,' she said at last. Tears began to roll down her cheeks and he saw how tired and scared she was. 'Nobody will tell me anything. Holly talks at me, but there's no information, just fatuous empty words. Am I under arrest? Do you all think I killed Miranda Barton?'

'No!' As he had in her room the day before, he wanted to put his arms around her shoulders. If it hadn't been for the audience in the shadow of the cliff he might have done it. 'But you can't stay here. Come back with me, and I'll try to find out if you're free to go. Or at least if you can join the others in the hotel.'

'No!' She was standing very close to him. The refusal, an echo of his own word, reminded him of his daughter in one of her stubborn moods. At those times, nothing would persuade the child to change her mind. She'd just repeat herself: *No, no, no*.

'Don't you see?' Nina cried. 'One of those people is a killer. They slashed Miranda's throat. How can you expect me to sit in a room with them all? To drink tea and make polite conversation.'

She turned away from him and stamped back towards the house. He had to run to catch her up.

223

23

Vera climbed the narrow stairs in the Bartons' cottage and dipped her head under a low beam to reach a landing. A narrow passage with three doors off. It was almost dark; the only light slanted up from the kitchen below. She presumed Alex Barton was still there, sitting in the rocking chair, still not communicating with the uniformed officer she'd called back to mind him. Vera pulled on gloves before opening each of the doors and looking inside. There were two bedrooms and a bathroom.

She checked out the bathroom first. It was tiny, with a small corner bath and a shower built over it, a basin and lavatory. No room for a chair or a cupboard, except for a small unit fixed to the wall above the sink. Mirrored doors. Inside a wrapped bar of soap and some toothpaste. Over-the-counter medicines, remedies for colds and flu, indigestion. No sleeping tablets. Had Alex Barton come here last night and showered? Had he stood in the bath and washed his mother's blood from his skin? If so, they'd find traces of it perhaps, in the outflow pipe. But the room seemed spotless to Vera. There was a smell of bleach. Not in itself suspicious. Perhaps the Bartons were naturally very clean. She wasn't that way inclined herself, but it was known.

Alex had the smaller bedroom. It was built into the roof at the front, with a view over the yard. There was no double-glazing and Vera could hear the talk from below, could sense the. anticipation even from here. There'd been a discovery. She knew she'd be excited later, but at the moment the chatter was just background noise in her head and she tried to filter it out. Now she wanted to focus on these people and the strange relationship that there'd been between them. A single parent and an only child. It could make for the closest relationship in the world. But it could be a deadly combination.

The young man's bedroom was functional and so tidy that it made Vera uncomfortable. A psychologist might say it indicated a need to control. There was a three-quarter-sized bed against one wall, the duvet folded back at exactly halfway of its length to air the bottom sheet. Under the window, in the part of the room where the ceiling was most low, a small desk held a PC. There was no printer. Probably no need. All young people communicated electronically these days. Did Alex Barton have friends of his own age? People he texted and shared jokes with on Facebook? She couldn't see it. He'd grown up here, would have been to school with everyone of the same age in this part of the county, but it was hard to imagine him getting pissed on a Friday night on Newcastle's Quayside. It was as if this place had sucked the life and the youth from him and turned him into a loner. Yet when she'd first met him, she'd thought him confident, competent. Perhaps he was only comfortable in this house, on home territory. Perhaps work had been *his* saviour too.

Vera sat on the swivel chair in front of the desk. From here, Alex would see everyone who came down the track to the house, but there was no view of the terrace or the beach. Next to the bed was a chest of drawers. Not old like the furniture in the big house, but flat-pack from a major chain and self-constructed. Was that Alex's choice or had his mother needed to save money? On top of the chest stood a small, flat-screen television.

What did he watch? Vera wished there was some way of finding out. *Maybe that macho survival stuff. Living in the forest with only a knife and a water bottle.* She couldn't imagine him chilling out in front of soap operas or escapist drama. *Comedy?* He hadn't displayed a sense of humour in any of the interviews, even before his mother's death, but then not everyone thought it fitting to laugh about murder.

In the drawers, the clothes were ironed and neatly folded. Two sets of chef's whites and underwear in the top drawer. Casual T-shirts and jeans in the rest. A wardrobe in the same style held one suit, a formal jacket and two pairs of grey trousers. Four shirts, again immaculately ironed. Vera knew that a couple of women came in from the next village to clean the big house each day, and that the bed linen and towels went to a laundry at the end of each course. But Vera thought this was Alex's work. The control thing again. He'd want to look after his own possessions. Maybe she shouldn't make too much of the spotless bathroom. If this was how Alex kept his bedroom, it would be in character

226

for him to clean the bath and sink every day. It didn't necessarily mean that he'd been awake all night washing away his mother's blood.

She looked under the bed and felt behind the wardrobe. No porn. No girlie posters on the walls. In fact there were no pictures on the walls at all, only a framed certificate from his catering course. What did he do for sex? Probably used the Internet, like most of the UK's male population. It came to Vera that more than likely he was a virgin.

In contrast, Miranda's room was surprisingly big. Opulent and glamorous in an old-fashioned way. It held a double bed, piled with pillows and silk-covered cushions, in various shades of purple. These seemed to have been artfully arranged — another sign, Vera thought, that Miranda hadn't been to bed the night before. There was a small wrought-iron grate, just for decoration now. Where the fire would once have been laid stood a candle in a big blue candle-holder, identical to the one on the table on the terrace. Was that significant? Vera tried to remember if she'd seen one like it in the main house. On one side of the chimneybreast, bookshelves had been built into the alcove, and on the other stood a big Victorian wardrobe. There was a dressing table with an ornate framed mirror under the window, and an upholstered stool in front of it. No PC.

So what did Miranda do for sex? The question came, unbidden, into her head. Vera sat on the stool and gave a wry smile into the mirror. She knew her team had sometimes asked the same

227

question about her. But not recently. As you got older, folk seemed to think you could do without.

This is where Miranda would have sat to prepare herself to meet the residents. Again Vera was reminded of an ageing actress. Her dressing table was scattered with make-up. The woman hadn't shared her son's obsession with order and cleanliness. And beyond the mirror there was a view to the coast. It wasn't possible to see the terrace from here — it was in the shadow of the big house. But the beach was visible. What had Miranda been thinking as she put on her face, as she brushed her hair and held it in place with spray? That her life as a writer was over? Or did she still hope for the big break, the posters on the Underground and the reviews in the Sunday papers? Was she still writing?

It seemed to Vera that this question was so important, so fundamental, that she'd been a fool not to consider it before. If Miranda had written a new book, and Tony Ferdinand had offered to help her find a home for it, of course Miranda would be shattered to find him dead. The stabbed body would symbolize her shattered dreams. It wouldn't be easy for a middle-aged woman, considered a has-been, to find success again. If the police service was beginning to put its faith in bright new things, wouldn't the publishing industry be even more that way inclined? It would want beauty, as well as talent, to promote. The scream of anguish Vera had heard on the afternoon of Ferdinand's death was an expression of Miranda's desperation about

228

her own future. She would see nothing left for her now but to provide bed and board for younger, talented writers. She hadn't cared for Tony Ferdinand in a personal way at all.

That, at least, was how it seemed to Vera. But she did have a tendency to get carried away by her own theories. Best not get too excited. Best to find out if Miranda had written a new book first.

She turned her attention to the bookshelves. One row was devoted to Miranda's own work and most of the rest to paperback fiction. Some crime. There seemed to be a complete set of Giles Rickard's novels. Had Miranda felt the need to read them, once the author had agreed to be a tutor on the course? Vera picked one up and looked at it. No dog-eared pages or coffee stains. A small square of paper slid onto the carpet. A comp slip from Rickard's publicist. So Miranda hadn't paid for the books or even, it seemed, read them; they'd been sent to her in the hope that she'd promote Rickard's work on the course. Vera supposed that was how the thing worked.

Vera turned away from the shelves to consider the matter. Her head was still full of the notion that Miranda had started writing again. The first afternoon Vera had arrived here, looking for Joanna, she'd seen Miranda in the kitchen reading a manuscript. Her own book? Ideas chased each other in a crazy jig, and she could make no sense of them. Looking down at the beach, she was distracted for a moment by the sight of Nina Backworth almost at the water's

229

edge. Joe Ashworth came into view. They looked like a pair of lovers having a row. Vera smiled at the notion and turned back to the books.

She took Miranda's novels out and laid them on the bed. A couple had been translated into foreign languages — one might have been in Polish and one was in German. There was a small pink version that must be Japanese. Vera set these aside. The rest she arranged in date of publication. There were four. *Cruel Women*, the book that had been adapted for television, was the third. She slipped it into her bag and put the others back on the shelf.

If there was no computer in the room, where would Miranda have done her writing? There was an office in the main house. When there were no students present, that would be a reasonably quiet place to work. But Miranda had been a romantic. The swept-up hair and the long skirts, the velvet and the silk, the rich colours in her bedroom, all were calculated to give a certain image, to portray a style. Vera could picture the woman sitting with a notebook and fountain pen in the grand drawing room of the big house, looking out to the coast, concentrating on the words perhaps, but also pleased to present herself as a writer. The inspector opened drawers and began her search for a manuscript or paper.

Half an hour later she gave up. There was lots of frilly underwear. The sort you might expect in a Paris whorehouse in the 1950s. An octopus of tangled coloured tights. But no notepad or exercise book. And no handkerchiefs with red hearts embroidered in the corner.

When she returned to the kitchen Alex seemed startled. It was as if he'd forgotten she was in the house. Vera sat at the table and turned towards him. 'Was your mother still writing? She read the beginning of a story the evening she died. Was it from a new piece of work?'

'I'm sorry?' He looked at her with those soft, little boy's eyes.

'It's ten years since she had a book published. Had she given up writing? Retired, like? I saw her reading something at the kitchen table once. Would that have been her own work? Or had she given up?' The time spent rifling through Miranda's belongings had made Vera impatient. She wanted to shake Alex Barton and scream at him.

He seemed not to give her question any importance. He shrugged. 'I don't think so. She always thought of herself as a writer. She wouldn't ever stop. But I don't have any details of what she might have worked on recently. Really she didn't discuss that sort of thing with me.'

Why did you stay? Vera wondered. *You had nothing in common with your mother, so why didn't you move out?* But she'd stayed with Hector. Perhaps things were never quite that easy.

24

The house was quiet. Nina Backworth had been allowed back into her own room. Vera had sent a female officer to sit discreetly on the landing with a view of the door. She didn't think Nina would make a run for it — she was too intelligent for that — but Vera wasn't taking any chances. Alex Barton was still in the cottage, with a bored plod and the cat that he hated as his only companions. Holly and Charlie were in the Coquet Hotel taking statements from the other residents. Vera knew that soon she'd have to put in an appearance there too, but she couldn't bring herself to leave the Writers' House yet.

After walking out of the cottage she'd gone to the beach to see where the knife had been found. She pictured the scene following Miranda's murder. The early hours of the morning. A thick frost, and cold that would take your breath away. There'd been a half-moon, but as Vera had discovered on the afternoon of Ferdinand's death, visibility in the garden would be poor. She'd ask the search team if any of the residents had a torch in their room. Had the killer removed the waterproof jacket on the terrace, or worn it down to the beach? If he — or she — had taken it off at the terrace, there should be a blood-stained bag: he'd need to carry it and the knife in something. Where was the bag? If he'd left the jacket on, they should find traces of blood along the footpath.

Now, though, she was more interested in the contents of the jacket pocket. And food. And coffee. She and Joe sat in the Writers' House kitchen.

'Make us a few slices of toast, pet. You can't expect a woman to work on an empty stomach.'

The bread was fresh, the slices thick and the marmalade was home-made. Joe couldn't work out how to operate the fancy coffee machine, so they had instant, but Vera thought she hadn't been this happy for ages. Joe still seemed subdued, but he'd been moody for a couple of days. If he were a woman, you'd say it was his time of the month.

'So what's this all about?' She set the newspaper cutting in its plastic sheet on the table between them. 'Have we identified the magazine yet?'

'Billy's scanned it and sent it off to HQ. They're tracking it down there.'

'We'll not hold our breaths then.'

'I can't take it seriously,' Joe said. 'It's like somebody's been watching too many crap cop shows on television. Or reading too many of those books where there's a body on every other page, but the police still can't track down the killer.'

'A joke then, instead of a real message?' She emptied the mug of coffee and wondered if she could get him to make some more. She didn't like playing the demanding boss.

'Not so much a joke. More like an attempt to

distract us? To make the whole thing more complicated than it really is. Surely the most likely scenario is that Miranda Barton was killed because she saw the first murder. Or guessed the identity of the killer. Arranging the body on the terrace, the magazine cutting — that's just an attempt to make us chase other links between the victims. Triggered by Nina Backworth's short story.'

'Aye,' Vera said. Half her mind was still on a need for more coffee. 'I dare say you're right.' A thought occurred to her. 'How did the killer persuade Miranda Barton to go to the terrace last night? It must have been late. Joanna, Jack and Rickard were still there when I went home. And it was bloody freezing, even earlier. She must have had a good reason to agree to the meeting.'

'Maybe she made the arrangement,' Joe said.

'We're back to blackmail then?' Vera leaned back in her chair. 'Miranda knew or guessed the identity of the killer and made the appointment herself? It makes sense. She wouldn't invite the killer to the cottage. Alex was in there and might have overheard their conversation.' She peered at the magazine cutting, sliding it away from her along the table until the words came into some sort of focus. It had very small print, and she thought again she should get to an optician's and sort herself out some specs. It wasn't that she was vain. If you had a body the size and shape of a barrage balloon there was no sense in vanity. But until recently her eyesight had been perfect. Hector hadn't needed glasses until he was in his late sixties. She imagined him jeering at her. *Feeling your age, Vee?*

'Read it out to me will you, pet,' she said to Joe. No excuses and no explanation. Challenging him to ask why she couldn't read it for herself.

He shot her a look, but said nothing. He'd always known when to keep his mouth shut. It was one of the things she liked about him.

On Tuesday night the television adaptation of *Cruel Women* will appear on BBC television, starring Sophia Young as businesswoman Samantha. Author of the novel, Miranda Barton, takes time out from her busy schedule to talk to our reporter. We meet in the library of St Ursula's College, London, where Barton once worked.

'So Miranda maintained her contact with the college,' Vera said. 'I suppose in a sense this piece links both victims. By that time Ferdinand would have set up his writing course there.' She could see the photo okay: Miranda posing in front of a pile of books.

'Ferdinand isn't named,' Joe said. Vera could tell he thought she was allowing herself to be distracted again. He didn't understand that she took pleasure in complication.

She glared at him. 'Go on then.' She put on her cross voice as if he'd been the one to interrupt the flow. 'Let's hear the rest.'

Miranda explains that the central character in the book is in no way autobiographical.

'In one sense the book is an allegory,' she says. 'A study of greed in contemporary Britain. Tony Ferdinand was the first reviewer to recognize that. Samantha puts her career in front of everything — her family and friends, her relationships. Of course I want to be successful, but I hope I have a more balanced attitude to life than that. For example, nothing is more important to me than my son.'

Joe looked up. 'Then there are some details about her latest novel, date of publication and that sort of thing. It's a very short piece.'

'What's the title of the novel she's plugging?' Vera thought it wouldn't be *Cruel Women*. The script would have been written and the film shot and edited months before transmission.

'*Older Men*.' Joe looked up at her. 'Do you think that's relevant?'

'No, probably not.' Vera thought there were too many small details to consider. Too many possibilities. 'That was the last book to come out. She had copies of all her novels in her bedroom, and I checked the dates. There was the TV film that year, an interview in a national magazine. You'd think she'd want to make the most of her success. So why did she stop publishing?'

'Maybe the last book wasn't very good,' Joe said.

'Aye, maybe.' But Vera suspected the book business didn't work like that. She wasn't sure the quality of the work had so much to do with sales figures. 'Let's track down a contact at her publisher's. We might find somebody who remembers her.' She paused and looked again at the paper. 'I think there was more to the article than this. Look, the edge has been neatly cut. Originally wouldn't there have been two columns?'

Joe was sceptical. 'How can you tell?'

'The placing of the headline. It's not symmetrical. And the headline itself. *One Cruel Woman?* There's nothing in the piece that answers the question.' Vera spoke almost to herself. 'Did the killer want us to realize the article had been cut in half? Or has he underestimated us?'

'This isn't a game.' Joe was losing patience. 'It's not one of their stories.'

'Oh, it is,' Vera said. 'That's just what it is.'

They sat for a moment staring at each other. The room was filled with the cold morning sunlight. Vera half-expected Joe to demand an explanation, but he just looked at her as if she were mad.

'I think Miranda was still writing,' she said.

She made the announcement as if it were a revelation and was disappointed by Joe's reaction: 'Is it important?'

'If Ferdinand was in the process of helping find a publisher for her, it would explain the grief at his death. Not personal at all. Professional.'

Now Joe did look up. 'Backworth said that they were all going to read pieces last night over dinner. Even Miranda Barton. Although Jack broke up the party, most of them carried on in

237

the lounge. Nina might know if Miranda read, and if she explained the background to her story.'

'So she might.' Vera gave him a long, lazy smile. 'Why don't you nip upstairs and ask her, pet? Take your time. You've got a way with the women. We need all the details she can give.' She nodded towards the cutting on the table. 'Take that with you. Our Nina might know where it came from. She was being taught by Ferdinand after Miranda became rich and famous, after all. She might just remember if there was more to it than we've got here. I'll wait for you.'

When Joe Ashworth had left the room, Vera switched on the kettle again. She made more coffee and found a tin with a few home-made biscuits still inside. It'd be a shame for them to be wasted. Her phone rang. Holly.

'I've just had a call from the incident room. A member of the public wants to talk to you.'

'Oh, aye.' People who fancied they had vital information always wanted to speak to the senior investigating officer. They didn't trust the person at the end of the phone to pass it on. Not without reason. If Vera read every scrap of gossip, she'd get nothing else done. 'So what's so urgent that they contacted you?'

'It came from a politician. An MEP.'

'Let me guess,' Vera said. 'Paul Rutherford.' *Joanna's ex-husband.*

25

Joe Ashworth knocked on Nina Backworth's door and waited to be invited in. She'd been lying on top of the bed and was scrambling upright when he opened the door. He felt as embarrassed as if he'd walked in on her in the shower. He knew she would hate to have her private space invaded.

'I'm sorry,' he said. 'Were you trying to get some sleep?'

'Trying,' she said. 'Not very successfully.' She swung her legs onto the floor. 'I can make you some tea or coffee, if you'd like. Miranda always made sure the rooms were well stocked.'

'Better at running this place than she was a writer, you reckon?'

'Would it be very bitchy if I said she was?' Nina had gone into the bathroom to fill the kettle and looked round the door to get his answer.

'You've already told us you didn't think much of her books.'

She plugged in the kettle and switched it on, giving herself time to form a reply. 'That was while she was still alive. I thought they were pretentious and over-written. Like poor copies of other people writing literary fiction at the time. But it seems much worse to be rude about her when she's dead. And perhaps I got her wrong.'

'I need you to be honest with me,' Joe said.

239

'That's the most important thing now.' He sat on the desk chair and watched Nina play with the small cartons of milk and the teabags on strings. Her fingers were very long and white.

'I haven't lied to you at all,' she said. 'Why would I do that?'

He left the question unanswered. She poured boiling water into a mug and looked at it. 'How strong do you like it? Do you want to fish it out for yourself?'

'Last night,' he said. 'After Jack Devanney kicked off in the dining room, you went with the others to the lounge to listen to them read their stories.'

'To the drawing room.' She corrected him absent-mindedly. A teacher correcting a bairn's grammar. 'Yes, I didn't think I could get out of it.'

'Did they all read from their own work?'

'I didn't,' she said. 'Inspector Stanhope has already asked me that. I couldn't face it, after the scene over dinner. It just seemed like a sham. Whoever set up the scene on the terrace must have looked at my notes without my realizing.'

Joe saw she was blaming herself for Miranda's death; somehow she felt she had made it happen by imagining the crime scene and writing it down. Like a bizarre kind of magic.

'It wasn't your fault,' he said.

'It feels as if it is. I was writing for entertainment. A bit of fun. I didn't expect my story to be brought to life.' She fished in her pocket for a tissue.

'At the moment I'm more interested in the

240

others.' Joe kept his voice low and leaned towards her. 'For example, you said Miranda read from her own work last night.'

'Yes!' Nina's eyes were feverish and Joe thought she needed to get away from this place. She'd have some sort of breakdown if she was locked in here for much longer. 'Miranda did read. I wasn't taking much notice. I was very tired and I kept looking at my watch, hoping that it would be over soon. All the students had done their pieces and I thought: *Hurrah! At last! I can escape to my room.* And then Miranda stood up and my heart sank. But it was good. The writing, I mean. Only a couple of paragraphs, but so good that I even wondered if she'd written it. I thought she might have stolen it. We all hope that we'll get better as we practise, but this was so different from her published novels that I couldn't believe it came from the same person.'

'What was it about?' Joe wondered briefly if stealing fiction was a crime in the technical sense. There'd be copyright law, but surely that would be a civil matter.

It took Nina a while to answer. 'I'm not sure what it was about,' she said. 'Not really. You can see for yourself. She left her reading copy in the drawing room and I picked it up. She'd have it saved on her PC of course, but she'd probably want it back. You can't be too careful about copyright.'

Nina got to her feet and fetched a sheet of paper from a drawer. It was A4, double-spaced, and still the writing only covered three quarters of the paper. Although Joe could have read the

241

words for himself, Nina continued describing them. He thought it was the teacher in her.

'Miranda described a woman walking into an empty house. No furniture except one kitchen chair. There was little background or context. We didn't know who had lived there before or why the writer was there, but in a few words she managed to conjure up such a sense of bleakness. Despair. Just by following the woman as she opened the door and walked inside.'

'How did the group react?'

'It was astonishing. Miranda made everybody forget Jack Devanney's tantrum in the dining room. The first couple of sentences hooked us in. And from then we were completely silent. Listening.' Nina paused. 'Partly it was shock, I think. We hadn't expected her to come up with anything so moving. When she finished there was a moment of complete quiet and then somebody said: *Come on, Miranda, read some more. You've got to tell us what happens next.* But she just shook her head and said goodnight to everyone. People started to clap. I went to bed.'

Joe tried to picture the scene. The residents were all tired and this was their last night. Jack had disrupted the meal. Everyone had had his or her few minutes in the spotlight, and tried to be generous when the others had theirs. Then the dumpy, middle-aged woman had begun to read and had immediately grabbed their attention. Another bizarre kind of magic.

'Who asked Mrs Barton to carry on reading?'

Nina looked at him strangely, as if the

question could have no relevance. 'It was Joanna.'

'I thought she, Jack and Giles Rickard were on the terrace while the reading were going on.' Vera had told Joe she'd seen the three of them outside.

'So they were at the beginning. But they came into the drawing room later.' Nina gave a little smile. 'Joanna handled it very well. *Jack here's sorry for being a prat.*' Nina spoke using Joanna's grand voice. If he'd had his eyes shut, Joe thought he wouldn't have been able to tell them apart. Nina continued, as herself this time: 'Then Jack gave a little bow. You could imagine him as a performer of sorts. He reminded me of a circus ringleader. By then we'd all had a lot to drink and we were willing to be forgiving. Both Joanna and Jack listened to the other readers and stayed until the party broke up.'

'Did Miranda read more of her work?'

'No,' Nina said, 'and that surprised me. I always thought she loved being the centre of attention.'

'What about Giles Rickard?' Joe asked. 'Was he there?'

'Mr Rickard didn't come in with Joanna and Jack,' Nina said. She stood up and walked to the window. Joe thought she was playing the evening before in her mind like a film, as he'd done earlier. 'But he must have slipped in quietly at some point later, because he was there while Miranda was reading. He went up to speak to her. I presumed he was congratulating her on the work. It seemed a kind thing to do. He's

243

something of a celebrity and it would have meant a lot to her.'

They looked at each other. Joe pictured Miranda Barton flushed with pleasure at the response to her work. Perhaps she'd see the moment as a new start to her career. A few hours later she'd be dead.

'Did you know that Mrs Barton was still writing?' Joe asked. 'It's ten years since she's had anything published. You'd think she'd have given up.'

'I don't think writers ever really give up,' Nina said. 'But I didn't know she was writing seriously. We weren't close in any way. She wouldn't have confided in me. She left the paper she was reading from in the drawing room. I picked it up to give back to her. Now she won't have the opportunity to finish her story. Would you like it?'

He took it from her. It would be something to keep Vera happy.

'The handkerchief that was under the table on the terrace,' he said. 'It had a little red heart embroidered in one corner. I don't suppose you've seen anything like that while you've been here?'

She shook her head.

'Aye, well, worth a try.' He put the magazine article in its plastic bag onto the dressing table. 'Would you mind looking at this? Does it mean anything to you?'

She looked at it and he thought there was a moment of recognition. 'Nothing beyond the obvious,' she said. 'Miranda obviously tried to cash in on the publicity for the television film. I don't remember seeing the article.'

'Nothing else?' Something about the way she stared at the photo made him think there was more on her mind.

'I remember seeing her around St Ursula's occasionally when I was there,' she said. 'I'd forgotten how attractive she was in those days. Like a different woman.'

He turned to go.

'When can I leave?' she cried suddenly. 'When can I go home?'

He paused at the door. Bugger Vera, the woman was in pieces. 'Have you got your own car?'

She nodded.

'Go now then,' he said. 'We've taken your statement and we know where to find you. I'll tell the guys on the gate you're free to leave.'

She smiled and for an instant he thought she would take him in her arms and kiss him. Walking down the stairs to meet Vera, he found himself trembling at the idea.

★　★　★

Vera reacted remarkably well to the news that he'd sent Nina Backworth home. There was a poke in the ribs. 'Eh, Joey, you've always been a soft touch when it comes to a pretty lassie. Though I wouldn't have put her down as your type.' But it was all good-humoured. There was no edge to it. She was preoccupied by the prospect of her meeting with Paul Rutherford.

245

'You're going all the way down to London just to chat to Joanna's ex?' Not hiding the disbelief. The disapproval. He thought Vera had her own agenda here. How could she be objective, interviewing the man who'd beaten up her neighbour? Her friend.

'No need, bonny lad. He's coming to see me. The mountain to Mohammed. Well, he claims he had a meeting in Newcastle anyway. I'm not so sure.'

'What do you want me to do now?' He could tell there was no point in trying to persuade Vera against the meeting. Through the kitchen window he saw Nina Backworth walk across the yard towards the car park. She had a little suitcase on wheels that juddered over the cobbles. It was red, the same colour as her lipstick.

'Get off to the Coquet Hotel and see how Holly and Charlie are getting on with the statements.'

'What will I do with the residents, once the statements are taken?'

'Send them home,' Vera said. 'We can't have one rule for Nina Backworth and one for the rest of the party.'

★ ★ ★

The Coquet Hotel in Seahouses had been built in the Seventies when there were still pits and shipyards, and the Northumberland coast had seemed an exciting place for Scottish workers to come for their holidays. Joe had been taken to

246

the hotel once by his nana. She'd dragged him along on an over-sixties coach trip one summer, when he was off school, and he'd complained of being bored. Even to a seven-year-old the place had looked shabby. They'd had afternoon tea in the lounge after being shown round Bamburgh Castle. He remembered a knickerbocker glory so tall that his spoon wouldn't reach the bottom of the glass. His nana had complained that the scones were hard. In the coach on the way home she'd pulled off her shoes, and her feet were swollen to twice their normal size, her toes all twisted and bent.

'Never grow old, Joe lad,' she'd said, though she hadn't seemed upset and she'd joined in the singing of 'Ten Green Bottles' all the way back to Blyth. She'd never been able to carry a tune, and he'd stared out of the window pretending she had nothing to do with him.

The hotel was on the edge of town looking down over the harbour. It had been painted recently, so the stained concrete of his memory was a clean, bright white. But closer to, you could tell that it hadn't been well done. The paint of the fascia boards had leached into the white walls. The last throw of the dice, Joe reckoned, before the owner gave up. There were empty hotels all along the coast.

The Writers' House party was sitting in a lounge that reminded Joe of somewhere institutional. An old folks' home or a doctors' waiting room. Upright chairs set around the wall. There were huge picture windows and the sunlight showed the streaks of salt on the glass outside. He thought they probably hadn't been cleaned since the gales at the beginning of September. The room was big enough for Holly and Charlie to have set up camp at one end and not be overheard by the people at the other. There were empty cups, screwed-up napkins and on low coffee tables a couple of trays with a few sad remaining sandwiches. Lunch had been provided then. Joe wondered if that had come out of Vera's budget.

When he pushed open the door they all looked at him. Even Charlie and Holly. And stared, as if he was an exhibit in a zoo. The *detective sergeant*, a strange and alien specimen. Did they expect him to bite or scratch? He must be tired. His mind was working in peculiar ways.

'Everyone who has already given a statement can go home,' he said. 'We'll provide lifts back to the Writers' House so that you can pick up your cars. We're sorry to have inconvenienced you. If you wait outside, a minibus should be here in a few minutes.' He'd expected cheers of jubilation but they all seemed subdued and there was little response. They gathered up bags and started to wander out. Joanna and Jack were last to leave. Joanna had her arm around Jack's shoulder, a protective gesture. You'd have thought *he* was the one who'd been accused of murder.

It seemed that Holly and Charlie only had Lenny Thomas and Mark Winterton still to interview. The men sat at opposite sides of the room. Lenny grinned and shrugged and moved closer to the ex-policeman. 'And then there were two, eh, Mark?' He waved at Joe to show there were no hard feelings. As he joined his colleagues and began to read through the witness statements, Joe heard Lenny's voice in the background, asking questions about crime scenes and procedure, and Mark's patient replies. Tired and strung-out, he thought the muttered voices sounded like waves on shingle, and he remembered again his earlier encounter with Nina Backworth. It came to him that he had her home address and that he might find an excuse for going to visit her.

26

Joe Ashworth turned to his colleagues. 'So everybody went to bed once the party had broken up, and no one saw or heard anything,' he said. He kept his voice low, but Lenny and Mark were still deep in conversation at the other end of the room and were taking no notice of them. He looked at Holly and Charlie and waited for an answer.

'Pretty much,' Charlie said. 'Jack got up in the middle of the night for a piss and thought he heard music. The Beatles' album *Sergeant Pepper*.'

'What time was that?'

'About two in the morning. Does it really matter?'

'It shows someone was still up. A possible witness.'

'If you think you can believe anything that man says.' Charlie rolled his eyes.

Holly jumped in. 'And they all thought Miranda Barton was a wonderful woman, and nobody had met her before this week.'

'Not even Giles Rickard?' Joe Ashworth asked. 'They were writing at the same time.'

'Different sort of material, apparently. She was considered a literary novelist. He wrote detective stories. They'd have no reason to bump into each other.' Holly paused. 'And nobody can remember seeing a handkerchief with a red heart in the corner.'

'You need to have a word with the boss,' Charlie broke in angrily. It seemed to Joe that he hadn't even been listening to this last exchange. He got that way sometimes, for no reason. Since his wife had run off there were times when he was angry at the whole world.

'What about?' Joe said, though he could guess.

'She's making a fool of herself over those hippies.' Joe thought Charlie had eaten lunch too. Tuna sandwiches, from the smell of his breath. 'It's obvious that they're behind it all. The woman's tried to kill before, and the bloke's as mad as a snake. *Sergeant Pepper!* And look at the way he stormed into the place last night, shouting the odds.'

'Everyone says that he calmed down and apologized before the end of the evening.' Joe didn't know why he was standing up for the hippies. Because Vera didn't think they were behind the murders? Is that what he'd become? Vera Stanhope's representative on Earth?

'Doesn't mean the chap still didn't have murder on his mind.' Charlie was chuntering just loud enough for Joe to hear him.

Joe thought if they didn't get on with the next two interviews they'd be here all day, and the hotel, with its Seventies colour scheme and his nana's ghost, was already freaking him out.

'Why don't you get off, Charlie?' he said. 'I can sit in with Holly for these. It won't take three of us.'

Charlie brightened. 'I've arranged to go over to Carlisle tonight to have a beer with my mate. The one who worked with Winterton. Despite

251

what the boss says, I don't see why I should do it in my own time.'

'Off you go then.'

And when Charlie shambled out of the room Joe felt a sudden sense of relief.

They took Mark Winterton first, because he had furthest to travel home and Lenny seemed to be in no hurry. The ex-policeman took a seat opposite them. The hotel had provided a trestle table, and Joe thought this felt more like a job interview than taking a witness statement. *Tell me, Mr Winterton, why did you decide to apply to be a writer?*

And his first question was almost like that. 'Why the Writers' House course? It's not cheap, is it? And pretty intensive for a beginner. I'd have thought there'd be places closer to home, if you were interested. Evening classes. That sort of thing.'

Mark Winterton blinked at him through the small, square spectacles. 'I thought I'd already explained that to your colleague.' He nodded towards Holly. He kept his voice patient and polite, but the blinking eyes suggested a repressed irritation. 'I'd always enjoyed writing, and this seemed like a great opportunity to kick-start the crime novel I'd thought I might write.' He paused. 'As to the money, I don't have many extravagances.' He gave an awkward smile. 'I paid maintenance for the children of course, when I was first divorced, but they've left home now. My ex-wife married again very quickly and her husband's a wealthy man. My pension seems rather generous for a man of simple tastes.'

Joe wondered why Winterton felt the need to share all this personal information. Perhaps he was just lonely. Perhaps that was the explanation for him attending the course.

'I was sorry to hear about the death of your daughter,' Joe said.

'You know about that? Of course, you'll have checked up on us all. Nothing is ever the same afterwards.' He looked up. 'I discussed that with Miranda yesterday afternoon. The loss of a child. How that affects absolutely everything that happens later. Miranda was immensely understanding. I'd never really talked about it to anyone else in the same way. She was a sympathetic woman.'

'When did you have this conversation with Miranda?' Joe kept his tone light. The woman had never struck him as particularly sympathetic. Beside him, Holly was twitching like a hunting dog scenting prey. He hoped she'd have sense enough to keep her mouth shut.

'Before dinner. I'm always early. At work I was a tyrant about punctuality, and I see now that it was my obsession. I'd showered and changed and was waiting for the others in the drawing room when Miranda came in. She brought me a sherry and we began to talk. She was nervous, I think. She wanted the final evening to be a success, despite Tony's death. I'd never been alone with her before and I was surprised at how well we got on.'

'Did she ask for your advice?' Joe remembered that Miranda had invited Nina into her cottage the same day.

'I had the sense that she wanted something from me, but I never quite worked out what it was. You must have come across that, Sergeant: acquaintances with vague anxieties wanting reassurance. About children mixing in unsuitable company, or neighbours who seem suddenly to have come into money. I suspect it goes with the job, but of course we have no answers. We can't always keep our own family safe.' Winterton looked up. Joe had the sense that he wanted to prolong the discussion and that he was in no hurry to return home to his empty house. Joe wondered about the ex-wife. Had she had a lover even before the separation? Was that the cause of the divorce? Joe thought it would be interesting to meet her.

'What anxiety did Miranda have? Did she have concerns about her son?'

'Certainly we talked about our children. But I don't think Alex was causing her any problems. He always seemed the sort of boy you'd be proud of. I did wonder . . . '

'Yes?'

' . . . if she'd had a daughter. Perhaps who'd died when she was still a baby.' He put his hands on the table in front of him. Ashworth saw he still wore a plain gold wedding ring. 'Miranda spoke with such understanding about losing a child,' Winterton said, 'and last night there was a slip of the tongue that made me think she'd had a baby girl. She was talking about the experience of giving birth. *I'd never known pain like it, but once I'd taken the baby into my arms it was all worth it. She was so tiny.*' Really, I'm sure she said *she*, but I didn't want to follow it up.' He looked up and frowned. 'Of course none of this is evidence. Perhaps I shouldn't have mentioned it. But sometimes in an investigation small snatches of gossip can make a difference. I thought you should know.'

Joe's attention was caught by a bright-yellow coach that had pulled up outside the hotel. Elderly people climbed stiffly out. The driver began to unload luggage. Joe dragged his focus back to the room.

'Of course,' he said. 'Thank you. Would you mind waiting until we've finished talking to Mr Thomas? Then we can give you both a lift to the Writers' House.'

'No problem at all.' Winterton stood up and gave a polite little nod. 'I'm not in any rush to get home.'

Lenny Thomas sat awkwardly looking at them across the table. 'I wouldn't have killed her,' he said without introduction. 'I mean, I wouldn't have killed either of them. But Miranda picked me to go to the Writers' House and I loved every minute of it. I'll always be grateful to her for giving me the chance. For taking me seriously. As a writer, like.'

'We're not accusing you, Mr Thomas,' Holly said. They'd agreed that she should take the lead on this one. Only fair. But Joe wished he was asking the questions. Sharp, bright Holly would make Lenny nervous and tongue-tied. 'We're just trying to find out what happened.' She paused. 'Last night you read your piece early in the

255

evening, while the group was still in the dining room.'

'Aye.' He looked at her. 'You were there. What did you make of it?'

The question obviously threw her. 'It was very good,' she said at last. 'Very moving.'

Lenny grinned widely at them both. Joe was reminded of his youngest child, coming home from nursery with a gold star on a painting.

'What did you do later in the evening?' Holly asked. Joe sensed her, tense and impatient. Under the table her foot was tapping on the floor.

'After Jack Devanney came in, shouting his mouth off, I moved out of the dining room with the others and listened to their readings in the drawing room.'

'And after that?'

'They all went off to bed, but I didn't. It was my last night there and I wanted to make the most of it. To make it last. Do you understand?' He directed the question to Joe. He'd think Holly was too young and too confident to understand.

Joe nodded.

'What *did* you do, Mr Thomas?' Holly broke in immediately. 'Did you sit all night in the drawing room?'

'I sat there for a while. Then I thought I'd take a walk, clear my head before going to bed. Outside it was dead still. And there were all those stars. In the town, with the street lights, you never see the stars. And the moon making a road over the sea. I wanted to remember it. One day I might write about it.'

'Where did you walk, Mr Thomas?' Holly managed to sound bored and hostile at the same time.

'Onto the terrace. But there was nobody there. No body, either.'

'Are you sure?' Joe asked. 'It was dark.'

'Aye, but like I said, there was a moon.'

'And it was cold,' Joe said. He was aware of Holly firing furious glances in his direction, but he took no notice. 'Did you go upstairs to get a coat before you went out?'

'No, there was a jacket in the cloakroom downstairs for folk to borrow. I took that.' Lenny looked at Joe as if he were daft.

'What did you do with it when you came back inside?'

'I put it back!'

'And then?' Holly asked, determined now to have the last word. 'What did you do then?'

'I went to bed,' Lenny said. 'I couldn't make the night last any longer. It was going to end, wasn't it? I had to get ready to go back to the real world.'

'What time was that?' Joe wondered if the week at the Writers' House had been a good thing for Lenny. Had it set up expectations that would never be realized?

'Twelve-thirty. I looked at my watch when I got into my room.'

'Did you listen to any music when you were sitting in the drawing room?' Joe asked.

'No. Why?' Now he just looked confused.

Joe looked at Holly. She shook her head to show that there were no further questions.

★ ★ ★

Joe ended up giving Lenny a lift back to his flat in Red Row. Lenny said he didn't have a car any more. His ex-wife had offered him her old one, but he couldn't afford to run it. They dropped Mark Winterton at the Writers' House to pick up his Volvo. The lane was blocked with vehicles. A reporter from BBC *Look North* was doing a piece to camera with the house in the background. They watched him straighten his tie, then nod to the cameraman. At last the media all moved aside to let the car past. Joe thought Lenny might be interested in the activity, but he sat in the passenger seat, listless and unengaged.

Red Row had once been a mining community just inland from the big sweep of Druridge Bay. Recently there'd been a new private development, big houses all looking out to the sea, but the village itself still looked sad. As if there were no longer any point to it. A main street with red-bricked terraced houses and a small council estate. A boarded-up shop.

'Do you want to come in?' Lenny sounded eager, but he expected refusal.

'Aye, why not? I could use a cup of tea.'

And before the words were out of Joe's mouth, Lenny was knocking at his neighbour's door to scrounge some milk. The old lady who lived there seemed pleased to see him: 'Eh, Lenny lad,

258

it's good to have you home.'

Sitting in the small, cold room, Joe wondered what he was doing there. Was this about pity for a lonely man? 'We talked to your wife,' he said. The words were out of his mouth too quickly. He hadn't thought them through. This sounded like interference.

But Lenny didn't seem offended.

'She's a grand woman,' he said. 'A great mother.'

'You don't think you could still make a go of it, the two of you?' Joe wondered what Vera would make of this. *You've turned counsellor now, have you, Joey boy? Well, maybe you could always get a job with Relate.*

Lenny looked up at him and grinned sadly. 'Likely too much water under the bridge,' he said. 'And I can't fancy being a kept man any more. It might have been different if I'd got the contract with the publisher. That would've put us on an equal footing. You know what I mean?'

Joe nodded.

'Not that I don't dream about it,' Lenny went on. 'Late at night. Not that I wouldn't do anything to make it right.'

Driving back to Police Headquarters, Joe Ashworth thought Lenny was a romantic, the sort of dangerous romantic who might kill for the notion of the perfect relationship. But Joe couldn't see how the deaths of Tony Ferdinand or Miranda Barton could help him achieve his aim of a perfect marriage.

27

Vera had agreed to meet Paul Rutherford at the Lit & Phil Library in Newcastle. She'd suggested the venue. He'd said he'd only have an hour spare before he took the train south, and the library was just round the corner from the Central Station. The Lit & Phil was a Newcastle institution, a private subscription library. Hector had been a member, had dragged her there for lectures and meetings until she'd been old enough to leave alone in the house in the hills. Usually Vera despised the things and places Hector loved, on principle, but the library still held a place in her affections. Each year she renewed her membership. If she was struggling to make sense of a case, occasionally she'd go down the stairs to the Silence Room in the basement, and ponder the details of the investigation away from interruption. She recognized some of the regulars — the tall, skinny man who was never without a hat, the glamorous art historian, the famous poet — and nodded to them whenever they met, as if they were friends.

Upstairs in the magnificent main Georgian library, with its domed roofs and balconies, silence wasn't expected. Today two elderly men sat at the big table and talked about shipbuilding, re-creating the life of the Tyne with books and memories. Vera bought herself a cup of coffee and a sticky bun from the woman behind the tea counter and waited. She found a quiet table with a view of the door. She'd googled Paul Rutherford. He had a slick website and there was a photo of him beaming out of the home page. When he arrived she probably would have picked him out anyway, a stranger, hesitating very briefly at the top of the grand stone stairs, before preparing to make an entrance.

He was wearing black. Informal black, so that she found it hard to believe the meeting that he'd used as an excuse for being in the North-East. Didn't politicians always wear suits? Rutherford wore black jeans, a black T-shirt under a black jacket. She thought he'd find it cold outside without a proper coat, and then wondered if he'd dressed deliberately to create an air of menace. Was he out to intimidate her?

But it seemed he intended to try charm first. She stood up to greet him and he approached her as a long-lost friend. 'Inspector Stanhope. Thank you for taking the time to meet me. I know how busy you must be.' The voice clipped. Posh south, but without the drawly vowels. He gave a thin smile that had no warmth or humour in it. His eyes never quite met hers. The elderly men walked past them and out. The library was empty apart from the tea lady and a librarian at the front desk.

'Coffee?' Vera asked. 'Or are you a tea man?'

'Oh, tea,' he said. 'Every time.'

She bought him tea. He didn't offer to pay for it. Meanness or arrogance? Did he believe that the small social niceties didn't apply to him? They sat round the corner out of sight of the librarian. Rutherford took no notice of the beautiful surroundings or the shelves of books.

'I'm not quite sure,' Vera said, 'why you wanted to see me.' She smiled brightly at him.

'I still feel some responsibility for Joanna,' he said. 'It's some time since our marriage ended, but one can't turn off one's feelings. I hate to think of her in trouble.'

'Is she in trouble?' Vera looked up at him, wide-eyed.

That threw him. 'I understood, from the newspapers, that she'd been questioned about a murder. Tony Ferdinand's murder.'

'Questioned,' Vera said, 'but not charged. We've *questioned* everyone who was staying in the house. Even your old friend Giles Rickard.'

'That's ridiculous,' Rutherford said. 'Giles Rickard wouldn't hurt a fly. I've known him since I was a child.' He held his teacup, sipped and gave a small grimace to show that he was accustomed to better. Vera saw that his hands looked older than his face. Rutherford went on, 'He was like a second father to me.'

'But you think Joanna would be capable of murder?' Vera asked. She looked at him, as if the answer was of considerable interest to her.

'She tried to kill me!' he said. A flash of almost childish anger.

'But that surely was rather different. As far as I know, Professor Ferdinand hadn't kept her prisoner or beaten her up.' Vera kept her voice even. She wouldn't get this chance again and she didn't want to lose her temper in front of the man. Besides, she was enjoying herself. This was

262

an interesting experience. She didn't come across psychopaths very often. It occurred to her that there might be a greater proportion of psychopaths in Parliament than in prison.

He paused for a moment and gave another tight smile. 'You do know, Inspector, that your words are slanderous.'

She leaned forward across the table, made her voice intimate, almost flirtatious. 'Somehow, Mr Rutherford, I don't think you'll sue.'

They sat looking at each other. It was very warm. The hot water in the radiators gurgled. At the desk a phone rang.

'We'll stop playing games, shall we?' Suddenly she'd lost patience with him. 'Why are you here? What did you want from me?'

'I wanted to warn you,' he said, 'not to be taken in by my ex-wife. She tells stories. Not just to the people around her, but to herself. Eventually I think she comes to believe them. Do you really think that I locked her in our apartment in Paris? That I hit her? It's the stuff of melodrama.' His words were scathing. 'She's plausible, vulnerable. And very clever. She has a knack of making people love her. Then she makes fools of them. Don't let her make a fool of you, Inspector.'

He began to stand up as if he was about to leave, but she nodded for him to remain seated and he stayed where he was.

'When did you last hear from Joanna, Mr Rutherford?'

He paused and she thought he was deciding whether or not to tell her the truth. Or perhaps

263

he too was enjoying the drama, and the hesitation was to add to the suspense.

'About a month ago.'

'Would you tell me what she wanted from you?'

Now he did get to his feet. 'Money, Inspector. That's what she wanted. Joanna was blackmailing me. Of course I refused to pay. It does seem a coincidence that suddenly I find her picture all over the popular newspapers. Though I find it hard to believe that even she would commit murder to spite me.' He turned suddenly and walked out. Vera sat where she was and watched him go.

★ ★ ★

As she drove north into the country, it occurred to Vera that she might have been wrong all along about Joanna. Perhaps Rutherford was no psychopath, just a man who suffered from stress and was being harassed by a flaky ex-wife. The idea was shocking: Vera wasn't used to being wrong. *But why did you want the money, Joanna pet? Why stoop to blackmail?* Vera really couldn't get her head round that one. The Joanna she knew boasted about the charity-shop clothes, the bartered veggies, the Freecycle fridge. Joanna despised money as common, vulgar, and thought an obsession with money displayed the worst possible taste. What had she called greed? *The meanest of vices.* So why was she so desperate for cash that she'd got back in touch with the man she hated?

264

Vera was so puzzled that she almost missed the lane to Chrissie Kerr's place. Vera had tracked down Nina's publisher the day before. Holly had spoken to her earlier in the investigation. After all, Chrissie had been in the Writers' House the morning of Ferdinand's death. Holly had reported back that the woman had no useful information, but Holly wasn't brilliant at picking up unspoken messages. Besides, Vera had her own reasons now for wanting to speak to the publisher.

Chrissie Kerr still lived with her parents, it seemed, and had given Vera directions. Once it would have been a farmhouse as scruffy as Jack and Joanna's, but the land had been sold off and the house and a barn conversion were all that was left. The house was rather grand now, solid and double-fronted, with long sash windows and a view out to the National Park. The barn had been turned into a stylish office, one wall made almost entirely of glass, the roof covered in solar panels. A sign, black on green: *North Farm Press*. Between the two buildings, where once there would have been a mucky farmyard, white lines marked parking places on a paved courtyard.

No shortage of money here. Vera climbed out of the car and waited. Chrissie was expecting her and would have heard her coming. It was mid-afternoon, still a beautiful day, but already the sun was low. Vera hesitated, unsure whether to knock at the house or the office.

'Inspector Stanhope!'

A young woman still in her twenties, but

confident and loud. Big-busted and wide-hipped, dressed in a black frock that hid most of the bulges. Vera didn't know much about clothes, but thought that sort of magic wouldn't come cheap. She could do with something similar herself, but would probably shrink it the first time she washed it. Anyway she wouldn't have the aplomb to carry it off.

'Come into the house and have some tea.' Chrissie's foghorn voice carried from the door of the office. 'I usually take a break at about this time. Mummy and Daddy are in town, so we'll have the place to ourselves.'

By the time tea had been made and carried into a living room Vera knew all about Chrissie Kerr. About how Mummy had been an academic, a classicist, and Daddy a scientist, and they'd both given up posts in the university to move out to the country. 'They both got a bloody good redundancy package, actually. They were at the top of their pay scales and the university couldn't wait to get rid of them.' Chrissie poured tea, but she didn't stop talking. Vera looked around her. A pot of chrysanthemums stood on the windowsill. The carpet was red and there was an expensive-looking rug by the fire. On the walls original paintings: a couple of large oils. 'They didn't stop working of course. They're still writing. And as my business has grown, they're more involved in that.'

'You're a publisher?' Finally Vera managed to get in a question. Obvious, but at least it stopped the flow of words.

'Yeah! Crazy, isn't it? When you think of

266

publishers, you think of London. Huge offices. Men and women in sharp suits. But I do very well.'

'And you publish Nina Backworth?'

'She was one of the reasons why I set up the company. I did English as an undergraduate at Oxford and then came home to do an MA at Newcastle. Nina was one of the tutors. Her writing is brilliant! I mean, really outstanding. But she couldn't find a publisher. So I thought: *How many more people like you are there out there? Wonderful writers overlooked by the big presses.*' Mummy put the money in to set up the business, but I've nearly paid her back. I've already had an author on the Man Booker longlist. Imagine! And Nina's reviews have been astonishing. But really, choosing the right books is just the beginning. In the end it's all about marketing. If readers don't know about the books, how can they read them? We need publicity. To get the word out. I'm working on it, but it's a tough market.'

There was a silence, startling after the flow of words.

'I'm investigating two murders,' Vera said. 'I don't understand this world. That's why I wanted to see you.' *At least that's part of it.* 'You're not a suspect or a witness. I thought you might help.'

'I will if I can.'

Vera believed her. This cheerful, unflappable young woman would be a dream to work with. She thought of Holly, competitive and tense, and she sighed.

'The first victim was Tony Ferdinand. You'll have heard of him. Met him, of course, because you gave a lecture at the Writers' House the morning he was killed. The second was Miranda Barton, the author who set up the place.'

'I know,' Chrissie said. 'It's been all over the papers and one can't help reading. Like a dreadful soap opera involving people one knows. And one of your officers came here to take a statement after Ferdinand was killed.'

'How well did you know Professor Ferdinand?'

'Not at all. I only met him that once. My knowledge of him came from what I read in the papers and saw on the television,' Chrissie said. 'And from what Nina told me. But she was hardly an impartial observer.'

'Why would anyone kill him?'

'You don't know how influential that man was,' Chrissie said. 'He wasn't a publisher or an agent, but boy, did he have power! I sent a number of my titles to him, but never got a response, more's the pity, and all the big London literary people will have been doing the same. If he liked an author's work he could persuade an editor to take it, and his reviews made a real difference to sales.' She saw that Vera looked bewildered. 'Think the Simon Cowell of the publishing world.'

Vera thought about that. Lenny Thomas had seemed laid-back about his writing. He'd dreamed about being an author, but had never believed it would happen. Mark Winterton had clearly become aware of his own limitations. Neither would have been provoked to murder if

268

Tony Ferdinand refused to help them. But what about Joanna? She'd been passionate about her writing. She'd wanted her story — her abuse at the hands of her respectable ex-husband — to be made public. Vera shook her head. 'Nah, I can't see it. Nobody wants to see their name on a book that badly.'

'Don't you believe it!' Chrissie grinned. 'That's why the Writers' House did such great business. All those wannabes convinced they'd become the next best-sellers.'

'Did it do great business?'

'Yeah,' Chrissie said. 'It had a terrific reputation. A couple of young writers found publishers during their time there. I picked up one myself.'

'You were a tutor there?'

'Yes, last spring. And of course this year I was a visiting lecturer. I was speaking the morning Tony Ferdinand died.'

'What did you make of Miranda Barton?' Vera found herself holding her breath as she waited for the woman to answer. She valued Chrissie's opinion and decided the woman might have thoughts to move the investigation on.

'I thought Miranda was rather overrated as a writer. She must have caught the public mood to sell so well — Tony's recommendation alone wouldn't have made her a big-hitter. But she dated very quickly. As a person, I found her seriously weird. I felt sorry for the son. He's a good cook and he could make his own life in a flash restaurant anywhere. I tried to persuade him, but he said his mother needed him around.

Perhaps that was just an excuse and he didn't have the confidence to set out on his own.'

Vera stood up. She was disappointed. She'd hoped for more from this meeting. It seemed she'd come away with nothing new at all. Chrissie walked with her out of the house, past the umbrella stand in the hall, the boots and the Barbour jackets.

'I was wondering . . . ' For the first time the young woman seemed diffident.

'Yes!'

'I don't think the Writers' House should fold. As a concept, I mean. As an idea. I thought I'd start a foundation to keep it going. Buy Alex out, if he doesn't want to be a part of it.'

'Don't ask me, pet. Like I said, it's not my world.'

'Nina showed me the writing that came out of 'Short Cuts'. Some of it is very good. I wondered about putting together a pamphlet, a sort of sampler to show what the Writers' House has achieved. Actually it was Nina's idea. She was here earlier; you must just have missed her in the lane. North Farm Press would sell it as a fund-raiser. All profits to the project. What do you think? I wouldn't want to prejudice the investigation in any way.'

They were already in the yard. Vera stopped in her tracks and squinted into the sun. 'When were you planning to launch it?'

Chrissie seemed embarrassed. 'As soon as possible.'

Vera nodded her understanding. 'To make the most of the publicity surrounding the murders?'

'Do you think that's really crass?'

'Probably,' Vera said. 'But I've come to realize writing's not a noble calling. Like you said, it's all about marketing, isn't it? I'll not stop in your way.' As she climbed into Hector's Land Rover she was smiling. She wound down the window. She'd had one last thought. 'Why don't you throw a party, to set it on its way?'

28

When she got home Vera phoned Joe Ashworth. 'What was he like then?' Joe asked. 'The monster MEP.'

'Ah, Joe, you know I don't believe in monsters.' *Though if anyone might make me change my mind, it'd be him.* 'And I kept my cool. You'd have been proud of me.' She ran her finger along the window ledge. It made a track in the dust. The house was muckier than it had been in Hector's day, and that was saying something. She knew Joe wanted the full story, but she wasn't sure what she herself made of Rutherford yet. She needed to think it out. 'What are you doing?'

'I'm still in the office,' he said. 'I drove Lenny Thomas back to Red Row after taking the statements in the Coquet Hotel.'

'And?' Vera thought Joe was a soft-hearted sod, but she liked him the better for it.

'Nothing. He seems like a nice guy. Genuine. The interviews didn't take us much further forward, though Winterton was interesting on Miranda Barton. Wondered if she'd lost a child. Maybe a daughter. No evidence, but something she let slip.'

'That's something we can check.' Vera had no patience for speculation. Unless she was the one doing the speculating.

'And that's why I'm still here, when the wife's

272

desperate to get us home. No record that she ever gave birth to a daughter. Her only child is Alexander. Winterton must have got it wrong.'

'I need to talk to Joanna,' Vera said. She'd had enough of Joe's flights of fancy. 'And I can't do that on my own.'

'I don't suppose it would wait till morning . . .'

'Aye, why not?' She could tell that her immediate agreement had surprised him and she found herself grinning. She wasn't going to let on that she was rather dreading the interview with Joanna, that she wasn't yet sure what she was going to say. Let him believe that she had his family's welfare at heart. 'Work/life balance. Wasn't there a memo from the Chief about that a few months ago? More to do with saving the overtime budget than marriages, I thought, but you know me, pet. I always take these missives from on high to heart.'

She grinned again, enjoying the shocked silence at the other end of the line, and replaced the receiver.

⋆ ⋆ ⋆

She was still eating breakfast when she heard Joe's car outside. Another clear, frosty day. A bit of mist over the lough in the valley, but that would soon burn away. She got up to let him in and saw that Jack's van wasn't in the yard. It was market day in Alnwick, so he'd have left early. She hoped Joanna hadn't gone with him.

She pushed the teapot in Joe's direction and

273

got up to fetch him a mug.

'You'll have had breakfast.' Not a question. His wife looked after him, however early the start.

'I wouldn't mind a bit of toast, if there's one going.'

'Tough, there's no bread.' Not quite true, but she couldn't be arsed to make it. Now Joe was here, she wanted to get on.

'Rutherford claimed Joanna was blackmailing him,' she said.

He set his mug down slowly. 'Did you believe him?'

'Yes,' she said. 'It's a bugger, but I did.'

'Does that change anything?' Joe's attention was caught by the view from the window and he seemed preoccupied. He lived in a modern semi on a quiet executive estate. Vera knew he regarded the open countryside with awe and something like suspicion. 'I can't see what it's got to do with our investigation,' he said. 'All the witnesses will have stuff going on in their private lives.'

'Of course they will,' Vera said. 'But they won't all be turning the stuff into stories and putting it out for the public to read.' Then she wondered if that was true. By all accounts, the piece Lenny Thomas had read on the evening of Miranda's death had been personal too. 'Anyway,' she went on, getting to her feet, feeling again the strain in her knees, 'why don't we go and ask her?'

They found Joanna hanging out washing.

'That'll be frozen stiff in half an hour,' Vera said by way of a greeting.

Joanna only laughed and said she was fed up with having it all over the kitchen. 'I like to get the air into it.'

'Do you fancy a bit of a walk?'

Joanna looked at Joe. 'What's this, Vee? Do you need a bodyguard these days? Are you frightened I'll slash your throat too?'

'Eh, pet, you know how it is. I can't talk to you on my own.'

They walked down the track a way, then along the edge of a newly ploughed field. The soil was hard, but Vera could see that Joe was worried about the state of his shoes. She was glad to be outside: this case had made her feel claustrophobic from the start. It was being shut in the Writers' House for days on end. Like being remanded in custody. A hawthorn hedge marked the field edge and there were redwings and fieldfares feeding on the berries. She followed Joanna and Ashworth in single file until they came to a gate and a wide track through woodland. Then Vera joined Joanna and started her questions.

'You didn't tell me you'd been in touch with your ex-husband recently.' The tone was conversational, but she saw that Joanna had picked up the steel beneath it. 'In fact you told me you were frightened Rickard might tell him where you were.'

'You've spoken to Paul,' she said. 'Of course I should have realized you might.' She slowed her pace and turned to Vera. 'We all get taken in by you.'

'I didn't make the contact,' Vera said. 'That

was your ex-husband. I think he came all the way to Newcastle especially to tell me what you'd been up to.' The ground under the trees was dry and there was a smell of pine. 'Cocky bastard, isn't he?'

'Is he? It's so long since I've seen him that I really can't remember any more. Perhaps he's just a creature of my imagination.' Joanna scuffed her feet through the pine needles. The sun formed a series of spotlights, catching her face as she walked through the trees.

'Oh no, trust me, he's real enough,' Vera said. She was aware of Joe, walking a few paces behind them, making himself unobtrusive as only he could. 'But those stories you told me. About him hitting you. Locking you up. Were *they* real? I'm not quite sure any more.'

'You know what, Vee?' The words were angry and Vera saw that the woman was close to tears. 'Neither am I. Perhaps I'm a liar and a fantasist. Perhaps you can't believe a word I say. All those pills they make me take, it's hardly any wonder I don't know what happened all those years ago.'

They came to an area of clear fell, a pile of tree trunks waiting to be hauled away. Vera sat on one and patted the log beside her for Joanna to join her.

'Why did you need the money?' Vera asked, her voice gentle, almost maternal. 'I can get my head round all the rest, but not that. Not the blackmail.'

Joanna shook her head, a gesture to indicate that there was no point trying to explain: Vera wouldn't understand.

'Is it gambling? Drugs?'

'No! What do you think we are? Jack and I have the most tedious existence possible. I've become a housewife like my mother. Except I don't have the staff to do the boring stuff. And I love it. Really, I love it.'

'So why did you need the money?' This time the question was firmer.

Joanna shook her head again. 'It was a mistake, talking to Paul. Crazy. I did it that time when I stopped taking my meds and I wasn't thinking clearly. And I wasn't lying about Giles Rickard — I didn't speak to him, because I was scared Paul might find me. I made sure Paul wouldn't be able to trace me from my phone call. It didn't seem like blackmail to me. It was more like asking for what I was owed. When we divorced he gave me nothing. But I shouldn't have got in touch with him again. I should have realized it would lead to trouble.'

She pushed herself off from the tree trunk and began to run off, back towards the farm, her long plait bouncing behind her. She was too fit for Vera to follow, and Joe stayed where he was too. They saw her flickering figure through the trees, the movement seeming jerky because of their interrupted vision, like an old silent movie playing out before them.

★   ★   ★

Vera had set back the morning briefing to accommodate her meeting with Joanna, but now she wondered what had been gained by it. Had

277

she achieved anything at all? Suspicion of the woman ate away at her like a worm in her gut and made her feel sick. Had Joanna deceived Jack? Was she a manipulative liar, untrustworthy? Had she made a fool of Vera, as Paul Rutherford had suggested? That would be unforgivable. Deep down, though, Vera still thought of Joanna as a good woman.

Vera tried to set these questions aside as she came before the team. They'd be tired and anxious because so little had been accomplished. This was the point in an investigation when desperation led to mistakes and jumping to conclusions.

'Well then.' She beamed at them. An encouraging teacher, showing her students that she knew they wouldn't let her down. 'What have you got for me? Holly?'

'I've done as you suggested and phoned round the major literary agents and publishers to find out if they'd been approached recently by Miranda Barton. Or by Tony Ferdinand on her behalf.' Holly had a sheet of paper in front of her. Vera could see a list of names, a neat tick by each one. Organized and efficient, that was Holly.

'And?'

'Nothing. And they say they'd have remembered if Ferdinand had been in touch.' She paused. 'But according to the people I spoke to, it's not unusual for authors who haven't been published recently to use a pseudonym. Apparently editors are more willing to take a chance on a new writer than someone who's been knocking around for a while.'

Vera thought that was much the same in most professions. Easier to pin your hopes on the bright young things than cynical has-beens. 'So?' she demanded again.

'Nina Backworth collected Miranda's script after the reading session and gave it to Joe,' Holly said. 'I faxed it to the list of contacts to see if anyone recognized it, in case it had been submitted under a different name.'

'Well done!' Occasionally her team needed encouragement as well as a boot up the backside. 'Any joy?'

'Not yet. But they promised to get back to me.'

'Chivvy them if you haven't heard by the end of today.' It would be a boring and time-consuming task for some editorial assistant and Vera doubted if it would come top of anyone's to-do list. 'Anything else?'

'I managed to track down a couple of Alex Barton's teachers, as you asked. One from school and one from the catering course at Newcastle College.'

'And?'

'He was never in any bother, but they both described him as a strange lad. At school he was withdrawn. Not many friends. Not a high-flyer academically, though he always showed . . . ' she looked at her notes ' . . . an interest and aptitude in English literature. It was at college that he seemed to come into his own. He was always the top of the group. A brilliant chef, apparently. Meticulous. Occasionally given to an outburst of temper if things didn't go according to plan, but happy enough if he felt he was in control. His tutor was pleased when he went to work with his mother. He thought Alex might not stand the stress of a restaurant kitchen, where there's always pressure of time and unexpected demands. 'Not a great one for teamwork.' That was how the tutor described him.'

Vera nodded. She wondered how Alex would manage now he was on his own. She looked up at Holly. 'These outbursts of temper, were they ever violent?'

'The tutor never said.'

'Get back to him and find out.'

'I did wonder . . . '

'Aye?' Vera made sure her voice wasn't too encouraging. She didn't always like folk thinking for themselves.

'We've always assumed that both murders were committed by people staying in the Writers' House, but that's not necessarily the case, is it? Jack Devanney managed to find his way into the place on the night of the dinner. Ferdinand was murdered in the middle of the afternoon when the doors weren't locked. And Barton was outside when she was stabbed. I'm not saying that they *weren't* killed by a resident, but that perhaps we shouldn't make that assumption.'

'Quite right, pet.' Vera narrowed her eyes. 'And we shouldn't be afraid to teach our grandmothers to suck eggs, either.'

Holly flushed and Vera thought she'd been hard on the girl. She'd never liked being told how to do her job. Especially when the person doing the telling had a point. 'No, really,' she said, 'it's a good point, and one that Joe made earlier. Maybe we've focused too much on the residents.' She looked around the room, spreading blame. 'I suppose we've checked all the CCTV in the area.'

'There's not much.' Joe shot a small triumphant glance in Holly's direction, glad that he'd been there before her. 'One petrol station on the road towards Seahouses. I've checked registration details. Nothing belonging to anyone related to the case.'

'Charlie. What have you been up to?'

'I was over in Carlisle yesterday evening. Doing a bit of research on Winterton. In my own time.'

Vera threw up her hands in mock horror. 'He has a night in the pub and he wants a medal! I hope you didn't drive back last night, Charlie. You know what I think of drunk driving.'

'I stayed at my mate's.' Charlie was sulking. 'On a bloody uncomfortable sofa.'

'What did you come up with?'

'Winterton's ex-wife's just got divorced for a second time and has taken up with a toy boy. A solicitor half her age. He practises criminal law, so the team all know him.'

'Winterton'll be a bit of a laughing stock among his former colleagues again then,' Vera said. 'He's a respectable citizen, a bit of a God-botherer, and his former wife's making a spectacle of herself. I bet they all love that.'

Charlie shrugged. 'I think they just feel sorry for the poor bastard.'

281

'Did you come up with anything else during your wild night out with the sheep-shaggers?' Vera knew it was irrational, but she'd never really thought much of Cumbria. Hillsides grazed to buggery by too many sheep, arty tea rooms and too many trippers. Give her the east side of the Pennines any day.

Charlie shook his head.

Vera was just about to give her 'boost the morale of the troops' speech, to send them out to do great things, when there was a knock at the door. It was a small constable with a Lancastrian accent so broad that Vera had to struggle to understand her.

'Ma'am.'

'What!'

The woman continued bravely, 'There's been a call, Ma'am. About Nina Backworth. The locals have been in, but it sounds as if it could be important.'

29

Nina had expected to feel more at ease once she returned home. More comfortable. Here, she'd thought, it should be possible to distance herself from the nightmare of the Writers' House. But as soon as she unlocked the door of her flat and picked up the post from the floor, she saw that a change of place would do nothing to calm her. If anything she was more restless and tense. The flat, which she'd bought with a legacy left to her by her grandparents, was usually a refuge from the petty irritations of university life. It was on the first floor of an end Victorian terrace. The rooms had high ceilings and looked out over a cemetery: a green space in the middle of the city. From first seeing it, she'd loved the view over trees and the old grey gravestones. She liked watching the elderly women laying flowers. Now the flat seemed rather lonely. She switched on the radio and the inane lunchtime phone-in that usually drove her to distraction at least provided some background conversation.

She'd stopped at the supermarket on her way home and emptied the bag into the fridge and the larder. Sitting with a sandwich and a glass of juice, she switched on her laptop to check her emails. There'd been no Wi-Fi at the Writers' House. A deliberate decision, Miranda had said. She didn't want her students distracted. There was nothing exciting to read: a load of spam and a couple of student assignments. Lenny Thomas had already sent his novel to her as an email attachment. The only message of any interest was from her editor Chrissie, suggesting that they should arrange a meeting to discuss marketing of the new book.

On impulse Nina got out her phone and rang the woman. 'I don't suppose you're free this afternoon. I'm back at the university tomorrow and it might be tricky then to get away.'

'Ooh, yes, do come over. As soon as you like. I've got a pile of admin, but nothing that won't wait.'

Nina could hear the woman's excitement. It was nothing to do with the novel, Nina thought. It was murder. It brought out the voyeur in everyone.

She'd liked Chrissie as soon as she'd met her at the interview for the MA. There was nothing pretentious about her, despite the classy degree and the obvious intelligence. She had a passion for books that was basic and visceral. A hunger for reading. Not for writing, though. She completed her MA, but wasn't tempted to do further research. 'There are enough bad writers out there,' she'd said to Nina when she'd pitched the idea of forming her own publishing house. 'The world doesn't need another one. I'd rather spend my time and my energy promoting the good ones. Like you.'

The formation of North Farm Press had started a partnership that had worked well for them both. Nina felt cherished, and that gave her the confidence to experiment in her work. Chrissie had begun to make a name for herself. And even a little money.

Chrissie came out of the office to greet Nina as soon as she came into the yard.

'What a nightmare!' she said. 'You must have been terrified. I would have been: in that creepy house with a killer on the loose.'

But Nina thought that Chrissie wouldn't have been terrified at all. She was the sort of Englishwoman who was scared of nothing. You could imagine her as an indomitable missionary making her way across Africa with only stout boots, a Bible and an umbrella to protect her.

And as if she was reading Nina's thoughts Chrissie said, 'I do feel a bit cheated, though. Driving away from the place just as the excitement was about to start . . . '

'It's hard to believe that it really happened,' Nina said. 'It seems now like a bit of theatre. Something from a Revenge Tragedy. Webster. All that blood.'

'Brilliant timing, though!' Chrissie couldn't keep her exuberance in check. 'With the new book out, I mean. I've sorted out a few interviews with the national press. And Radio Newcastle, of course.' She must have realized she sounded callous and frowned. 'That is all right? I don't think Miranda would have minded. She could be pushy enough when she wanted.'

Nina, following Chrissie into the office, didn't answer directly. She sat on the small red sofa that stood against one wall.

'Did Miranda ever approach you about

285

publishing *her*. The police asked me if she was still writing. It's only just occurred to me that you might know that better than me.'

'No,' Chrissie said absent-mindedly. She was scrabbling through the papers on her desk looking for the list of interviews she'd arranged for Nina. 'Shame, really. She'd be selling like hot cakes now.'

They talked for a while about publicity. 'There's a woman from *The Times* in Scotland. They won't read it in London, I'm afraid, but it'll be on their website for the world to read. Seems lovely, and she's prepared to come down from Edinburgh. And how do you fancy a piece on *Woman's Hour?*'

Nina thought that a month ago she'd have gone out to buy champagne to celebrate all this attention. Now it seemed as if she was profiting from two people's deaths. 'I suppose they all want to talk about the murders in the Writers' House?'

'Of course they do, darling!' Sometimes Chrissie affected an arty voice just for show. 'But can you blame them? You were talking about crime fiction, and suddenly two people die in dramatic and horrible circumstances. It's too delicious for words.' She was perched on her desk and leaned forward. 'You will do it, won't you, Nina? It's not as if you actually liked either of them as individuals, is it? And really this could be the breakthrough you need. It's just a pity we're not promoting a crime novel.'

'I started writing a crime short story,' Nina said. 'While I was there . . .'

286

'Did you? Is it finished?'

'It's not ready to show. And it's only a short piece.'

'But still, one of the more intelligent women's magazines might take it. In fact I know just the person to talk to.' Chrissie was already flicking through her address book looking for a phone number. Nina thought she'd never seen her so excited.

'A couple of the other students were very impressive,' she said, hoping to create a distraction. She wasn't sure she wanted Chrissie selling her story to a magazine. The writing was good, but surely it was too close to reality to turn into entertainment. Certainly she didn't want to hear the publisher make the pitch. 'You might want to look at their work before they're approached by one of the larger publishers.'

That stopped Chrissie in her tracks. 'Tell me about them.'

'One's called Joanna Tobin. She and her partner run a smallholding in the wilds. Hers is a sort of woman-in-jeopardy story. The other is a guy called Lenny Thomas. He used to work on the open-cast until his back gave up. He spent six months in prison, so he knows what he's talking about.'

And that was when Chrissie came up with her idea for a collection of the work from the course, but somehow making it sound as if the brainwave had been Nina's. 'Of course! I see just how it would work. A sampler to show the sort of writing you were doing.' And a few seconds later she dropped the bombshell that she'd been

287

thinking of finding a way to keep the Writers' House going.

'Inspector Stanhope will never wear it,' Nina said.

'I'll ask her, of course.' Chrissie looked at her watch. 'In fact I'll ask her very soon. She'll be here in a quarter of an hour. She phoned up and made an appointment. Though I'm not sure how she thinks I can help her. I wasn't even there.'

Nina thought the last thing she needed was to bump into Inspector Stanhope again so soon. If it had been the sergeant, she might have hung around. She still hadn't thanked him for allowing her to leave the Writers' House that morning, and she would have been glad to see him. She said goodbye to Chrissie and drove away.

★   ★   ★

That night she persuaded a friend to go out for dinner with her. He worked at the university and harboured, Nina knew, hopes that one day they might be more than friends. She found him sweet, but ineffectual, and despised herself for using him when she was desperate for a companion. They had a pleasant Italian meal together, in a small restaurant not far from her flat. He was sympathetic about her ordeal and allowed her to talk about it all evening. They shared a bottle of wine.

Afterwards he offered to walk her home, but he'd taken her hand over the table and told her to phone him at any time, that he was always there for her, so she knew there would be an awkwardness on her doorstep when he fumbled to kiss her. She even thought she might feel so lonely that she'd invite him inside and sleep with him. That would lead to horrible complications. So she squeezed his hands and thanked him and said she'd be fine. It was only half a mile, after all.

'You do understand, don't you, Ian, why I need to be alone tonight?'

He nodded gravely and said that of course he did. Though that was ludicrous, because if he'd been anyone else, being alone would have been the last thing she'd have wanted.

She left him outside the restaurant and walked off briskly, suspecting that he'd be watching her at least until she reached the corner. It was freezing again and her breath came in white clouds. She put her hands in her coat pockets. It was only eight o'clock, but the cold seemed to have kept people indoors. Away from the main street the roads were empty. All the curtains were closed. She thought she heard footsteps behind her. Ian perhaps, risking her displeasure by playing the gentleman after all. But when she looked, nobody was there.

She walked so quickly then, almost running for the last hundred yards, that when she got inside she felt suddenly very warm. The heating had come on while she was out. She locked her door, glad that she lived on the first floor. There was no danger of an intruder climbing in through the window.

I never used to think like that. I never used to worry. Is that what violent death does to the people left behind? It makes us victims too, of our own anxiety.

She ran a bath and lay there, running over her meeting with Chrissie. How robust she seemed! If she'd been at the Writers' House over the past week, would she be imagining footsteps in the dark? Nina thought probably not. She wondered if Chrissie would take on Joanna and Lenny as North Farm writers and what she, Nina, would make of it if that happened. In one sense they'd become her competition. She thought suddenly that she never wanted to see either of them again. Lenny had already sent her his whole novel as an email attachment: *I know it's a cheek, but would you mind having a look and telling me what you think?* She hadn't opened the attachment or sent a reply. She wished them both well as writers, but she didn't want anything to remind her of the past week.

When she went to bed she switched on the radio beside it. It took her a long time to fall asleep and she listened to the BBC World Service talking about floods in Pakistan, a riot in the streets in Rio, an earthquake in Mexico. Other tragedies that made the ones close to home less enormous. But still important to her because she'd met the people involved. She'd known their names. And she'd disliked them.

She woke suddenly and still the radio was murmuring in her ear. She knew it was the middle of the night, reached out and switched it off. Silence. Then footsteps in the living room next door. *I'm imagining it.* She remembered waking suddenly in the Writer's House and the images of blood and death that had terrified her then. *That was nothing, and so is this. I'm being ridiculous. It was all a bad dream.*

It had always been impossible to move quietly about her flat. The floorboards creaked. The front door jammed and had to be slammed shut. It occurred to her now that the banging front door must have woken her. *If I lie still, they'll take what they want and go away.* But the footsteps moved out of the living room and towards her bedroom. She found herself screaming. Then, mingling with her screams, came the sound of a siren, a police car or an ambulance racing down the street outside. The footsteps pounded down the stairs, the front door slammed shut and there was silence again.

Nina climbed out of bed and pulled on her dressing gown. Had a neighbour seen the break-in and called the police? She ran into the living room and looked out of the window. But the street was quiet. The arrival of the emergency vehicle had been coincidental. Luck. And there was no sign of the intruder. Further down the street there was the sound of an engine starting.

She tried to breathe more calmly. Perhaps, after all, the incident had been a nightmare, the result of the violence she'd experienced second-hand. She'd make herself some camomile tea and try to sleep. She switched on the light to make sure that there was no sign of a break-in. The room was tidy. It seemed that nothing had been moved or taken. But on the middle of the table sat a crystal bowl full of ripe apricots.

30

Vera sent Joe Ashworth to deal with the incident at Nina Backworth's flat. The rest of them had been excited by the news of the break-in. The investigation had achieved so little that they were glad of anything that might move it on.

'Too much of a coincidence surely, Ma'am, if it isn't related to the Writers' House case.' Holly, bright-eyed, was ready to leave immediately.

But Vera seemed preoccupied with some project of her own. Joe thought she'd had an idea during the team briefing, had made some connection or seen something they'd missed. Occasionally she had these sudden flashes of inspiration; usually they came to nothing, but sometimes they were important and developed the case in an interesting way. Now she flapped her hands to send him on his way.

'Use your judgement. You'll know if it's just a coincidence — some yob trying his luck — or if it's related to our investigation. Probably nothing. The CSIs have already been in. Holly, you start chivvying the publishers. I need to know what Miranda was up to. That's our priority at the moment.'

Joe went, secretly pleased to have an excuse to see Nina again, but offended too that Vera hadn't decided to confide in him. Usually she was happy enough to share her daft ideas. When he arrived in Newcastle he sat for a moment outside the house where Nina lived. By now it was lunchtime and girls from a private school at the end of the road were walking along the pavement, giggling and scuffing the fallen leaves with their feet. He waited until they'd passed, then he got out of the car and rang the bell.

He thought Nina must be dressed for work. She seemed to him very smart.

'This is such a nuisance.' Her voice was peevish. 'I've already had to cancel my class at the university, and I'm supposed to be doing a radio interview this afternoon.'

'It won't take long.'

Suddenly she put her head in her hands. 'Oh God, I'm sorry. It's not your fault and it was good of you to come. I'm scared. Absolutely bloody terrified. Waking up in the middle of the night to find someone in the flat. I thought I was going to die like the others.'

'Of course you're scared.'

She led him into a large living room with a deep bay window. All the furniture was old. One wall was covered in books. There was a table under the window, where long blue velvet curtains reached almost to the floor. And on the floor a grey carpet.

'It looks very tidy,' he said. 'You've not moved anything?'

'Don't you believe me?' She turned on him and he saw how close she was to hysteria.

'Of course I believe you. Has anything been taken?'

She shook her head. 'Not that I can tell.'

He thought she would know if anything was

missing. This was an ordered place. She was an organized woman.

'They did bring something, though.' She pointed to a glass bowl, containing small fruit. They were so perfect that if it hadn't been for the smell, he'd have thought they weren't real, that they were wood or china, painted. 'They were there, left by the intruder. He *meant* to leave them. That's why he came in here first. He was on his way to the bedroom when the siren frightened him off.'

'Apricots, are they?' He wondered if she was losing her mind. She'd been so tense when he'd last seen her, so strung out, that he wouldn't have been so surprised.

'Yes.'

'Why would a burglar bring you apricots? You must have bought them before you went away and forgotten all about them.' He kept his voice gentle. 'You can tell by the smell that they're very ripe. They could have been here a week.'

'I didn't buy them,' she said. She was frowning and a little angry, but he thought that she was quite sane after all.

'There's no sign of a break-in.' He took a seat on a scratched leather chair.

'No, and I don't get that, either. It's like he's some ghost who can walk through walls.'

'More likely someone who's got hold of a key,' Ashworth said. 'Did you have a spare? Have you ever given one to a friend?' He was thinking that the fruit could be a message. From a lover, maybe. Or a drunken student thinking it would be funny to scare his teacher. This might have

294

nothing to do with the Writers' House investigation after all.

'No, I've never given a key away. I've always lived here alone.'

'But you'll have a spare? Could you check it for me, please?'

'My neighbour has one in case of emergencies. But Dennis has been here as long as I have. He wouldn't play this kind of stunt.'

Dennis was a small, tidy man in his sixties. He'd worked as an engineer in the shipyards, moved into the garden flat below Nina when his wife had died. Nina filled in the background information as they went downstairs. They found him sweeping leaves in the yard at the front of his flat. Nina told him about the break-in and asked about the key.

'It's hanging up in the kitchen where it always is, pet.' He seemed affronted, as if Nina had accused him of committing burglary. 'See for yourself.' He led them through an arched gate at the side of the house and in through the open kitchen door. Over the sink there was a row of hooks, each neatly labelled. The one marked *Nina* was empty.

★ ★ ★

'Not a ghost then,' Ashworth said. They were back in Nina's flat and she'd made coffee and a sandwich. It was a poor sort of joke, but he wanted to make her more cheerful. He wasn't sure how he'd cope if she started to cry. 'I'll wait until the locksmith comes before I leave.'

'But why go to all that bother?' Now she was furious and he thought it was only the anger that was holding her together. 'Wait until Dennis was in the back garden and slip into the flat and steal the key. And how would the intruder know he'd have my key in the first place?'

'Did you tell anyone that Dennis kept the key? A friend?'

She shook her head.

'A good guess then,' Ashworth said. But he was thinking that they were dealing with someone intelligent. Or an experienced burglar. Someone had planned this carefully, reccied both flats in advance. And, like Nina, he was wondering why anyone would go to all the bother. 'You're sure nothing was taken?'

'Absolutely certain.' She looked up from her coffee. You do realize I was a target, like Tony Ferdinand and Miranda? If he hadn't been scared off by the siren, he'd have killed me like the others.'

Ashworth didn't answer. He sensed her growing paranoia and couldn't think what to say that wouldn't feed it. 'Were there apricots in any of the stories written during the course?' he asked at last.

'I see what you mean.' She gave him a quick nod of appreciation. 'You think the intruder was copying a scene from a piece of fiction, in the same way that the murder on the terrace was stolen from my work. But no, I don't remember anything like that. Of course I didn't see everything the students wrote. Though when I first saw the apricots they reminded me of something I'd read, it was nothing recent.'

'Where will I find that written material?'

'Lenny sent me his novel as an email. I can show you that now, if you want. And I've already given you the few paragraphs that Miranda read at the party.'

Joe nodded. 'No soft fruit there,' he said. He was pleased to see her give a small smile. 'And I'll ask Lenny to let me have a copy of his book.' He looked at her. 'Is there anywhere you could stay for a while? A friend who might put you up?'

'You think it's not safe here? Even with new locks?'

Again he tried to keep his tone light. 'I'd worry about you.' Not really a joke, but she tried another smile.

He thought she'd dismiss the idea out of hand, but she considered. 'I'll ask Chrissie, my publisher. She has lots of room.' She picked up her phone, but didn't dial immediately. 'I think someone was following me last night,' she said. 'How do I know they won't follow me to North Farm?'

'I checked the street before I came in,' he said. 'There was nobody there.'

★ ★ ★

He stood in the road and waved her off. Now the children in the posh school were spilling out of the gates at the end of the day. A couple of small boys were playing conkers, swinging the nuts hard on long shoelaces. A few parents waited in smart vehicles to collect their children, but none of the cars pulled off when Nina did. Joe drove fast, back to the police station.

Holly was on her own in the office, eyes fixed on the computer monitor. She looked up when she heard Ashworth come in. 'Was Nina all right?'

He shrugged. 'Shit scared, but putting on a brave face.'

'What was it? A run-of-the-mill burglary.'

'No,' he said. 'Anything but that.' He thought the place seemed very quiet. 'Where's the boss?' He still couldn't bring himself to call her Vera, found it difficult even when they were on their own in the pub or she was bending his ear at her house.

'She spoke to Alex Barton on the phone and then disappeared up the coast. She didn't tell me where exactly, or why. You know what she can be like. A drama queen. She said she'd see everyone for the briefing tomorrow.'

Joe always felt disloyal complaining about the inspector behind her back. 'And Charlie?'

'God knows.' She stretched and rubbed the back of her neck.

He nodded towards the screen. 'What are you up to?'

'I'm trying to trace Miranda's publisher. The books are out of print and they're not on Amazon. Nobody recognized that piece she read at the Writers' House. There's no support for Vera's theory that she'd been writing again.'

'Except the piece that she read.'

'Mmm,' Holly said. 'That could be years old.'

'The boss has got one of the books in there.'

He nodded through to Vera's office. 'I saw a copy on her desk. *Cruel Women*, it was called. I thought it was appropriate.'

Holly was still grinning when he came back with the novel. 'I think she pinched it from Miranda's cottage. The publisher should be listed on the title page.' He opened the book. '*Rutherford*. Not much use to you, if you're trying to find out if Miranda has been trying to sell a new book. Giles Rickard told the boss that Rutherford Press got taken over by a multinational years ago.' He turned to Holly to check that she was listening. She hated being told what to do. 'Though I suppose some of the same staff might still be there. Worth a punt.'

He closed the book and slipped it into his jacket pocket. He wondered if this was another coincidence. Rutherford, who ran the company that published Miranda's novels, had been Joanna Tobin's father-in-law. He wondered too if Vera had known the name of the publisher all the time, and had been waiting to see how long it would take Holly to track it down. *Nah*, he thought. *Not even Vera would be that petty.*

'Where are you off to with that book?' He should have realized Holly was so sharp she'd notice what he was up to.

'I'm going to read it,' he said. 'See if there's anything in it about apricots.'

31

Further north the weather changed suddenly; the sun disappeared and there was a mountain of cloud to the east. A brisk northerly breeze blew against the Land Rover and found its way through the gaps in the windows. Winter had come early. Vera hadn't warned Giles Rickard that she was coming, but he didn't seem surprised to see her when she knocked at his door. His holiday cottage was in Craster and looked out over the harbour. There was a narrow front garden, everything brown and salt-blown. The first splashes of rain.

'My Dad used to come here every winter,' she said, looking down at the exposed sand. 'To get Mediterranean gull for the year. There's one that turns up in the autumn, regular as clockwork.'

He didn't respond.

'You're not a birdwatcher then? Aye, well, it's not much of a hobby and I expect your writing has taken up most of your time. They're bonny birds, mind, Med gulls. Get someone to point it out to you if you get a chance.' She followed him into the house.

The cottage was small and unpretentious. The front door led straight into a living room with a wood-burning stove, a table under the window and a couple of armchairs. She looked round, making a show of it. 'No computer?'

'I don't write any more, Inspector. I've retired.'

'How does that work then? You just wake up one day and decide you're not going to tell any more stories.'

'Yes,' he said. 'That's exactly how it happens.'

'What do you do here all day?' She was genuinely interested. She and Rickard had a lot in common. No family. Few friends, it seemed. She might learn something from him that would help her come to terms with her own retirement.

'I read,' he said. 'I think. I remember.'

'Aye, well, it's your memory I'm interested in.'

'I really don't think I can help you further, Inspector. I've told you everything I know.' His voice was firm. 'I bought this place so that I'd be undisturbed. In London there are always people who expect me to be pleased to talk to them: journalists, students. I'd thought that would end when I stopped writing, but it seems not to have been the case. This is where I escape from unwanted conversation.'

'Indulge me,' she said. 'I've come a long way.' She sat in one of the armchairs, wedged herself in, making it clear she was there for the long haul.

He looked at her and decided that further argument was futile. He opened the door of the stove and pushed in a log. 'Can I offer you a drink, Inspector?'

'Eh, pet, I thought you'd never ask. Whisky with a dash of water. Unless you've got a single malt, and then I'll take it neat. Just a small one. I'll be driving.'

He poured whisky for them both. No water. She saw that his hand was still and didn't tremble. His movements seemed stronger than they had in the Writers' House. Perhaps he felt happier on home territory. He pulled a small table between them and set the drinks on it, then took the other armchair. It came to Vera that anyone looking in from the outside would see them as a couple. Happily married for decades, sharing a drink before dinner in front of the stove. For a moment she imagined herself into the fiction. What would it have been like? To have this domestic ritual? This comfortable silence? Boring, she decided. It would be bloody boring.

'I spoke to Alex Barton earlier,' she said.

'How is he?' They could have been discussing a mutual friend. A neighbour perhaps. Nobody too close or dear to them.

'I don't know. He seems a strange young man to me. I'm not sure if that's because his mother has just died or if he was always like that. I don't like the thought of him in that place on his own. But he claims he's fine. He's an adult. I can't force him to find some company, and I can't see him being happy away from the house. Seems to me he only ever leaves it to go to the shops.' She turned slightly in her chair so that she was looking at Rickard. Before pouring the drinks he'd switched on a wall light. Now he stared at the wood-burner and his face was in shadow.

'Some of us function better on our own,' he said.

'You never fancied marriage?'

'No.' He paused and seemed entirely lost in

302

thought. She might not have been there. Then he jerked back to the present and realized more was expected. 'There was somebody I was very fond of at one time,' he said. 'It never worked out. Now I'm accustomed to being on my own.' A gust of wind rattled the sash window. He got slowly to his feet and drew the curtains.

'Alex told me you turned down their offer to tutor at the Writers' House at first. You changed your mind at the last minute.'

'An old man's prerogative. But we've discussed this already, Inspector. I was intrigued when I saw that Joanna Tobin would be one of the students.'

'So it had nothing to do with Paul Rutherford?'

He turned to face her. 'What are you saying, Inspector? We're both too old for games. What do you really want to know?'

'Joanna tried a bit of blackmail,' Vera said. 'At least your friend Rutherford called it blackmail. She said she was making a claim on what she was owed. I'm still not sure what that was about. Did he ask you to have a word with her? Scare her off maybe.'

For a moment Rickard didn't answer. He sat facing the stove, his chin on his chest. *Good God*, she thought. *Perhaps he's dead. He's had a stroke or a heart attack. What do I do now?* 'Mr Rickard?'

He turned slowly to face her. She thought his face was like a tortoise's. Impassive and grey. He gave nothing away.

'What are you suggesting? That I scared

303

Joanna away by killing two strangers?' His voice dry, laced with sarcasm.

'I'm not suggesting anything! I'm asking if you went to the Writers' House because Rutherford asked you to. I need to clear the decks here and work out what's really important. There's too much stuff getting in the way.'

He was staring into the stove again and she thought he might refuse to answer, but after a moment he started speaking.

'Yes, I came to the Writers' House because Paul asked me to. Joanna had contacted him at work and demanded money. He said she was crazy again. He was worried about what might come out, if she decided to go to the press with an election only months away. *You're up in Northumberland anyway. It'll only be for a few days. See what's happening. What's rattling her cage after all this time.*'

'What I don't understand,' Vera said, 'is why you agreed. You've retired. You hate meeting readers, all the marketing bollocks. Don't you? You've just said that's why you bought this place.'

He nodded his tortoise head. 'As you say, I hate the bollocks.'

'So why didn't you tell Rutherford to deal with his own shit?' Vera wondered why she felt the need to be crude. It wasn't like her. She could swear like a trooper in her own home, but was professional enough when it came to work. Did she hope the coarse language would shake Rickard from his slow and solid resistance to her questions?

He paused for a beat and then he started talking. He didn't look at her and the words came with difficulty. She saw he had never told anyone this before and he wanted to be precise, to describe the situation accurately. Vera kept her mouth shut and listened.

'Paul Rutherford is the closest thing to a son I ever had.' He shut his eyes for a moment and then opened them. 'I loved his father. Not as a friend. Or at least as a friend, but as much, much more than that too. He was my passion. Do you understand what I'm saying, Inspector?'

Vera nodded slowly. No comment needed.

'I think Roy realized, but he never said anything. I never made a move on him. I wouldn't have known where to start. It wasn't uncommon at school: crushes on other boys, on the younger teachers. But as an adult I was lost, out of my depth. It was considered beyond the pale then, of course, but that wasn't what prevented me . . . ' He hesitated and put the following words in conceptual quotation marks ' . . . exploring my sexuality. I was a coward and I didn't want to stand out. And sexual experimentation was never really what it was about, despite my fantasies. Though I had fantasies that would have made your hair curl, and which certainly shocked me. It was about Roy. I wanted to be with him. To serve him. There was never anyone else. Physical contact has never been so important to me. I was happy to make do with the occasional touch: an arm around the shoulder, a handshake.' He looked at her. She noticed that his glass was empty. 'I'm sure you think I'm foolish. He married after all. He had a son.'

'I think you're fortunate to have found someone you were able to love.'

He looked at her sharply. 'Did that never happen to you?'

There was a moment's silence. 'We're not talking about me,' she said at last. 'I think you should value what you had.'

'Yes, I suppose that I should. But now Roy's dead, and all I have left of him is Paul. I see his father sometimes in Paul's expression, the way he stands. Like an indulgent parent, I can deny Paul nothing. As I've said, I'm a foolish old man.'

'Does he know how you felt about his father?' Vera asked.

'No! I don't think so.' Rickard was shocked. 'Do you think he guessed?'

'Younger people are more sexually aware than old ones. And he seems to have been prepared to exploit your affection for his father.' She swirled the remainder of her whisky in her glass. It was unlike her to have made it last so long. She thought this had been a peculiar encounter. She'd even been tempted to make a confession of her own. 'Just be careful what he's dragging you into, eh?'

'Joanna had told Paul that she'd won the bursary for the Writers' House. Paul asked me to go there and report back on her state of mind, Inspector.' The acerbic and witty tone returned. 'He didn't ask me to commit two murders.'

'Did you know that Rutherford published

306

Miranda Barton?' Holly had texted Vera with that information; the message had been on her phone when she got out of the Land Rover at Craster.

'Everyone's entitled to make mistakes.' Rickard pulled himself to his feet and took the bottle of whisky out of the sideboard. He offered it to Vera, but she shook her head. He poured a splash into his own glass. 'Even Roy.'

'Was it a mistake?' Vera asked. 'To publish Miranda?'

'She was never a great writer. Not dreadful, and the market was less demanding in those days. But Roy had founded his business to champion traditional story-telling and she was never particularly good at that.'

'Was Roy susceptible to her female charms, do you think? Is that why he decided to publish her?' Vera tried to imagine how that had worked. Had Ferdinand become involved even at that stage? Had he approached Roy Rutherford on Miranda's behalf? *There are too many connections in this case*, she thought now. The Writers' House had sucked them all in together and created too many suspects with a shared history.

'When it came to publishing, he wasn't susceptible to charms of any gender.' Rickard gave a little smile. 'He was extremely hard-headed. He must have believed that her books would sell. And he was right for a while. For a year, after Tony Ferdinand's article in *The Observer*, she became almost a celebrity.'

'As you are now,' Vera said.

307

'Ah, she was much more famous than me. And she enjoyed it.'

Vera got to her feet so that they were both standing, facing each other. Outside the wind was even stronger and blew around the chimney. There was a loose slate on the roof.

'Do you know what happened at the Writers' House last week?'

He looked at her sharply. 'If I knew, Inspector, don't you think I would tell you?'

She didn't answer that, but pulled her jacket around her and headed out into the storm.

32

In the Land Rover Vera saw that she had missed calls from Joe. She called him back.

'Where are you?' he asked immediately. As if she were a teenage girl out on the town without permission. Vera thought his daughter would have a tough time when she was old enough to think for herself.

'I came to visit Rickard,' she said. 'I'll tell you about it later.' *Maybe.* She wasn't sure she wanted Rickard's sexuality the subject of canteen comment. She imagined Charlie sniggering and couldn't stand the idea.

'The break-in at Nina Backworth's wasn't a coincidence.'

Vera listened as he explained about the fruit in the glass bowl, the fact that nothing had been stolen.

'The CSIs haven't found anything?'

'All clean,' he said. 'No fingerprints on the bowl or the table.'

'And nothing stolen?' She couldn't see how this could be relevant, how it could relate to the Writers' House killings.

'Nina claims not.'

So it's Nina now, is it? Is this our Joe with ideas above his station?

The tide had come in since she'd arrived in Craster and, with the wind behind it, the waves were breaking against the harbour wall. The

Land Rover was suddenly covered in spray.

'Nina couldn't have set it up herself?' she asked suddenly. 'She'd know about the key in the neighbour's flat. And the whole scene sounds like something she'd write. A good way to mislead us, if she were involved with the murders.'

'No!' He sounded horrified. 'She's scared. Scared enough to go and stay with that publisher at North Farm for the night.'

When she switched off the phone Vera sat for a moment. She could go home. Light a fire and watch a few hours of bad television to unwind. There was nothing cosier than Hector's house with the wind and the rain outside. She could stick some washing in the machine and have a couple of drinks to help her sleep. Rickard's malt had given her the taste for it.

But she didn't take the road inland towards the hills and home. She turned down the coast towards the Writers' House. In the lane leading to it the path was covered with small branches, already snapped by the wind. At one point she had to drive on the verge to negotiate the debris. There were no lights in the main building, but two of the windows in the cottage — one downstairs and one up — were lit. The curtains hadn't been drawn, but she saw no silhouette. And there was a light in the chapel. Alex Barton was still rattling around this enormous space on his own. She thought if he hadn't been mad to start with, he certainly would be now.

When she got out of the vehicle the wind caught her and she almost lost her balance. Even from this distance the sound of waves on the shore was deafening. There was something exhilarating about being part of the noise and the gale. She ran towards the cottage and knocked on the door. No answer. She pushed it open. The kitchen was as she had remembered it. The rocking chair by the Aga, the small table with its oilcloth cover. No fat tabby cat, though. And no clothes airing. Alex had kept the place tidier than Miranda had done, but there was a dirty plate, some cutlery and a frying pan on the draining board and that seemed out of character. There was no sign of Alex. She opened the door to the stairs and shouted up. He might not have heard the Land Rover over the noise of the wind.

When there was no reply she climbed the stairs. His place was as clean and impersonal as a room in a hotel. The bed was made. His computer was still switched on and had reverted to standby, a screen-saver showing a mixing bowl and floating wooden spoons. Vera pressed a button and Alex's Facebook page appeared. The photo showed him in his chef's whites. A list of messages expressed condolence. Vera supposed there was no way of telling whether these were real friends or people he'd met through the Internet. Virtual friends. She'd never been on Facebook before, though she'd caught Holly on it once at work. On Alex's wall, written two days earlier, was the post: *The wicked witch is dead.* Had he really disliked his mother, or was this his way of dealing with his grief? A young man playing at being cool? Vera still wasn't sure.

Outside the wind was as strong as it had been

before. Still no sign of Alex, but she saw his car was parked outside the cottage. He couldn't be far away on a night like this. From the top of the bank Vera had seen a light in the chapel and she made her way there. It was possible, she supposed, that the violence in the house had persuaded Alex to turn to religion. She'd always thought it would be comforting to have faith, had tried it in her youth because Hector had despised it, but had never found it possible to believe. Rationality had been the one perspective on which she and her father agreed.

She pulled open the heavy door, remembered Alex bringing her here the morning following Tony Ferdinand's death to set it up as an interview room. Inside there was one light, suspended from the high ceiling on a long chain. As she opened the door the wind caught it and made it swing, scattering the light over the dark wood chairs, throwing moving shadows. Vera tried to remember that she was a rational woman. Still she couldn't see Alex. She called his name and her voice echoed around the space.

There was an object lying on the stone floor in front of the table at the end of the nave. Not Alex. Too small for a grown man. And besides, it glittered, reflecting the swinging light. She walked towards it. The sound of her feet on the flags sounded very loud.

She knelt to look at the object on the floor, and felt suddenly sick. Like some new PC, she thought, called to her first corpse. *Pull yourself together, Vera. This is a crime scene and you don't want to throw up all over it. You'd never live it down.* It was Miranda's tabby cat. As a way of focusing away from her nausea, Vera tried to remember its name. Ophelia. A stupid name. Why call a cat after a mad lass in a play? The animal looked fat and ridiculous, lying on its back. A kitchen knife had been stuck in its belly. Part of the blade was exposed and that was reflecting in the hanging light. There wasn't much blood, but the guts were spilling out.

She stood up and saw another corpse on the white table, this time tiny. A robin. No blood. She remembered the bird feeders outside the drawing-room window of the big house, and Alex filling them with nuts and seed. Had he been attracting the birds, just to kill them? Or was stabbing the cat a kind of retribution because it had caught the robin? Mad, either way.

The chapel door banged and she stood up.

'What are you doing?' Not her voice. The voice of Alex Barton standing at the back of the nave. He looked wild and windswept. No coat. A thick jersey and baggy jeans. Baseball boots on his feet. He stood, blocking her exit from the building.

'We'll go back to the cottage, shall we?' Vera said. 'I could murder a cup of tea.' She thought she could make a phone call from there. Get the mental-health team out. He probably just needed a few nights in a psychiatric unit to sort him out. Unless he turned out to be a murderer. And now, alone with him, she didn't want to think that way.

'Didn't you see the cat?' he demanded. He almost ran up the aisle towards her. 'Did you see what happened?'

'Did you do that?' She tried to keep the judgement out of her voice. She'd never liked cats much anyway. 'Tell me about it.'

'No!' He almost spat out the word in his frustration, his determination to make her understand. 'Of course it wasn't me. Somebody was in here. I heard them outside.' When she didn't answer he continued, 'Look at that bird! That has nothing to do with me. You know how I felt about them. And I hated the cat, but it reminded me of my mother. I needed to have it around. I wouldn't even have given it away to a good home!'

Vera saw that he was quite overwrought, on the edge of tears. She thought a couple of nights in hospital wouldn't do him any harm anyway. She'd persuade a sympathetic medic at the Wansbeck Hospital to admit him later. But not until she'd had a few words with him. 'Let's get out of here,' she said. 'I'll deal with all this in a little while. Let's get you home.'

★ ★ ★

In the cottage he curled up in the rocking chair like a baby. It was hard to remember him as the confident young man in charge of the kitchen in the big house. She found milk in the fridge and heated it up on the Aga, made mugs of hot chocolate for them both. 'They say you need tea for shock, but chocolate always cheers me up.'

314

Wittering as usual. Outside it was still windy, but she thought the worst of the storm had passed. She felt awkward in front of his grief. A real woman — a woman who'd had kids — would know how to deal with him.

She sat on a hard kitchen chair and leaned towards him.

'Are you up to talking me through what happened here tonight?'

He nodded. Big eyes over the rim of the mug. He looked like a boy who'd woken from a nightmare, still confused and unsure what was real.

'You made yourself something to eat,' she said.

He nodded again. 'An omelette. Fried potatoes. Broccoli.'

'Then you went up to your room to use the computer.'

He didn't seem surprised or upset that she could guess his movements. 'I was just going to check my Facebook. I knew I wouldn't be long. I thought I could do the washing up afterwards.'

'What happened then?' She kept her voice gentle. She didn't want to scare him or stop the flow of the story.

'I heard a noise outside.'

'A car?' How else would an intruder get here? She tried to remember if she'd passed a vehicle in the lane. Certainly there'd been nothing coming the other way up the track.

'No,' Alex said. 'Footsteps.'

'And you could hear those over the noise of the wind?'

'They were on the gravel path just under my

315

window. And we don't have double-glazing in the cottage.'

She nodded to show that she believed him and to encourage him to continue talking.

'But by the time I got up to look outside, there was nobody there. I thought I'd imagined it. It's easy to get spooked all by myself in this place.'

'Of course,' she said. 'Anybody would be. I shouldn't have let you stay here on your own.'

They sat for a minute in silence. She wiped the milk from around her mouth with the back of her hand.

'Where was the cat?' she asked. 'Was it in the kitchen while you were eating? Cats seem to know when there's food about, don't they?'

'She wanted to go out,' he said. 'I opened the door for her to go into the garden. She hated the bad weather and I thought she'd be scratching to come back in straight away, but she didn't. I went upstairs and thought I'd shout her in as soon as I came back down.'

'I'm sorry I interrupted you.' Vera sat back and waited for the rest of the story.

'I was still at the window,' he said. 'I'd looked out and there was nobody there. Then a light came on in the chapel.'

'My God! You must have been petrified!'

'I was going to bolt all the doors and call the police,' he said. 'That was the first plan.' She thought he was beginning to recover from the shock. He uncurled his legs, seemed almost embarrassed by his previous outburst. Sat upright. Set the half-drunk mug of chocolate on the table with something like disdain. Too cool for chocolate too.

'That would have been a sensible plan.'

'But I couldn't do it,' he said. 'I couldn't sit here. Some sitting duck. Helpless, waiting for the killer to come.'

Vera thought he'd seen too many horror movies. Or he could tell a good story.

He looked at her with something of the old competence. This was the man who had greeted her on her first visit to the Writers' House. 'I had to *do* something.'

'So you went into the chapel?' she said.

'Outside the storm was so wild I could hardly think. It was brilliant actually. Liberating. It reminded me of when I was a boy and used to swim in the sea. Nothing but the noise of the surf. For a while I stopped being scared. After all, what did it matter?'

'So you went into the chapel?' she asked again. She preferred the quiet, scared Alex to the manic one.

'Yes.'

She thought she would have to prompt him, but he continued almost immediately. 'There was nobody there. The light was still on. Then I saw Ophelia.' He looked up at her and gave a quick smile. 'That was what we called the cat. Mother's idea.' He paused for a beat. 'I couldn't take it in. I couldn't believe anyone would do that. Like it was a sacrifice. And then there was the robin on the table.'

'What did you do then?' Vera had finished her drink. It was obvious that Alex didn't want his.

She wondered if he'd notice if she took it.

'I couldn't stay there. I went outside. Screaming. Something like: *Where are you? Come out!* I ran round the house to the terrace, in case he was there.'

'It was dark,' Vera said. 'How could you see?'

'I've lived here since I was nine. I could find my way round with my eyes closed. Literally.'

'And then?'

'I stood for a moment on the terrace. Letting the wind blow against me. Listening to the sea. I wondered . . .'

'What did you wonder?' She took his mug and finished the drink. Enjoyed it immensely. More than she had her own. Stolen pleasures.

He looked up at her again. 'I wondered what it would be like to run down the path to the shore and run into the sea and keep on running until I drowned.'

'Bloody cold,' she said. 'That's what it would be like.'

'I didn't do it.'

'No,' she said. 'You had more sense.'

'I came back round to the yard and I saw the door of the chapel closing.'

'That would have been me,' she said. Her voice comfortable. Ordinary. She thought he could do with more of the ordinary in his life.

'Yes, it was you.' He curled his legs under him again and sat there in silence. He didn't object when Vera told him she'd like him to spend a few days in hospital. 'Shock does weird things to us.' Perhaps he was relieved after all to have an excuse to leave the house. When the hospital car

318

came to collect him he was docile. He carried a small bag with a pair of pyjamas and a toothbrush inside it and reminded her of an obedient child.

33

Joe Ashworth couldn't get worked up over a dead cat. Or a dead bird. The inspector wanted him, immediately, to drive out there in the worst storm of the autumn, and for what? In these conditions it would be dangerous just getting to the end of the road.

He explained all this to Vera Stanhope, keeping his voice reasonable. There was never any point in losing his temper with her. She liked it when she provoked a reaction. In the end he came up with a lie, 'Anyway, I can't drive. I've had a couple of drinks.'

Even she couldn't order him out after that.

He wasn't sure what had kept him at home, because he would have enjoyed the drama of the drive through the windy night, being Vera's confidant and right at the heart of the case. That evening he would even have been glad of an excuse to get out of the house. The wind always made the children wild and the weather meant they'd been cooped up all day. Guilt, he thought. Nobody did guilt like good Catholics. Not that he had anything to feel guilty about, except a vague attraction to a female academic.

All the same he did his penance: cleared the dishes after supper, pulled apart the squabbling children, took on bathtime single-handed, read each of the bedtime stories. When they were alone at last, he sat with his wife on the sofa, his arm around her shoulders, cuddling together like teenagers. Thought there was nobody in the world he would feel so at ease with. He couldn't imagine Nina Backworth watching old episodes of *The Simpsons* and laughing with him at the same jokes. Later he took Sal to bed and they made love. Afterwards he lay awake, listening to her breathing, loving her with all his heart and soul and pushing away the feeling that there should be more to life than this.

In the morning he was first in the incident room for the briefing. Guilt again. Maybe he should have responded to Vera's call after all. Holly was there before the inspector too.

'Did the boss phone you last night?' he asked. He wouldn't have put it past Vera to drag Holly out, after he'd refused to go.

'No, why?'

'She was out at the Writers' House. Somebody had killed Miranda Barton's cat, laid it out in the chapel, like a sacrifice, she said.'

'Gross!' Holly wrinkled her nose, as if she were there in the chapel with the smell of damp stones and dead cat in her nostrils.

'Gross indeed.' And there was Vera, breezy and energetic, as if she'd had twelve hours' sleep, though she'd probably been up all night. Followed by Charlie, who looked as if he'd been up all night, though he'd probably fallen asleep in front of the television at nine o'clock and had been pretty well comatose until about half an hour before.

Vera stood in front of the whiteboard and pinned up a photo of the animal, a knife in its belly and the guts exposed. 'Now here's the big question: has young Alex gone loop the loop and killed the poor beast himself, or is someone trying to scare the shit out of him? And if it's the latter, why?' She took another blown-up photo from her canvas bag and stuck it on the board too. 'And if you've got a thing about cats, why kill a small, inoffensive bird too?'

'It's like someone's sending us a sort of message,' Holly said. 'The apricots, the dead animals.'

'And the hankie at the Miranda Barton scene,' Vera said. 'Don't forget the hankie!'

'But nothing left with Ferdinand's body in the glass room,' Joe said. 'Why was that different?'

'There was something left, though, wasn't there?' Joe thought he'd never seen Vera this hyper. She looked around at them and waved her arms. 'Come on, people! Think about it!'

'The knife,' he said slowly. 'We always thought the knife was left to throw us off the scent and implicate Joanna Tobin, but it could have been a sign or a message as well as that.'

'So what's going on here?' Vera demanded. 'And who's behind it? Let's have a few ideas. It doesn't matter how daft they sound.'

'Alex could have done it,' Joe said slowly. 'He has a car and had access to Nina's address through the Writers' House bookings. He's not stupid and could have worked out where her spare key would be. We don't know where he was the night before last. He could have been watching and waiting. He could have broken into her flat.'

'Why would he do that, though?' Holly asked. Joe thought she would have contradicted him whatever he'd said. Before he could think up a cogent reply, Charlie broke in: 'Because he's a loony, like the boss said. If he killed his own mother, why would he think twice about sticking a knife into a cat? Or having a thing about expensive fruit? He's a cook, isn't he, and it's food. Sort of related.' He paused. 'And if we're talking about crazies, does anyone know what Joanna Tobin was up to that night?'

'If you carry on talking like that, Charlie, I'll make sure you're sent on the next diversity-awareness course.'

Joe could tell that Charlie was about to make another flippant remark when he realized that Vera wasn't joking.

Another silence while she drummed her fingers on the desk and looked exasperated.

'Lenny Thomas has a conviction for burglary,' Holly said. Her voice was tentative. She remembered the inspector's earlier pronouncements about jumping to conclusions. 'He might have played the trick with the key.'

'Lenny doesn't have a car.' Joe felt an irrational need to defend the man. Just because he'd sat in his flat and drunk his tea? Because his elderly neighbour liked him?

'He has friends, though.' Holly's voice, bright and triumphant cut into Joe's thoughts. 'Friends who also have convictions for burglary.'

'Stop behaving like a bunch of bairns.' Vera could have been a long-suffering parent. 'We're all supposed to be on the same side here. If it comes to that, I dare say Winterton would know a thing or two about breaking into houses. We need to know where he was the night someone got into Nina's place. And Chrissie Kerr, though I'm damned if I can come up with a motive for her. She's on the periphery of the case too.' She looked at them. 'Good old-fashioned policing, eh? Let's ask some questions, check out the movements of our suspects. The boring stuff that leads to convictions.'

The boring stuff, Joe thought, *that you've spent all your career avoiding.*

'What about Jack Devanney?' he said, partly to spite her. 'He wasn't on our original list of suspects, but we're all agreed that he could have been at the Writers' House for the murders. Can we see him killing the cat and the bird, playing the stunt at Nina's place?'

'Oh, aye,' Vera said. 'I wouldn't put anything past our Jack if he thought he was protecting Joanna. And in his mind the objects cluttering up the crime scenes might be all about distracting us. He could be devious if he wanted.'

'So that leaves Rickard,' Joe said. 'The only one on the list that we've not discussed yet. Didn't you go to see him yesterday?'

'And he's the only one we can dismiss.' Vera wrote Rickard's name on the whiteboard and put a cross beside it. 'There's no way he could have driven from Craster and got to the Writers' House before me with enough time to set up the theatricals in the chapel. Even if he were fit, which he isn't. He can hardly walk.'

Joe was going to push the point, to ask what

Vera had discussed with Rickard. Why had she gone to see him anyway? But then she looked at him and he kept his mouth shut. He'd ask her later when they were on their own.

'Are you saying we can dismiss Rickard from the murders too?' Holly looked up from her notebook. Kept her voice bland so that she wouldn't incur Vera's wrath by getting it wrong.

'I don't see how he could have done the stabbing,' Vera said, 'with the arthritis in his hands. But maybe if he was angry enough or desperate enough — ' She broke off and looked at them. 'But that's speculation. So let's sort out the actions for the rest of the day. The greengrocers and the credit cards — any news on that, Joe?'

'Only negative. If anyone bought the apricots in Jesmond, they paid cash.'

'Of course,' Vera muttered almost to herself. 'They would. Our killer's too clever to be caught out like that. I don't think we're looking for what Charlie would call a loony. Not in the conventional sense, at least. So it's a question of driving round and asking who bought a big bag of apricots for cash. Flash a few photos around. Try the supermarkets too. Charlie, that sounds like one for you.'

Charlie nodded.

'Joe, you go out to Myers Farm and speak to Joanna and Jack.'

He looked up surprised. 'You want me to go on my own?' He thought Vera would want to be around too.

'It's all right,' she said. 'They don't bite.'

He thought he wasn't so sure, where Jack was concerned.

'And, Holly, get on the phone to Cumbria. Get them to check out Mark Winterton's movements over the last few days. If they're arsey, refer them to me. Or if you fancy a trip out west, go and do the legwork yourself.'

Charlie looked up sharply. 'I've got contacts out west.'

'I know you have,' Vera said. 'And that's why I've asked Holly to do it.' She smiled serenely in Joe's direction. 'We need to take care about apparent conflicts of interest.'

★ ★ ★

When Joe arrived, Jack was digging over part of the vegetable plot. The soil was wet and it must have been heavy going. A row of black sprout stalks had been flattened by the wind of the previous day. For a while Jack pretended that he hadn't noticed the detective's car on the track, though he must have seen it coming for miles. Then he looked up. Despite the raw weather he'd worked up a sweat.

'Your boss is out,' he said.

'It's you I've come to see. You and your Joanna.'

Jack weighed the spade in his hands, held it like a weapon. Then made an effort to keep his temper.

'You'd better come in then. She's writing.' He spoke the last word as if it were a strange and unnatural activity. At the house he sat on the

326

doorstep and began to pull off mud-caked boots. Joe saw that the man would insist on being present at any interview and thought this might be the only chance to talk to him alone.

'This must be a quiet time on the farm.'

Jack looked up at him, suspicious. 'It's not really a farm, like. More a smallholding. And there's always stuff to do.'

'You don't manage to get the odd day away then?'

'Look, I've been dealing with pigs like you since I were a scally lad in Liverpool.' He sounded tired. 'And I'm old. As old as the hills. Why don't you just ask what you want to know?'

'Someone broke into Nina Backworth's flat and then into the chapel at the Writers' House,' Joe said. 'The night before last, in Backworth's place in Jesmond, and late yesterday afternoon at the Writers' House. Where were you and Joanna?'

Jack looked up at him. He was still sitting with one boot on. 'Nina Backworth is helping Joanna get a publisher. They're putting together a book. A kind of collection of Writers' House work. Why would we do anything to get in the way of that?'

Joe wished he weren't towering above the man. He felt like a bully. 'I'm not accusing you,' he said. 'I just want to know where you were.'

'I was out yesterday afternoon,' Jack said. 'I went to the agricultural suppliers in Kimmerston. Layers' mash for the hens. I'm a regular and they'll remember me. The night before, Joanna and I were both at home.' He pulled off his second boot and led Joe inside. 'Come in and talk to Joanna. She's been at that computer since she woke up this morning. Maybe at least if she's talking to you, it'll be a break for her. I'm worried. She seems lost in it. Driven.'

And Joe realized that Jack must be worried, because he almost seemed glad to let the policeman into the house.

Joanna was sitting at the kitchen table working on a laptop. She was wearing big, round glasses that had slid down her nose. There were two mugs half full of coffee next to her; both were obviously long cold.

'Sergeant Ashworth has come to speak to us,' Jack Devanney said.

She glanced up, but Joe could tell she was miles away, caught up in her story.

'I'll make him some coffee, shall I?' Jack persisted.

'Yes.' But she frowned, looked at Joe. 'Will you be long?'

'Just a couple of questions.' He sat at the table beside her.

'I've got a deadline,' she said. Her voice was excited. He thought she sounded unwell. Had she stopped taking her pills again? 'Chrissie Kerr is bringing out a pamphlet of our work. A kind of sampler. To raise publicity for the Writers' House and its work. Only a thousand words each, but it has to be good. It's an opportunity to prove I can write. A showcase. I'm writing something new. A crime short story.'

'Alex Barton is in hospital,' Joe said.

At last she did drag her attention away from the screen. 'What's the matter with him?'

328

Joe made sure Jack was listening too. 'Someone stuck a knife in his mother's cat and laid it out like a sacrifice in the chapel, along with a dead robin. It freaked him out. I suppose it would.'

'And you think we would do something like that?' Jack was round the table squaring up to Joe.

'You wouldn't be squeamish about killing animals,' Joe said. 'It's something you do all the time.'

'That isn't like wringing the neck of a hen that's stopped laying.' Jack's face was so close to Joe's that he could see the hairs in Jack's nostrils, the gold cap on one tooth. 'That's sick!'

'Is Alex okay?' Joanna asked. Both men looked at her, distracted for a moment from their hostility. 'He's young and he's been through so much.'

'Sergeant Ashworth wants to know where we were late yesterday afternoon,' Jack said.

'Jack was out.' She smiled. 'His weekly trip to Kimmerston. The one day he gets an escape from me. Shopping for the farm and then supper in the Red Lion. Quiz night with his mates. The highlight of the week, eh, Jack? What exciting lives we lead!'

'And you?' Joe wasn't sure how he should address her. Ms Tobin? Joanna? In the end he left the question as it was and thought it sounded blunt, almost rude. 'Where were you yesterday?'

'I was here,' she said. 'Where else would I be? We only have one vehicle, Sergeant. Without that I'm stranded.'

Joe thought she'd escaped by taxi once before, but said nothing.

Before leaving the house he glanced over Joanna's shoulder at the computer screen and read the first paragraph. It was a description of a dead man lying on a beach. His face was covered in scratch marks. 'As if he had been attacked by a wolf.' Joanna's idea of an entertaining read.

34

Chrissie wouldn't hear of Nina going back to the flat in Jesmond.

'Really, you can't! Not with some nutter about. I wouldn't forgive myself if anything happened to you.'

So Nina allowed herself to be persuaded. And after a few days she found she was really enjoying her stay in the big house in the country. There was no cooking or shopping to do, and the Kerrs employed a cleaner, so there were none of the chores that distracted her from her writing at home. It was like staying in a friendly hotel. She was given a guest room on the second floor, had her own bathroom and even a little study in which to work. Chrissie's mother was a good cook; she studied recipes with the assiduous concentration of an academic. Her father was pleasant and mild-mannered. Nina felt almost that she was recreating the working atmosphere of her grandparents' house and imagined herself back during that summer when she'd produced her first book. The crime story was growing. She could see how it might become a novel. Different from anything she'd written before, but perhaps even better. The form of the mystery gave her the structure that had been lacking in earlier work.

At mealtimes the talk was about the collection of short pieces Chrissie aimed to put together to celebrate Miranda's work and establish her own claim on the Writers' House. From the beginning Nina saw that this was the prime motive for the book. Chrissie wanted to spread her empire, and for some reason the Writers' House was at the centre of her plans. She could talk of little else. It had become an obsession.

'That detective phoned,' Chrissie said.

They were eating dinner. Nina had been at the university all day. She'd been given a glass of wine as soon as she got through the door and now there was a lasagne on the table as good as any she'd tasted. Bread from an artisan bakery in Morpeth. Salad in a big glass bowl.

'That fat one, Inspector Stanhope. She wants us to fix a date for Miranda Barton's memorial celebration. It was her idea in the first place — a party to launch the book and remember all the good work Miranda did to encourage new writers. She said that Alex is okay with the idea. He's back at home, much better. I suggested a week on Friday and said I'd go to see poor Alex to discuss the details. What do you think?'

'Can you get the book out by then?' Nina had other objections, but thought Chrissie would only care about the practicalities. The work had by now turned from a modest pamphlet to a substantial anthology; Chrissie had approached former tutors and students for contributions, had been up for nights in a row proofreading. They'd chosen the jacket together. It was a black-and-white photo of the Writers' House in winter, the trees bare, the sea flat and grey.

'It went to the printer's today.' Chrissie poured red wine into her glass and lifted it in mock celebration. 'So what do you think? Friday week for the party?'

'Where will you hold it?' Nina thought it would be one of the usual places: the Sage, the cafe in the Baltic or the Lit & Phil.

'The Writers' House, of course.' Chrissie looked at her as if she were mad. 'Where else? I thought you'd understood that was my plan from the start.'

Until now Nina had been swept along by her friend's enthusiasm. She'd listened to Chrissie's ideas about the important people in the literary establishment and the media who should be invited, how the evening should be run. But now she set down her glass. 'You can't! It's a dreadful idea. Besides, the inspector would never allow it.'

'She already has.' Chrissie looked at Nina with amusement. 'Of course I asked her permission first. It has to be at the Writers' House. All this press coverage, we'll fill the place as soon as I send out the invitations. I've even had interest from *The Culture Show*. They're doing a special memorial programme on Tony Ferdinand.' Then: 'But we won't have readings. There's nothing more tedious than listening to new writers reading from their work. A couple of very short speeches will be quite enough. You'll speak, won't you, Nina? You'll tell them how important the Writers' House is to literature in the North-East?'

And Nina said yes because she felt she had no alternative. How could she refuse Chrissie when she was sitting in this house, enjoying her parents' hospitality; when Chrissie had been the person to save her from joining the ranks of the great unpublished?

But later, sitting in her room, plotting out the chapter she intended to write the next day, her unease about the whole event grew. Two people had died. The killer had not been brought to justice. Chrissie's excitement, her zest for business and for making sales seemed inappropriate. Besides, Nina thought she never wanted to set foot in the Writers' House again.

In the days that followed, as the date for the party approached, her anxiety about the event increased. She didn't want to see the players in the drama. Lenny and Giles Rickard, Joanna and Jack, Mark Winterton and Alex Barton, they belonged elsewhere. Now they lived not in Cumbria or Red Row or Craster, but in her imagination. They provided the cruel fuel that fired her story. She hadn't created characters exactly like the real people, but the sense of menace that she remembered from her time in the house, the odd friction — all that was feeding into her book.

All writers are parasites, she thought.

She was anxious that if she met the real people, the magic would die and the heart of her story would disappear.

But that's crazy. Are all writers mad too?

The next day she had a free morning. She should be writing her students' assessments, but the weather was beautiful, sunny and clear and she joined Chrissie as she took the family dog for a walk. This was a ritual and Chrissie's only exercise. She would take the animal on a circular trip along footpaths that crossed former North Farm land. It was hardly a mile, but Chrissie would return red-cheeked and out of breath as if she had run it. In fact it seemed she did walk very quickly, resenting perhaps the time away from her desk, and now Nina struggled to keep up with her.

'Do you think it's a good idea to launch the book and the appeal so quickly?' Nina said. Another attempt to stop the juggernaut that seemed to be rolling towards the inevitable party. 'Shouldn't we wait until the killer has been caught? It seems rather tasteless to go ahead now.'

Chrissie stopped in her tracks, bent to release the dog from her lead and watched her gallop away.

'Of course we must do it now!' she said. 'Absolutely.' She turned to face Nina and her eyes shone with excitement — almost, Nina thought, with a kind of madness. 'These days there's no reason why all the major players within publishing should be based in London. I'd have to pay a fortune to get this quality and quantity of publicity. To get noticed. I heard this morning that *The Bookseller* has agreed to do an article about North Farm. They're heading it 'Regional publishing: the saviour of the industry?' It's in your interest too, you know. You want to see your books in the high-street shops, don't you? You want to give up work at the university to write full-time?'

Nina had to agree that she did want both those things. As she marched in step with

Chrissie along the edge of the newly ploughed field, it occurred to her that she was being manipulated by her editor in much the same way as Tony Ferdinand had tried to manipulate her in the seminar group all those years ago. The difference, she told herself, was that Chrissie had Nina's best interests at heart.

★ ★ ★

One day not long afterwards, walking out of her office in the university, she met Joe Ashworth. She'd had a supervision session with a mature student, a middle-aged woman with fixed ideas who should never have been accepted onto the course. Nina was so cross and frustrated that she almost walked past the detective. He was in the corridor, staring at a student notice board. There were old posters about elections for NUS officials and new ones advertising end-of-term parties and performances. Soon the undergraduates would be leaving and the place would be quieter. He turned so that she saw his face, and she stopped in her tracks.

'Are you here to see me?' Then could have kicked herself. Why else would he be there? It made her sound ridiculous. 'Is there news? Do you know who broke into my flat? Have you caught the killer?'

'No,' he said. She thought he looked older than she remembered. Certainly more tired. 'Have you got time for a coffee?'

'Sure!' She was in no hurry to get back to North Farm. Chrissie had threatened to drag her to the supermarket to buy wine for the Writers' House party if she got back in time. And Chrissie, with her restless energy and constant enthusiasm for the project, was irritating her more each day.

Nina took him to a small coffee shop in a back street between the university and the hospital. It was dark, like walking into a Victorian parlour at dusk. The place was run by an elderly man. He baked great cakes and scones and the coffee was very good, but he had no sense of how to treat customers. Perhaps he had Asperger's syndrome, or some other condition that made him awkward in social situations. 'What do you want?' he would ask very brusquely as soon as anyone walked in. He hated waiting to take an order. He loved to read, and it was as if the customer had wandered into his home and disturbed him in the middle of his book. But, once served, the customer would be left alone, unbothered.

They sat by the window. Outside the street lights came on suddenly. Already the shops in the main street at the end of the alley had Christmas displays in the windows. Nina smelled the camomile tea as it was set before her, watched Ashworth drink his coffee as if he needed it to stay alive, then he spread butter on a warm cheese scone and took a bite. She wondered when he had last eaten.

'How can I help you?' Because Nina thought the man did want her help. He sat across the table from her looking tentative and anxious, the scone poised near his mouth.

'This do at the Writers' House . . . '

'Yes?'

'How's it going to work, like?'

'It'll be a party,' she said. 'Like a launch party, only for a group of authors instead of an individual. And the idea is to start a fund to keep Miranda's vision of the Writers' House alive.' Across the street she saw a mother holding the hand of a little girl. The girl was skipping, almost dancing along the pavement. Nina imagined what it would feel like to be holding the hand and thought that probably she'd never really know.

'Have you talked to Alex about the idea?' Ashworth had swallowed the scone and had almost finished his coffee. He stared at her.

'I haven't. I'm sure Chrissie has; she talked about going to see him the other day. It's her project.' Still Nina couldn't work out what the detective wanted from her. Had the fat woman sent him to get information? Was Alex having second thoughts about hosting the party? Nina wouldn't blame him if he was. Chrissie might dress it up as a memorial celebration, but it would be a party nevertheless. Had Alex complained to the police that he was being bounced into something he didn't care for?

Ashworth said nothing. He gazed out of the window and she saw that he was watching the mother and daughter too.

'Is there any news on the investigation?' she asked. The silence between them was becoming awkward. 'I suppose I should think about moving back to my flat. I can't hide out at North Farm for ever.'

He turned towards her sharply. 'Stay there for a little while longer. At least until after the event at the Writers' House.'

'Why until then?' she demanded. 'What difference would a book launch make?'

'Probably nothing.' He gave a strange little laugh. Nervousness? Or to cover the fact that he was lying to her? 'We just hope that we'll have a result by then.'

'You're close then?' He looked at her as if he didn't quite understand and she added, mimicking his words, 'To getting a result?'

He didn't answer and instead came back with a question of his own. 'Who will be there from the 'Short Cuts' course?'

'Everyone who's contributed to the anthology: Giles Rickard donated a special story; Mark Winterton has written a true crime piece; Lenny Thomas, Joanna Tobin, me. And Chrissie will be there of course, even though she hasn't written anything for the book. Is it important?'

'Probably not.'

But it seemed to Nina that it was the most important thing in the world to him at the moment.

'Why did you come to the university to find me?' The words seemed to be propelled by a blast of energy inside her mouth. They emerged sharp and staccato, like gunshots.

He seemed shocked by her bluntness. 'I wanted to check you were all right.'

'Did the inspector send you?'

'No!' he said. 'I suggested it.'

'But she knows you're here?' Nina thought he

was here to gain information after all. Why couldn't Vera Stanhope do her own dirty business? She was in touch with Chrissie. She stood up. It seemed to her that the exchange was going nowhere. 'I should be getting back to North Farm. I promised Chrissie I'd go shopping with her. Stuff for the memorial party.'

He got up and they stood for a moment side by side. The elderly cafe owner continued to read his book — oblivious, it seemed, to any tension, though Nina could feel it. Physically, like static electricity.

Ashworth put a hand on her arm. 'Take care,' he said. 'Yeah?' And he hurried off and was swallowed up by the Christmas shoppers. She stood for a moment, still unsure of the purpose of his visit. Had it all been about those last few words? Had he come into town just to warn her?

35

Joe Ashworth hurried through the busy streets and thought he should never have come into town. What had he hoped to achieve? He stopped for a moment outside Fenwick's department store, drawn by the crowds staring at the window. It was a Newcastle institution, Fenwick's Christmas window. He and Sal always brought the bairns in to see it and the trip marked the start of the festive season. This year it had a space theme: mechanical astronauts bouncing on the moon, whirling stars and a rocket that took off in one window and landed in another. Real sparks from the engine. Santa Claus and his reindeers all wearing space helmets. The kids would love it.

But he was only distracted for a moment and pushed on, past the grandmothers with wide-eyed toddlers strapped into buggies, the street pedlars, the working people who'd sloped off early to avoid the rush. Usually he liked being in town, but now he felt hemmed in. He'd spent too long with Vera and her need for the hills.

He'd paid the visit to Nina Backworth because Vera had asked him to: 'Just call in on your fancy friend in the university.' Her voice amused. 'Find out what she's up to. Or what her publisher's up to. It's one way of making things happen, this party on the coast. Like a chemical reaction. Shake the bottle and wait for the fizz.' Then she'd paused. 'I need to know that all the elements will be there. All the suspects. I don't want to contact the Kerr woman again. She already thinks I'm taking too much of an interest. But your Nina will know.'

She's not my Nina, he'd wanted to say, but he knew that would only provoke another caustic comment.

Instead he'd fought back the only way he knew, by turning Vera's own words against her. 'I thought we were going to sort this one with traditional detective work. Knocking on doors, talking to witnesses.'

'Aye, well.' She'd looked at him, frowning. 'That's getting us nowhere quickly, and you know me. Patience was never one of my virtues.'

So he'd phoned the university and found out that Ms Backworth had tutorials all day. And had driven in immediately, knowing he might bottle it if he gave himself time to think. He'd replayed his last encounter with Nina in his head since the group from the Writers' House had broken up. Lust that felt like adultery. How his colleagues would mock him if they knew! They took one-night stands and affairs in their stride, and he hadn't even touched the woman.

He reached the multi-storey car park and tried to decide how he felt about Nina Backworth now. There'd been the sudden thrill of attraction when she'd come out of her office in the university. So upright. Her body held straight by the tailored jacket, the narrow skirt, the black leather boots. And then what? Only an anxiety that he was making a fool of himself. She'd sat in the cafe, cool as ice, and he'd burbled questions that seemed to come from nowhere.

His phone rang as he reached his car. Vera, of course. Still impatient. Still not trusting him to carry out the simplest of instructions.

'Yes?' He stood, leaning against a concrete pillar, looking down at the city.

'Well,' she said, 'how did it go?'

'They'll all be there. Rickard, Winterton, Thomas, Joanna Tobin, Chrissie Kerr.'

'And your friend Nina?'

'Of course,' he said, though it was impossible to consider Nina a suspect. She'd been a victim. That's why she was camping out in a strange house, why she couldn't return to her own home.

'I'm going to the Writers' House tomorrow morning,' she said. 'I want to talk to Alex. And get a feel for the place again. If you fancy coming.'

'Sure.'

'What are your plans for the rest of the afternoon?'

'Why?' Joe could tell from her voice that she had plans for him. He didn't say that it felt like evening to him, not afternoon, and that his shift was nearly over.

'I want you to call in on Lenny Thomas,' she said. 'He's got no alibi for the dead cat or the break-in at Nina Backworth's place, and Holly said he seemed shifty when she talked to him. But you know Holly: she hasn't got the gentlest of interviewing techniques. She makes *me* feel shifty. I'd like a second opinion.'

Ashworth felt himself smiling. Above him a plane was approaching Newcastle airport to the west, dual landing lights flashing as regular as a lighthouse beam. He knew Vera was as fickle as any lover, but he liked it when he was in favour. Couldn't help himself.

'Sure,' he said again.

* * *

The flats in Red Row were quiet and most of the curtains were drawn. Climbing the stairs, he heard the occasional murmur of the television behind closed doors. A new headline on the national news to replace the Writers' House murders. There was still heavy press interest, though it was mostly local now. On one of the doors someone had hung a Christmas wreath. Joe thought it'd be dead and brown by the beginning of December, but coming closer he saw that the holly leaves were plastic. A sudden squawk of a baby reminded him of his wife and the kids at home. Then silence again.

Lenny answered as soon as Joe knocked. He was in the narrow corridor in the flat, wearing a coat.

'On your way out?' Joe said.

'Nah, I've just got in.' He stood for a moment, then his eyes slid away from Joe's face. Even Joe thought he looked shifty. 'What is it?'

'A couple of questions. You know how it is.'

'Not really.'

Lenny frowned, and Joe wondered what was bothering him. What was giving him the guilty

344

conscience? Maybe he'd found another woman and, despite the divorce from Helen, he considered that a betrayal. Helen had said he was romantic, a dreamer. *Like me?* Joe thought, and then: *For God's sake, man, you've got sex on the brain.*

'Shall we sit down?' Joe moved further into the flat and shut the door behind him. Still Lenny showed no sign of moving or taking off his coat.

'Aye, all right.' Lenny seemed to have lost his puppy-like energy and enthusiasm. 'It's cold in there, though. I've only just turned the heating on.'

'I could murder a cup of tea. That'll soon warm us through.'

The living room *was* cold. Lenny switched on the light and pulled the curtains shut. The place was tidy enough, but there was dust on the mantelpiece and biscuit crumbs on the carpet. Lenny saw Joe looking at the muck on the floor. 'Sorry.' For a moment he was himself again, apologetic and eager to please. 'I haven't done the hoovering this week.' Still wearing his coat, he went through to the kitchen and filled the kettle.

Joe remained standing. He considered what it must be like to live alone; he'd gone straight from his mam and dad's place to setting up home with Sal. Under the window there was a table, spread with a few sheets of printed paper and a glossy image of a house surrounded by bare trees. The angle was unfamiliar and it took the arty writing of the title — *Short Cuts from the Writers' House* — to make him recognize it.

345

He turned and saw Lenny watching him from the kitchen door.

'That's the page proofs,' he said. 'You get them from the publisher and check for mistakes. The picture will be on the cover.'

'You'll be at the launch party then?'

'I will.' Lenny hesitated. The kettle boiled and clicked off, but he took no notice. 'I wondered if I'd ask Helen. My ex. She never thought I'd make it, and here I am with my name on a book. But would she think I was showing off — putting her down, like. *I told you so. You were wrong all along.* I wouldn't want it to be like that.'

'I think she'd like you to ask her,' Joe said. 'She'd be proud. Really.'

'Maybe I'll risk it then,' Lenny said. 'Maybe I will.' And he disappeared to make the tea.

Later, a mug on his knee, Joe asked, 'What have you been up to lately?' Hearing his voice, he almost winced. It was patronizing and with that forced jollity that bachelor uncles and priests put on when they are talking to children.

Lenny was immediately suspicious. 'What am I supposed to have done?'

'Nothing!' But surely the man deserved an explanation. 'Someone killed Miranda's cat and laid it out in the Writers' House chapel. A sick joke maybe, and nothing to do with the murder, but we're asking everyone what they were doing that afternoon. And at the time someone broke into Nina Backworth's flat. You do understand. It might help us track down the killer.'

There was that frown again. 'I wouldn't do something like that. And I couldn't even get to the Writers' House. I don't have a car.'

'An officer came to see you before, to ask you where you were that day. You told her you couldn't remember.'

'That young lass,' Lenny said. 'Snotty cow. She wouldn't even sit down. Worried maybe that she'd catch something.'

'Where were you, Lenny?' Joe tried to keep his voice light. He liked the big man. 'You don't have such a hectic social life that you really don't remember.'

Lenny paused and for a moment Joe thought he was preparing an answer. But at the last minute the man shook his head. 'Sorry,' he said. 'When you're home all the time like me, one day seems just like another.' He stood up. 'But I wouldn't do that. I wouldn't upset Nina or Alex. They're good people.'

Joe realized that Lenny hadn't answered the question. Perhaps he couldn't bring himself to lie. But he knew fine well where he was, those days of the bizarre happenings. He just wasn't saying.

Joe found a card in his pocket. 'This is my mobile number. Give me a ring if anything comes back to you.' He could tell that forcing the issue now would just make Lenny more stubborn. Lenny left the card on the table where Joe had put it, but he nodded.

Outside, Joe thought the day was turning into a disaster. One failure after another. He'd wanted to bring Vera good news to justify her faith in him. At the car something made him turn back to look at the flats. He saw Lenny, holding the curtains a little apart, looking down at him.

He wants to tell me, Joe thought, *but he's scared. What could a big man like him be frightened of?*

⋆ ⋆ ⋆

When Joe got home the kids were ready for bed, but still up and waiting for him. Sal had put on a DVD for the big ones and she was sitting beside them, feeding the baby. They all looked up when he came in, but none of the children seemed excited to see him. They were drowsy after their baths and their attention was on the screen. A cartoon about giant insects. He was pleased to find the house calm, but oddly disappointed all the same.

'I ate with the kids,' Sal said. 'I wasn't sure what time you'd be home.'

Her voice was flat and he couldn't tell if she was apologising or if it was a complaint.

'No problem. I'll get something when they're in bed.' He scooped up the middle child, the boy, and put him on his knee. His thumb was in his mouth and he was almost asleep.

I need to spend more time with them. When the investigation's over . . . All evening — with the kids, and later eating scrambled eggs on a tray, with Sal sitting next to him — Joe felt that he was a peeping Tom, snooping on his own family. It was as if he was in the garden, peering in through the window. He wasn't part of it at all.

Sal went to bed early, but he said he'd stay up for a bit. He was all wired up and he'd only keep her awake too.

'You drink too much coffee.' Her only comment, but he could tell she was hurt. He heard her upstairs, her footsteps on the bedroom floor, the flush of the toilet. Every sound a reproach.

He'd been reading Miranda Barton's book *Cruel Women* and finding it heavy going. Too many words that he didn't understand. Not very much happening. It was about a single mother making her way in London. The first chapter described the woman giving birth and he thought she made a lot of fuss about something that Sal took in her stride. The rest of the novel followed her encounters with work colleagues and lovers. Even the sex scenes were boring.

It was eleven o'clock, but there was only one chapter left. Joe read on; he wanted to be sure Sal was fast asleep before he went up. In this scene Samantha, the businesswoman central character, had just been rejected by a lover. The book ended with Samantha slumped on the floor. The conclusion was ambiguous. Perhaps she'd committed suicide or perhaps she was just sleeping. To Joe, that felt like cheating.

But despite that, Joe reread the final chapter, making sure he didn't skip a word. Not because the story held his attention — he couldn't, for a moment, believe in Samantha or her desperation — but because the setting of the final scene was so familiar. The encounter took place in the home of a friend, in a conservatory. The

349

arrangement of the furniture and the plants, the colour of the new rug on the floor, the newspaper on the table, all these matched exactly the room in which Miranda had found Tony Ferdinand's body. And the position of Ferdinand's body, in a corner, had mirrored that of the fictional Samantha. Once again, it seemed, a scene from a story had been brought to life.

Joe's first impulse was to phone Vera Stanhope. Other detectives saw intricate complications in a case as distractions or put them down to coincidence. Vera was excited by them. She hated things to be too easy. Where was the challenge in that? Then he decided there was no rush. Let his boss have her beauty sleep. The notion of 'Vera' and 'beauty' in the same thought made him smile, and he was still smiling when he went upstairs. When he climbed into bed beside Sal and felt how warm and soft she was, he no longer felt like a stranger in his own house.

36

'Of course I knew the book was important,' Vera said. 'That's why I took it from Miranda's cottage.' She didn't care if Joe believed her or not. His description of the final chapter of *Cruel Women* was firing sparks in her brain. Confusing sparks. She'd thought she was groping towards a solution. Did this new information confirm her theory or would she have to think again? They were in Hector's Land Rover, breaking all the rules about officers using their own vehicles, but she had plans for later in the day and didn't want to be tied to a pool car.

She looked at Joe, expecting him to challenge her, but he let the comment go. He probably realized she'd have got round to reading Miranda's book in the end. She changed into four-wheel drive to go down a steep bank. In the night there'd been hail and the roads were still greasy.

'So that's why Miranda was so hysterical when she found the professor's body,' Vera said. 'It would have been like walking into one of her own books. Or into a nightmare.'

'Like Nina finding Miranda on the terrace and recognizing her own short story.'

Vera looked at him sharply. She couldn't work out what was going on between Joe and the Backworth woman. This was something else that confused her. A month ago she'd have bet her home on Joe Ashworth's fidelity. Now she wasn't so sure. And she'd never have thought he'd go for someone intellectual and skinny.

'Aye.' They'd reached the bottom of the hill and she changed gear again.

'Is that coincidence, do you think?' Joe said. 'The writers discovering the bodies? Or did the killer organize it that way?'

'Joanna could have found the first one.' Vera thought she shouldn't have had to remind Joe of that. He was losing his focus on the case. 'And she was meant to. All that business with the different knives and the note. Miranda came along later and screamed the house down. I don't think that was intended.' It wasn't grief that had caused the hysteria, Vera saw now, but shock because she recognized the scenario; she'd created it. And Miranda had recovered from that more quickly than anyone would have expected. It seemed she hadn't really cared for Tony Ferdinand at all.

'Why didn't she tell us that the scene came from her book?' Joe frowned and looked like a school kid doing difficult sums. 'That's been bothering me since I read that last chapter.'

'Perhaps she was worried that we'd see her as the killer.' Vera paused. 'And then she decided she could use the situation to her advantage. If she worked out who was playing games with her stories.'

'Blackmail?'

'It's always seemed likely as a motive for the second murder.' But Vera thought that wasn't the big question. The big question was, why had the killer created the fictional scenes in the first place? A warped sense of fun? Or was there a greater significance? And you could ask the same questions about the objects he'd left behind.

Now they'd reached the highest point of the road and there was a view of the coast and the house below them. The earlier storm had stripped the trees of leaves, so the outline of the building was clearer than Vera had remembered. It was strange being back here with the place almost empty. No CSIs, no students, theirs the only car in the visitors' car park. Alex had heard the Land Rover and came out of the cottage to meet them. He seemed calm enough, but slightly dazed. Vera thought he was probably still on tranquillizers. Or maybe it was losing a mother he'd never been close to.

'I've just had Chrissie Kerr on the phone,' Alex said, his voice distant and uninterested. 'She seems to ring about three times a day. This time it was about what time the caterers can get here on Friday. I don't understand why it's such a big deal for her.'

Oh, I do, Vera thought. *It's her big chance.*

'You're not doing the cooking yourself then?' Joe was concerned for the young man. He probably thought Vera was a callous cow to allow the party to take place here. Vera saw that he wasn't sure what they were doing here now. Why was it so important for them to visit the Writers' House? And she didn't know that she had an answer for him.

'Chrissie asked if I'd like to do the cooking,' Alex said. 'She told me that she'd pay the going rate. But I didn't think I could take it on. These days I wouldn't know where to start.'

'Are you sure you're up for the party?' Vera knew she was going through the motions even as she put the question. She was desperate for the event to take place. Like Chrissie, she saw this as *her* last chance. Her only opportunity to get this killer. How would she react if Alex said he wasn't sure, that the last thing he wanted was his home invaded by a bunch of strangers?

But Alex reacted exactly as she'd hoped: 'My mother would have loved it. All this fuss in her name. It's the least I can do. Then maybe I can move on.' The last phrase sounded trite and uncertain, as if it had been suggested by one of the doctors in the hospital.

'Show us round then, will you, pet? Show us where it's all going to take place.'

And Alex did as he was told, leading them through the grand rooms as if he were an estate agent and was showing around a prospective customer, as if he had no emotional tie to the Writers' House at all.

It was only as they were drinking coffee in the kitchen that they discussed his mother's book. Vera was aware of time passing. She had another place to be. 'Have you ever read your mother's novel?' she asked. 'The famous one that was adapted for telly?'

Alex seemed confused by the question. 'Years ago, when I was a teenager. At least I tried. I'm not sure I actually finished it.'

And Vera left it at that. She could sense that Joe wanted her to push the point. Why else were they there? They'd achieved nothing by trailing round the house after Alex. Joe even opened his mouth to ask more questions, but she hurried him out of the house. 'Come on, Joe, man. I've got a train to catch.' And she drove straight to the station at Alnmouth. They got there just as the London train was pulling in, so she left Joe to park her Land Rover and to arrange for a taxi to get himself back to the office. Looking out of the window as the train moved away from the station, she saw that he was still frowning.

★　★　★

London. She could find her way round well enough. If Hector had taught her anything it was to read a map. And the city didn't scare her. She knew you could get scary people anywhere. She just didn't like it much. She didn't like any city. Even a visit to Newcastle was a bit of a chore and she was glad when it was time for her to leave.

First stop was St Ursula's College. A mellow red-brick built around a north-London square. The horse-chestnut and plane trees had shed their leaves and the late-afternoon sun threw shadows of the branches onto the pavement. Vera had arranged to meet Sally Wheldon there and found the poet in a small office, sitting at her desk behind a pile of books. Vera had picked up a copy of her work from the independent bookshop in Kimmerston, had been surprised that she'd enjoyed it. Much of it concerned the domestic and was funny. One poem had moved her to tears. Sally was tiny, dark-haired and dark-eyed. From her voice, Vera had expected a larger woman and it took a few seconds to reconcile her imagined picture with the reality.

Vera had just introduced herself when a student knocked at the door. A young man with thick glasses and wild hair.

'I'm busy, Ollie,' Sally said. Her voice was amused and a little impatient. 'I'm sure it can wait until the tutorial.' He sighed and left the room, and she turned to Vera. 'Sorry about that. Some of them are so intense. Occasionally I'm tempted to tell them to get a life so that they'll have something real to write about.'

'You're keeping things going then? Without Tony Ferdinand?'

'We're just about managing.' A smile to show she was being sarky, but not malicious. Vera liked that in a woman. Sally went on, 'Shall we go for a walk in the square? That way we'll be sure we'll not be interrupted.'

They wandered across the road and found a bench to sit on.

'I've been asked to take it on,' Sally said. 'To run the creative-writing MA.'

'Will you do it?'

'I think I will. Just for a limited time. It saps the energy, working with students. They suck the life from you. But I'll consider it as a sabbatical, a time away from my own writing. I'd like to change the ethos of the course, make it gentler and more positive. It'll be worthwhile, I think, if I can pull it off.' She paused. 'And of course it'll raise my profile professionally.'

'What do you know about Tony Ferdinand's family?' Vera asked. 'Did he talk about them? We haven't been able to trace anyone.'

'He doesn't have one. He was an only child and his parents died ages ago. No wife.'

'No children?' Vera couldn't help herself.

'If he had, he never acknowledged them.' Sally gave a quick smile. 'I told you, when he was mugged that time I was his only visitor. Most of the writers and editors in London would recognize him, might even describe him as a friend, but there was nobody really that he was close to. Rather sad.'

'Where did the attack happen?' Vera didn't know where all this was going or how it could be important.

'Just about here. He was crossing the square on his way back to his flat. It wasn't particularly late, about eight o'clock at night, but the square is quiet in the evening once all the students have gone home. It was last February, foggy. He would have been very badly hurt, but one of our office staff came along and frightened the guy away.'

'It was definitely a man?'

'Must have been, mustn't it?' Sally looked at Vera strangely. 'How often do you get female muggers?'

'Yeah.' But Vera was lost in thought. 'Yeah, of course.' It was beginning to get cold and she pulled her coat around her. 'Did you know Miranda Barton? She worked in the library here before she became a full-time writer.'

'No, that was before I started.'

'An odd coincidence.' Vera could have been talking to herself. 'Both victims connected to St Ursula's.'

'But surely it must be a coincidence,' Sally said. 'It's years since Miranda worked here.'

'Aye.' But Vera wasn't convinced. 'There must have been talk about them, even when you started here. Tony and Miranda. Him turning her into a star overnight. Like a kind of fairy story. What was it with the two of them? And what held them together after all this time? What persuaded him north, to do her a favour by being a tutor in her house in the wilds?'

'I'm sorry, Inspector. I try not to listen to departmental gossip.'

'An affair, do you think?'

'Maybe, but Tony was never romantic, even with women he took to bed.'

A group of students, laughing and teasing, crossed the square in front of them. They seemed not to notice the two middle-aged women sitting on a bench.

'Did Miranda ever come back to St Ursula's?' Vera asked.

'Occasionally. Tony would take her out to lunch. He never invited her to the SCR or to any of the college dinners.'

'Like he was ashamed of her?'

'Perhaps.' Sally stood up. 'But really I'm not prepared to speculate. I didn't know enough about the pair of them to do so. Now I'm sorry, Inspector, but I have to go back to work. I've got a meeting this evening and I need to prepare.'

'Is there anyone in the college who might remember Miranda?' Vera got to her feet too. She felt that the encounter had been unsatisfactory. She'd arranged a meeting with an admin officer to look at college records, and that might prove more fruitful, but so far it had been a long train journey for so little.

'Jonathan Barnes, our senior librarian, has been there for years. You might talk to him.'

★ ★ ★

St Ursula's library was housed in a new building behind the college and hidden from the square. Barnes was a small, round man with a huge belly. He made coffee for Vera in his office and he, it seemed, had no qualms about passing on gossip.

'Of course I remember Miranda. She was rather glamorous at that time. All shiny make-up and big hair. We knew she had ambitions as a writer. The day she found a publisher she brought in champagne. She thought it would change her life. Unfortunately the book sank without trace.'

'Until Tony Ferdinand wrote an article about it.' Vera sipped her coffee.

'That's right! He must have seen something in the work that none of the rest of us recognized. He always had a knack of picking up on the mood of the reading public. It wasn't that he created best-sellers. More that he could tell which books readers would like, if they came to them. That's a little different, don't you think?'

Vera didn't answer. She had other things on her mind.

'Were Ferdinand and Miranda lovers?' she asked.

'Oh no,' he said. 'Really, I don't think so. She had a baby by then, and no way was Tony going to be saddled with a child.'

'Who was the baby's father?' Vera looked up at him. His face was round and, for an older man, it was remarkably smooth.

'Miranda would never say. It was her one big secret. She always implied that it was someone grand in the publishing world, but I never believed that.'

'Why not?'

'Oh, my dear, she would never have kept that to herself. I suspected the boy was the result of a rather sordid one-night stand and that was why she refused to speak of it.'

It was clear that Barnes would have been prepared to talk to her for hours, but Vera had an appointment with a woman in HR to keep, and a boring trawl through college records in the hope of finding another connection between Miranda, Ferdinand and any of the other suspects in the case. She drank the rest of her coffee and left.

★ ★ ★

Later Vera met up with a lad who'd worked with her until he'd got ambition and moved to the Met. They ended up in a pub behind King's Cross, so she wouldn't have far to go to get her train at the end of the night. They were drinking brown ale because the man was homesick and she wanted to keep him sweet. At the end of the evening she was a lot more sober than he was. One more bottle and he'd be singing 'The Blaydon Races' and applying for a transfer back north.

But the trip to London had provided her with the information she wanted. Hurtling through the night in the carriage with exhausted businessmen and a couple of pissed housewives who'd spent the day Christmas shopping for themselves, she thought she knew what had happened in the Writers' House. Now, she just had to prove it.

37

Nina Backworth took the Friday of the Writers' House party as a day off work. She was tempted to throw a sickie, but in the end she played it straight, went to her head of department and explained.

'Take a day's compassionate leave,' he'd said. He was old and tired and counting the days to retirement. He didn't have to play games with the management. 'You were there when the woman died, it's not unreasonable that you'd want to pay your respects at her memorial service.'

Memorial service made Nina think of a cold church and gloomy hymns. Chrissie's plans for the event were a million miles away from that. The farmhouse had been full of preparations for days. She'd had her mother and a couple of the other women from the WI making floral decorations, great glowing balls of dahlias and chrysanthemums, berries and coloured leaves — very similar, Nina thought, to the flowers that had been in the Writers' House on the evening of Miranda's death. The flower arrangements were already loaded in a van hired for the occasion. 'Alex wants a celebration for his mother,' Chrissie said. 'We have to respect that, don't we?'

Now, sitting in the kitchen at North Farm, Chrissie was as high as a child looking forward to a birthday party. She couldn't sit still. Nina found the excitement distasteful and wished the evening was over, wished she'd spoken up against it when she'd had the chance.

The present conversation was about clothes. 'What will you wear, Nina? Not black. Really, darling, I know it's your statement style, but please don't wear black tonight. It's so funereal.'

Nina thought funereal might be appropriate, but to her relief Chrissie broke off to answer her mobile phone and she was saved the need for an immediate answer. It was the producer of the local BBC news programme, confirming that he'd send out a reporter and a cameraman. As soon as the call was over, though, Chrissie persisted. 'What about that red frock? The one you wore to the launch of the novel. It makes you look stunning.'

'I can't wear that dress. I had it on the night Miranda died.'

'That makes it rather suitable then, doesn't it?'

'No!' Nina thought Chrissie must be mad, wondered if she'd already been drinking. 'No, really. We're not trying to re-create that night, are we? You're not hoping for another murder?'

'Of course not, darling! This is a party. A celebration.'

Nina thought it was time to move back to her flat in town. She wasn't made for communal living. This house in the country, with its shared meals and lack of privacy, was already starting to lose its attraction. She longed to be on her own. The possibility of an intruder suddenly seemed less threatening.

Chrissie had arranged for a big taxi to pick up the contributors to the anthology and to take them back at the end of the event. She would have liked them to stay over in the Writers' House, but Alex had refused to countenance that. He'd insisted that the party should start early in the evening, and that everyone should be away from the place by ten. As if, Chrissie said later to Nina, reporting back on the conversation, he was a sort of male Cinderella and would turn into a pumpkin at the strike of the clock at midnight.

Nina had decided she would take her own car. She felt the need of an escape route. She allowed the van driven by Chrissie's father, with Chrissie sitting beside him, to drive ahead of her, and was relieved when it disappeared from view and she felt at last that she was alone. She drove slowly, putting off the moment when she'd arrive and be drawn into discussions about canapés and the arrangement of chairs, when she'd have to fix a smile onto her lips and greet the other guests.

She drove down the bank to the house in the last of the sunshine. The house itself was already in shadow and for a moment she was tempted to turn the car round and drive away. Since finding the body on the terrace, the picture of Miranda's head — her throat slit across — had slipped into Nina's mind on occasions when she was least expecting it. Now the image returned and, terrified, she brought the car to a stop in the middle of the road. Only the caterers' van coming down the lane behind her, lights flashing and horn blaring, made her drive on. There was, after all, no turning back. Chrissie hurried out of the house to greet them. She was wearing a gold dress, knee-length, with a tight-fitting bodice and a wide skirt. Over it an apron, so that she looked like a perfect housewife from a 1950s film.

Nina forced herself to focus on the detail. She polished glasses and opened bottles, set copies of the anthology on tables in the entrance hall and drawing room, watched as Chrissie positioned the flowers to best effect. Chrissie was talking a lot, but the words washed over Nina and only occasionally did the woman demand a response. Alex Barton was there too, but distant, as if he'd handed the house and its contents over to Chrissie for the night, as if he was perfectly happy to be an observer. Once Nina looked over and caught his eye. He gave her a look that was at once conspiratorial and dismissive, as if to say, 'You and I both know how unimportant all this is.'

Soon it was almost dark and Nina felt able to draw the curtains across the drawing-room windows that looked out on the terrace. She'd been itching to do that since they'd arrived. Outside a stray piece of police crime-scene tape, one end trapped beneath the wrought-iron table, blew and twisted in the breeze, like a blue and white kite tail. She shivered slightly, pulled together the velvet drapes and told herself that the terrace could hold no fear for her now.

She'd expected a police presence. Vera Stanhope, big and unmovable, and Joe Ash-worth, and perhaps the sharp young woman who'd pretended to befriend her the night

Miranda was killed. But there was no sign of them. Perhaps Chrissie had made it clear that they wouldn't be welcome. The guests began to arrive, hurrying across the cold space from the car park to the house, holding their coats around them, everyone a little tense and brittle, excited to be in this place that had headed up the news for the last couple of weeks.

Many of the guests were acquaintances. Academics and poets, arts administrators and arts funders. Nina had met them on similar occasions, talked books and politics and publishers, usually standing, usually with a glass of white wine in her hand. Today, though, she was holding orange juice. All that kept her going was the knowledge that her little car was waiting outside and that she could escape whenever things became too heavy.

Today the talk was of Miranda, of the importance of keeping the Writers' House alive as a base for literary talent and encouragement. But Nina knew that few of them would have made the trek north from Newcastle if the place hadn't been made notorious by the murders. These calm men and women with their references to high fiction and classical theatre were inquisitive, as voyeuristic as readers of tabloid newspapers. Nina remembered Jack Devanney's outburst at their final dinner here and could understand what had led to his outrage. She felt like shouting too and creating a scene. *You don't care about Miranda Barton. You don't even care about keeping this place going, though you have a vested interest, of* course. *You'll come along as tutors and advisors, promote your own work and earn fees for the privilege. You just want to see where two murders took place.* But she didn't have Jack's courage. So she stood with her back to the wall, watching and smiling.

Chrissie was beginning to panic because the big taxi with the writers hadn't yet arrived. Mark Winterton was there; he'd driven from Cumbria and looked rather dashing, Nina thought, in a dark suit. He smiled at her across the room and was making his way to join her when the others burst in, with tales of a driver who'd completely lost his way, all of them laughing: the companionship of people who'd shared a minor drama. Chrissie was pouring wine for them and taking their coats, and suddenly the room seemed warmer and the atmosphere more natural. Perhaps, after all, the evening would go well.

Lenny was there with a woman. Girlfriend? Not a wife, surely, because he'd told her he was divorced. She seemed very small in comparison to him and Lenny was proud. Of her and himself. He took the woman to the table where the books were laid out, picked up a copy as if it were something precious and delicate, and opened it to the title page to show her. She smiled and took his hand.

All these stories, Nina thought, played out in front of me.

Joanna and Jack were in fine form, both flirting with the other guests, shaking hands, kissing cheeks, hugging. They were performing,

Nina thought. They'd prepared their script ahead of time and decided that all this physical contact was necessary to the role. But there was a watchfulness too, despite the good humour. Occasionally Joanna, taller than most of the men in the room, would look around her. Like an animal sniffing for danger. A meerkat in the desert.

For a while Nina thought that Giles Rickard had decided to stay away. What reason would he have to be there? He didn't need the publicity. He had fame and money enough, and during his stay at the Writers' House he hadn't formed a real attachment to any of the residents — those now dead or those still living. She didn't see him as a sentimental man who would feel that he should be there to support the rest. Yet here he was. He'd arrived in the taxi too, but perhaps he'd been to the cloakroom and avoided the mass arrival of the rest. Chrissie, flushed with the success of the evening so far, went up to greet him. She'd discarded the apron and looked beautiful. Nina was reminded of a fictional character and struggled to remember which one, and then it came to her: Samantha, the eponymous cruel woman in Miranda's novel. Nina had found her old copy at home and was in the process of reading it. Her tribute to the writer, who had died. She still thought it a bad book, but the visual description of the central character had stuck with her.

Now Chrissie was calling the event to order. She clapped her hands and the conversation died away. *Why was I so nervous about tonight?* Nina thought suddenly. She could have come in the taxi with the others, drunk wine, relaxed and laughed and shared memories of the dead. *Nothing terrible will happen here.*

Chrissie's speech was short and well judged: a perfect soundbite for the local television news. She praised Miranda's qualities as an author and as a mentor for new writers. 'We're selling this book in her memory, and to help maintain and continue the work that she started here.'

Chrissie had asked Nina to say a few words about Tony Ferdinand.

'We can't ignore him altogether, darling, and he was once your tutor, even if you didn't last the course.'

Nina couldn't bring herself to praise Ferdinand even after his death, but spoke briefly instead about the quality of the writers who had grown out of St Ursula's, the prizes they had won, the breadth of the talent. There was applause at the end of her speech. Gratitude that she'd kept it short, so the guests could return to the wine, rather than appreciation of its quality.

And soon afterwards things started to wind down. Books were sold. The reporters left. It was a long drive back to Newcastle and the weather was closing in. The caterers began collecting glasses. In the drawing room only the main players in the drama remained: the group who'd been present through the tragedy, and Lenny's ex-wife Helen. Alex reverted to type and brought out a tray with jugs of coffee. The party had finished earlier than they'd expected and there was half an hour before the taxi would arrive.

They sat rather awkwardly, unsure what to say to each other.

Mark Winterton made the first move. He said he had a long drive back to Cumbria, and he was sure they'd excuse him. Then there was a sudden flurry of activity. Jack and Joanna said they'd help in the kitchen, Lenny asked Alex if he might show his ex-wife something of the house. Nina thought that now she could decently go too and stood up to say goodbye. Chrissie, though, had other ideas.

'Alex says we can store the books in the chapel for now. Could you give me a hand to take them over?' Then classically, after issuing the request, Chrissie was distracted elsewhere and Nina was left to put the books into boxes, onto a trolley and out into the yard. The cold made her wheezy and turned her breath into a white fog. The chapel was unlocked, but dark. There was enough light from the big house to pull the trolley inside, but there she felt for a switch. Before she could find it, the door behind her swung shut and everything was black. She thought she heard a key turning in the lock and felt the first bubbles of panic. But perhaps her mind was playing tricks. Just a few yards away the house was full of people. Chrissie knew she was here. She let go of the trolley and moved along the wall, still trying to find the switch. Then came the footsteps, slow and deliberate. They were behind her, cutting off her route to the door. And a sudden bright light, as a torch shone directly into her face, so that she could see nothing. And, faint but distinctive, the smell of overripe apricots.

'Chrissie? Is that you?'

Because who else could it be? Who else knew she'd be in the chapel? Nina told herself she was being ridiculous, that she was overreacting. Her imagination was creating the plot of an overblown horror novel, all weird noises and unexpected smells. This was her friend and publisher, coming to help her with the books at last. Or playing some tasteless prank.

'Chrissie, shine the torch the other way, will you? You're blinding me.' She stumbled on.

But the footsteps got even closer and still Nina couldn't see.

The footsteps stopped and the light went out. After the brightness, the dark was thick and deep. Nina listened. Nothing. Outside the caterers must still be loading their van and laughing and shouting, but the walls of the chapel were too thick for her to hear. If she screamed, nobody would hear her, either. And she had the sense that whoever was standing beside her on the stone floor wanted her to scream. So she kept silent. A small act of defiance. A stab at courage.

The footsteps moved on, past her towards the table that took the place of an altar. She didn't move. Not courage this time, but the understanding that it would be useless. The turned key hadn't been a creation of her wild imagination after all. There was a click that in the silence sounded as loud as a gunshot. Then music, recognizable from the first bars. A favourite of her mother's, sung to Nina as a lullaby: 'Lucy in the Sky with Diamonds'. This time panic made Nina want to laugh. She felt a giggle rise inside her. If a student had presented a situation as melodramatic as this, for her consideration, she'd have covered the writing with red ink: *Tension should be created sparingly and with subtlety.*

The music stopped. There was another sound, of a match being struck. A flash of light so small and fleeting that all she could see was the hand holding the match and the wick of the candle towards which it was carried. Then a steadier beam as the candle was lit. This provided a narrow circle of illumination. A white cloth on the table. A glass bowl of apricots. A long, sharp knife. The impulse to laughter faded away.

'This is ridiculous.' She always had a tendency to be haughty when she was scared. 'How can you hope to get away with this?'

'You'd be surprised what one can get away with.' The killer's voice was matter-of-fact. Mad. 'And really, you know, it doesn't matter. I don't care about being caught. Not once you're dead.'

The hand appeared in the circle of light again and lifted the knife. This time Nina screamed.

38

Vera and Joe Ashworth arrived at the Writers' House once the party was in full swing. By then there were so many vehicles in the car park that theirs wouldn't be noticed. Joe had been fretting to go all day.

'We could get there early. Hide in an outbuilding or something.'

'Don't be daft,' she'd said. 'Holly had a quick look round earlier. We know what we're waiting for. My bladder won't stand long surveillances any more. I've never pissed in front of a subordinate yet, and I don't intend to start now. It's bad for discipline.'

He'd grinned, but she could tell he wasn't happy. There was something going on between him and the writer woman. The last thing she needed was emotion getting in the way and Joe going all chivalrous on her. That was why she hadn't entirely taken him into her confidence. She couldn't face the aggro.

'What do we do now?' he said.

They were still in her Land Rover; Vera had taken to driving it more often throughout this investigation. 'The seats are higher up than in the pool cars,' she'd said when Joe had queried its use. 'We'll have a better view.'

Now he made to climb out of the passenger door.

'We stay here,' she said sharply. 'And we wait.

The hardest thing there is.'

'We can't protect them while we're sitting here.'

'And if we go inside, nothing will happen and we'll never have a conviction.' Vera turned so that she was looking at him. 'Is that what you want? A double killer on the loose?'

She'd driven to the far edge of the car park, so they had a view down over the courtyard. They could see the main house, all lit up, the Barton cottage in darkness and the corner of the chapel. Vera reached for her bag and pulled out a flask of coffee, two plastic mugs and a packet of shop-bought apple pies. 'Don't say I never give you anything.'

'Won't the coffee make you wee?'

'Cheeky monkey,' she said, but her mouth was full of pie and she wasn't sure he heard.

As people began to leave, Vera could feel Joe becoming tenser by the minute. He watched the visitors' cars pull away, following them with his eyes up the track through the trees. The park emptied. Soon only a handful of vehicles were left. He rattled his fingers against the dashboard, a sign of his stress.

'Take it easy, lad. Nothing was going to happen in front of an audience.'

A moment later Vera's phone pinged, showing she had a text. She read it, without showing it to Joe. 'From Joanna,' she said. 'My contact on the inside. It looks as if we're on.' She tried to keep the complacency out of her voice, but couldn't quite manage it. 'Just as I expected.'

Her eyes had become used to the dark and the

lights from the bare windows in the big house allowed her to make out the figure slowly crossing the courtyard towards the chapel. She nudged Joe and found herself whispering, despite the distance between them and the yard. 'What did I tell you?' Felt the exhilaration of finding herself to be right.

'Let's go then, before any damage gets done.'

'Not yet. Wait.'

And they waited. The caterers were loading their van and each time one emerged from the kitchen, Joe seemed to become nervier, more wound up.

The main door opened again and this time Nina Backworth came out, struggling to pull something behind her. Vera had expected her, but would have recognized the silhouette anyway: no one else was so tall and slim. 'What's going on there then?' The words muttered to herself. Then again to Joe: 'Wait!'

The woman reached the chapel door and disappeared within. There was a light inside and then darkness. With a sudden burst of activity, Vera fell out of the car and ran towards the chapel. Joe, having been told for so long to wait, took a while to realize what was happening. He was behind her out of the Land Rover and didn't catch up until she'd reached the building. Despite her size and her age, she'd covered the ground as quickly as him. Excitement and fear had sent her flying.

The door was fastened by a latch. She pressed it and pushed, but nothing happened. It had been locked from inside.

I should have told Holly to take out the key. She'd never have thought of that for herself. My fault, then, if it all goes tits up.

Joe Ashworth seemed to lose his reason. The tension of the wait in the Land Rover and his anxiety for the woman, the frustrations of the case, all came together and he put his weight behind the door, swearing under his breath. Words she'd never heard him use before. She knew it would be no good. The chapel had been built to withstand the border reivers, the wild raiders from the north. One man wouldn't shift the door. The opaque glass in the windows glowed with a gentle light. Candles had been lit. Then a woman screamed. The thickness of the walls made the noise faint, but they could make out the terror in the voice.

Joe battered on the door with his fists.

'Police! Let us in!' He was yelling so loud that Vera thought his throat would be scratchy and sore in the morning. He'd not be able to speak for days. He turned to her, furious that she was so calm. 'Isn't there another way in?'

She shook her head. She couldn't bring herself to speak. No point in letting him see she was as scared as he was.

'You do realize,' he said, suddenly still, 'that you've sacrificed that woman for the sake of a conviction. You do realize that I'll never be able to work with you again.'

She felt the words physically like a punch in the belly. Then there was the sound of a key turning in the lock. The door was pushed open and Nina Backworth, white and shaky, fell

376

towards Joe Ashworth. There was blood on the hand that reached out to clutch his shoulder, and she lost consciousness.

Vera left Nina to Joe and pushed her way inside. She still had her suspect to think about. The room was barely lit, with one candle on the altar. There was the bowl of apricots on the white cloth. And on a high-backed chair sat Mark Winterton. In his dark clothes he looked almost like a priest. But Holly had her arm around his neck and a knife at his throat. He'd stopped struggling.

'I was too slow,' Holly said, almost in tears. 'He got to the woman before I could reach him.'

'Is she badly hurt?'

Vera thought that she'd blown it. Joe had been right all along. She was an arrogant fool. She'd pulled her phone from her bag and was punching out 999 for an ambulance, and then the number of the team in the van parked in the layby up the bank.

'I don't know!' It came out as a scream. Then Holly was repeating the words 'He got to her before I could stop him.'

Vera's pulse was racing.

Winterton was still, staring straight ahead of him. Holly set the knife on the table, and he allowed her to fasten his hands behind his back.

Vera finished her call and turned to the young woman. Her voice was angry. She always needed to take it out on someone when she'd cocked up. 'Why didn't you take the key out of the door? You always leave yourself a way of escape.' She allowed a moment of silence filled with fury, and then brought her feelings under control. This wasn't Holly's fault.

'Joe!' Her shout echoed round the bare chapel. 'Talk to me, Joe. How is she?'

But Joe didn't answer.

39

Early the following morning they were in the police station. Vera and Joe, who hadn't had any sleep, Winterton and a solicitor, who'd arrived from Carlisle. Vera wondered if this was the ex-wife's toy boy. The woman wouldn't want the publicity of a high-profile trial, and Vera thought that the solicitor was there to make them see Winterton as a man unfit to plead, rather than to put up any form of defence.

Nina Backworth was in hospital, but she'd be allowed home later in the day. The knife had caught the fleshy part of her upper arm. Joe still hadn't talked to Vera. Since his refusal to answer in the chapel he'd maintained a moody silence. She thought his feelings were mixed. Of course he was furious that the inspector had put Nina in danger, but he was even angrier that Holly had been the person to save her. Vera should have allowed him to be hiding in the chapel. He should have been the rescuer, the gallant knight.

Winterton was dressed in a paper suit. He struggled to hold on to a tatter of dignity, but sitting beside his lawyer, he was falling apart. He curved his fingers so that his nails touched the table in front of him like claws. Vera leaned towards him.

'Why don't you tell me about Lucy?' she said. 'Your Lucy.'

'She was my youngest,' he said. 'My baby.' He

took off his glasses for a moment to wipe them on the synthetic fabric of the suit and his eyes were unfocused and cloudy.

'A bright girl,' Vera prompted. 'Everyone says how bright she was.'

'She was always lost in a book.' He nodded fiercely. 'Always telling stories.'

'So that was why you enrolled in the English-literature evening class when you retired. To connect with your daughter.'

'Yes!' He nodded again. 'My ex-wife could never understand that. She said I should move on.'

'We all have our own ways of dealing with our grief.' *But what*, Vera thought, *would I know about grief? When Hector died I felt like celebrating. Heartless cow that I am.* 'Tell me about Lucy's death,' she said.

'She was never very good at handling stress.' Even Winterton's voice was different. He ran the words together. 'In the run-up to A levels, Lucy had an episode. That was what the doctors called it. A stress-related psychotic episode. She had to go back and resit. Margaret, my ex-wife, couldn't understand. She always thrived on stress.'

'But you *did* understand?' Vera had met police officers like Winterton before. The ones who stuck to rules. Rigid and unbending. They were the people who were so anxious about getting things wrong that they let the system take decisions for them. They were the ones who had nervous breakdowns when the rules let them down.

'I didn't have the care of Lucy,' he said. 'When

Margaret left, she married again very quickly. They formed a new family. The children even took their stepfather's name. But she was always my baby.'

'Lucy must have passed her exams,' Vera said. 'She went off to university.'

'To do English in Manchester,' Winterton said in the same frantic tone. 'At first she did well. She phoned me occasionally, full of her news. The end of the next year she came home for a bit and I saw her then. I thought she'd lost weight. Later I found out she'd already started taking heroin. I should have realized, shouldn't I?' He paused for breath and scraped his nails over the table. 'A police officer with all those years of experience. I should have seen the signs.'

'It wasn't your fault,' Vera said.

But Winterton seemed lost in thought and didn't hear her. 'She told me she was writing a novel,' he said, his voice suddenly bright. 'I was so proud of her. It explained her nerviness, you see. Writers aren't like everyone else. They're more sensitive.'

Vera said nothing.

'She finished her degree,' he said. 'I went down for the graduation, but they didn't let me in. There were only two tickets and Margaret and her husband took those. Lucy came back to Carlisle, but she never really settled. She was still working on her book.' He looked at Vera. 'She had her heart set on doing an MA at St Ursula's. An obsession. She'd seen Tony Ferdinand on the television. She thought he could get her a publisher.' The galloping words seemed too much for him and he lapsed into silence, rested his chin on his chest.

'What happened next, Mark?' Vera needed it for the tape recorder.

He lifted his head, took off his glasses again and looked at her with his wild eyes. 'She got a place on the course,' he said. 'I was so pleased. I thought it would make her well again. I took her down to London and she was as excited as a small child. 'This is my fresh start.' That's what she said when I dropped her off.'

'And then?'

Vera knew what had happened. She'd spent a couple of hours reading the student records in the St Ursula archives. The change of surname had thrown her at first — that had wasted them all a lot of time — but she'd known what she was looking for and she could be persistent when she set her mind to it.

'They killed her,' Winterton said.

Vera stared out of the window. The room was on the first floor of the police station. It looked out over the river. She saw the street lamps on the other side. Soon it would be daylight and the town would be busy with folk on their way to work. She turned back to the room. 'That's not entirely true, is it, Mark? She killed herself.'

'They tormented her,' he said. 'They tore her apart.'

'It was a tough regime,' Vera said. 'Not everyone could cope. Even Nina Backworth left before she completed the course.'

'Her!' Winterton shot to his feet and was rearing over her. 'She was one of the tormenters.

Lucy thought she was a friend — her only friend in the place — and Backworth ended up killing her. It was the worst sort of betrayal.'

'Tell me about it,' Vera said.

'They had this session,' he went on. 'Everyone on the course there. Ferdinand had brought in a visiting tutor, an old friend. And they chose Lucy's work for discussion. There she sat facing them all. Like it was some sort of interrogation. And they picked her writing apart. Sentence after sentence for three hours. She'd put her heart into that book. By destroying it, they were destroying her.' He paused. 'She told me that it was like exposing herself, as if her skin was made of glass and they could see into her soul.'

'What was the name of the visiting tutor?' Vera asked. She knew fine well, but she needed it for the tape.

'Miranda Barton.' He spat out the name. 'The great novelist. The cruellest woman.'

'Lucy left.'

'That evening. She didn't even go back to her room to pick up her stuff. She phoned me about midnight. She'd tried earlier, but I was at work and her mother was away on a cruise with her fancy man.' He paused. 'She was crying as she told me about it. Sobbing. And there was nothing I could do to help.' He looked up. 'I never heard from her again. I tried to get hold of her, but there was no answer on her mobile. A week later she was found in a squat in a flat near King's Cross. Dead. A heroin overdose.'

Vera said nothing. She had no questions about that. Her former colleague, now working in the

Met, had filled in all the details.

Vera shot a quick look at Joe Ashworth. He'd left the interview to her. Still sulking. Now his face was white. Chalky. She could tell that he was thinking of his kids, understanding that one day they'd leave home and be outside his control and his care.

Winterton was still talking. 'There was an inquest, but the result was inconclusive. Lucy might have intended to take her own life or the heroin overdose could have been a terrible accident. Really, it doesn't matter. I know who was responsible. If she hadn't been bullied at college she'd still be alive.'

'You can't know that,' Vera said.

But Winterton hadn't heard. He'd convinced himself that the killings were justified. He'd spent his career working for the criminal-justice system. Now he'd formed his own.

'So they all had to die,' Vera said. 'Ferdinand, Barton and Backworth. To avenge your daughter.'

'It wasn't vengeance,' he said. 'It was justice.'

It was only a book. Not worth killing yourself for. Not worth committing murder for.

'This evening class that you took when you retired,' Vera said. 'English literature. I spoke to the teacher. The title of the course was 'Classic Tragedies'. That would have appealed to you.'

'Shakespeare,' Winterton seemed a little calmer. '*Macbeth* and *Othello*.'

'Not light reading then.'

'Lucy did *Othello* in her first year of university. We'd talked about it. About the jealousy that drove Othello to madness.'

'Then the class moved on,' Vera said, 'to the Revenge Tragedies. Webster. *The Duchess of Malfi* and *The White Devil*. Very gory. Makes today's violence on telly look restrained.' She looked at him. 'But you already knew you wanted revenge, didn't you? It didn't take the play to make you carry it out.'

'I'd dreamed of it since Lucy died,' Winterton said and his voice was dreamy now. 'I'd spent my whole career bringing killers to justice. Those people had killed Lucy as surely as if they'd injected the heroin into her vein.'

'No, they didn't,' Vera said. 'They were flawed and cruel, but there was no intent to kill. Not within the meaning of the law. And the law's all we have to hold things together.'

Winterton shook his head and she knew he was mad. As mad as the Webster character who believed that he was a wolf and dug dead bodies from the earth.

'You tried to kill Tony Ferdinand before,' Vera said. 'Last February.'

'That didn't feel right,' Winterton said. 'I felt like a thug. It wasn't how it was supposed to be.'

'Then you found out that he would be at the Writers' House.'

'It was fate,' he said. 'A sign. The teacher of the evening class brought in a flier for the courses.'

'And you recognized the names,' Vera said. 'Tony Ferdinand, Miranda Barton and Nina Backworth. All of them there together. So you enrolled.' Suddenly she felt very tired. What would have happened if Winterton had missed that lesson? If he'd had flu or a dodgy stomach, and had never seen the Writers' House flier? Would Ferdinand and Barton still be working and writing?

'When I arrived at the house on the coast it seemed so *right* for my purpose.' Winterton's voice was manic again. He wiped his face with the sleeve of his paper suit. 'The atmosphere, the grandeur. It was a fitting place for justice to be executed.'

Vera looked at his face and saw there was no point arguing with him. Let him just bring his story to its conclusion.

'You stole Nina Backworth's sleeping pills from her room and put them in Ferdinand's coffee at lunch. You knew he always sat in the glass room immediately after the meal. After you'd killed him, you set up the room to look like a scene from Miranda Barton's book.'

He nodded. 'And I left the knife. To buy me some time, but also as a sign of his guilt. Like in *Macbeth*.'

'Oh, pet,' she said. 'The world couldn't read your signs and messages. I struggled and I'm almost as daft as you are.'

He looked at her, but again she saw that he would only hear what he wanted to.

'You played music,' Vera said. ' 'Lucy in the Sky with Diamonds.' Was Ferdinand supposed to hear it? To remember and realize what he'd done?'

'It was her song,' Winterton said. 'It was for her.'

'You wrote the note for Joanna and hoped that she would pick up the knife.' *Let's move this on,* Vera thought. *Get it over with.* The futility of his actions made her want to weep. And if she didn't get her breakfast soon she'd faint. 'Tell me about the handkerchief on the terrace after you killed Miranda,' she said briskly. 'Another play?'

'*Othello.*'

Vera smiled as if she'd known all along; she thought Google was a wonderful thing. 'Desdemona's hankie,' she said. 'White cloth embroidered with strawberries. And we thought it was a heart. Embroidery's not one of your talents, pet.'

The solicitor cleared his throat. They all looked at him. It would be his first utterance. 'I don't quite understand the significance of the apricots,' he said.

Vera gave him a superior smile. 'They feature in a play too,' she said. '*The Duchess of Malfi.* A Revenge Tragedy. And the dead robin's from *The White Devil.*'

Winterton lay back in his chair and closed his eyes, reciting:

Call for the robin-redbreast and the wren.
Since o'er shady groves they hover,
And with leaves and flow'rs do cover
The friendless bodies of unburied men.

He sat upright. 'That's Cornelia mourning her dead child.'

The room was very quiet. Nobody knew what to say. Vera broke the silence. 'You certainly gave Miranda a fright. Killing Ferdinand in a scene from her most successful book. Very weird.'

'When I heard her screaming,' Winterton said, 'it was the happiest I'd been since Lucy died.'

'While everyone believed that Joanna killed Tony Ferdinand, Miranda could persuade herself that the scene was a coincidence,' Vera went on. 'It was only after Joanna was released from custody that she began to reconsider.'

'She was a stupid, greedy woman,' Winterton said.

'She tried to blackmail you.'

'She had grand ideas. For the Writers' House and her own work.' Winterton looked disdainful. 'She needed money. She thought it was only Ferdinand I blamed for my daughter's death.'

'And this time you used the scene from Nina Backworth's short story.' Vera thought that by then his lust for revenge had taken over. Though he'd held it together in public — slipping ideas to Joe about Miranda Barton having lost a daughter, sending them in quite the wrong direction.

Winterton looked up. 'It seemed fitting,' he said. He gave a little smile. 'They care so much about their fiction, after all. For Lucy it was a matter of life and death.'

Vera said nothing. She looked at Joe to see if he had any further questions. He shook his head. On the other side of the table Winterton was sitting upright and still. Now he didn't care at all what might happen to him.

Vera thought it was time for breakfast. Maybe if she bought him a decent fry-up, Joe would forgive her.

40

Joe Ashworth caught up with Nina at her flat, in Jesmond. He'd expected her to be with Chrissie Kerr at North Farm, thinking she'd want company after her ordeal with Winterton. But she was alone. She'd been sitting by the window looking out over the cemetery. Her arm was bandaged and she wore a red cardigan over her shoulder like a shawl. In the street outside, schoolgirls were making their way into the playground.

'Perhaps you don't want to be disturbed,' he said. 'There's nothing that won't wait.'

'No, please! Do come in.'

She made him coffee and he sat beside her at the table.

'Of course I'd gone over the events in my head, wondering who the murderer might be,' she said. 'Mark was at the bottom of the list. He seemed such a gentle man.'

'Who did you have at the top?' Joe thought they'd never have had this conversation while the investigation was still running.

She paused and seemed ashamed for a moment. 'Lenny Thomas,' she said. 'Dreadful, isn't it? The assumptions we make. Just because he'd been in prison.'

'We had our suspicions about him for a while.' Joe supposed he should be more discreet, but he didn't think Nina would be talking to the press.

'He wouldn't tell us where he was the night of your break-in and the afternoon the cat was found in the chapel. Turned out he'd been working for a mate, a plumber from Ashington. He was being paid cash, nothing on the books. He hadn't told the benefit people.'

'Mark was so respectable, so courteous,' Nina said. She turned to Joe. 'Do you know how he got me into the chapel?'

Joe shook his head. This was a comfortable room. It occurred to him that he'd never had this. A space of his own. Quiet. Peace. He'd never thought he needed it.

'He told Chrissie that he thought he was in love with me. We all knew he was divorced. He'd been too shy to talk to me during the Writers' House course, but he said he didn't want to drive back to Cumbria without telling me how he felt. Chrissie knew he was an ex-detective and didn't think for a moment that he could be the killer. And she's such a bloody romantic, always playing matchmaker. So she set me up. She asked me to take the books into the chapel, knowing he'd be there.'

Nina looked up.

'He would have killed me, you know. He thought I'd caused his daughter's death.' She paused. 'I remember it, that session when we pulled apart Lucy's work. I thought about it again when you showed me the magazine article they found on the beach. Miranda looked much younger, and it reminded me that she was the visiting tutor that day. I've always felt guilty about the way I allowed myself to be dragged into the criticism. Lucy and I were friends, and until then we'd always supported each other. I hated the person I became that day. It was horrible.'

'The inspector should have had more sense than to allow you into the chapel.' Joe tried to contain his anger. 'Playing God with other people's lives. I told her she was crazy.'

'She came to see me in hospital after you'd finished with Winterton,' Nina said. 'Apologized. I told her I understood. She was doing her job.'

'She's bloody lucky you don't sue. Or make a formal complaint.'

Nina smiled at him. 'She told me you were sulking.'

Joe didn't know what to say to that.

''Lucy in the Sky with Diamonds',' Nina said. 'That's what he was playing in the chapel. His song for his daughter, I suppose.'

They sat for a moment in silence. A bell rang to mark the beginning of school.

'I feel such a fool that I didn't recognize the reference to the apricots,' she said suddenly. 'It's years since I've seen the play, but all the same. And the handkerchief.'

'The inspector googled it.' They looked at each other and grinned. A moment of intimacy. Joe got to his feet. 'I should go. I told my wife I'd be home.'

41

Vera had a late breakfast at Myers Farm with Jack and Joanna. Joe had turned down her offer of a fry-up and she felt that she owed them an explanation. And that Joanna at least owed one to her. There was local bacon and sausage, and eggs from the Myers hens, and it was a while before she could give her full attention to the case.

'So it was all about revenge,' Joanna said when she'd heard the story. 'Mark saw himself as a great avenging angel, acting on behalf of his daughter.'

'Aye.' Vera wasn't sure she believed in Winterton as an angel. 'Something like that. Though I suspect the shrinks will say he's too mad to plead and he'll go straight to the loony bin.'

Joanna said nothing to that, and Vera thought she was remembering her own stay in a psychiatric clinic.

It was cold again outside, but snug in the kitchen, and there was condensation clouding the windows, so she couldn't see into the farmyard.

'What about you?' Vera asked. 'Was your story all about revenge too?'

'No!' Joanna was indignant. 'I wanted to make sense of it. And keep a record.'

'She's a great writer,' Jack said. 'I've told her, if

she keeps at it, she'll be rich and famous one day. She'll be keeping the pair of us.' He reached out and touched the woman's hand, then got to his feet, went to the door and pulled on his boots. 'But I can't sit here gassing all day. I've got work to do.'

Vera waited until the door had closed behind him. The warm kitchen was making her feel as if she could fall asleep at any minute. Joanna seemed about to go back to work too.

'So what was going on?' Vera asked. 'The demands for money, stopping your medication. What was all that about?'

'I don't think,' Joanna said, playing the grand lady again, 'that it's any of your business, Vee. It's not a police matter.'

'I want to know. I can't stand unfinished business. Is it another man?' Vera couldn't bear to see Jack hurt. And she couldn't bear the thought of him dripping around the place, disturbing her with his misery.

'No!' Joanna threw back her head and laughed. 'What would I want with another man? I'm perfectly happy with the one I've got, and anyway, who else would have me?'

'So what then?' *I can be as stubborn as you, lady.*

Perhaps Joanna realized that Vera wasn't going to give up. Or perhaps she wanted to discuss the idea, put it into words. 'I want a baby,' she said. 'Before it's too late. I can't be pregnant on the medication. And I thought I should have some financial security before bringing a child into the world. So I asked Paul for money. That's what it's all about.'

'Does Jack know?'

'No point telling Jack until I've made up my mind,' Joanna said. 'He'll be so excited he won't be able to contain himself. He'll talk about nothing else.'

'What's the next move?'

'I've made an appointment with the doctor to talk through the options. Very sensible. You should be proud of me, Vee.'

Vera stood up and yawned. She needed a few hours' sleep before she went back to the station. Joanna followed her to the door.

'What about you?' Joanna asked as they stood together, looking out down the valley. 'Did you never want a child?'

'Eh, pet, what sort of mother would I have made?'

Vera stomped off towards her house. Both of them knew that wasn't any sort of answer to the question.

We do hope that you have enjoyed reading
this large print book.

Did you know that all of our titles
are available for purchase?

We publish a wide range of high quality
large print books including:
Romances, Mysteries, Classics
General Fiction
Non Fiction and Westerns

Special interest titles available in
large print are:
The Little Oxford Dictionary
Music Book
Song Book
Hymn Book
Service Book

Also available from us courtesy of
Oxford University Press:
Young Readers' Dictionary
(large print edition)
Young Readers' Thesaurus
(large print edition)

For further information or a free
brochure, please contact us at:
Ulverscroft Large Print Books Ltd.,
The Green, Bradgate Road, Anstey,
Leicester, LE7 7FU, England.
Tel: (00 44) 0116 236 4325
Fax: (00 44) 0116 234 0205

SILENT VOICES

Ann Cleeves

When DI Vera Stanhope finds the body of a woman in the steam room of her local pool, she wonders if, for once, it's a death from natural causes. But closer inspection reveals ligature marks around the victim's throat. Vera pulls her team together and sets them to interviewing staff and those connected to the victim, while she and Sergeant Joe Ashworth work to find a motive. While Joe struggles to reconcile his home life with the demands of the job, Vera revels in being back in charge of an investigation. Death has never made her feel so alive. When they discover that the victim had worked in social services — and was involved in a shocking case centred on a young child — it seems the two are connected. But things are rarely as they seem . . .

THE SEAGULL

Ann Cleeves

When prison inmate and former police officer
John Brace says he's willing to give up
information about a long-dead wheeler dealer
in return for protection for his family, Vera
knows that she has to look into his claims.
But opening up this cold case strikes much
closer to home than Vera anticipates as her
investigation takes her back in time to The
Seagull, a once decadent and now derelict
nightclub where her deceased father and his
friends used to congregate. As Vera's past
collides dangerously with the present, she will
have to confront her unwanted memories and
face the possibility that her father was
involved in what happened. The truth is
about to come out — but is Vera ready for
what it will reveal?

DEAD WATER

Ann Cleeves

When the body of journalist Jerry Markham is found in a traditional Shetland boat down at the marina, young Detective Inspector Willow Reeves is drafted in from the Hebrides to head up the investigation. Since the death of his fiancee, Inspector Jimmy Perez has been out of the loop, but his interest in this new case is stirred and he decides to help the inquiry. His local knowledge is invaluable as the close-knit community holds many secrets. Willow and Jimmy are led to Sullom Voe, the heart of Shetland's North Sea oil and gas industry. It soon emerges from their investigation that Markham was chasing a story in his final days. One that must have been significant enough to warrant his death . . .